The Runaway Daughter

Joanna Rees, aka Josie Lloyd and Jo Rees, is a bestselling writer of fourteen novels, including rom-coms, blockbusters and big-hearted adventures such as *Come Together*, *The Tides of Change* and *A Twist of Fate*. With nearly twenty years' writing experience, Joanna regularly teaches creative writing in schools and libraries and she also contributes regularly to online station Radio Gorgeous. Based in Brighton, Joanna is married to the author Emlyn Rees, with whom she has three daughters. They have co-written seven novels, including the *Sunday Times* number one bestseller *Come Together*, which was translated into twenty-seven languages and made into a film. They have written several bestselling parodies of their favourite children's books, including *We're Going on a Bar Hunt* and *The Teenager Who Came to Tea*, as well as *'Twas the Fight Before Christmas* and *Shabby: The Jolly Good British Guide to Stress-free Living*. Joanna is always delighted to hear from readers, so please visit her website www.joannareesbooks.com. She's also on Twitter @joannareesbooks

BY JOANNA REES

The Runaway Daughter

Joanna Rees

PAN BOOKS

First published 2019 by Macmillan

This edition published 2019 by Pan Books
an imprint of Pan Macmillan
20 New Wharf Road, London N1 9RR
Associated companies throughout the world
www.panmacmillan.com

ISBN 978-1-4472-6670-9

1 3 5 7 9 8 6 4 2

A CIP catalogue record for this book is available from the British Library.

Typeset by Palimpsest Book Production Limited, Falkirk, Stirlingshire
Printed and bound by CPI Group (UK) Ltd, Croydon CR0 4YY

For Roxie, with all my love

The
Runaway
Daughter

1

Inventing Miss Casey

The shrill whistle woke her. For a second she didn't move, feeling the rattle of the steam train jolting her as she remembered her midnight flight across the moonlit field. How she'd spotted the stationary train impatiently puffing silvery clouds into the night air, how she'd managed to prise open the wooden carriage door with her shaking fingers and how she'd curled up in a tiny space behind the industrial cargo and packing boxes from the mill. How the exhaustion and terror had transported her to blackness.

Now her legs were stiff and her cheek was sore from where she'd been leaning against the cold metal machinery. And she was cold. So very cold. Her teeth chattered as she shivered in the icy air. She had that same fluttering feeling she'd had when she'd fallen asleep, as if the fear were darting around inside her, like the birds in her mother's aviary.

How long since they'd last stopped? How far till she was far enough away?

Would she *ever* be far enough away?

She thought of the drama that was bound to be unfolding by now. She imagined her parents' drawn faces when they discovered Clement's body in the stable . . . her mother's muffled scream.

Would they even be thinking of their daughter? Would they have noticed her absence yet? *Probably not*, she thought bitterly. Her mother had always been a muddled, ethereal presence – prone to lengthy bouts of illness, and concerned only with her birds and her absolute insistence on quiet. Her father, on the other hand, had always been as tempestuous as her mother had been timid, and he'd made it perfectly clear that Anna, like her mother, had always been an irritation to him. Lower down on his pecking order than the dogs.

Perhaps, though, her parents had drawn the correct conclusion straight away. Helped, no doubt, by Mark, the stablehand. He'd never liked her and she had no doubt that he'd readily describe how he'd seen her running for her life. And if he had, then the police were bound to have been called. Perhaps they were already chasing her . . .

Again, she fought down the fluttering fear. She'd got away, hadn't she? She'd escaped.

Underneath the wooden carriage door, she could see an inch of the world outside. It was late February and the tracks flashed by with tufts of frosty grass.

She got to her feet, hobbling as they were so numb with the cold. She stretched her arms up with difficulty, the full sleeves of her mother's best Sunday woollen coat stiff with the layers of clothes beneath it. Her breath steamed in front of her face as she stamped her feet, pressing her hands into her armpits and shivering again. Then she rubbed her face and felt the indent of the machinery's steel stamp on her skin from where she'd been leaning against it. 'Casey,' she read now on the brown-grey iron.

Casey.

That could be her name.

Miss Casey. It was good to make a new decision for a new day. Like the decision to hide on this train. Fast and life-changing. Where there'd only been despair, this was a whole new way of living. Impetuously. Impulsively. The opposite of who she'd been until now – pushed down, trodden upon, so suppressed that life had been an agonizingly slow grey. But not any more. Because now that she'd run away from Darton Hall, she – Anna Darton – could be anyone. Anyone at all.

Casey . . . yes.

She'd take it. Isn't that what she'd decided? That she would reinvent as she went along. Because that was the only way she could cope with this terrifying descent into her future. Like she was sand pouring through an hourglass.

Verity. It came quite suddenly. She didn't know why. She'd certainly never known a Verity before. Apart from the mill worker who'd once danced around the maypole on that holiday long ago. The full-breasted girl's smile flashed in her mind's eye.

Verity. Yes. *That worked*, she decided. Because, as of this very moment, for the first time in her life, she was free to be the truest version of herself. And, since this was 1926, she could be as modern as she dared to be. As modern as those brave suffragettes who made her father furious.

'Verity Casey,' she said aloud. Around her, the rhythm of

3

the train sounded like the start of a song. Verity Casey didn't have to be scared. She could be fearless.

She *would* be fearless.

2

Sixty Seconds

The train slowed as it entered the suburbs of the city, the brakes on the huge wheels making a deafening screech below the boards of the carriage. After fiddling with the catch for twenty minutes and some serious hefting, she'd managed to slide the door open several inches, and now she – *Verity* – stood and watched the slums slide by. The sun had come up and she bathed her face in it, longing for some much-needed warmth.

She hadn't dared to hope that the train might have been travelling south, but during the last hour they'd slowed and passed through a station and she'd heard someone calling out that this was a freight train to London.

It was a gift. The train might have been going anywhere – she hadn't cared a jot, only that it was somewhere other than that oppressive Lancashire valley she'd always called home. But this wasn't somewhere else. This was London. The home of artists, poets, flapper girls, musicians and the kind of people of consequence that she longed to breathe the same air as. Somehow, coming to London changed everything.

She peered out at the tracks below her and at the high brick walls banking them, stained black with soot, thinking how inhuman it all seemed and not at all like the lively hub of activity she'd imagined from the occasional copy of the *Daily Sketch* that she'd read. She didn't care, though – anything to distract her from the constant thoughts of Clement, which seemed to burn through her mind. *Don't think about him now*, she told herself. *Don't think about it at all. You've ended it. Clement's lifelong reign of terror is over.*

She took a deep breath of the smoggy air, breathing in the sulphurous tang, which reminded her of the smell of struck matches, and she wondered whether Martha would be lighting the fire in the drawing room this morning. For a heady moment, as she thought of Martha *there* and herself *here*, the lightness of her freedom soared inside her. She was free, *wasn't she?* At last.

Above the railway embankments, brown tenement blocks rose to the white sky. She saw a line of drying washing – tatty grey bloomers stretched between two grubby high windows. *Talk about airing your dirty linen in public*, she thought.

She smiled, remembering how she'd added some lace trim to a pair of her own bloomers, then dyed them pink with beetroot juice – much to Martha's horror. But what her mother's stern housekeeper didn't understand was that having jaunty bloomers and that tiny bit of pretty lace below her dowdy skirts had the capacity to infinitely brighten a girl's day.

But then Martha, with her grey hair and grim scowl, had always belonged in the same camp as her mother – the one that believed all clothing should be utilitarian and functional. Just like the way they approached life. Afraid of doing anything that might attract even a tiny bit of attention. And it was dull, dull, dull.

Should she be feeling guilty that she was free of them now? Probably, but she wasn't. Instead she smiled, silently blessing the people in the tenement blocks, despite their terrible underwear. *God bless you*, she thought.

She ached to be right there. In the city. Amongst the people. The shops and theatres and cafés. They were all here – tantalizingly close. She could almost smell it. But how? How could she become a part of it? Now that she'd run away, what on earth was she going to do to get by? And, as if directed by her thoughts, her stomach let out an almighty growl of hunger.

She ducked out of sight now, as another train pulled up on a parallel track. It had dark-green livery, its windows embossed with gold lettering. Sneaking a peak, she saw a man in a smart suit stretching up to retrieve a leather suitcase from the overhead rack in one of the busy carriages.

Who knew where that train was going? Or this train, for that matter? In fact, now that she thought about it, perhaps this one wouldn't stop at a passenger station at all. And how would she explain herself, if anyone caught her here amongst the machinery? She might get punished – or, worse, found out.

But on the other train, in a crowd, she could blend in and disappear. Quickly she grabbed her carpet bag from the corner. She had to get on that train right now. Her heart hammered with the decision she'd made. It was so risky. If anyone looked out of the window, they would see her.

Take everything one minute at a time, from now on. She

forced the words into her head, as if she were spelling them out on the typewriter in Papa's study.

'Sixty seconds,' she whispered, bracing herself. 'Come on, Verity Casey. You can do it.'

She yanked her red woollen beret down low over her head and pulled up the collar of her coat. Then, quick as she could, she threw her bag onto the track and, willing herself to be all right, she jumped.

3

King's Cross

She landed on the hard gravel, her heart pounding. She'd never felt so exposed, or so small. But her survival instinct kicked in as she looked at the great iron underbelly of the train with its terrifying pistons.

You can do this.

She picked up her skirts and hopped across the tracks onto the wooden sleepers, as if she were running away from Clement on the stepping stones across the brook. She'd always been faster than him. She always would be now.

The outside door of the train was higher than she'd expected. She hauled herself up onto the latticed metal step with difficulty, in order to reach the wooden handle. She heard a rip coming from one of her skirts as she yanked it free.

The door swung open towards her, almost making her lose her balance.

Sixty seconds. Nearly there . . .

She threw her bag into the carriage and then hauled herself up. Once through the door, she stood quickly, brushing herself down, realizing she was shaking all over. Had anyone seen her? It was hard to know, but suddenly the train was moving. Passengers began stirring in the compartments on either side of her.

'Are you well, Miss?' It was a man – a conductor, she realized with a jolt, his brow furrowing beneath his peaked cap, as he walked between the carriages and spotted her in the small walkway. A second earlier and he'd have seen her ungraceful entrance.

She watched him now as he looked from her to the wooden door, but she saw immediately that he had dismissed the thought that she could possibly have come from outside. She looked down at her knuckles, which were still scuffed and bloodied. She'd forgotten to put on her gloves and she needed to smarten up. To not look like . . . like – goodness, she could hardly even think the word – like a *criminal*.

She pressed herself against the corridor wall and shoved her hands behind her.

'Taking some air, that's all,' she said, trying to mask the tremor in her voice with a haughty lift of her chin – just one of the things she'd picked up from those ghastly elocution lessons that her mother had insisted upon. She was aware that a strand of her long hair had fallen out of the bun she always wore it in, and she had to resist the urge to blow it away from her face.

'Be careful, Miss. It's a long way down to the track. Wouldn't want a pretty young lady like you to fall out and ruin that nice coat,' the conductor said, tipping his hat, before moving along into the next carriage. 'King's Cross in two minutes,' she heard him say.

She looked down at her mother's lilac checked wool coat. She realized now for the first time how conspicuous her clothes made her look, how the guard would already be able to identify her by her coat and hat, if anyone were to ask. But they wouldn't, she reassured herself. She was about to be just one person in a teeming metropolis.

She opened the window, leaning out as the platform came into view. Railway porters hauled trolleys along it through the crowd of passengers. The train slowed and shuddered to a halt in a bellowing hiss of steam beneath the round clock, the hands of which now clicked to half-past nine.

Anna – no, *Verity*, she reminded herself – opened the door and jumped down, before hurrying along the platform to a wooden bench. There she hastily pulled on the kid gloves she'd stolen from her mother's tallboy. Then, pretending that she had somewhere important to be and holding her head high, she made her way with the crowd towards the ticket barrier.

A portly inspector with a bushy grey moustache was punching tickets as he ushered passengers through to the busy concourse. What would he do to her when he caught her without a ticket?

But she was Verity Casey and she was all brand new, she reminded herself. Verity Casey could very well have lost her ticket. She could very well be down from, say, York, and visiting her aunt in a smart London townhouse.

Believe me, she willed, approaching the inspector and smiling shyly at him. Cook had always told her that she could get anything by batting the eyelashes of her baby-blue eyes.

'Ticket, Miss.'

'Oh yes, of course,' she said, laughing at her own silliness at not having it ready. She put her hand in the coat pocket of her mother's coat, holding eye-contact with the guard and then frowning. 'Oh, that's strange. It was here a second ago,' she said. She made a show of checking the other pocket and then her bag. 'Oh no! Don't say I've dropped it.' She looked behind her at the ground, then back at the guard, believing her lie so thoroughly that she might actually be able to summon tears.

'Excuse me. Excuse me!' A woman directing a porter with a trolley full of luggage bustled up from behind. 'Whatever is the hold-up? We're in a hurry here.'

The inspector met Anna's pleading eyes and made a decision. 'Go through, Miss. But be more careful next time.'

4

Headlines

Clutching her bag and trying to look like she had a purpose, Anna headed out of the station, looking at the motorcars and omnibuses, the taxi cabs and the bicycles. It was noisy and quite overwhelming, and the air felt thick with fumes. But it was intoxicating to be in the city, nonetheless.

She passed signs to the Metropolitan Railway and saw people disappearing down steps into the pavement to the Underground, then stared up at a hoarding advertising a show at Drury Lane. Wasn't that a fancy theatre in Covent Garden? She would *love* to go there, she thought. And she would do so! From now on, she could do whatever she wanted.

She was jostled along in the crowd on the pavement to the queue for the taxis and couldn't help feeling how purposeful everyone seemed to be, as two large women in black dresses and with grand plumes in their hats bustled by with two dogs on a lead, followed by a boy pushing a wooden cart filled with clanking milk churns, and then three gentlemen, all with walking canes. The one with the busy moustache tipped his hat at her.

All of these lives, she thought, *all these people with so much purpose* – they made her feel so insignificant. Darton Hall suddenly seemed like a very, very long way away.

She was nearing the front of the queue and wondered whether she should get into a taxi. But to go where? She didn't have a clue where to head for in London, or where to stay.

Giving herself time to think, she left the queue and walked along to where a boy was selling newspapers, but it occurred to her now that she herself might well make the news soon. She imagined the headlines, and the boy yelling them out: 'Heir to Darton Mills Fortune Found Dead. Sister Missing.'

She stopped still and scanned the newspapers for those very words, her heart in her throat, before reassuring herself that it was far too soon for the scandal to have gone to press. But it wouldn't be long. With the high level of resent amongst the mill workers about their working conditions, any misfortune that befell the hated Darton family would most likely be celebrated and gossiped about in the newspapers.

Her attention was caught by a report on the front page of the *Daily News*. The word flashed out at her, as if she'd been snapped by a press photographer: 'MURDER'.

Clement's bloody face flashed before her, like another pop of the photographer's bulb. Is that what the newspapers would say? When they found out what had happened to him? Because she knew for a fact that they wouldn't understand that she'd had to do what she'd done. That she'd had no choice. But nobody had ever believed her in the past. Not over Clement.

She imagined herself in the dock, her hands cuffed, the

judge stern in his white wig, his sentence unforgiving. But if she were faced with the same situation again, she'd do the same thing. Over and over. Of that she was sure.

Even so, she was aware now that the knowledge of it – her crime – was, with each passing hour, expanding into a *thing*. Something that was difficult to label: guilt, terror, disbelief – at all the decisions she'd made and everything she'd left behind. But, mostly, a sense of righteous indignation. Clement had got what he'd deserved. *Hadn't he?* If she hadn't have done what she'd done, he'd have tormented her forever. It was a choice: his life or hers.

Don't think about it. It's gone. It's over, she told herself, forcing herself to keep moving.

'You looking for something, Miss?' the boy on the newsstand asked. He had a strange cockney accent and she felt startled that he'd addressed her, but saw that he was only being friendly.

'Oh, no. Well, perhaps a hotel.'

'Try the Midland Grand. Just up there,' he said, nodding along the street to an imposing red-brick building with a clock tower. 'All the smart people go there.'

'Thank you,' she mumbled and he nodded, before hollering out, 'Extra! Extra! Read all about it.'

5

The Grand Hotel

Anna walked intrepidly up the stone steps of the large hotel, catching the eye of the doorman in his smart grey livery. He was older than her, but not by much, and he was handsome, she realized. She wasn't used to seeing such clean-shaven, groomed men and she felt herself flushing as he smiled at her.

'G'day. Welcome to the Midland Grand,' he said, tipping his hat.

'Hello,' she said.

'Can I help you with your bag?'

'Oh no. Thank you. It's not heavy.'

But just then she tripped up the last step and he caught her elbow as she stumbled. She recovered quickly, feeling embarrassed.

'I'm sorry,' she apologized.

'Don't be.'

He steered her inside the wooden revolving door and told her to walk straight on, and she had to suppress the urge to laugh nervously. A revolving door! The doorman caught her eye as he came in after her and grinned.

'You want to go again?'

16

'No, no, thank you,' she said, although another turn would be fun.

'I'll find you the bellhop,' he said, standing on tiptoe, as if looking for someone.

Her attention was caught now by the inside of the hotel. A vast staircase rose from the prettily patterned tiles and split into two, gliding upwards, all lit by windows that must be at least fifty feet tall. The walls were painted red and there were large urns filled with sumptuous ferns.

The foyer was busy – a group of older women heading for the lounge area, waiters passing by carrying silver trays aloft. There was the faint sound of a string quartet playing.

'I am meeting my aunt,' she explained to the doorman, hoping her lie sounded plausible, 'but she's been delayed. So I need a room. A single room. Just for the night.'

'Very good, Miss,' the doorman said, as if this were a perfectly reasonable explanation. 'I can't see the bellhop. Follow me and I'll take you over to reception.'

He made a path easily through the crowd, carrying her carpet bag in front of him, but Anna almost had to run to keep up with him. When they got to the imposing reception desk, he summoned one of his colleagues to attend to her. Then he withdrew, tipping his cap again.

'I'm Wilf,' he told her. 'If you need anything – anything at all during your stay – I can help,' he said and his smile was so friendly that she grinned back. Maybe London wasn't going to be so difficult after all.

The man at the reception desk made a show of checking his bookings, before agreeing to find her a room. To stay just one night was going to cost her one-third of what precious little money she had, but it was too late to back out.

'If you'd sign in here,' the man said, twisting a heavy leather-bound book towards her. But when he looked up at her, she saw a narrowing in his eyes, as if he'd seen right through her.

Unsettled by his scrutiny, she wrote her name – Anna Darton – and her address, almost without thinking; and then, realizing her mistake, she hesitated, but it was too late to cross them out. The man gave her a quizzical stare, but didn't question her any further.

She felt her cheeks burning as she followed the liveried concierge into a lift and then along the carpeted corridor on the third floor. Why hadn't she written 'Verity Casey'? She was supposed to be all-new, she remembered, but at the first test she'd failed.

The concierge opened a door into a comfortable-looking bedroom and placed her shabby carpet bag on a wooden suitcase stand, before tipping his cap. He didn't meet her eye and, as he backed out, she wondered whether she should have tipped him.

'Wait!' she said, delving in her pocket. She pulled out a note. 'Here,' she said, handing it over.

'It's far too much, Miss,' he said, looking surprised.

It was, but she didn't have any change and she couldn't exactly ask the boy for any. So instead she swallowed the rising feeling that she was way out of her depth and decided that, on this occasion, she could be generous. She waved her hand as if such tips were commonplace.

The boy grinned and left. Finally alone, she shut the door and leant back against it, letting out a long breath.

The room was small with a tiny tiled fireplace, and a mantel above it with an oval mirror to reflect the light from the window. By the window was a wooden bed with a light-blue silk eiderdown and a prettily upholstered chair to match. Compared to her bedroom at home, it was gloriously modern and comfortable. A wooden rail housed a set of folded monogrammed towels. Just for her.

She stared at the room with its fancy cornicing, wondering what she should do now. And all too soon her mind was buzzing. *She'd done it. She was really here, in London. In a grand hotel, where she'd given an equally grand tip.* It made her feel both flamboyant and deliciously reckless.

She grabbed a towel, checked both ways along the corridor and then walked along to the communal bathroom. She locked the door and stood by the large porcelain sink, staring at herself in the mirror, feeling that her blue eyes belonged to a stranger. How different she was from the child she'd been just days ago. It was as if she'd grown up ten years overnight, and her face showed it.

She turned away from her reflection and changed quickly out of her clothes, washing herself in the bath and then putting on her smartest blue dress. It was such a relief to shed the layers of clothes.

She went back to her room and took down her long hair, brushing out the knots. Her hair still smelt vaguely of home and she quickly plaited and pinned it. Then, satisfied with her appearance, she looked out of the small window at the other windows facing the back courtyard of the hotel and decided to be brave. Now that she'd come this far, she had to explore. Who knew how much time she had before someone caught her out? And when they did, she wanted to have some memories – good ones – to show for her time on the run.

Feeling too nervous to use the lift alone, she shrugged on her coat and walked slowly down the staircase, admiring the art on the walls and the smooth wooden handrail. She passed several other guests and wondered what they made of her. Did they see Verity Casey, a smart young woman who might fit into London society, or Anna Darton, a frightened girl who had committed a terrible crime? She hoped it was the former.

'Your first time in London then, Miss?' the doorman, Wilf, asked, as she stepped outside again.

She nodded, bowing her head down. Was it that obvious?

'How far is it to Piccadilly Circus?' she asked.

'Take a bus. From just there,' he said, pointing to the omnibus stop. 'You'll see all the sights, that way.'

6

Eros

Anna was used to hearing her father's suspicious ranting about the 'flagrantly immoral' types in London, but looking at everything from the top of the omnibus – the sheer colour and magnificence of the city – had resolved everything in her mind. She was going to be a flagrantly immoral type herself. As soon as possible.

She was so absorbed in looking at all the people and buildings that she only just made it down the outside steps of the omnibus in time to get off at the bottom of Regent Street.

She stood on the pavement, taking in the honking motor-cars, the statue of Eros and the curved foyer of the Criterion Theatre. She'd only ever seen Piccadilly Circus on a cigarette card that she'd stolen from Clement's bureau, but now she wanted to pinch herself. She was actually doing this. She was actually here.

Pigeons applauded themselves into flight and a tiny, foolish part of her felt they might be congratulating her, too. Because she realized now that she hadn't actually expected to get away. Not really. Not *disappearing* like this. It filled her with a strange, nervous euphoria.

She stared at a pair of women draped in fox and mink furs, and at a small child in a fawn three-piece suit and matching cap, skipping along beside a nanny pushing an unwieldy navy-blue pram. A veteran soldier limped along on crutches. *The poor man.* Another brave soul wounded by that dreadful war. Why had it taken all the good men, and spared monsters like Clement?

She crossed the road and went right up to the statue of Eros, her dark thoughts about Clement unsettling her so much that she shuddered. Perhaps if she touched the famous statue, it would bring her luck. Perhaps it would make Verity Casey real. She willed it to be true, as she walked up the steps and reached out her trembling hand to the curved, blackened brass. The fish-heads in the intricate design eyed her coldly.

She trailed her hand along the smooth edge of the trough, walking round the statue, reading its inscription: *The strong sympathies of his heart and the great powers of his mind . . .*

Clement's strong heart had stopped now. And his sharp mind was dead, too. Caught by the enormity of these granite-like facts, Anna stared up at Eros's bow against the grey clouds. She'd done that to him. Her brother was gone forever. Because of her. And suddenly an image of Clement as a little boy giggling at Christmas, with the cream from the trifle around his mouth, made her gulp and caused tears to spring to her eyes.

A light drizzle was starting to fall and people were hurrying along the pavement, putting up their umbrellas. From her vantage point, each black disc seemed like a personal rebuff, a reminder of her guilt and hopelessness.

Now the heady euphoria she'd felt earlier popped, and

the facts seemed to slap her one by one, as tangible as the raindrops. She was on the run from everything, and from everyone she knew. A lone fugitive in this terrifying metropolis, with just two pounds to her name and not a friend in the world. Terrible things could happen to a girl like her. She had assumed that she'd land on her feet, but what if she now fell flat? What then?

She stared up at the tip of Eros's bow, her face in the rain, and made a wish: *Please, someone . . . please save me.*

But nothing happened. Anna waited for a full five minutes, feeling the drizzle getting heavier and soak through the wool of her coat, willing it on like a punishment. She knew she should find somewhere to shelter, but somehow she was rooted to the statue. At least standing here, in the centre of London, she could imagine that, momentarily, she was the calm in the eye of a storm. Were she to step away, then a whirlwind of trouble and indecision would surely sweep her up.

She sneezed loudly, then shivered, her teeth chattering. She remembered the train now, and how she'd spent the night feeling frozen to her core.

'Come on,' she said, out loud. 'Pull yourself together.'

What would Martha tell her to do? No doubt she'd prescribe a hot meal and a good night's sleep. Yes, that was probably the best solution. She caught the bus back to the hotel and was disappointed that her new friend, Wilf, wasn't on the door. She had an early supper of steak-and-kidney pie and beans, alone in the dining room. It was delicious, but she couldn't help calculating how expensive each mouthful was.

As she ate, she tried to focus on the events that had

happened before she'd fled Darton Hall, but they seemed to be blurring in her memory, as if they were being smudged out.

When she thought of home now, she could only see the blurred grey blocks of Darton Hall in the evening rain. She remembered everything that had preceded her flight as if it had happened to someone else in another time. How she'd argued with her father about Clement, and he'd slapped her face and sent her to her room, where she'd flung open the musty drawers of her tallboy and pulled her clothes into her carpet bag on the bed, tears coursing down her face.

She wondered now what would have happened if she'd managed to leave just with that resolve. Whether her anguished fury would have held. Or whether she'd have crumbled and slunk back to the Hall, before anyone had noticed she'd gone. Whether she'd have succumbed to the pattern that had shaped her life: fear and guilt leading to remorse and penance.

But instead Clement had intercepted her flight, and her resolve had turned into a necessity.

And now it was done. She'd gone for good.

After dinner, she walked slowly around the public areas of the hotel, marvelling that there was a Ladies' Smoking Room and wishing that she had the nerve to go into it. There was a lecture going on in one of the large rooms and a cello recital in another, but she couldn't bring herself to step into the crowd, for fear of being noticed. Yet she longed for someone to talk to – anyone who might stop her being alone with her conscience. But everyone ignored her. And later, as she crawled into the single bed, Anna felt so alone that she cried herself to sleep.

7

The Waitress

Anna woke up shivering, although the room was quite warm, the maid having lit the fire last night. At first she thought she was still in Darton Hall and then she remembered and leapt out of bed, as if she could distance herself from the terrible sense of guilt. She dressed quickly, counting her money and realizing that she was going to have to make a plan.

She hadn't been thinking straight yesterday, but now it seemed glaringly obvious: if her parents had alerted the police and they worked out that she might have got on a train, then surely they'd come straight to the nearest hotel and find her. And there would be the evidence: her name in the book.

No, there was only one thing for it. She had to find somewhere else to stay. And fast. And that wasn't all; she was going to have to find some kind of a job. It had never occurred to her that existing in the city would be so expensive. She had no qualms about getting her hands dirty. She'd learnt all about the young society women who had worked at Guy's Hospital during the war, and she knew that she wouldn't have a problem 'mixing with the masses', as her mother would say. But how?

At breakfast, she sat at the small table between two leafy aspidistras, looking at the other diners, wondering why her head was aching so much. She caught the eye of several people, wondering if any of them might take pity on her and talk to her, but they resolutely continued to mind their own business.

She felt overwhelmed by the choices she was going to have to make by herself, without any guidance. She tried to remember her pledge to live impetuously, but it was so much harder than she'd imagined, now that she was here.

She'd been so desperate to get away, but now the impulsive decisions she'd made – one after the other, in the last forty-eight hours – suddenly felt overwhelming. And foolish, too. There'd been no plan. There still wasn't a plan.

'I hope you don't mind me asking, but is it difficult to get a position at a hotel like this?' Anna asked the waitress as she poured her tea.

The young girl look startled. She had a plain face with large brown eyes. 'I couldn't say, Miss,' she said, sounding defensive, as if Anna were questioning her right to her job. 'I know there's a waiting list. Always is.'

Anna nodded, smiling at the girl. 'I see.'

She felt stupid that she'd offended the waitress. And pathetic for even attempting to cross the class boundary that the girl clearly felt lay between them.

'You see, I can't afford to stay here,' she confided, hoping to salvage the situation. She longed for the girl to see her through sympathetic eyes.

'Not many people can. It costs more for one night than I earn in a month.'

This was sobering news. How would she survive, if someone like this girl, with a decent job, earned so little?

It was only now that Anna realized how pitifully ill-prepared her life so far had made her, for her present situation. Her ability to ride a horse, or to execute some balletic pliés and pirouettes, was obviously going to be useless in London, as was her mediocre ability to play the piano. She could sew and she loved the idea of fashion, but how could she use any of these skills to earn money?

'I need to find somewhere else to stay. Before my aunt joins me,' she said hurriedly, remembering her lie. 'Do you know where I might happen to find cheap lodgings?'

'I live with my parents,' the girl replied, with a shrug. 'I couldn't say.'

8

The Boarding House

Anna packed her bag slowly, eking out her stay in the hotel until the last possible minute. She'd thought she'd be able to come to London and reinvent herself, and fall effortlessly into a life of glamour and plenty. She'd been so convinced that there was a space in this city, just waiting for her to fill it, but now she saw what a fool she'd been.

Cramming her clothes into the carpet bag, she tried to steel herself for the outside world. This had probably been the easy bit, she concluded. Now the real test of her strength would begin, although every part of her longed to crawl back into the comfortable little bed and pull the quilt over her head.

When she checked out, she was pleased to see Wilf at the door.

'Where are you off to?' he asked her.

She looked up at the grey sky and the busy street. 'I don't know.'

'You don't know?' he checked, with an amused grin, and she realized how naive she must seem.

'My aunt is delayed and I've decided to stay in London, but I'll need a cheaper place to stay.'

'You'll need a boarding house,' he said. 'Hard to find a good one. I know that much. I heard there were places in Brunswick Square.'

'Where's that?'

'Bloomsbury.'

'Thank you,' she said, as if she'd heard of Bloomsbury. She wished she had some money to spare to tip him.

'Take the Tube, I would,' he said, seeing her confusion. 'You'll find the maps at King's Cross. Good luck, Miss,' he called after her as Anna set off, and she felt a pang at leaving such luxury and kindness.

She bought a map, but it was difficult to find Brunswick Square, especially as the Underground was much more confusing and frightening than she'd expected.

She sat on the edge of the upholstered seat, gripping the armrest, watching her reflection in the dark window. As the lights flickered, she felt fear race around inside her. What if the Tube train got stuck, or stopped? She didn't like the feeling that the man who was hanging onto the leather strap was giving her, or the noise of the train as it whistled through the tunnels. She felt terrified that she might get lost, then remembered that, technically, she was already lost. She sneezed and shivered. She really didn't feel very well.

By the time Anna found Brunswick Square, her head was pounding. Walking along the pavement next to the black railings, she looked up at the row of dirty terraced houses. This was a far cry from the Midland Grand.

But she had no choice, she reminded herself. And she so desperately wanted to lie down. She could feel chills racing up and down her spine. She had always been strong and never prone to sickness, so now the thought that she might be ill came as a shock. How would she look after herself if she became poorly? Because what would happen if she got *really* sick? What if she died?

In the front window of the third house Anna saw a sign saying 'Vacancies' and she opened the iron gate, which squeaked loudly. She knocked on the door, praying that it might be opened by a friendly face. She was met by a red-faced woman with rough hands and a dirty apron. Her eyes were cold as she looked Anna up and down. When Anna explained that she was looking for accommodation and had seen the Vacancies sign, the woman tutted.

'You're a fine little one, ain't you?' another woman leered. Anna realized that the voice belonged to a woman on the doorstep of the next-door house, who was addressing her over the railings. She was wearing a shawl with red fringing, her hair dyed the most alarming orange, her lips smeared red to match her shawl. 'You looking for lodgings?'

'Yes,' Anna admitted, taking a step towards her.

'Oi, Rose, leave her alone.' This was the landlady, who now stepped forward and grabbed Anna's arm. 'Come in here, Miss,' she said.

Anna looked in confusion at Rose, the other woman, who laughed knowingly and licked her lips. She followed the land-lady through the grubby front door.

'You don't want to be talking to the likes of her, believe me,' the woman said. 'She'd eat you for breakfast, if she could.'

Anna felt confused. Apart from Wilf, Rose had been the most friendly person she'd met since arriving in London.

The whole house smelt of suet cooking, and the wallpaper was black with streaks of damp. Anna reassured herself that it wasn't that bad, but even so, it took all her effort not to put the cuff of her coat over her nose to mask the smell.

In the kitchen at the back, a giant pot bubbled on a black stove, and the sink was piled with dirty plates.

'I'm Mrs Jackson,' the woman said.

Anna nearly introduced herself as Verity Casey, but thought Mrs Jackson might laugh at her, so she said her name. 'I'm Anna.'

Mrs Jackson looked suspicious. 'You staying long? You got work?'

'No, I haven't. You see, I've just arrived and—'

'You don't look very well. Are you in the family way? I'm not taking you, if you're in the family way.'

'No!' Anna said, astonished that the woman had made such extreme assumptions about her. 'I seem to have a headache. That's all.'

'Yes, well, I'm sorry to ask, but one of my last tenants caused a terrible commotion.'

'Who's this then?' Anna turned to see a man with arms like hams coming through the back door, in a grubby collarless shirt, his braces hanging down.

Anna backed away. This wasn't good – these people . . . they were the wrong sort. She could sense it now, as the hairs on the back of her neck stood up, and the man looked her up and down. She shouldn't have come in, she realized. She should have looked around and found a respectable place.

'New one. Fresh in,' Mrs Jackson said.

The man came right up to Anna and looked into her face,

before feeling the wool collar of her coat between his grubby fingers.

'A month up front,' the man said. Anna recoiled from his breath. 'And she can have the room on the third.'

She wanted to run, but she forced herself to stay calm, although her stomach churned with misgivings. She handed over almost all the rest of her money to the man, who terrified her nearly as much as Clement had. She was furious with herself as they climbed the rickety stairs, but she felt as if all her energy had drained away.

They passed a girl with blonde hair on the way. She was wearing a fashionable dress and looked at Anna appraisingly.

'Oh, a new girl,' she said, but Anna was unsettled by the knowing smile that she gave her. 'Good luck in *that* room.'

'Don't mind Suzanna,' Mr Jackson said. But Anna looked after her, as she flounced down the stairs. She could hear the voices of other young women and felt slightly heartened. Could she possibly find friends here?

Mr Jackson opened the door to a small room at the end of the corridor. A chipped chamber pot was balanced on a chair, catching drips from a leak in the ceiling. The air was acrid with stale smoke and damp. So this was what the girl Suzanna must have meant, about needing luck for this room. It was dreadful. She couldn't even begin to think what Martha would say about her staying somewhere so awful, but it was too late to back out now.

She shivered and tried to smile and tell Mr Jackson it would do nicely, but he just slammed the door. Anna bit her lips together, telling herself to be strong, as she put down her carpet bag. How could she have been so stupid as to have handed over all her money before checking the room? She felt annoyed with herself that he'd taken advantage of her so easily. And that girl, Suzanna, must have thought she was a complete fool.

On the other side of the wall, she heard a couple arguing. And then she heard the sound of someone being struck, and a scream. Anna gasped, ran to the door and opened it. Mr Jackson was standing on the other side, leaning against the rickety bannister, as if he'd been waiting for her.

'You mind your own business, Miss,' he said, nodding for her to go back into the room. 'There's a good girl.'

9

Robbed

The fever struck with such alarming intensity that Anna was unable to get up the next morning. She lay alternately shivering and sweating in the damp bed, listening to the strange noises of the house, wondering what was real and what had been in her dreams.

She told herself to pull herself together, but her bones felt as if they were made of lead and she gave up trying to get dressed. At some point Mrs Jackson had been up to the room and had reluctantly delivered soup, and Anna had tried to reassure her, through chattering teeth, that she was going to be better soon. But in the dead of night, with drunk people lurching around in the street below and the couple arguing on the other side of the thin wall, she felt so wretched that she wondered whether she might die. And when morning came, her fever kept on getting worse.

Days passed as she slipped in and out of consciousness, delirious dreams about Clement racing around her mind. At one point she was convinced that Clement was in the room with her, telling her to be quiet; and even though a part of her knew that she was alone and miles away from home, she still shook with terror. At times she cried – for Martha, of all people. As the nights bled into the days, Anna became convinced that this was the end.

She was woken nearly a week later by the sound of church bells and birdsong. It was early on a Sunday morning and Anna realized she was ravenous – and better enough to get up.

Her legs were wobbly as she made her way to the dirty bathroom, glad of the cold water to wash away the acrid sweat. But when she looked in the mirror, there were dark circles under her eyes and her skin was sallow. 'You didn't die,' she told her reflection. 'That's something, at least.'

Back in her room, she sat back on the bed with a sigh and gathered her clothes to get dressed. She reached into her pocket to count the rest of her money to make a plan, but the notes weren't there. She searched through her bag and her clothes twice more, but her money had gone. She felt a hollow despair grow and grow inside her.

Downstairs in the kitchen, Anna lost the nerve to challenge Mrs Jackson about the lost money. The landlady didn't seem particularly bothered that she was better, only relieved that she hadn't died. She asked for some breakfast, but Mrs Jackson said she didn't have much in and that Anna was to wait in the living room. Suzanna, the girl she'd seen on the stairs, smiled at her as she went into the small room. She was lying on one of the sofas, her feet up on the arm, smoking a cigarette.

'You had quite a fever,' she said.

'I know.'

'We were worried about you.'

Worried enough to rob me, Anna wanted to say. 'I'm better, I think.'

They must have been around the same age, but Suzanna seemed so much more worldly. They talked about the weather, and then Anna plucked up the courage to tell Suzanna that she'd been robbed.

'Of course you were. You didn't lock the door. You can't trust anyone in this place.'

Anna nodded, feeling stupid. 'I don't know what I'll do, now the money's gone. I need a job – and fast.'

Suzanna leant forward, looking towards the door as if frightened of being overheard by Mrs Jackson. 'You could work for Rose.'

Anna remembered the woman next door, who had leered at her. 'Work doing what?'

'Oh, you're a green one all right,' Suzanna laughed.

Anna felt confused, so Suzanna enlightened her. 'She runs a bespoke service. We . . .' she paused, sucking on her cigarette, 'entertain certain gentlemen.'

Anna felt a flush starting right inside her. 'I couldn't, I mean—'

'It's not for everyone, I'll grant you that,' Suzanna said, letting her off the hook. She stood and crossed her arms over her slender waist, appraising Anna. 'If you're really short of money, I'll buy that coat from you,' she offered, looking at Theresa Darton's checked coat, which hung over Anna's arm.

'This?' Anna asked, holding it up.

'Yes. I need a new coat, and I rather admired that one when you came in.'

Anna couldn't help feeling that the money Suzanna handed over a few minutes later was rather grubby, but she didn't care.

When Mrs Jackson brought in tea, Anna loaded sugar into it and then took the paper that was folded on the small wooden table by the fire and pored over it for news of Darton. She read all the obituaries, too, looking for any mention of Clement.

But there was nothing about Lancashire at all and she put the paper down, then saw an advertisement for a show. She ran her finger over the picture of the chorus line. The girls, with their long legs and bright smiles – if only she could be one of them. If only she could belong to something. Instead, she felt like a ghost. Here, but not here.

She wandered out and found a church on the corner of the street. The service was over and Anna went inside and sat in the pew, staring up at the wooden cross above the altar.

She'd so hoped to become Verity Casey, with a bright future, but instead she'd lost all of her money and, with it, her hope. And now, having spent the worst week of her life, alone and sick, she prayed things would start to get better. But a churning sense of fear overcame her. The sale of her mother's coat would only sustain her for a short time, and fairly soon she was going to be completely penniless. And what then?

The boarding house was bad, but being on the streets would be a hundred times worse. The word 'destitute' sprang to her mind. Anna knew all about the shame of being destitute. Her father believed anyone who lost their home to be degenerate and feeble-minded, and thoroughly deserving of the fate that befell them. He and Clement had always been quick to mock the poor and unfortunate. But perhaps they were right. Perhaps she would be thoroughly deserving of her fate, too.

She thought briefly of Suzanna's offer and how she could work for Rose, but she couldn't ever do that, could she? Was that the only option? To sell her body, in order to eat?

Maybe she should telegram her parents. Admit what she'd done. Get them to pay for her ticket home, where she would have to face the police and her punishment – although this felt like punishment enough.

But then . . . she'd got this far, hadn't she? To London. To a place she'd only ever dreamt of. She thought of the advert in the paper and of the smiling dancing girls.

'Please, God,' she whispered, 'I know we probably don't believe much in each other any more, but please, if you're there, give me strength.'

10

Blackness

Noises . . . voices and pain. *Pain*. He gasped as he felt himself swimming up into consciousness from the darkness.

He saw a blurred face above him. A woman with a white hat. A nurse?

Voices.

'I think he's coming round. Clement? Clement, can you hear me?'

Shadows coming closer. Slowly focusing now: Mother . . . in a black dress, her face pale, leaning down. He tried to move, but couldn't. Something was on his face. What? A bandage . . . Where was he?

'Can he speak?' His father's impatient voice.

'Give him time, Darius.' Another man's voice. A glimpse of his face. Was it Doctor Whatley? 'It's a miracle he's made it.'

The people all went blurry again, then a sharp scratch. A needle in his arm.

Pain, but it subsided. A warm, fuzzy feeling set in.

Then a memory: *her* . . . Anna – that *bitch*.

11

The Girl in the Green Coat

Determined not to have to succumb to Suzanna's proposal to work for Rose, Anna took to the streets, resolved to discover the city – her eyes open for any kind of possibility. Surely it was only a matter of being positive, she told herself. *Something would turn up, surely?*

She'd gone further afield each day, first to the British Museum and then down to Trafalgar Square, wandering around the National Gallery and marvelling at the artworks.

Today she walked along Shaftesbury Avenue and, as she walked, she hummed 'Bye Bye Blackbird', trying to keep herself steady and to ignore the rain.

Her mother, Theresa, had always told her that singing of any sort – apart from in church – was vulgar and unnecessary, but Anna had always loved music, pressing herself against the wireless when she was alone, to devour the romance of the latest songs. Now she stopped to shelter under the awning of a theatre.

It wasn't open yet, so she peered in through the glass doors to the foyer, looking longingly at the red carpet and imagining the theatre beyond. What if she stayed until opening time: might she meet the manager and get a job selling tickets? Or even become a cleaner? She would do anything. Anything at all.

It was only now that she noticed a girl running through the traffic, dodging the umbrellas as she held on to her green felt cloche hat. Anna didn't want to stare, but the girl looked impossibly glamorous, as if she had stepped right off the cover of a fashion magazine.

She was wearing a long green coat embroidered with what looked like Chinese figures, with fur trimming grazing her emerald suede shoes, which were adorned with sparkling rhinestone buckles. Anna had never seen anything so extravagant. But the girl seemed to be wearing this outfit as easily as if it were a factory tunic.

She was still gorging her eyes on every detail as the girl came right up to the front of the theatre, just along from where Anna was standing, and she had to rip her gaze away before she seemed rude. *Oh my goodness. Did the girl work here? Could she possibly be one of the actresses, or one of the dancers on the poster?*

But as she sneaked another glance, she saw the girl looking at the silver watch on her wrist and then over in Anna's direction, as if she were looking for someone. Her eyes were heavily lined in kohl, her lips an alluring, glossy red, her pink cheeks bright from the rain.

Anna stared ahead, banging her carpet bag against her knees, feeling dull and grey by comparison, her humming fizzling out as her heart hammered. It was ridiculous standing here, pretending to have a purpose, when she had anything but. And she'd been caught staring, so she had to go on pretending.

But it was so hard not to stare. *Goodness, the girl was lovely.* How did you get to *be* like that? How did one get to look so carefree and yet so styled?

'I say – you're not waiting for anyone, are you?' the girl called over to her, as if she'd suddenly been struck by a thought. It took a moment for Anna to realize that the girl was addressing her. She had a twangy American accent. 'You Edith's friend, by any chance?'

The girl's eyes searched out Anna's, and she realized this was her moment – the moment to cut her off and deny any knowledge of what she was talking about.

Or not. The moment to do the opposite – to truly become someone else. The moment to become Verity Casey.

The young woman suddenly darted forward and put her hand out and grabbed Anna's arm and, without waiting for a reply, laughed. 'Because what if you are? Wouldn't that be a hoot? And so typical of naughty old Edith to stand you up, but then after last night, I doubt she's even been to bed,' she added in a confidential aside. Then she laughed.

Do it. A voice inside Anna spurred her on, stronger than her fear. *Go on. Do it.*

'You know Edith?' Anna said. She'd never pretended such an audacious thing before, but she couldn't bear the girl to leave. She was so desperate that taking such a monumental risk seemed worth it.

'Ha! I knew it. I just knew it. The moment I saw you. Edith said you were pretty in that . . . well, *understated* way. But she's quite wrong, of course. You're simply lovely,' the girl said, before linking her arm through Anna's and leading her along the pavement. Simply being near her was like being lit up by starlight. 'We'd best hurry. You don't want to know what a beast Mr Connelly is, if we're one moment late. Edith will just have to meet us there. Taxi!'

12

Taxi

'Hot diggity dog. It's turning into quite a squall,' the young woman exclaimed, as she sat back on the maroon leather seat in the taxi cab and sighed with satisfaction, having given instructions to the driver to go to the Savoy Hotel.

Wasn't that where rich, society people went? Anna thought. *The Savoy! She was on her way to the Savoy with this amazing, sophisticated young American.*

Anna watched, spellbound, as the girl opened the clip of her snakeskin handbag and pulled out an embossed gold compact and checked her perfect make-up, dabbing pressed powder onto her shining cheeks. She was tempted to tell the girl that this light London drizzle was nothing like a squall. Nothing like the horizontal rain that drove down the Pennine hills at the back of Darton Hall, and which could drench you in seconds. That was a squall. This was . . . well, this was . . .

Nothing short of a miracle.

But this had to stop! Right now, Anna told herself. *Didn't it?* But with each passing second she was tumbling deeper and deeper into this wonderful young creature's misguided assumption. Just when she'd had nothing at all but possible destitution facing her, or worse – the prospect of having to become one of Rose's 'ladies' – this was a lifeline, one that she couldn't bring herself to break by telling the truth.

'Now,' the girl said, 'I can't remember your name. I'm Nancy, but you probably knew that already,' she said, followed by that tinkling laugh of hers.

'Oh, I'm Verity. Verity Casey,' Anna lied, deliberately trying out an accent – one that she hoped seemed modern and didn't given even a hint of her northern roots. She wanted Nancy to think the best of her.

'Verity? Oh. I thought Edie said it was something else.' Nancy's perfectly arched eyebrows puckered together for a minute, and then the thought was gone. She looked up from the compact and Verity noticed that her eyes were green, her nose slightly turned up. She was younger than her chic clothes had implied. 'Hmm, well, I shall call you Very. No, no, that's quite wrong – you can be Vita. Yes. That's much better. My very own little Vita. I do so admire Miss Sackville-West.'

Anna had never heard of the woman that Nancy mentioned, but she was too entranced by the girl. 'Vita,' she said. 'I like that.'

She rolled the innovation around her mind as she looked out of the window, smiling to herself as they drove down Charing Cross Road, past the Hippodrome towards Trafalgar Square. Vita. She could be Vita. Couldn't she? *I'm Vita. Vita Casey*, she said to herself. *Vita, Vita, Vita.* The more she said it in her mind, the more she liked it. As if she were trying on a fanciful new coat and finding that it fitted.

If Nancy believed it was possible, then surely it was. She pressed her lips together hard, a heady feeling rushing up her chest that suddenly made her want to laugh and then to blurt everything out. But she couldn't. She wouldn't. Not ever.

Nancy snapped the compact shut. 'So, tell me, dear *Vita*, how many auditions have you been to before?'

Auditions?

'Um—' she began, bracing herself to speak up, but Nancy immediately interrupted.

'Well, don't worry. It's more to do with whether your face fits than how fast you can dance. Since Loretta ran off with that *ghastly* little man, our troupe has been quite up the swanny. And Edith has vouched for you,' she added, 'although I don't know *why* Mr Connelly has such a soft spot for Edith. I suppose you might know better than me why she's stuck on that old lounge lizard . . .'

In the confusing monologue that followed, the only thing that became clear was that Nancy had taken it for granted that 'Vita' knew all about Edith, who sounded – as far as Anna could make out – like some sort of lapsed society girl. The implication was that Edith's relationship with this Mr Connelly person was more personal than was strictly professional, and this wasn't the first time that 'wicked' Edith had used her 'considerable charms' to finagle her way into work.

Anna listened, awestruck. It was like she was suddenly part of a thrilling game. How wonderful to be embroiled in such trivial gossip, when her mind had been so occupied with much darker thoughts.

She glanced out of the window to hide her blushing cheeks, as Nancy continued, chattering on about Mr Connelly. There was Nelson's Column, sliding by beside her, and she craned her neck to look out of the cab window to see the top. It was huge. Almost as huge as the deception she was creating.

'I mean, I'm American, so I'm hardly shockable, and not one to judge anyone commandeering a sugar daddy, but how Edith could bring herself even to touch that man, I can't imagine.'

But now she became aware that Nancy had finally paused and it was her turn to respond. Amazed at herself – that she was *really doing this* – Anna cocked her head conspiratorially towards Nancy.

'Well, Edith has mentioned a *few* things about him,' she ventured, letting her comment hang. Nancy's eyes widened with the heavy hint of gossip that she'd implied. Then, really going for a dramatic tone, she added, 'But I can't really say more. It wouldn't be right.'

Nancy raised her eyebrows and gave a wicked smile, clearly intent on finding out the 'more' that Vita might be hiding.

Anna felt giddy with the boldness of the lie. Its decisiveness, its unknowable consequences. And proud, too. That she could be this risqué person.

'Stop here,' Nancy said suddenly, and the driver pulled over in the traffic. Anna saw the Savoy Hotel on the other side of the road. 'It'll take ages to turn.'

'Right-ho, Miss,' the driver said. He'd been listening in to the conversation. He caught her eye in the driver's mirror and smiled.

Anna stood on the pavement as Nancy paid for the cab, and watched a smart car turning into the driveway of the hotel. That was a Rolls-Royce Phantom, she was sure of it.

Her father had said that he was going to order one, now that production in the mills was at an all-time high.

This was her moment to bolt, but it was already too late. Nancy grabbed her arm and linked hers through it and then, holding onto her hat with her other hand, walked along the pavement. There were a few appreciative honks from the cab drivers. A tram bell clanged, along with the church bells of St Martin-in-the-Fields.

'Oh, goodness,' Anna murmured under her breath. It was as if she were on a helter-skelter going far too fast. And she knew, with absolute certainty, that sooner or later she was going to crash.

13

The Dressing Room

She would never have noticed the side-alley along the Strand, or the unassuming stage door set back from the street, but Nancy led her right through it, into a tunnel-like corridor. The walls were of plain brick, lit only by sparse gas lamps. Anna had to squint to get used to the sudden gloom.

'Welcome to the Zip Club,' Nancy said, her heels clicking on the stone floor. 'It's nothing much back here, but we have quite a reputation.' She laughed and did a pose over her shoulder, putting a finger to her pout.

'Oh?' What exactly did she mean by *reputation*? Anna – *no*, Vita – was finding it difficult to breathe.

'Darling, didn't Edith fill you in? We're only one of the best nightspots in the whole of this crazy town. You must have heard of us?'

Nightspot? Anna remembered how she'd wanted so badly to become a flagrantly immoral type, but she hadn't really believed it might happen. And now all her bravado deserted her. Her parents would positively kill her, if they knew she was here. *But they would never know*, she remembered. Even so, *what on earth was she getting herself into?*

She was saved from answering by a man with a clipboard,

wearing turned-up tweed trousers and rolled-up shirt sleeves, who bustled down the thin corridor towards them.

'Onstage in five. You're late,' he barked at Nancy, who rolled her eyes and pulled a funny face.

'Don't mind Jerome. He's musical. And highly strung,' she said, as she threw open a dark-green door and ushered Anna in.

A dressing table ran all along the back wall, the surface of which was covered in various pots of powder and jars of make-up brushes, along with several impressive bunches of flowers in china vases, which were now past their best. The space above the dressing table was covered with mirrors, with elaborate headdresses hanging on hooks between them. The air was thick with perfume and the smoky smell of electrics.

Nancy, entirely missing how awestruck her guest was, walked over and collected a pile of envelopes, then slung her bag on the dark-green leather armchair and plucked a dress that was hanging over the back.

'Looks like the others have already changed. Here, you can put this one on,' she said, throwing it over to Anna, who caught it with difficulty, as she was still holding onto her carpet bag. 'It's a spare. You can change behind there,' she added, now distracted by the envelopes. She gestured to a black enamelled screen in the corner, over the top of which hung several pairs of pink stockings, 'Although around here there's really no point in being modest. We've seen it all before.'

Anna looked down at the cream silk slip-dress draped over her arm. It was the most daring garment she'd ever seen.

A dancer's dress. She was actually holding it. And it was so flimsy. Barely more than a petticoat slip with sparkling fringing. She couldn't put that on . . . could she?

'You heard what Jerome said. We'd better get out there,' Nancy added, throwing down the envelopes on the chair and starting to strip off herself. 'Connelly's got himself in a bit of a stew about our routines.'

She threw the coat away with wild abandon, to reveal a very fancy green-and-black lace dress, daringly cut just below the knee. A black silk sash was tied in a floppy bow around her slim hips, which made her figure look enviously boyish.

But before Anna could admire the detail further, Nancy lifted the dress over her head in one easy movement and stood there unashamedly in her pretty pink slip, like she was the model on the front of a pattern.

Anna had hardly ever been face-to-face with another girl in their underwear, let alone one so clearly confident in her own skin. Nancy looked . . . well, stunning. She never knew that such a lovely garment could exist. She longed to touch the silk and run her fingers over the lace. Her pulse throbbed in her cheeks.

Quickly averting her eyes, and terrified that Nancy would see her blushes, Anna ducked behind the screen. Her hands were shaking as she fumbled with her gloves and unbuttoned her thin cotton jacket. She looked down at the worn assortment of clothes she was wearing. Her long skirt underneath her dress was still stained with the mud that had gathered on the hem on her flight from Darton Hall. Her best Sunday blouse, which had always been her favourite item of clothing, now seemed hopelessly dowdy and old-fashioned. She thought about the worn boned corset she was wearing, its fabric yellowed with age and sweat. *This had to stop. She had to tell Nancy the truth. Right now.*

But she'd gone too far. How could she extricate herself now?

Maybe she could just get changed very slowly, and kill time while she worked out what she was going to do. But then she heard a new voice. A man's voice.

'I was sent to look for you. The others are already out there.'

She craned her neck and looked in the mirror, realizing she had a clear view to the door. A young man with smooth boyish skin stood there, with a tape measure around his neck. He was wearing small tortoiseshell glasses, a blue shirt with the sleeves rolled up, a woollen sleeveless jumper and natty light-blue slacks, the kind that her father might consider appropriate attire for a golf course.

'Howdy-doody, Percy. I was collecting Edith's friend,' she heard Nancy say.

Anna realized that Percy had a direct view of her in the mirror.

'Vita, come and meet Percy. He's a perfect lamb,' Nancy called.

Percy nodded to her and, as his eyes met hers, she wondered if he could tell how terrified she felt.

14
Right Foot First

I'm Verity Casey . . . Vita. Vita for short, she told herself, trying not to succumb to rising panic as Nancy pulled her towards the middle of the stage. She should have taken her chance and bolted before she'd put the costume on, but Nancy hadn't left her alone – or stopped talking – for a second.

But now each long moment stretched out, as Anna's eyes adjusted to the lights and she took in the Zip Club, wanting to pinch herself that she was actually in a London nightclub – albeit during the day. And not just in it. *Onstage.*

She could see a shadowy area in front her, and empty tables dotted further back around a sprung dance floor. At the back were dark booths. The air smelt dusty in the lights, and of stale alcohol and smoke. It was simply wonderful.

'Where *is* Edith?' Nancy said, in a confused whisper, as if Anna should know. 'She's a flake, *as we all know,* but she's never usually this late.' She was clearly vexed that Anna's introduction had fallen to her.

In her costume, Nancy looked astounding. She had perfect skin and, although she was short, she seemed to have very long legs. She appeared to exude class and effortless style and, next to her, Anna felt painfully self-conscious. Knowing that she was hurtling towards the moment when she'd be found out felt terrifying, but oh, she *so wanted* Nancy to like her.

Anna watched as Nancy fluffed the fringe of her jet-black bob with her fingertips, and she had to suppress the urge to copy her.

Quickly she looked around, to the wings of the stage, as if she too were perplexed by Edith's absence, but actually looking for an escape route, should she need to run . . . which was getting more likely by the second.

She saw the other girls – four of them, dressed just like Nancy – fanning out behind her, taking up positions on the stage. They were all looking at her with intense curiosity. Beneath the glare of the lights, she might as well have been naked. A tight knot of anguish grew and grew inside her, until she almost couldn't breathe. One of the girls, with lustrous wavy black hair, gave her a friendly wave. Anna smiled weakly back. Did they honestly believe she could be one of them?

'Mr Connelly, this is the new girl. Edith's friend,' Nancy piped up, grabbing Anna's wrist and pulling her towards the front of the stage, putting up her hand to shield her eyes in the lights. 'You said she could have an audition. She's a doll, don't you think?' She pronounced it *dahl*.

Nancy turned and held her hands out towards Anna with a big grin, like a magician presenting his assistant, but there was no response from the dark shadows, only a low murmur of male voices. Nancy's arms dropped and she shrugged, then winked at her for reassurance, but there continued to be a distinct lack of response.

Anna didn't know what to do with herself. The shimmery dress swished around her legs, the sequins catching the light. Surely it was sinful to have her shoulders so exposed? She resisted the urge to tug at the top of the fringed dress, where it strained across her breasts in an unbecoming way. Goodness only knew what would happen if she started to move. Not that she was planning on dancing! Anything but that. A trickle of sweat slid down her back to her buttocks and she clenched her fingers into her palms, feeling her skin goosebump.

'Name?' a gruff male voice demanded from the shadows, startling her.

'Ann— I mean . . . er . . . Verity.'

'Speak up.'

'Verity. Verity Casey, sir. My friends call me Vita.' She half-smiled across at Nancy, feeling a lump in her throat. *Oh, this was so bad*. She was going to be in so much trouble.

'You in a contract, Miss Casey?' the voice from the dark demanded.

Nancy flicked her head, encouraging her to speak.

Anna shaded her eyes from the light, straining to see who was talking to her. 'No, sir.'

'You could work right away?'

'Uh . . . yes.'

There was the muffled sound of voices, and then she noticed a man sitting down at a piano near the edge of the stage and saw that it was Jerome. He opened a file of music and balanced it on the stand. He took a drag of his cigarette and then rested it on the top of the piano. The smoke curled up into the darkness.

Anna stared at the polished black floor of the stage, which was pitted with tiny heel-marks.

'He'll want to see you dance,' Nancy whispered, sidling closer to her. 'Just follow me. We start the warm-up with the Charleston. Right foot first. Eight bars in.' She demonstrated the dainty move, and Anna saw straight away that she was an excellent dancer.

Anna had danced on and off all her life, but nothing that might have prepared her for this. There'd been ballet lessons with the awful Miss Scott, who banged her stick on the ground as the girls tried to plié and jeté, and had made the girls parade around with heavy encyclopaedias on their heads to encourage graceful deportment. She'd once whacked Anna's hand with a ruler so hard that the ruler had broken. Then there had been some ballroom-dancing lessons, but her mother had put a stop to them, after Clement had heard that some of the workers were spying on the girls.

Anna had been to the dance hall in Preston once, so she knew all about the Charleston and had practised it when she could; or at least a version of it, behind her mother's back, listening to Clement's gramophone record in the drawing room. But she'd had no idea if she'd been doing it right. Now, flailing her arms around, as she had done then, was only going to make her look like the foolish child she was. She had to say something.

She braced herself, stepping forward right to the edge of the stage, her toe almost off it, but just then Jerome started playing a few tinkling bars of introduction, making her jump back. The girls shuffled, getting ready to dance.

'Five, six, seven . . .' Nancy mouthed.

'Wait a moment, Jerome,' someone called and the piano stopped abruptly.

This was it: her moment of humiliation. From the gloom, it sounded as if two or three people were deep in what was becoming a heated conversation. There was the noise of a scraping chair. She glanced towards the other girls, who now seemed to retreat further back on the stage. The heat of the stage lights seemed to bear down on her.

'Goddamn it, Jack,' she heard someone say. A man's voice. American. 'You've got two months, max, or this place will fold. I'm telling you.'

'What's going on now?' Nancy whispered. She cocked out her hip, staring at Jerome, who shrugged.

'That's all for today,' she heard a voice from the back. The man, whoever he was, sounded angry.

'But, sir,' Nancy piped up. 'What about . . .' She gestured to Anna.

'Fine. You'll do. That's all. See Mrs Winters about a contract. Next call, tomorrow at twelve.'

'Oh, well, that was easy,' Nancy said, clapping her hands with glee. 'Looks like you're one of us. Come and meet everyone.'

15

The Girls

'This is Emma and Jane, Betsy and Jemima,' Nancy gushed, as the girls all jostled around. 'This is Verity, but we're calling her Vita.'

This is actually happening. They really believe I'm Vita.
'How do you do. Vita, is it?' one of the girls said, wanting to get in first. Was she Emma, Jane or Betsy? She was the one who'd given her a wave earlier. 'I'm Emma,' she said.

Anna – no, *Vita* – shook her proffered hand, and tried to remember that Emma was the one with the wavy black hair and deep-blue eyes. Then there was Jemima, with the freckles. She felt like a small chick in a nest, as the plumed, groomed girls stared down at her. She hooked the stray hair from her hairband over her ear. How did that one – Jane, was it? the tall brunette – get her hair to stay in those lustrous curls? She'd never seen such lovely young women. Where she came from, so many women were downtrodden and grey. These shiny, glorious girls were like a whole new species. It was as if she'd stepped into a Greta Garbo film.

'Where you from, Vita?' Jane asked.

'Oh, I, er . . .'

'How do you know Edith?' It was another one of the

girls; Betsy, was it? She had fiery red hair in pin-curls and rouged cheeks.

'Well, I . . .'

'How old are you? If you don't mind me saying, you look frightfully young.'

'Great gams, though,' Nancy chipped in, gesturing to Vita's legs and giving her thigh a friendly slap.

She jumped at the contact and blushed. Nobody had ever complimented her about her figure before. 'Nineteen . . . nearly twenty,' she lied. It was like being pecked by questions.

Suddenly the girls shushed each other, nodding over Vita's shoulder. Another girl with a fur stole over her shoulders, but in one of the dancers' dresses, was strutting towards them across the stage. Her blonde hair was cut short like Nancy's, her feline eyes heavily ringed in black, her fashionably thin brows pencilled in, and her mouth a glossy red with a particularly pointed cupid's bow.

A much smaller girl in day-clothes followed, shy and almost cowering, but it was the girl in front who exuded authority, her gaze making the other girls shrink away from Vita.

'Oh, Edith honey. *There* you are,' Nancy said, breaking away from the group. 'Wherever were you? We waited and—'

'You will never believe the ghastly morning I've had. And you made me late. I've been waiting all this time, Nancy.' Her tone was harsh and accusatory, her plummy accent cutting. It was the voice of a bully.

So this was Edith, Vita realized. Meaning what? That the girl behind her was the girl whose job she had just stolen?

She wasn't 'pretty in an understated way', as Nancy had implied earlier – she was stunning. The girl had exotically dark skin and a perfectly slender figure. How had Nancy ever mistaken Vita for her?

'But it's no bother, darling. I found your friend, Vita, and Mr Connelly has given her a job. The spot in our line-up. Just as you wanted. Isn't that the berries?'

Edith's eyes flashed with fury. 'Who? Who did he give a job to?'

'Verity . . . Vita,' Nancy said, but her voice quavered now with uncertainty. 'I thought she was your friend?'

'*Her?*' Edith's lips curled as she spoke, her eyes blazing at Vita. 'I've never seen her before in my life.'

In the silence that followed, Vita felt everyone staring at her. Nancy spoke next, slowly, as the realization sank in. 'That is too devilish,' she said, arms akimbo. 'Vita, are you not . . . ?'

Her eyes bored into those of Vita, who swallowed hard, sheepishly meeting Nancy's astonished gaze. 'No, I'm sorry. I sort of—'

'You perfect idiot, Nancy!' Edith's mouth was a thin line of fury, as Nancy gasped. 'Can't you see that she's clearly an imposter? As if I would ever be friends with someone like *her*. You Americans!' She threw her arm up in disdain, before marching over to where Vita was standing. 'Where are you from?' she demanded, jabbing her roughly on the collarbone with a forefinger, the shock of it making Vita stumble backwards. 'The Troc? The Kit Kat? Those sneaky girls are always trying to get in here.'

'I'm sorry, I promise I'm not, I . . . I'm so sorry.' Vita

pulled away, too frightened to cry. Edith looked furious enough to hit her. Vita had seen that look enough to know.

A small woman with curly grey hair in a dowdy black dress walked onto the stage, a bottle-green knitted cardigan balanced on her shoulders. 'Verity, is it?' she said in an exhausted voice, looking at her notepad. 'Miss Casey?'

This must be Mrs Winters, whom she'd been told to see. 'Yes, that's me,' she piped up, before she'd even known she was going to speak. It was the only thing to do. To get out of Edith's line of fire. She quickly sidestepped Edith towards Mrs Winters, but Edith moved quickly too, barging Vita out of her way as she beat her to it. The elderly woman looked up, dismayed at the unseemly scuffle.

'What's going on?' she asked, staring between Edith and Vita.

'This is intolerable. She's an imposter. She's not meant to be here at all. Call Jack back,' Edith demanded, her voice rising hysterically. 'I insist. We need to clear this terrible mess up at once. Don't let her sign anything.'

'Mr Connelly has left the building,' Mrs Winters said, her tone icy. It was clear she wasn't happy about taking instructions from Edith. She also disapproved of Edith being on first-name terms with Mr Connelly.

'Well, get him back,' Edith snapped, as if the woman was an imbecile.

Mrs Winters drew up her formidable chest and positioned her spectacles on her nose.

Vita glanced behind her into the wings and saw Percy standing with his arms folded, taking it all in. He was trying to suppress a smile.

'Ugh!' Edith made an exasperated growl and flounced towards him, her shoulder shoving against Percy's. 'Do I have to do *everything* around here?'

'Edith, wait!' Nancy said.

Vita looked down at her feet, wishing the stage would open up beneath her and swallow her whole. But then Jerome dropped his music book on the piano keys and a discordant sound rang out.

Percy strolled over, as the girls erupted into shocked gossiping. Vita felt close to tears. She looked at him, imploring him to take her side.

'Ignore her,' he whispered to Vita. 'Mrs Winters, my dear, Mr Connelly was quite clear that he wants to sign up Miss Casey. She's exactly what the girls have been looking for. And, as we all know, time is of the essence. So let's make this simple, shall we? Vita will sign the paperwork, and then I'm sure one of the girls will find you a cup of tea and a biscuit. You look run off your feet, as usual.'

For the first time, Mrs Winters smiled. A little kindness went a long way, even with her, it seemed.

16

Wisey

Vita wanted to pinch herself as the girls took her backstage, after she'd signed Mrs Winters's forms.

'You're being so nice,' she said to Jane, as she led her down the narrow corridor back to the dressing room.

Jane gave her a sideways smile. 'I've been a rabbit caught in the headlights myself, darling, but I've rarely seen anyone braver than you. Nobody ever stands up to Edith Montgomery.'

'I didn't really stand up to her,' Vita said, feeling oddly close to tears. It felt nice to be called 'darling' by someone so glamorous. 'I honestly didn't mean it to go this far. I sort of got swept up with Nancy and I wanted to tell her the truth, but she didn't stop talking and . . .' She hung her head. 'But the truth is, my life has been so *awful* recently and I *so* desperately need a job – so I lied.'

'Cheer up. Everyone tells a few fibs,' Betsy said.

'Especially in this business,' Jemima agreed, and they all laughed as they bustled into the changing room. There was no sign of Nancy or Edith.

'Look, it doesn't matter how you got here – you're in. You heard the man, and you've signed Mrs Winters's forms now.

Forget Edie, and whoever that other girl was. Frankly, she would never have cut the mustard,' Jane assured her.

'Honestly?'

'Honestly. There's no room for shrinking violets around here, but your face fits.'

All the girls started to undress, stripping off with the same abandon that Nancy had shown. Nervously Vita headed for the corner, grabbing her Sunday blouse and skirt.

Betsy's voice now took on a serious tone. 'Who's taken the Q-tips?' she asked, looking around on the dressing table. Jane slid a box across. 'Thanks, honey,' Betsy went on, prodding a stick at her eyeliner in the mirror. 'Did you hear what they were talking about? Those men? Do you really think we've only got a couple of months?' she asked the others.

'Take no notice,' Jemima said, spritzing some perfume under her arms and sniffing. She put on some glasses and inspected her hair in the mirror, licking her forefinger and rubbing her hairline. 'The Zip Club is fine. We're full every night. You know how dramatic Connelly is.'

Vita slipped behind the screen as she listened to their animated chatter.

'So, where are you staying?' Jane asked, just as Vita had finished dressing and emerged from behind the screen with her carpet bag.

The girls were ready in their street clothes, and Vita immediately felt dowdy next to them. Emma was wearing a sky-blue wool coat and matching hat, and Jane had a brown coat and a turban with a large jewel brooch on the front.

'In Brunswick Square. At a boarding house.'

'Oh. Is it nice?'

Vita let out a bitter laugh. 'No. I'd rather be anywhere but there.' She knew she sounded too honest, too needy, but she couldn't help it. Betsy and Jane were looking at her. 'There's a couple next door and they fight all night long,' she continued. Then she did an impression of the fight. 'You come here . . . wallop . . . no, Billy, no.'

'Dear Lord, that sounds awful,' Jane said, with an alarmed laugh at Vita's impression.

'It really is. And there's a brothel next door. The woman, Rose, who runs it is, frankly, terrifying. But I can't afford anywhere else.' She stopped herself saying more, even though she longed to tell the other girls how difficult life had been, without any references or a job. How frightening it had been to be ill and alone. It felt *so* good to be talking to them. For them to be listening to her. It was as if she were a wilted flower and their attention was water, bringing her back to life.

'What about Mrs Bell's?' Betsy suggested to Jane.

'Where's that?'

'Oh, we all board together,' Jane replied, adjusting her turban in the mirror. 'At Mrs Bell's. It's the best value, although she's rather formidable. Percy put us on to her.'

'That sounds lovely,' Vita said, feeling a stab of jealousy. It did sound lovely – all of them being together.

'There's still a spare bed in our room in the attic. It's freezing in the winter, but the worst of that's passed,' Betsy added.

'Do you think I could have it?' Vita asked, pouncing on the possibility. 'I'd be so very grateful. And I'd be no trouble – no trouble at all. I don't mind where I go, or how uncomfortable the bed is . . . I really can't bear another night in the place I'm in.'

Jane looked at Betsy and then wrote the address down on a piece of paper. 'Here. Tell her we sent you,' she said, handing it over. 'There's no guarantees, though.'

'Thank you. That's very sweet of you.' Vita didn't know how she was ever going to find the boarding house by herself, or what she would say to Mrs Bell, but as she pressed the paper to her chest, she didn't care. All that mattered was that she'd been given another precious lifeline.

An older woman entered the dressing room. She was wearing a pale-yellow day-dress and had dyed blonde hair, held in place by hairclips and covered in a pink hairnet. There was an air of faded glamour about her, and Vita wondered if she'd been a showgirl herself once. She wasn't old, but she had a weathered air about her as she surveyed Vita from the door, her bright-red lips puckering around a cigarette.

'Where are you off to in such a hurry?' she asked, as Betsy grabbed her handbag and threw in her cigarette case. The woman tutted and walked over, before confidently adjusting the turban on Jane's head. 'That's better.'

'Thank you, Wisey,' Jane said, checking her reflection approvingly. 'We're going to Lyons Corner House and I'd ask you,' she said, looking at Vita, 'but it's a double date.'

'Oh no, of course, it doesn't matter,' she replied, amazed that they'd even think of including her.

Jane linked arms with Betsy, who made an excited face. 'Alex and Tommy.'

'Have a nice time,' Wisey said with a wry look.

'Oh, Wisey, this is our new girl, Vita,' Jemima said, putting on her coat. Then she went off with Emma.

Vita didn't want to be abandoned, or left alone with Wisey, who now assessed her with a suspicious eye.

'I know all about you,' Wisey said. 'Nancy's language was particularly blue. Running after Edith like that – I ask you. Edith says "Jump" and they all jump around here. Only not you, it seems.'

'I did rather deceive poor Nancy. I'm not surprised she's cross.'

Wisey nodded and said nothing. She started tidying up, gathering up the dresses. 'I take it your parents don't know you're here?' When Vita didn't answer, she grunted, as if she'd expected as much. 'Well, you're here now. And for as long as you are, if you obey the rules, you'll get along fine.'

'I will try. I promise,' Vita said, but she heard the warning note in Wisey's voice. One bad move and she'd be out, just as fast as she'd got in.

'How old are you?' Wisey asked, eyeing her suspiciously.

'Twenty.'

Wisey pulled a face.

'Eighteen.'

'Well, keep that pretty nose of yours clean, Verity.'

'I will. I promise.'

'I don't know where you're from, and I don't want to know, but you won't have seen the nightlife around these parts, I'm guessing. There's all types that come in here. They want to dance and get drunk. You have to keep your wits about you, and don't let anyone take advantage of you.'

She thought of Clement, and of the million ways in which he'd taken advantage of her all her life.

'I can look after myself.'

'Well,' Wisey squinted at her as she crushed the cigarette stub into the ashtray on the dressing table, 'we'll see about that.'

Now Jerome stuck his head around the door, while putting on a brown trilby. He threw up some keys in the air and caught them. 'I'm off, if you still want a lift, Wisey,' he said.

'I can't,' Wisey said with a sigh. 'I still have to return these costumes to Percy. He had to leave, and I promised I'd drop them into his workshop.'

'I'll do it,' Vita offered. She liked Percy, and the idea of visiting his workshop sounded intriguing.

'Oh, well, if you don't mind,' Wisey said. 'Only my mother is in hospital. I have to see her, and Jerome needs to get over to Hammersmith.'

'Of course, it'd be my pleasure,' Vita replied, pleased to have found a purpose and to be able, at least in part, to pay these people back.

'Well, there's a turn-up,' Wisey said to Jerome, as she handed over the pile of costumes. 'A nice girl, for once.'

17

Percy's Chaos

In the tiny cobbled lane in the maze of streets around Covent Garden, Vita looked up at the wooden door and then back at the piece of paper that Wisey had written on.

Next door, the wooden workshop doors were open and a tanner was bashing a long animal skin. He wolf-whistled at Vita, who hardly noticed, her attention drawn instead to two Italian men who were arguing. A boy on a bicycle drew up next to them, long loaves of bread sticking out of the top of his basket, and Vita's stomach growled. From an open window above came the sound of a violin being tuned and she saw the sign for an instrument repair shop.

She dropped her carpet bag, then shifted the costumes over her arm and knocked on the glass panel in the wooden door.

She could hear music coming from inside and then Percy's voice. 'It's open. Come in.'

With difficulty she turned the handle and opened the door, ducking to go through the smaller doorway in the big wooden entrance.

'Aha, it's you. The new girl,' Percy said, pushing his glasses up his nose. 'Welcome to the chaos.'

Vita stood on the threshold, taking in the amazing scene before her. There had been nothing from the outside to suggest what might lie behind the wooden doors, but now she was quite astounded. Percy's 'chaos' was actually a treasure trove.

The room had a high ceiling, a skylight illuminating a high wooden workbench in a horseshoe shape below. The brick walls were painted white, but on one side of the room they weren't visible as they were entirely covered with hanging rails, from which hung every conceivable colour of costume. At one end there were a few headless mannequins wearing enormous crinoline dresses, and on one of the benches there was a whole row of wooden heads covered in feathered headdresses and wigs.

'Wisey said to bring these,' Vita said, realizing that Percy was waiting for an explanation. 'Sorry, it took me ages to get here.'

'You came the long way. You know there's an alley down the back that takes you almost to the Zip?'

He stood up from where he was sitting at the workbench and squeezed past a large ironing board to reach her, taking the costumes from her. Vita shook out her arms, relieved the weight was gone.

She had to suppress the urge to bury her face in the row of bright feather boas and soak up the delicious rose-scented colour of the costumes. She put her fingers out and ran them over the flowing white ostrich feather that lay on the top of a pile of fans on the bench.

'Do you really make all of these?' she asked.

'Mostly. I help out all the theatres, and siphon the best

pieces off to Wisey for the girls at the Zip. But don't tell anyone that. Those ones you've brought are for the girls at the Adelphi next week.'

'It's amazing. What you do, I mean. This is all—'

'Don't be too impressed. I usually have to cobble things together at home, or here in my studio – with never enough money, and with a deadline that's usually already past.'

She smiled. Percy might not think this was exciting, but she did. She ran her hands over pieces of red silky fabric on the large wooden bench.

'I've always dreamt of making something like this – of having someone to make it for . . . It's something I've always wanted to learn,' she said.

Even saying it out loud felt foolish. Where she came from, such lofty ideals would have been smacked down by her parents, who had dismissed every sign of creativity she'd ever shown. It was only Meg and Ruth, on the cutting-room floor of the mill, who had ever let her watch them at work; and John, who had occasionally helped her mix the dyes for the cotton. But she'd always been fascinated by the fabric that the mill produced, dreaming about the millions of uses for the bales of material that her father exported to America.

She was half-expecting Percy to mock her, as her father would have, but instead he smiled warmly.

'So where are you from?' he asked.

'Nowhere.'

'Nowhere?' Percy said with a grin, before piercing the cloth with a pin. 'I like it there. Great views.'

Vita laughed. 'You don't want to know about my past.'

'Don't I?'

'No. I've left it behind. There, in the past.' She felt empowered saying it like this. Like it might actually be truth.

'Oh, I see. Nothing stays in nowhere. Got it.'

She laughed for the first time in weeks and, as her eyes met his, realized that he was just being kind.

'I should go. I've got to find this place the girls told me about. Mrs Bell's. Hopefully she'll take me on. I cannot tell you how appalling my boarding house is.'

'Ah, I see,' Percy said. 'Well, let me telephone her first. I'll put in a word.'

'Would you?'

'Yes, but in return, I could do with an extra pair of hands, if you don't mind helping. You're not in any rush, are you?'

18

Mrs Bell's Boarding House

In the front parlour of Mrs Bell's boarding house, in the little street just off Tottenham Court Road, Vita spooned down a second helping of apple pie and custard, thinking this might be the most delicious thing she'd ever eaten. She couldn't seem to get it into her mouth fast enough. It had been a very long time since she'd eaten a decent meal. After everything that had happened today, her spirits were immeasurably lifted and, having felt so weak after the fever, her appetite was now back with a vengeance.

Mrs Bell, whom the girls had described as formidable, was in reality terribly sweet, Vita thought. She had a buxom figure, her waist cinched in by her flowery apron, and neat grey curly hair, and glasses on a chain. She smelt of lavender.

'Och, he's a good boy, my Percy. A kind heart,' Mrs Bell said in her thick Scottish brogue, after Vita had explained how he'd helped her out at the theatre and how she'd spent the afternoon with him in his studio. How he'd made her tea and put her to work unpicking some hems, and then ironing costumes for the players at the Shaftesbury Theatre. She reported how she'd been entranced by the steady stream of flamboyant theatre folk who'd come to the studio; and how, eventually, she'd left to come to Mrs Bell's, leaving Percy to meet some friends. She'd decided to come straight here and never go back to Brunswick Square ever again.

'Aye, steady on there, Miss,' Mrs Bell said, 'you'll be giving yourself indigestion.'

Vita put the spoon down with a clatter, remembering her manners, and Mrs Bell laughed softly and picked up her plate.

There were four small tables laid up with shabby, but ironed tablecloths. The walls were covered in candy-striped wallpaper and there were several framed photographs of the royal family, the largest of which was a portrait of the Prince of Wales, his eyes made to look a particularly intense aquamarine-blue. Next to the portrait was a large wooden clock with a brass pendulum, which ticked loudly. The whole place felt homely and solid and safe, and so unlike Mrs Jackson's, it seemed as if that had all been a horrible dream.

'It was so kind of you to give me that extra pudding. It was just divine.'

'You don't have to thank me like that. It's not Holyrood Palace, dear. It's only tea. It was always my James's favourite pudding, too.' Mrs Bell pulled at her gold chain, and a large pendant housing a photo of a soldier flopped out of the top of her apron. She held it in her fingers and kissed the image.

'May I see?' Vita asked.

Mrs Bell turned the pendant for Vita to look. A man in military uniform looked sternly out from the black-and-white image.

'He looks so very smart. Is that Black Watch tartan or Stewart?'

'Would you know the difference?'

'Of course.' Vita looked closer. She'd grown up knowing all about the difference between the warp and weft of fabrics like tartan. The patterns and their provenance had always intrigued her. 'It looks like Hunting Stewart to me.'

'Fancy you knowing that,' Mrs Bell said, impressed. 'His regiment was with the Ninth Royal Scots. He looked so very smart going off to war,' she went on proudly, before taking Vita's bowl over to the sideboard.

Vita watched now as a very fat, fluffy fawn-and-white cat with one eye scarpered through the door across the dark-green carpet towards her. It purred loudly, pressing against her legs.

'Och, that's Casper,' Mrs Bell said. 'He's not usually fond of strangers, so I'd take that as a compliment.'

Vita smiled and reached down to stroke the cat, remembering with a stab of pain what had happened to Spot. How Clement had punished her for some minor indiscretion by drowning her beloved cat, and her litter of kittens, in a sack in the stream at the back of the mill. Anna had only been ten and it had broken her heart.

Don't think about Clement, she told herself sternly. *Just don't.*

'Ouch!' she exclaimed, feeling something sharp in the cat's fur pricking her palm.

She picked up the cat and investigated the fluffy patch of fur. 'Goodness. Look,' she said, pulling out a dressmaking pin.

She handed it to Mrs Bell, who tutted, before taking the cat from Vita's arms. 'You've been in Percy's room again, haven't you, you naughty boy?' she scolded, her voice full of affection. 'You won't believe the things Percy makes in there,' she added to Vita. 'All sorts of creations. But he's terrible with those pins. Gets them everywhere. You should thank Miss Casey, Casper,' she added, addressing the cat. 'That would have given you a nasty wee shock, wouldn't it, if you'd started licking yourself.'

Mrs Bell chuckled as she put the cat down. She jabbed the pin into the top of her apron.

'There's a bed in the attic, with the girls. It'll be a week's rent – in advance, on a Saturday. And I'm not having any fancy-man callers around. Understood?'

'Oh, understood,' Vita said. 'Only, can you wait for the first rent? I've only just started at the club with the girls today.'

Mrs Bell shook her head. 'Well, no, dearie. If you don't have any money, I can't give you the room.'

'But I will have soon, I promise,' Vita implored. The cat meowed and circled round her legs. Vita stared at Mrs Bell, knowing that she couldn't bear it if she had to go back to that horrible place in Bloomsbury. 'I'll be no trouble, I promise – please let me stay.'

'Well, Casper likes you, so this once I'll bend the rules, but you'd better not let me down.'

19

Rudolph Valentino

Vita lay on the bed in the tiny attic room, watching a band of light pass from the high window across the apex to the chimney breast, where the shadows of the row of hanging stockings reared like the silhouette of a chorus line.

She stretched on the bed, then sat up and unbuckled her shoes, feeling the relief as she kicked them off and they fell on the floorboards with a thud. She knew she ought to get undressed, but as she lay back heavily on the salmon-pink satin eiderdown, feeling her body rise and fall in a gentle ricochet on the springy mattress, it felt like bliss.

Now that she was finally safe, she realized she was bone-tired. Possibly more tired than she'd ever been, but somehow in a completely different way. It was as if she'd been living with a high-pitched annoying noise in her head, and now it had suddenly gone and there was peace for the first time.

She sighed, putting her hands behind her head on the pillow and examining the other two beds across the room, where Jane and Betsy slept. The mirrored dressing table between them held an array of perfume bottles; and necklaces and hats were draped over the mirror, where a picture of Rudoph Valentino was pinned, a red-lipstick kiss on his cheek. The drawers below were slightly open, revealing colourful slips and blouses, and the cupboard door was draped in a silk dressing gown, with a hairnet on the Lloyd Loom chair.

She was still in a boarding house and it was hardly the Ritz, but the difference between this and her room at Mrs Jackson's was so complete that she was reminded of the illustrated Dickens book she'd had as a child. She remembered the pop-up scenes, and it felt as if she'd stepped through the pages of her own story into an entirely new scene.

It had only been in her most wishful thinking that she would ever fall in with people like Nancy, Percy and the girls. That they might actually swoop her off the street and save her seemed like an act so utterly overwhelming, it felt religious. And not just save her – *look after her*. Wisey and Mrs Bell had already shown her more care and concern than her mother ever had.

But it *had* happened. She'd only been in this bed for a couple of minutes, and yet already she felt like she belonged to this world. To these girls. To this house. And that Vita Casey's life, not Anna Darton's, was the one she'd been destined for, all along.

She raised her legs, circled her feet and examined her slender ankles. *Are you dancing feet?* she wondered. Was it possible that she could find a way to stay? In her heart, it was a yes; but even so, she felt a thud of fear when she shut her eyes.

She couldn't dance.

She'd got away with it so far, but what would happen

when the girls and Mr Connelly found out? She took a long, deep breath, forcing herself to calm down. She'd survived today, on her wits alone, and look how far she'd come. Who knew what tomorrow might bring?

20

Casper Gets His Way

When she woke up, the room was bathed in silvery light seeping through a crack in the curtain. Vita sat bolt upright, realizing that someone had covered her with a woollen blanket, which smelt musty.

Betsy and Jane were both asleep, tucked up in their beds – at least she presumed it was those two. They seemed different without their make-up. Betsy had rags in her hair and a large greasy smear of cold cream on her cheeks. Jane lay on her side, her hands bunched into fists, like she might fight off anyone who came near.

They must have made some noise when they'd come in, but Vita hadn't heard them. She must have been in the deepest sleep.

She swung her legs out of bed, standing up gingerly as the bed springs creaked. She needed to get undressed, but she was going to have to find a lavatory first. She didn't dare use the chamber pot and wake the girls, when they were so soundly asleep.

She crept down the wooden staircase from the attic to the top floor, groping along the dark, unfamiliar corridor and down another flight of stairs. On the first-floor landing she jumped when she saw Casper, the cat. He purred loudly, circling around her ankles.

'Hello, you,' she whispered, scared of displeasing the cat, which was somehow managing to usher her along the corridor towards the door at the end, his purr getting louder by the second.

A light was coming from underneath the door and she was relieved that she wasn't the only one awake in the house. Perhaps this was Mrs Bell's room. Or maybe this was where Emma and Jemima's room was.

Casper meowed, nudging the door with his nose, clearly wanting to get in. He looked up plaintively at her with his one eye.

She knocked softly on the door, but there was no answer. The cat pawed at it, desperate to get in, and Vita turned the handle tentatively. 'Sorry,' she said, as she pushed ajar the door into the room, 'the cat wanted to come in and—'

She poked her head around the door as the cat scuttled through the crack, but then stopped suddenly, taking in the scene, a deep blush pulsing fast from her toes to her hairline.

Percy was standing by the bed, his back to the door, kissing . . . a man . . . who was dressed only in trousers, with braces over a vest. Now the cat jumped on the bed, startling the lovers, who sprang apart. Percy whipped his head round and his eyes met Vita's. His cheeks were flushed, his lips red. He looked different without his glasses. The other man hastily grabbed his shirt from the bed.

She was so stunned that she hadn't thought to close the door, but now she jumped.

'I'm so sorry,' she gasped, wishing she'd never seen what

she'd just seen. She closed the door quickly, screwing up her face and wanting to cry.

The door opened behind her.

'Wait,' Percy said in an urgent, hissed whisper. 'Come in, and for God's sake close the door.'

Vita did as she was told, pressing her hands and then her back against the painted wooden door, the brass handle sticking into her spine. She looked round the room, which was filled with racks of clothes, with a small bed pushed up against the chimney breast. A wine bottle and two glasses stood on the mantelpiece and next to the bed was a wooden table, which housed a sewing machine and a lamp.

She held her breath, watching as Percy paced away from her, then back again, rubbing his jaw. He was clearly furious. But the young man with him simply smiled at Percy's distress. Not cruelly, but amused. He didn't seem to mind this awful situation at all. Instead, he buttoned up his shirt calmly.

But how could he be so calm? This was awful. She'd heard of men . . . of certain men . . .who – she didn't even know the right words to describe what it was that they did – men who kissed . . . who kissed each other like this.

There'd been talk of it at the mill once. Her father had had a man whipped, she remembered, and had called him a 'faggot', and he'd disappeared shortly after that. And there was the case of Oscar Wilde, too, which was so often referred to in the papers. Clement had talked of homosexuality as absolutely the worst kind of sin.

But what she'd stumbled upon here wasn't bad and sinful, surely? Because this was Percy. Dear, lovely Percy, who'd been so kind to her today.

She saw in his expression such shame – and such longing for understanding – that her heart ached. Did Percy think she might hurt him in some way?

It was the young man who broke the tension, and his deep-blue eyes were fixed on Percy as he did up the buttons of his shirt. 'So you know *our* secret, pretty face. What's yours?'

He turned his gaze suddenly on her and, caught out, Vita stared at him and then at Percy, seeing what was required here. Some sort of return for the information she now knew. A secret. They wanted a secret from her. And it sprang into her mind. Big and bold.

The truth about what she'd done. Who she was. What she'd run away from. And why. Because the truth was what they deserved. But she wouldn't tell *that* secret. Not to anyone.

But they needed something. And fast.

'I can't dance.'

Percy suddenly looked punctured, his shoulders slumping as he stared at her. 'What? That's it? That's all you're pre-pared to trust us with?' He said it like she'd betrayed them. Like she *would* betray them.

'You don't understand,' she blurted. 'What I mean is: I'm a liar – an imposter. A fake. I made everything up. I lied to Nancy, and I've never even been in a theatre before, or a club, let alone been a dancer.'

'I'm confused.' It was the other man, who held up his hand for Vita to stop. 'Enlighten me, please.' He had a fine accent and very fine skin, Vita noticed. In fact he was quite beautiful. Where she came from, she hardly ever saw men up close, and the ones she did see had dirt under their nails and phlegm in their lungs. But this man looked like he'd stepped out of a Renaissance painting. Like he could have been the model for an angel.

'This is Vita. The little seamstress I told you about, who helped me. Somehow – *God knows how* – she got a job today with Connelly,' Percy said.

'And you really can't dance?' said the man, a smile now wrinkling his bow-shaped lips.

'Not properly. Not like they think I can,' she said. 'I'm certainly not a dancer.'

She should never have told them, never revealed what a liar she was and how much she'd betrayed Percy's trust. He had every right to blow the whistle on her. Tell Mrs Bell and the girls. He could get her thrown out of the house. Tonight even . . .

'Well, well.' It was the young man. He bit his bottom lip, as if making a decision. 'Then maybe we can trust one another to keep each other's secrets safe, after all. But,' said the man, 'if we're going to keep you out of trouble, too, then I suppose the least we can do is teach you. And fast.'

'Teach me?'

'Yes. There's only one thing for it. We'll have to go out dancing. What d'you say, Percy?'

She noticed a charged look between the two men.

'Fine! Come on then,' Percy said suddenly, making a decision. He turned to the clothes rail in sudden furious concentration. 'Get dressed.'

'What – now?' Vita asked, stunned not only at his suggestion, but because this meant that he'd somehow forgiven her – for her intrusion and for lying. Because they were now equal. Because they really were friends now.

'Yes, *now*,' Percy said, pulling a peacock-blue dress off a hanger on the rail and looking it up and down critically, then at Vita, as if sizing her up. 'Edward's right. You're going to have to learn by tomorrow morning – otherwise, believe me, those girls will have your guts for garters.'

21

Pilchards

It was half an hour before they were ready to leave. Vita had quickly washed and changed in the bathroom into the dress that Percy had given her, as quietly as she could, her stomach fluttering with butterflies. He really had given her a chance, and now that feeling she'd had on the train was back. That feeling of tumbling head-first into her future, with absolutely no control.

Back in Percy's room, Edward whistled when he saw her, and Vita held out the skirt of the dress and did a curtsey.

'Suits you,' Percy said, raising his eyebrows.

Edward quietly slid open the sash window.

'Shhh,' he whispered. 'Mrs Bell is right below. Follow me.'

'Where are you going?'

'We're not going out of the front,' Percy said. 'He's not supposed to be here.'

Vita remembered Mrs Bell's stern warning about gentlemen callers, as she watched Edward put one leg over the windowsill and onto the brick ledge running away from the window outside. He put his lit cigarette between his lips and held out his hand for her.

She stared round at Percy, who was now dressed in a light

tan jacket and a boater hat. He patted his pockets, as if checking the whereabouts of his things, and then turned out the lamp by his sewing machine. She saw him lift a couple of pillows from under the bed and arrange them under his eiderdown into the shape of a sleeping body. He opened the door to the corridor an inch.

The dress that Percy had chosen for her was tight, and she hitched it up now as she tried to get over the window ledge in the most ladylike way possible, but it wasn't easy. Percy had pinned the dress at the back so that it would stay in place, and she was terrified it would tear. God only knew how much a garment like this cost. More than she could afford to replace, that was for sure.

Percy put his fingers to his lips for Vita to be quiet and gestured for her to follow Edward.

Outside, the night was cool and her arms puckered into goosebumps, but it was also adrenaline making her teeth chatter. The high wall was just a brick wide, with a long drop on either side. Edward held her hand as she sidestepped along it, until she'd reached the safety of the roof of a large shed.

'There's a knack,' Edward whispered. 'Watch.'

He skittered down the sloping roof to the wide ledge at the bottom and she followed suit. He caught her at the last minute.

Soon they reached the low wall at the back of the alley. Edward jumped down, and Vita jumped down into his arms and he stood her softly on the grassy cobbles.

'Where's Percy?' she whispered, alarmed that he hadn't followed them.

Edward nodded up at the window. Percy was straddling

the windowsill and scooping out something into a bowl. Even from down here, Vita could hear the thrumming purr as Casper licked the spoon.

'Pilchards – that's how he keeps in with Casper. And because Casper thinks he's the bee's knees, Mrs Bell does, too,' Edward said and Vita laughed. No wonder the greedy cat was so enamoured with Percy. 'Come on. My car is just along here.'

She looked towards where he was pointing with his cigarette, to a maroon Crossley under the street lamp.

22

Blanchard's

The debate about where to go carried on during the short journey in Edward's car into town, but Percy decided that Vita would get the best tuition from listening to the Ginx Five, the house band at Blanchard's, a club where Edward was a member. They stopped the car outside a building that looked, to Vita, like a bank.

Light spilled out onto the pavement, where men in top hats and overcoats escorted women in fur shawls through the entrance. The doorman greeted Edward warmly and smiled at her, as if it were perfectly plausible that she was one of his friends. She felt a frisson of excitement. Hadn't this been exactly what she wanted, when she'd come to London? To find people of note? People who mattered? She felt even more thrilled when Edward and Percy linked arms with her and escorted her through the door.

There was a large hallway and Percy explained that originally the building had been a coaching house. They walked towards the top of a richly carpeted staircase so that Vita could see the scene below.

There was a main ballroom and dance floor below, filled with couples dancing. It was an impressive room, with high ceilings, and everything was attractively decorated in brown, silver and grey. Coloured lights in rainbow pastels lit up the walls, which had mirrored panels in them, while mirrored columns supported the high ceiling.

She hadn't for a second expected to find anywhere so glamorous – or so lively. And the people! There were people everywhere. This late at night. In such fantastic clothes. Just dancing. Dancing like the world was ending. And it was simply wonderful.

They walked down the stairs and Edward ordered some drinks from a passing waiter, and they sat on a padded settee with a good view of the dance floor. When the drinks arrived, Vita took a deep breath and picked up the glass in front of her on the table, grinning nervously at her companions. This was it then, the latest part of her initiation.

'Take a sip,' Percy yelled over the wail of the clarinet and the splash of the drums.

'It's a Gin and It,' Edward added close in her ear, as she took a sip. She recoiled from the taste of the oily liquid in her glass. 'And you'd better get used to it, if you want to fit in. Down that one. I'm off to get us some more.'

Vita nodded, patting her chest with the shock of the alcohol. She'd barely ever drunk before – just a shot of brandy and lemon now and then, when she'd had a cold; a sip of mulled wine at Christmas perhaps. Nothing at all like this.

But this was going to be her drink from now on, she decided, storing away the information. Everything Percy showed her tonight was vital to her survival. He'd told her that, on the way here, and she believed him. She wouldn't let him down. Not now that he was giving her a second chance.

During all those grey, dreary long, cold nights at Darton Hall, when she'd read books, the silence punctuated only by the slow tick of the grandfather clock, she'd always suspected that there was life out there in the world. *Proper* life – happening somewhere. Not the kind of life her parents led, but the happy, hedonistic, *real* kind. And she'd been right all along, because here it was in all its colourful glory.

The jazz music coursed through her and she tapped her feet excitedly on the floor and knew that, if everything caught up with her and she was to die tomorrow, then everything had been worth it, to experience this.

'It's wonderful,' she gushed. 'Oh, Percy!'

'Well, you're here to learn. Pay attention,' he said, stubbing out his cigarette in the ashtray, and she wondered whether he'd really forgiven her. 'See her,' he added, picking up his Martini glass, eating the olive and then pointing the cocktail stick.

Vita followed Percy's gaze towards the crowded dance floor, where a woman in a gold dress, adorned with jangling loops of fringing, was dancing the Charleston, her feet and hands kicking out, her eyes half-closed. She didn't seem to care that her skin was covered in a sheen of perspiration, as she raised her knee up and hit it with the palm of her hand, then twisted her leg to hit her foot. She had an air of total abandon about her as the long rope of beads glittered and jumped on her chest. Vita watched in wonder as her dancing partner – dancing in perfect unison with her, from behind – kissed the curve of her neck. They seemed completely absorbed in one another. And they certainly didn't give a hoot who was watching them, or what they thought.

'She's got It. Whatever "It" is. You can see that right away, can't you?' Percy said in her ear.

Vita nodded, entranced, the gin making her head light. She imagined herself doing the move the woman was doing, like she was running on the spot. It wasn't so different from the dances she'd made up to songs on the wireless. She was a good mimic, she remembered, watching the woman closely. How hard could it be?

'It's about self-belief,' Percy continued. 'It's confidence. See?' he added. 'Just be like her. Dance like you're doing it for yourself – for the love of it. And don't give a damn what anyone else thinks. The key is not to be self-conscious.'

'But I've never danced. Not really. I mean, I've pretended. But it's not the same.'

'If you pretend hard enough at anything, you'll find it becomes real,' Percy said. 'Come on.'

He took her hands and lifted her out of her seat, before remembering his hat and chucking it onto the seat. He pulled her towards the crowd. Vita threw a nervous glance back at Edward, who was on his way back to their table, but he just winked and raised his glass.

'It's simple,' Percy said, spinning her round to face him on the dance floor. 'Right foot in front, then behind.'

Vita held on to his shoulder, concentrating hard on their feet. She followed his brown-and-white shoes moving slickly on the sprung floor, desperate to get it right.

'Now look up,' Percy instructed, lifting her chin. 'See if you can do it without looking down. Ow!' he exclaimed as she trod on his foot.

'Sorry. Sorry!' Vita gasped, mortified, but Percy simply grabbed her hand tighter in his.

'Concentrate,' he scolded, but he was smiling, clearly having fun, too.

She'd got through today on pure adrenaline, not really believing that tomorrow would happen, not thinking that she might really get that far without being found out, but with each step, she realized that Percy was dancing her into the future. And if he believed it, then it must be true. That she would be back in the club tomorrow with the girls. That she was Verity Casey – a proper member of their troupe.

But to make it happen, she knew she had to believe it, too. And so she danced like her life depended on it.

23

The Best Teacher

It wasn't long before Vita had mastered the knack of not looking at her feet, and Percy was impressed that she was such a fast learner. She only felt her confidence grow as she danced the Charleston for the first time and nobody around her noticed that she was a novice. All of those boring ballet lessons must have paid off, after all.

But when the music changed after the sixth song, Percy collapsed against her, his knees sagging.

'Can we sit down for a minute?' he begged. 'I need to get my breath back.'

'Of course.'

'Oh, and look at the time. The show will start any minute.'

'The show?'

'The "Midnight Merriments". There's usually dancers or this funny chap, Eddie, who juggles.'

Back at their table, he ordered two more drinks and a carafe of water from the waiter. The merriments, however, involved a barbershop quartet, who started singing in close harmony. Their song was called, 'I'm falling in love, one kiss at a time', and Vita listened, entranced by their voices. She was almost within touching distance of these exotic-looking men. Her father would be horrified at the mere thought of her being so close to 'Negroes', as he'd call them. He had a pathological hatred of anyone who wasn't white and English and rich, but Vita thought these men were simply wonderful. One of them caught her staring and winked, and she grinned back.

Across the club she saw Edward, his head thrown back, laughing. She watched Percy watching him for a moment, as he flitted to another group, who greeted him with hoots of delight.

'He's fun,' Vita said, following Percy's love-struck gaze. 'And so very handsome.'

She glanced across at Percy, who blushed as he patted his forehead with a folded-up handkerchief. 'You mustn't think, Vita . . . I mean, about earlier. Don't judge me, I—'

Vita put her hand on Percy's arm. 'I would never dare,' she said, meaning it. 'Really. I'm sorry I walked in.' She paused, smiling, as he gave her his handkerchief and she pressed the square of it into the sweat on her forehead. 'Actually, that's a lie. I'm not in the slightest bit sorry, otherwise I wouldn't be here.'

She shuffled back into her seat, closer to him. Percy was still watching Edward across the club.

'You really don't mind? I mean, you don't find it . . . shameful?'

'Why would I? You're both perfectly decent fellows. How you feel, and what you do, is up to you.'

Percy looked overcome with emotion for a moment, then

smiled and let out a relieved laugh. 'I wish more people were like you. I wish everyone else wasn't so damned judgemental.'

'Oh, believe me, I know enough about judgemental people. Enough to know that I will never be like that myself.'

'Good. You stick to your guns, Vita. Don't ever change the lovely ways you have.'

Did she have lovely ways? She flushed, so touched by his compliment. She longed to blurt out that whatever 'ways' she had, it was all brand new. Instead, she watched Percy watching Edward again.

'Are you two . . . ? I mean, it's none of my business.' She didn't know which word to use. *Together? Permanent? Friends?*

Percy sighed. 'Yes. We are – whatever that is. The awful thing is that I love him,' he went on, adding a wry laugh. 'I haven't told anyone else that. Especially not Edward. I don't even know why I'm telling you. Only perhaps because I'm so grateful to you.'

'Grateful? Why?' Vita asked, shocked.

'He uses me dreadfully,' Percy said. 'We meet in secret, but I never know when he's going to turn up. Usually I'd never get to come out dancing with Edward. We have to meet separately, and half the time he stands me up, or ignores me completely till the end of the night. And then, just when I'm losing heart, he's there waiting outside work, and he gets me to sneak him into my room; or he sends a message for me to meet him at the room he keeps in a hotel, and I'm sucked back into his web. But you being here makes it all legitimate.'

They watched Edward whispering into a man's ear, before he looked across to where they were sitting, his eyes locking with Percy's. Percy waved and Edward waved back, holding up a hand to signal that he'd be over in a minute.

'I don't even know why he does it,' Percy said, after the waiter had placed their drinks on the table. 'His father is a lord, you know. There would be the most frightful scandal if he realized. So Edward keeps it all terribly secret with his family and their people, but in places like this, he's the opposite. He takes terrible risks.' Percy sighed heavily. 'I must sound so jealous of him. But sometimes I just am.'

Nobody where Vita came from ever discussed their private feelings – only their public declarations of disapproval – so it felt good to lend a listening ear.

'Won't he get you into trouble?'

'Most probably,' Percy said, with a resigned shrug. She wished he would tell her more, but he suddenly changed the subject. 'What about you? Have you got someone?' he asked, lighting a cigarette, as Vita greedily gulped down the water.

'Me?' She guffawed.

'Yes, you.'

'No.' She gave him a horrified glance.

'I should've imagined someone would snap you up in an instant. Edward says you're the best-looking girl he's seen in years. So why not?'

There were so many reasons why there had never been a 'someone'. How could she begin to explain how outlandish today had been for her – and how very far from the person she'd ever been, or had imagined becoming.

Hold on, though – had Edward really said that about her? It didn't feel real. Not to her.

She was blushing as he came over and stood by the table.

She clapped politely as the barbershop quartet finished, not daring to look at Edward. *A lord's son thought she was good-looking.* Percy had said it so casually, but it still made her feel different. Because if Edward could see her like that – like she'd never imagined herself before – then maybe someone else might one day, too.

'Come on. Come and dance,' Edward shouted, as the music changed and he beckoned them to the dance floor.

'You go. Let me watch.' Percy said. 'Believe me, he's the best teacher you'll ever get.'

24

The Mysterious Man

Percy was right. Under Edward's careful instruction, Vita was soon getting the hang of it, despite treading on his feet several times.

'Don't apologize. Ever,' he laughed. 'The lady never makes the mistakes. If you muck up, carry on, like it was all deliberate. That's what Mama always taught my sisters.'

Vita laughed, soaking up his wisdom, and soon she was getting the hang of dancing with him, despite being out of breath. But she so wanted to impress him. She'd never been in the arms of someone so debonair and fun.

'That's it. That's it! Now you're getting it,' Edward encouraged and she beamed at him, before he swooped her into his arms again, singing along to the tune. 'Copy what I do.'

He whisked her into a fast foxtrot around the floor and kept introducing her, as faces whirled past them in a blur, and each time he made her laugh. 'This is Vita . . . Isn't she a doll? . . . Wouldn't you like to know, old fellow – she's mine, you know . . . She's a dancer, showing me how to do it.'

The music got faster and faster, and bodies pressed against her. Vita felt the pulse of the drums as if it were her heartbeat and the music was her blood. Everything seemed to fade away as she closed her eyes and surrendered herself to the rhythm. And then she felt Edward's breath in her ear. 'See? You're a natural, darling.' And then, 'What's that one?'

He watched her, then copied a move she'd just made up. Encouraging Vita, his eyes danced as she repeated the side-shuffle, and he danced in unison, as if suddenly *she* were teaching *him*. And then the others around them were joining in, too, copying her move, and Edward raised his eyebrows and smiled. She grinned at him, her cheeks aching.

The clarinets seemed to scream into a frenzy as the number came to a crescendo, the drummer almost standing in his seat as he crashed his sticks down on the cymbals.

Cheering and applause signalled the end of the number. A collective sigh of relief escaped as the band regrouped and the music softened and slowed. Vita gasped for breath and laughed, putting her hand on her chest. She felt slick with sweat and pure joy.

'Hold on – I'll be back,' Edward said, suddenly leaving her. Feeling dizzy, Vita tried to find the direction of their table, and Percy. She put her hand to her head, embarrassed by how much she'd let go. She couldn't believe how hard her heart was thumping. But then she felt arms go around her waist and a strong, large hand engulf hers.

'Hello,' a man said, turning her into his arms for a slow dance. He was good-looking, Vita realized, and he knew it, judging from the glint in his eye. The top button of his shirt was undone and he had a shadow of stubble under his chin. 'I've been watching you.'

'You have?'

'I haven't seen you here before. If I had, I'd have remembered.'

She was tongue-tied for a moment. She glanced down, aware of her clammy hand in his. He towered over her and she stared at the small badge on the lapel of his dinner-suit jacket.

'Well?' He stared at her. 'Who are you, mystery girl?'

'I'm Verity. Verity Casey. Although my friends call me Vita. I'm a dancer. At the Zip Club. You know? Near the Savoy,' she said, still out of breath.

Then she became aware of Percy cutting in, his arm around her waist, as he very indiscreetly pushed the other man out of the way. 'Come on, darling. You're not to give away our trade secrets. Time to go. Step aside now, old chap.'

Baffled, Vita allowed Percy to pull her away. She shrugged apologetically at the man, who was still staring at her. He put two fingers to his forehead and lifted them in a silent salute.

'Percy, whatever is it?' Vita asked.

'He's a reporter. The worst sort. Gutter press. You didn't say anything? Did you?'

25

The Breakfast of Champions

As Edward drove haphazardly around Soho, Percy explained to Vita that Edward was notorious for being possibly the worst driver in London – especially when he was half-cut. As if proving the point, Edward parked rakishly up on the kerb outside a dark townhouse in Gerrard Street and, stumbling and laughing, told Percy and Vita that he'd be back in a moment. 'I'm off to procure essential nourishment,' he slurred.

'Edward!' Percy said, giving him a look.

'I won't stay. Promise.'

They watched as he staggered down the steep basement steps and knocked twice on a plain grey door, with just the number 43 painted on the outside. Vita saw bright lights and heard voices and music as the door opened briefly and Edward disappeared inside. Then the night was quiet again.

She joined Percy on the pavement as he leant against the car and lit a cigarette. The sky was fading into a lighter blue. Was it nearly dawn already? This was only the second time she'd stayed up this late. The first time, she'd been running for her life.

'What's he doing?' Vita asked. She couldn't believe there could be somewhere open even later than Blanchard's.

'Gone to Mrs Meyrick's. She's quite famous, you know. She runs the '43,' he said, lighting a cigarette and nodding down to the basement door. 'We were in there when the police arrested her last month.'

'Arrested?'

'Oh, she's quite ingenious when it comes to getting round the licensing laws. She and Edward are great friends.'

Vita watched as shadows passed behind the glowing curtained windows. She could hear music faintly. *How exotic*, she thought, feeling a sudden affinity with this glamorous woman who deliberately kept her parties going all night.

But suddenly she shivered, the night air making her feel chilled, now that she was away from the warm embrace of the club. Percy took off his jacket and put it round her shoulders.

'It suits you,' he said, and Vita laughingly did a pose for him. He jokingly threw her his ivory-topped cane and she performed a theatrical twirl with it. 'You wear clothes well, you know.'

'You are too kind.'

Percy smiled and narrowed his eyes at her through the smoke.

'You enjoyed yourself, didn't you?'

'I loved every minute,' she said, meaning it.

'Tomorrow you'll have to be confident. Don't let Nancy or Edith bully you.'

'I'll try not to.'

'And this. All of this' – he waved his hands, *at what?* she wondered: this street? London? *Life?* – 'you can't tell them anything about it.'

Nothing about it. But she already knew that wasn't what Percy meant. He meant: not *about us*.

'You can trust me,' she said, putting her hand over her heart.

A burst of music and the door opened in the basement. Edward tottered up the steps, carrying a silver tray covered in a white tray cloth. 'She never disappoints,' he told Percy with a wink. 'Your favourite, Percy.'

'What is it?' Vita asked.

'The breakfast of champions,' Edward said.

She sat in the back of the car and Edward carefully passed her the tray, so that she could balance it on her lap. She could feel warmth seeping through the bottom of it, and the car filled with the aroma of smoked kippers as Edward started up the engine. Was that really what he'd just picked up?

'She wants the tray back this time,' Edward told Percy, and Vita realized this was a regular routine for the pair of them. It was like she was part of their secret.

She peeked under the tray cloth. There were two plates of kippers, eggs and toast. Her stomach growled.

'Don't be shy. Tuck in,' Edward said. 'A lady needs sustenance after such a lot of dancing.'

'She certainly does,' Vita agreed, her mouth watering.

'Especially one who has to be in rehearsals in the not-too-distant future.' Percy consulted his watch. 'We need to get you back before the girls wake up.'

'Pass me some toast,' Edward said, holding out his hand.

Percy righted the steering wheel, before they swerved across the street.

'Wait. You know the rules,' Percy told him, slapping his hand playfully. 'We always have our breakfast kippers in a royal park. We're civilized like that. Turn up here, to St James's. Honestly, Woody, how many cocktails did you have?'

26

The Rehearsal

Betsy and Jane had been full of encouragement on the bus on the way over to the club, and Vita almost blurted out that she'd had the most wonderful night of her life, but she remembered her promise to Percy and had kept quiet. She was riding high on adrenaline, and she almost certainly still had gin in her system, but as they made their way onstage for the rehearsal, Nancy didn't make eye-contact with her and Edith scowled. Vita started to feel the nerves, and her hangover made her mouth dry. She so desperately wanted to stay and earn her keep at Mrs Bell's, but what if she simply wasn't good enough for the line-up?

'Don't worry. Just copy what I do,' Jane said, but Vita felt her knees shaking. She tried to copy the moves, but she was too slow and she stumbled.

Jerome thumped his hand on top of the piano, making Vita jump.

'You see,' Edith said, holding up her hand and pulling an exasperated face at Jerome and then gesturing to Vita.

Jane put an arm out to steady her. 'Don't worry. You'll get there,' she said.

'I'll do it again,' Vita said. 'I'll get it right.'

She tried to suppress a rising tide of fear, forcing herself to concentrate as she stood back and watched the girls dance.

'And your part goes like this,' Betsy said, demonstrating some tap-dancing.

Vita bit her lip and swallowed, tasting gin at the back of her throat. It was so fast – and she'd never tap-danced before.

'Can you do it a bit slower?' she asked, going to stand next to Betsy so that she could copy the moves.

'No! Left foot,' Betsy said, but Vita still couldn't get it.

'We're wasting so much time!' Edith protested.

'Why don't we take a break and try the song,' Jerome said.

'I bet she can't sing, either,' Edith commented, furiously.

'I *can* sing,' Vita said, defensively.

'Scales?' Jerome asked.

'And arpeggios?' Edith demanded.

Vita nodded. She'd played them on the piano for hours in the drawing room in Darton Hall, although she'd never sung them. But how hard could it be?

'In C,' Jerome said, playing a flamboyant introduction on the piano and saying over the top of it, 'Loudly now, to "ah". This place has shocking acoustics.'

Vita looked around her, mustering her courage, finding the right pitch of the note.

'Ah, ah, ah, ah, ah, ah, ah,' she sang, belting it out at Edith, whose expression didn't change. Jerome nodded and went up a tone, and Vita followed his lead, singing arpeggios up a scale. He raised his eyebrows, clearly ready to test her.

'Faster,' he instructed. 'Now with a "mi" rather than an "ah". Cut the vibrato. Come on, louder.'

Vita felt herself sweating. She'd never concentrated so hard on anything in her life, and now the notes were getting higher and higher. Any second now, her voice was going to give out.

'That'll do.'

Vita stopped and turned to see a man in a dark-grey suit coming down towards the stage from behind the bar area. He clapped slowly.

'Oh, Jack, there you are,' Edith said, stepping forward.

So this was the famous Jack Connelly, the proprietor of the Zip Club, Vita thought. As he came into the light, he struck her as the kind of man who had most probably lived his entire adult life in nightclubs and bars and had rarely seen the light of day. He wasn't handsome exactly – more weathered, with thickly oiled black hair. In his flashy pinstripe suit he was undoubtedly what Vita thought her father would have described as a spiv.

'This is the girl. *The mistake*,' Edith said, but Jack Connelly's eyes were raking up and down Vita's figure.

'There hasn't been a mistake. She has a fine pair,' he said, with a twitch of his moustache, 'of lungs on her.'

Vita blushed, unsettled by his lewd compliment.

'But . . .'

'Sugar, don't cause an argument, my head can't take it today,' he said, his eyes flashing a warning, and Edith slunk back. 'She's just the ticket. Now come on, ladies. Why don't we all get along.'

27

Against Doctor's Orders

Clement stared at the breakfast plate on the silver tray on his lap, his mouth filling with sour saliva, but he felt too wretched to eat. His whole body felt like a bruise.

'Where is she?' he managed, through clenched teeth. The pain was intolerable, but he was eking out the injections, craving the sharp mind he relied upon, over the warm fuzz of relief that left him good for nothing.

'Nobody knows,' Martha said, in her timid whisper. 'She's gone. We've asked everywhere. Even at the mill. Nobody has seen her anywhere. It's been nearly a fortnight now and the police haven't had one lead. Your poor mother is sick with worry—'

Clement's fist came up under the covers and punched the breakfast tray violently, so that it tipped off the bed, everything clattering to the floor, smashing the china cup and saucer, as the fried egg slithered onto the rug. Martha yelped and backed away.

Crying out in agony, Clement lifted his feet out of bed and made to stand up, clinging onto the wooden bedside table.

'It's too soon,' Martha warned. 'Doctor Whatley said—'

'Damn Doctor Whatley,' Clement snapped. 'If none of you will find her . . . I'll find her myself.'

He pushed up from the bed, howling with pain. He took two steps, then collapsed. He hit the floorboards hard with his fist. Damn his sister. Damn her to hell. When he found her, he'd make her suffer this pain for herself. Only worse.

28

To the Roof

The rest of the week passed in a blur and Vita spent every moment she could practising the dance for the Friday-night show. And when she wasn't actually with the girls, she went over and over the dance in her mind. And now, finally, she'd done the routine several times without making a mistake.

The song that accompanied the number was coming together, too. Nancy, Edith and Jemima had the strongest voices and sang soprano, while Emma and Jane took the low tenor part. Vita had just about got the hang of the alto part with Betsy. It was the first time she'd sung close harmony in a group, and it felt thrilling.

Now, on one of the last rehearsals before the show that night, Jerome ran his fingers back over his thinning hair.

'All right, ladies. That'll do,' he said, blowing out a hot breath. 'Good work, Vita. You've really come on. Now, I don't want you too exhausted before tonight. Be back here for the rehearsal with the band at five.'

They relaxed from their static finishing poses – all of them wilting with a collective sigh. Vita felt her blisters stinging and her heart hammering from exertion. Tonight, if she made it through the first show, she hoped Mrs Bell would give her a bowl of warm water and some Epsom salts to soothe her ruined toes. But the pain and exhaustion were worth it. Every single minute that she was with these girls, she knew she had to do her very best. Because now that she was here, she never wanted to leave.

'Hey, girls. Let's go to the roof and get some air,' Jane said, but Nancy went offstage and Edith stayed behind, no doubt hoping for some time alone with Mr Connelly. She still saw herself as the main attraction, a whole rung higher up the ladder than the rest of the girls. *A real prima donna.* Wasn't that the phrase that Jemima had whispered only this morning, as they'd all been getting dressed?

All the other girls followed Jane, bundling along the corridor to climb up the iron fire exit, their voices bouncing off the back alley's bare brick walls. Jane was bemoaning the fact that Alex and Tommy hadn't called them.

'You said he had a big nose anyway,' Emma pointed out.

'Who? Alex?'

'No. Tommy.'

'That wouldn't put her off marrying him,' Betsy chipped in, and Jane gave her a shove. 'Even with a hooter like that.'

Vita laughed. She hadn't expected tough girls – working girls like these – to be so romantic. She'd always had her own romantic daydreams, of course, but she'd kept them very much to herself. Stupid fantasies about escaping . . . about falling in love . . . about being swept into another, more exciting life by a handsome stranger. But here in London the girls were serious, their fantasies tinged with pragmatism. As if their dreams and fantasies really could come true. And their nightmares, too, of course. Their fears, in a post-war city, with so few men around, of being left forever on the shelf.

'What about you, Vita? You've kept very quiet. Is there anyone you have your eye on?' Emma said.

'No,' she laughed, out of breath as they climbed up the last flight of steps to the door.

'Well, we can't afford to hang around for long,' Betsy said, with a sigh. 'We have to get hitched when we're at our best.'

'It's not all about getting married, though, is it?' Vita said. 'Surely?'

'Of course it is,' Jane replied. 'Making the right match, well, it's making a success of yourself, isn't it?' She grinned. 'And just think of the party, too. I want the whole works. A white wedding, champagne . . . a romantic honeymoon.' She burst into the lyrics of a song in her best deep voice and they all tumbled up onto the roof, laughing.

29

A Breath of Fresh Air

A high wall enclosed the small roof space and Vita breathed in the city air, standing on tiptoe and looking across the roof-tops. A church bell chimed in the distance. Pigeons cooed softly, traffic rumbled quietly far below.

Downstairs in the dark basement it was entirely possible to forget what time of day it was – or even that it was day itself. Let alone one as glorious as this, the kind of day that whispered the promise of spring after weeks of drizzle. To Vita – used to the dampness of Lancashire – this felt like how she imagined it must be abroad. In Rome. Or Venice. In any number of those marvellous continental cities that she'd read about in the racy novels the girls secretly passed around at school.

Watching the way they settled into easy sitting positions, and judging by the full ashtray, she guess the girls often came up here for a moment of fresh air. A couple of old tea chests and packing crates stood along the far wall, and Jane ran lightly over and jumped on them, sitting down, stretching out her feet and thrusting her face to the sun. Betsy was next, carrying today's newspaper.

Vita had scoured every paper she could lay her hands on every day, but today she felt like a rest from constantly looking for news from home. On the London rooftop, she felt free. She told herself over and over again that she'd escaped for good – so much so that she'd actually started to believe this wasn't a dream from which she was going to wake up any second, but it was actually happening. She copied Jane and turned her face towards the sun and breathed in. Maybe Percy was right. If you pretended hard enough at something, it could become real.

'Oh, my goodness!' It was Betsy. 'Look here. Vita, you'll never guess! You're in the paper.'

Vita's stomach lurched. What had she just thought?

'Right here. Look,' Betsy said, pointing.

Vita's feet felt like lead as she went over to where Betsy was spreading the newspaper on the wooden tea chest. Jane was reading over her shoulder.

What had they seen? Her picture? A report on the Darton family and their tragic loss? Had they worked out who she really was and deduced the truth about what had happened to Clement? Did that mean all the girls – and, worse, Percy – would now know her secret? And the terrible thing she'd done?

'You're a dark horse, aren't you?' Emma chipped in, reading over Jane's shoulder. 'Right under our noses.'

Vita didn't understand. What were they talking about? Why were they smiling? Why weren't they staring at her in horror instead?

'You should have woken us,' Jane said. Her voice was laced with envy. 'We had no idea you'd been out. How on earth did you get past Mrs B?' She stared round at Vita, as if seeing her in a new light.

Betsy now cleared her voice to read the column: 'Later on, I bumped into Edward Sopel at Blanchard's. Quite the man about town. He was dancing with Miss Verity Casey, a very fetching dancer in the latest new line-up at the Zip Club. A devilish young flapper, I must say. One would hope that such a perfect peach will not get bruised, if she's cavorting with Sopel and his merry-makers.'

It wasn't about her at all. Not the real her. But about Verity Casey. It must have been the man at the club – the reporter.

Relief made Vita's legs feel like jelly for a moment.

Devilish young flapper . . . perfect peach . . . Her cheeks started reddening with a mixture of pride and embarrassment. Was this good news? Or bad? She really had no idea. *No – good*, she decided. From the look on the girls' faces, it had to be good. Each and every one of them was looking at her now the way they only normally looked at Edith. With a mixture of jealousy and respect.

'How on earth do you know Edward Sopel?' Jane asked, her voice laced with envy. 'I've heard of him. Isn't he frightfully posh?'

'I thought you said you didn't have anyone. There's no secrets in the sisterhood, Vita,' Emma added, her brow furrowing in mock reproach.

Vita was about to tell them about meeting Edward in Percy's room, but then she remembered that they wouldn't have a clue about Percy. And after the other night, she would never betray his trust.

'He's an old acquaintance,' she lied. 'I bumped into him and told him I was in town, and he insisted I go out with

116

him.' There was no harm in riding the wave of their admiration. It clearly reflected well on her. Yes, she was sure of that now. She gave a little shrug, as if this kind of thing happened to her the whole time, while inside she was quaking, still counting her lucky stars that she was only in the paper because of this and nothing else. 'You were both asleep and I didn't know the rules, so I had to sneak out.'

If only they knew.

30

High Kicks

The girls were still gossiping about it five minutes later when Edith arrived. Maybe she was feeling left out, or maybe she'd been dismissed by Mr Connelly. It was difficult to know, from her haughty, superior glare.

Vita had been happy to bask in the glory of her sudden notoriety, but now her smile faded, as Edith's accusatory look ran between the girls.

'Did I miss something?'

'Vita is in Marcus Fox's diary,' Betsy announced, standing aside to give Edith a clear view of the paper.

Edith didn't say anything as she looked down her nose, scanning the column.

'It's nothing,' Vita said.

'You might be in the newspapers, but that doesn't qualify you as a dancer, just because it says so here,' Edith responded, but Vita noticed a hint of something in her voice. Jealousy? *Surely not respect? No, not that. Not from Edith.*

'I know.'

'I know,' she mimicked Vita's voice nastily.

And there it was. As quickly as she had thought Edith might be starting to thaw came the realization that it was quite the opposite. She couldn't shake the nagging feeling that Edith had seen right through her from the start.

'So if you're such a great dancer, why not show us your high kicks? I'm sure the others will agree that they were pathetic just now.'

It was a challenge. Vita realized that Edith was throwing down some sort of gauntlet, designed to show her up in front of the other girls. She couldn't help feeling affronted. She'd thought their run-through of the routine had been her best yet. But then she remembered: she wasn't a dancer. Scraping through wasn't what it was about. And the first show was tonight.

'Now?' she said, jutting her chin out and trying not to show the fear she felt.

'Why not?'

'Oh, Edith. Leave poor Vita alone,' Jane said. 'You've been on at her all week, and she's learnt the dance perfectly well. This is supposed to be our break.'

'I don't know why you're defending her,' Edith said, and Vita saw in the look that had passed between them that Edith demanded total loyalty.

'I don't mind,' Vita said, keen to deflect Edith's attention from Jane, who out of all the girls had been the most friendly. She had to do what Percy had told her: she had to front up to Edith and not be bullied by her. 'Actually, I love high-kicking. But could you hang on?' she said, an idea forming. 'Just for one moment?' Edith looked confused. 'Who has some scissors? Jane? Any in your vanity case?'

Edith backed away. 'What do you need scissors for?' She

119

sounded suspicious, and she saw Jemima and Betsy laugh in a surprised way.

'You'll see,' Vita replied, as Jane rummaged in her little leather pouch and produced a tiny pair that were hardly more than nail scissors. 'The best I've got.'

'They'll do.' Vita took them and ran over lightly to where a discarded windowpane leant against the wall, so that she could see her reflection. And, biting her tongue, she set about cutting off the legs of the dusky pink trousers she was wearing.

'What are you doing?' This from Jane. Vita saw her shocked reflection in the glass.

'Percy gave me these,' Vita said, with difficulty, contorting herself to reach behind her. 'But they're too flappy to high-kick.'

She didn't say it in so many words, but Percy had divined that she was lacking any sort of suitable clothes, so he'd helped her pick out an outfit for rehearsals from his rail.

'I need a new look. A sort of reinvention,' she'd told him, and he'd taken on the challenge, pulling out various options. Some – like these trousers – were rather outlandish and she'd been scared at first, but Percy had told her that, with the right attitude, she could wear anything. She simply had to experiment and be bold. And having never been bold before now, she'd grabbed onto his words. Because Verity Casey *was* bold and daring. Wasn't she? Even if she was quaking inside. It felt slightly sacrilegious to do what she was about to do, but then she thought of Percy – he would approve, wouldn't he?

'Here, I'll help,' Emma said, bending down and taking the

scissors from Vita, who felt the cold blade on the back of her upper thigh. 'Are you sure about this?'

'It's too late now,' Betsy said.

Vita stood tall, seeing her reflection in the pane. She adjusted Percy's pink paisley cravat, which she was wearing as a headband. Then suddenly the leg of the trousers was free.

'Oh, you do look funny,' Jemima laughed.

'Shall I do the other one?' Emma asked.

'Better had,' Vita nodded. 'So that I'm level.'

In a moment the trouser legs had both gone and Vita flipped them off her ankles.

'That's much better,' she declared, bending forward easily. 'I'm ready now.'

Edith strutted over and shrugged off the light cardigan she was wearing over her shoulders, throwing it so that Jemima had to catch it. She looked up and down at Vita's attire with disdain. 'It's just that we do need to check that you *can* high-kick.'

With that, she flung one of her superb legs high into the air, her eyes never leaving Vita's. She followed with a small part of the routine, a shuffle ball change and another high kick and a turn.

Vita followed suit. She probably couldn't kick as high as Edith, but she was damned well going to try. Putting her hands on her waist, she re-enacted the part of the routine that Edith thought was lacking, flinging her leg up into a series of high kicks. Soon her lungs were screaming, but she wasn't going to let Edith know that. Instead she met Edith's blazing gaze with a cool one of her own. She'd spent so long being cowed by Clement that it felt good to meet a challenge like this head-on.

'That's enough,' Jane said. 'She can dance just as well as the rest of us.'

Edith stopped and gave Jane a withering look that made it perfectly clear they all thought that particular statement wasn't true. Jane pulled a face back, as if daring her to say it.

'I don't trust her,' Edith pronounced. 'Not when we don't know where she's from or what she's up to.' Vita was about to speak and defend herself, but Edith put up her hand to stop her. 'But I believe in keeping your friends close and your enemies closer. I'm going to Annabelle Morton's twenty-first next Saturday night after the show,' she said, as if Vita should be impressed. 'Nancy's coming with me, of course, but you can come, *if* you bring Edward. You see, we're old friends,' she added, with an amused eye-roll at the others. She was clearly implying that she and Edward had been more than friends.

'I'll ask if he's free,' Vita bluffed, rising to the challenge, trying not to show how out of breath she was.

Edith's blue eyes narrowed and bored into hers. She didn't believe that Vita knew Edward Sopel. This was all a big test. 'I wouldn't tease him, though. He's a sensitive chap. He took it very badly when I ended our . . . dalliance.'

For a moment Vita thought about calling her out and exposing her for the liar she was, but she couldn't, without implicating dear Percy.

Edith puffed her chest out. If the high-kicking had tired her, it didn't show one bit. 'Come on, girls. There's work to do. This show is a shambles, and I won't have our reputation in tatters because of a few stragglers.' She looked over her shoulder at Vita.

'I really don't know what they see in her. She's so horrible. Here, have this. For your scrapbook,' Emma whispered, passing Vita the paper.

Vita was folding it up as Nancy arrived.

'What did I miss?' she asked, clearly disappointed that the others were on their way back downstairs.

'She's coming with us to Annabelle's,' Edith said. It sounded like an order.

'Who?'

'Verity. Your friend.'

Nancy took in this information, slowly turning her head towards Vita, who could see her trying to make sense of it all: that Edith was now not only speaking to Vita, but had invited her to a party.

Edith flounced through the door into the dark stairwell, followed by Emma and the others. Left alone, Nancy put her hand on her hip and looked at Vita through narrowed eyes.

'She's forgiven you and, therefore, so must I.'

Vita nodded. 'For what it's worth, I still feel terrible. About lying to you.'

Nancy smiled and flipped her hand. 'No, you don't. Anyhow, I like you. You have gumption and pluck.' She cocked her head on one side and twisted her lips. 'But I'm afraid, my little Vita, I'm going to have to take you in hand.'

Vita laughed suddenly, wondering what Nancy meant by this. But she didn't care. She was too busy mulling over what had just happened.

123

'By the way, whatever are you wearing?'

'Oh,' Vita said, stooping to pick up the trouser legs. She wasn't ever going to waste any material. 'I thought they were better like this for dancing.'

Nancy nodded. 'I like them. They look good,' she replied, linking her arm through Vita's as if they'd always been the best of friends.

31

Show Time

Despite her earlier confidence and the buzz of winning back Nancy's approval, by the time the evening came, Vita felt like a nervous wreck. Her headpiece fluttered in the hot draught of the open dressing-room door as Percy fixed the final details of her costume.

There was a charged atmosphere backstage, which only made Vita's stomach dance with butterflies even more. She could hear the band playing out at the front of the club and the hubbub of voices. Here, backstage, Edith and Jemima were singing arpeggios to warm up their voices, while stretching their legs on the small ballet bar in the corridor. Emma and Betsy were busy applying the gold sequins to each other's faces. Vita already had her show make-up on and stretched her face uncomfortably in the mirror.

'Stop worrying,' Percy said, turning sideways and admiring her profile.

'Oh, but I hate my arms,' she said, feeling exposed. She pointed to the large mole on her shoulder. 'It's ugly, don't you think?'

'I'd never have noticed it, unless you'd pointed it out. What do you think, Wisey?'

'Oh, go on with you. In the movies they paint those things on. As I always say, be proud of the skin you're in,' she said.

Vita laughed, amazed as always at the older woman's wise words. No wonder her nickname had stuck. 'Take it in just a bit more, maybe. Here.' She pinched the gold material and looked down to where Percy was kneeling by the hem of her dress, some pins in his mouth. She looked at herself a little less critically, deciding that she wouldn't be self-conscious about her arms from now on.

'Stop it,' he said. 'You'll ruin the line.' He stood behind her now, staring in the mirror at the dress he'd made. 'What about here,' he said, hitching up the strap on her shoulder and then taking a pin from his lapel and pinning the strap. 'That better?'

'That's it,' said Vita, delighted with the small adjustment. She'd been terrified about falling out of the dress, and Percy was the only one who understood. Maybe it was because of the secrets they already shared, but being around Percy made Verity Casey – the person she wanted to be – come alive. As if his very presence made her feel more vivacious and daring.

'Why do we need these bubs anyway?' she asked, staring down at her bosoms and cupping her hands over them, even though they were squeezed into a side-fastening contraption that Jane had found for her.

'You'll be glad of them some day, believe me,' Nancy said, passing by to the dressing table.

'I'm sure I won't.'

'You don't know how lucky you are. If I were a woman, I'd want to be just your shape. All your wonderful curves,'

Percy said, as he ran his hands down the side of Vita's costume, admiring her over her shoulder in the mirror.

Wisey nodded. 'He's right you know. There's nothing wrong with curves.'

'Well, you're welcome to them. As you well know, they're good for nothing. How I'd love to have a figure like hers,' Vita said, nodding towards Edith, who was limbering up at the wooden ballet bar in the corridor.

'Pah!' Wisey said, moving away. 'You girls are never satisfied with what you have. You wait till you're my age, then you'll be sorry you ever complained.'

'She's right,' Percy said. 'Art can't lie. If you look at any of the greats, they always celebrate the female form.'

'You've got a gorgeous figure,' Nancy added.

Vita smiled, buoyed up by her compliment. 'But surely there must be a way of making them more comfortable?' She wriggled her back, which was being squeezed by the itchy material, rearranging her front. 'Can't you magic up a design for something better than this thing of Jane's?'

'That's hard without . . . well, you know, having the equipment myself,' Percy said.

'So why don't I help you? We could design something that stretches, rather than squeezes. Something pretty and flattering,' Vita said.

She glanced over at Nancy, thinking about the first time she'd seen her in her lacy camisole. How she'd felt a tug of jealous longing. To touch the fabric? Or to touch Nancy? She pushed the shameful thought away.

'That's a swell idea,' Nancy said, smiling at Vita and

Percy. 'Why don't you design some thrilling lingerie for us all.'

'I suppose we could give it a whirl,' Percy replied, standing back and admiring Vita. 'There. You look divine,' and then he mouthed in the mirror, 'the best of the bunch.'

Vita smiled at him, delighted with the way she looked. She jiggled her shoulders, making the fringing on the dress dance. She turned round to hug him, as Nancy left and joined the others in the corridor.

'Oh, Percy, I feel so . . . I don't know. Nervous?'

'You're excited. It's the same as nervousness,' he said, reassuringly.

'But what if I mess it all up? Tonight, I mean?'

'Two minutes,' Betsy called, as she swung round the door. She took in Vita in the dress and did a whistle. 'Looking good,' she added with a wink.

'It'll go in a flash. Just enjoy it,' Percy reassured her. 'You, my darling, were born to be a showgirl.'

Vita tried to hold on to his words as she waited a few minutes later with the girls. Peeping through the gap onto the stage and the club beyond, she could sense the infectious atmosphere. She jogged her knees as Jerome called, 'Five, six, seven, eight' and their number started.

'Here we go,' Jane said. 'Good luck, Vita.'

She followed, blinded by the spotlight, as she ran out after Jane for the start of their routine. This was really happening . . . she was going out there in front of an actual audience – real people, out dancing in a nightclub – who had paid to see her.

She smiled along the line, as the girls linked up for the small cancan section. Even Edith smiled back.

Vita thought briefly about what her father, Darius Darton, would say if he could see her now, but it didn't matter. She was in the bright lights of London town and was totally anonymous. A sudden feeling of euphoria swept over her. Because she couldn't have found a better place to hide if she'd tried.

32

A Notice in the Paper

Darius Darton banged his wine glass down next to his side-plate at the dinner table, making the china jump.

'Damnation! For the last time, did you provoke her?' he said. He dabbed his moustache with his linen napkin, then threw it on the china side-plate.

'Provoke her, Father?' Clement said, keeping his cool as he buttered his bread roll. He wasn't clear about exactly what had happened on the night Anna had left. He remembered going to the stables and seeing her there, but the concussion had obliterated his memory, and only snippets of their argument had come back. The only thing he knew for sure was that his sister was responsible for his current predicament.

'To make Anna leave? To make her disappear into thin air.' His father sounded infuriated. 'I mean, where could she be? She can't have been able to support herself this long.'

'Can't we ask the police again? To try and find her?' Clement asked.

'You know as well as I do that they're not interested. The facts are that she stole money. She took a bag with her. She *deliberately ran away*,' Darius said.

There was a tense silence. His father looked down the

table at his mother, who lowered her eyes obediently. She didn't have the nerve to challenge either of them about the altercation over Anna's horse, Dante, which had preceded her flight, although he knew damned well that she wanted to.

Clement was beginning to suspect that, along with the intense worry that dominated every conversation they'd had over the past two weeks, his mother was also harbouring more rebellious emotions. The longer Anna stayed away, the less desperate she seemed for her daughter to return.

Without remembering the details of his argument with Anna, and without her being there to punish, Clement had fired Mark, the stablehand. The man should have been quicker at calling for help. It wasn't fair, he knew, but then life wasn't. Particularly when it came to his sister.

It wasn't fair, for example, that she had always been treated kindly – protected even – by their father, while he'd had to suffer.

'It's to toughen you up. Make you a man,' his father had said, that time he'd taken his trousers down and forced the boy to kneel in front of him. Clement couldn't have been more than ten. 'And because you're a man and know what a man feels like now, you must never tell anyone – your mother or your sister.'

He shuddered, feeling the familiar wash of shame when he thought of that time in his father's study, behind the locked door. It had been so wrong and was made even worse because Darius Darton had never mentioned it since. It was as if it had never happened. Except that it had, and sometimes the burden of the secret felt like lead in Clement's soul.

The grandfather clock ticked heavily. Theresa Darton had stopped eating.

Clement felt disgust for her weakness swamp him. She'd never stood up for herself. Or for him. Not even when he was a boy. When she must have suspected what her husband was doing to him. She'd done nothing to stop it.

He pushed the thought away. It was in the past. And things were different now. His father still had a temper, of course, but Clement had learnt not to provoke him. Now that Clement was a man, he could deal with his father better and, in time, he'd get his own back. Or, better still, get out – if his legs would ever carry him. In his innermost thoughts, he fantasized about finding a business that would take him away from the mills. But that, he knew, was wishful thinking. His father had groomed him for one purpose only: to do his bidding.

Eventually, when the silence became saturated with her husband's bad mood, Theresa cleared her throat. 'Let's not fret too much about Anna, dear,' she said. 'It is bad for us all. I have been praying that she's safe.'

'Praying. Ha!' Darius exploded, looking at the ceiling, as if that were ridiculous.

There was another long silence and then his mother tried a final time to lighten the mood. 'At least business is good. Didn't you say the mills were busier this year than ever?' She attempted to look up at her husband and then, hopefully, at Clement.

He hated it when she presumed to know anything about the business. He suddenly imagined reaching across the table and hitting her, and the sound that her head might make as it smashed against the fire grate.

'Well?' she persisted.

Clement decided not to rebuff her. 'The foreigners are in on the act, you mark my words, Mother,' he said. 'We need to get the monopoly now. It's the only way to ensure the future.'

He exchanged a look with his father. Neither of them was going to mention in front of Theresa their plan to secure the monopoly on the mills. And Anna couldn't have got wind of their plan, surely?

'Why don't we put a notice in the paper?' Clement suggested. 'Something Anna would recognize. An appeal, if you like.'

'The newspaper? I don't want people thinking—' Theresa began.

'Thinking what, woman? She could be anywhere,' Darius snapped. 'With anyone. You know how flighty and impressionable she is.'

Clement reached out and put his hand over his mother's small fist. 'Don't worry. She can't hide forever.'

'But what if she's . . . ?'

'What? With the wrong sort?' Clement asked. He met his father's eye. They both knew what might happen to a gullible girl like Anna.

'Stop fretting, woman. You're just making it worse. As if I didn't have enough to contend with, without the shame of our daughter being on the loose.' Darius stood up from his chair and it scraped angrily on the wooden boards.

'I will find her,' Clement said, in his most placatory tone.

'You can hardly move,' Darius snapped. 'In the meantime, sort out a notice in the paper.'

'Of course, Father. As you wish.'

33

Shingled

Vita hadn't realized the verve with which Nancy would throw herself into the task of 'taking her in hand'. She'd even written a list. And Vita's hair was at the very top, followed by other items, such as 'shoes', 'brows' and 'smoking lessons – get new holder'.

Despite being decidedly hungover after the weekend's shows and dancing afterwards in the club, Nancy had declared that Vita should meet her in Hanover Square at eleven o'clock sharp on Monday morning. Vita wondered how long she would be able to survive on four hours' sleep, or less, a night.

But she was too thrilled by Nancy's new-found attention not to do exactly as she was told. She was fascinated by Nancy's decree that Vita's outward appearance was not only worth investing in, but should be paid the utmost attention and care. And that this attention and care were to be fun. And daring. And defining.

In her previous life, as Anna Darton, her mother had never indulged in such extravagance herself, and abhorred the idea of paying such attention to her only daughter. There had been the occasional new outfit, of course, but that had always been out of necessity and Anna certainly hadn't been allowed any say in her fashion choices. Her mother, who had always had a phobia about going to the shops, let alone spending money, had barely noticed that Anna spent her childhood in clothes and boots that were perpetually too small. Anna's hair had been cut by Martha, who had always treated it like some kind of disobedient animal that she had to tame.

But now, freed from Martha's care and from her mother's disapproval, Vita was longing to see the kind of inner sanctum where pampered ladies came to get their hair cut. And she wasn't disappointed when Nancy guided her through the high white doors of a very grand building.

'Anyone who is anyone comes here,' Nancy whispered. She cupped her short bob in her hand and bounced it, before smoothing her pink lipstick, making it clear that she was one of Raymond's best clients. And she'd dressed up for the occasion. She was wearing a coat with a midnight-blue fur trim and long leather gloves to match, with silk-covered buttons up her wrists.

Vita hoped she was carrying off the hat with the long partridge feather that Percy fashioned on her head, but next to Nancy she felt decidedly dowdy. She'd had to admit to Nancy that she hadn't any money until she got paid, and Nancy had very kindly agreed to pay for Vita's haircut, but now Vita worried that it might be very expensive and that she'd owe Nancy a huge debt.

A glass vase of purple and white calla lilies stood on a table in the reception area, behind which sat a very chic young woman in a grey lace-topped dress and matching hat.

There were lots of gilt-framed pictures and light fittings and a lavender-coloured patterned carpet, the like of which Vita had never even imagined existed.

The air smelt unusual, too, as she gave her coat to a young man, who then ushered them through an ornate set of double doors to a brightly lit room beyond. Across a chequer-board floor of black-and-white tiles, a man in a dark suit stood by a floor-to-ceiling mirror. He was probably in his mid-thirties, Vita supposed, but his tan and his waxed moustache made him look older. She saw some scissors in the top pocket of his jacket. This must be the famous Raymond.

He kissed Nancy's hand, burbling in Italian. '*Bella, bella,*' Vita managed to pick up. She looked at Nancy, who was clearly basking in the attention.

'Raymond, honey, so . . . this is my good pal, Vita. She needs your magic touch,' Nancy finally explained.

Vita dutifully sat in the chair and Raymond placed a light-black gown around her neck. It felt odd to be so covered up by such unusual silky material. Especially now that Raymond and Nancy were staring down at her in the mirror.

'May I?' he gestured, before gently taking the pins out of her hair. It tumbled down around her shoulders. 'Hmm, I see.'

Then he pulled Vita's hair right down, looking in the mirror at the ends in his fingertips. The hair came below her ribs – almost to her waist at the back. She thought of Martha, drawn and grey, yanking the giant hairbrush through it. But now she felt a new sensation. Like she was actually being seen.

'It's the colour,' Raymond said. 'So much natural gold in it. Like the sunshine.'

Vita had to suppress the urge to giggle, biting down on her smile. He was so effusive and charming. But this felt wonderful.

'You're thinking . . . short?' Raymond checked with Nancy. It was clear that she was in charge.

'Short, yes. Of course. A bob. We were thinking a bob, weren't we?' Nancy's eyes met Vita's in the mirror, but it was obvious the only response required from her was to nod. She glanced down at the shiny barber's knife on the glass table in front of her.

'Just here, on her jawline.' Raymond's soft finger grazed Vita's jawline and she jumped at the unfamiliar contact. He leant down so that his head was level with hers. 'It will look . . . *fantastico*,' he said, kissing his fingertips.

'I'm sure it will,' she mumbled, when she thought anything but.

'If you're having it bobbed, you might as well go the whole hog and have it shingled. Don't you agree?' Nancy said.

Vita wasn't even sure what 'shingled' meant.

Raymond picked up the long tresses of frizzy browny-blonde hair, pulling it out, to create the kind of volume that Vita had spent the best part of her life trying to subdue.

'Let's begin,' he said decisively, putting his foot on a lever on the bottom of the chair. Vita squeaked with shock as she made sudden little jerking movements upwards, as the chair lifted. Then Raymond swivelled her away from the mirror and started snipping briskly with the barber's knife, as Vita watched the hair fall past her shoulders.

She stole a look down, her long tresses reminding her of fox brushes on the floor around her, and a sickening feeling rose up in her as she remembered the hunt at Darton Hall.

34

The Hunt

The end-of-season hunt was a tradition that the Dartons had grudgingly kept up, despite their frugal nature. It pained Theresa Darton to have horse-hooves churning up the prized front lawn, and she was suspicious of the neighbourhood landowners, who she felt came to Darton to snoop and possibly to steal. But Darius said it was good for morale and kept the good name of the Dartons at the forefront of everyone's minds.

The real reason was that competition between the Dartons and the Arkwrights, who owned the mills on the other side of the valley, was fierce – and Darius wanted to make sure that anyone with influence favoured Darton Mills. It also gave him time to bad-mouth Malcolm Arkwright – his arch-enemy.

Anna found the day of the hunt difficult – and this year was worse than ever. On the one hand, she welcomed the break in the tedious monotony of her daily life at Darton Hall, but it also made her furious that she was not allowed to take part. Clement wasn't as good a rider as she was and had little patience with the horses. She knew damned well that she would beat him, if only she were allowed to ride herself.

She had begged to take part on many occasions, but her father wouldn't hear of it, lumping her in the same bracket as her mother – a weak and feeble-minded female, too flimsy for the elements, or such a male pursuit. That might have applied to her mother, but not to Anna, who knew that she was robust and sturdy . . . not that her father would ever give her the chance to prove herself. And on the day of the hunt this year, once again, she had to contend with hearing the horns of the riders in the distance and the rumble of the horses' hooves.

She stayed at the landing window, hiding behind the thick brocade curtains in the box window, waiting for the riders return, wanting to be first out with the trays of sherry. Up at the Hall she had so little contact with anyone that even the red-faced chaps who'd turned up today were better than nothing. She stared out at the snow-covered hills, her breath clouding the cold glass, wondering if she might see the fox tearing across the field.

It was while she was waiting that she heard Martha and Elspeth, the scullery girl, whispering as they walked down the stairs. They had no idea that Anna was hiding.

'I heard talk from Jed at the inn. He said he saw Master Clement talking to him.'

'Who? Mr Arkwright.'

'He's brokering a plan. Those were Jed's words.'

'A plan?' Martha asked. She sounded sceptical.

'A plan for him to marry Miss Darton.'

Anna felt saliva flood her mouth, as her heart pounded. She peeped through the curtains as Martha and Elspeth walked on down the stairs.

What exactly had Elspeth heard? Surely it must be a mistake. Clement wouldn't possibly meet Malcolm Arkwright without their father's permission. And her, marry Mr Arkwright? He was her father's fiercest rival. Even the mention of him sent Darius into a rage.

She put her hand to her chest, trying to make sense of what she'd just heard. Malcolm Arkwright was well over fifty, with a pimpled, heavy face and a balding head. Although his manner was jovial, everything about him made her skin crawl.

Then she saw a movement at the edge of the far trees and Clement came into view. He was covered in mud and she was shocked to see him on Dante – her horse. Her fury at him taking Dante without her permission momentarily interrupted her disgust about Arkwright.

She ran downstairs and outside, just as Clement arrived at the gravel outside the front door. He was shouting, and it now became clear why. Dante had thrown him, when the fox had been in his sights, and he'd missed the kill.

She'd never seen Clement so incensed as he dismounted her horse, which, to Anna's eye, already seemed injured. Forcing Mark, the stablehand, to hold the reins, he started thrashing poor Dante until his flanks were bleeding.

The horse whinnied, foam frothing at the edges of his mouth. Anna screamed and tried to run and stop Clement, but Martha grabbed her and held her back.

'Leave him,' Martha said, a warning in her voice. 'If you know what's good for you.'

35

The Crystal Ball

Nancy's flat was in a new block near the canal in Maida Vale and Nancy didn't pause for breath while talking about Raymond's extraordinary skills, as Vita hurried to keep up with her across the marble reception area and into the lift, where the boy tipped his hat and blushed. Vita tried to copy Nancy, her hips swinging with a confident allure, her heels clicking on the tiles.

She caught sight of herself in the bevelled mirror and lifted her hand to feel her new hair. It was daringly, majestically, fantastically short. She no longer looked like a frightened child, but a confident woman. A London woman, at that. She thought momentarily of the horror Martha would feel if she could see her now, and it made her new transformation all the more pleasurable.

When they arrived at the fourth floor, Vita grinned as she saw the lift boy peaking around the corner in order to gaze at Nancy for a few moments more.

'I can see you, Freddie,' she called back, waggling her fingers in a wave and winking at Vita, who marvelled at the way Nancy charmed everyone in her path. 'Home, sweet home,' she said with a flourish, unlocking the white door. She threw the keys down on an ornate marble-topped table just inside the hall, before kicking off her heels. 'Come in.'

'Is this really all yours?' Vita asked.

She was aware that she might be gawping, as she took in the sumptuousness of Nancy's modern apartment. It was a large open-plan room, which had several white pillars holding up the ceiling. Over to one side there was a white grand piano, and several squashy-looking armchairs and some ornate tables with gold legs. In between the two pillars was a white marble statue of a semi-naked woman. When Vita looked more closely, she couldn't help noticing the resemblance to Nancy.

'My brother,' Nancy said, following her gaze. 'He's the sculptor in the family. Could have been quite good.'

'Could have?'

'Battle of the Marne. The second one,' she shrugged, with a sad sort of smile. 'Poor boy didn't stand a chance. First over the top, with his men. At least he didn't die a coward.'

It was on the tip of Vita's tongue to tell Nancy that she'd had a brother, too, but she was saved by the sound of yapping. A small white dog came bounding out of a doorway and Nancy's mood switched to one of pure joy. 'There you are. Oh, my baby, I missed you.'

She scooped up the dog into her arms and it licked her face enthusiastically. 'Meet Mr Wild,' Nancy said, pressing her face up against the dog's and turning to introduce it to Vita. She pronounced 'Wild' with a tremulous quiver, for added drama, and Vita wondered how the dog had come to get such a flamboyant name, but she was beginning to realize that everything about Nancy was rather dramatic. 'Come, come. I have lemonade in the refrigerator.'

She had her own refrigerator? Vita had been intrigued by Nancy from the first time she'd laid eyes on her, wondering how one got to be so styled and poised. And here was the answer: she had money.

Vita followed Nancy and the yapping dog, wanting to kneel down and run her hand over the thick carpet. Along one wall were stylish square windows overlooking the park. There was a balcony outside, with an array of urns housing tall leafy plants.

'So we might as well find you something interesting to wear to the party next weekend, now that you're here,' Nancy called from the kitchen. 'I'll have something, for certain.'

Vita knew she was being kind – and that very soon she'd have to do something to repay her. Nancy had already paid for her haircut and now she was going to give her a dress. She'd never known such generosity or kindness.

Imagine having a wardrobe of fashionable clothes. Enough to spare! And all of this space. This set-up of Nancy's was beyond anything she'd ever been able to imagine. She'd never thought it possible that girls could live totally independently and freely. Might this be possible for her? Could she live alone one day, in her own place? With her own refrigerator and cooker? The thought was so deliciously heady, it took her breath away. She leant against the doorway, trying to imagine how wonderful it would be to *be* Nancy.

'Isn't it odd living alone?' Vita asked. 'I mean, don't you ever get lonely?'

'Lonely? Why on earth would I get lonely? Mr Wild here keeps me company.'

Vita blushed, watching Nancy nuzzle her nose into the

dog's neck before setting him down on the floor, where he went up on his back paws and did a little dance, making Nancy laugh. She made him twirl round and round, before giving him a sugar lump.

'So why do you work? When you have all of this?' she asked as Nancy gave her a glass of lemonade.

'The club? It's not work. I like to think of it more as art. And it's fun.'

Vita hadn't considered that Nancy might have been working there by choice.

'Didn't you want to do something else?'

'Like what?'

'I don't know. I guess if you're . . . I mean, if money isn't an object, then you could do anything?'

Nancy sighed and pulled off her gloves. 'Money is *always* an object, darling, mark my words. But what else should one do? That's the question. It seems to me that I might as well do something I enjoy. Besides, it's a hoot, annoying my parents this much.'

'They know about the Zip Club?'

'Oh yes. But they can't do anything about it,' she said proudly.

Vita sipped the sharp lemonade and listened, enthralled. How brave Nancy was. And fearless. She'd never have had the guts to challenge both her parents.

'Since I'm such a "disappointment" to them,' Nancy continued, holding up her fingers as if quoting them, 'I thought I'd go all out and stay in London and get a job as a dancer, rather than go back to America. The Zip Club pays for my expenses, so I don't have the indignity of facing my father's wrath. And the discounted drinks are a godsend. That said, Goldie – that's Larry Goldblum, my lawyer – says I'm burning through my fund, but frankly I don't care. I enjoy it. I always wanted to dance and to party and meet interesting people. And this way I can do both, to my heart's content.'

It felt good to know that someone else had issues with their family, but the way Nancy was talking made Vita feel as if this was a game that she was playing for attention. Because despite her protests, Nancy was still connected to her family – even though they'd cut her off, for now. She still had property and a trust fund. And this . . . her own flat.

It was only now that the real significance of cutting herself off from her own family hit her. Because her status as Anna Darton had been part of her, for as long as she could remember. The fact that she would inherit money, as her father had done before her, had always been a given. As had the fact that she'd never have to work: a given, too. But not any more. Now she would never be able to pull the strings that her father had pulled. She'd never be able to play the card that she came from money, and ensure she had the kind of husband that she'd always assumed she might have.

In fact, she thought, the panic rising now, how was she ever going to find a husband? Because how would she live, if she didn't have one? She didn't have independent means, a trust fund – anything like the safety net Nancy had. In a world where status meant everything, she'd discarded hers entirely.

But now one thing was certain, she thought as she sipped her lemonade. She was going to have to come up with a plan

JOANNA REES

soon. Do something to support herself fully, because her job at the club couldn't sustain her forever.

But there wouldn't be a forever, she reminded herself. Not after what she'd done.

She put the glass of lemonade down on the table and, trying to distract herself from such a sombre thought, picked up a large glass orb that was sitting on a wooden stand next to the candelabra.

'What's this?' Vita asked.

'Oh, careful. Don't drop it.'

Vita put it back on its stand quickly. Nancy put a protective hand on it. 'It's my crystal ball.'

'You can read a crystal ball?' Vita said, thinking she must be joking.

'No. Not yet. But I will do one day. I think I have quite a gift. That's what Mystic Alice says.'

'Who?'

'My clairvoyant,' Nancy said, quite matter-of-factly. 'I go at least once a month.'

'She sounds frightfully intriguing. What does she tell you?'

'All sorts of things.'

'Like what?'

Nancy sighed dramatically. 'That I must move again, to another foreign city.'

'And you believe her? Surely it's utter nonsense?'

Nancy frowned. 'No, Vita, it's quite serious. The woman is a genius.'

Was she joking? Vita found it hard to tell. From the look

on Nancy's face, she was worried that she'd offended her friend.

'I'm sorry. It's just that I've never seen a crystal ball before.'

'Then maybe I'll take you with me next time.'

'Would you?' Vita said, a tad too enthusiastically, hoping to win back Nancy's approval, but as soon as she said it, she felt a sudden flush of fear. What would this Mystic Alice be able to tell about her? Might she reveal Vita's secrets? Would she be able to glean the truth about Clement?

'Maybe,' Nancy said, as if her good humour was still on trial. 'Now, come on. Let's find you something fabulous to wear.'

36

Nancy's Wardrobe

As Vita propped herself up in the small upholstered chair with the smart woollen cushion, she thought of her own bedroom in Darton Hall, with its ominous mahogany furniture and starched lace doilies, and marvelled at how different Nancy's was. There was a black fireplace, adorned with two more figurine sculptures, with tastefully framed covers of *Vogue* magazine on the walls. There was a jug of particularly bright daffodils next to the double bed, which was covered in a black silk eiderdown.

'Ha. Look at this!' Nancy said, from inside the walk-in wardrobe. She stepped out, pulling a white dress from a hanger before pressing it against herself. 'I wore this one when I came out.'

'You were a debutante?'

'Of course. Same year as Edith. That's how we met.' She jumped up on the bed so that she could see herself in the long mirror opposite it. 'Oh yes, her family are quite la-di-da, but she got herself into a scrape with an unsuitable sort, and that was that.'

Vita digested this new piece of information about Edith as she watched Nancy pose with the dress, ruffling the layers of white tulle. She would have killed to have been given the chance to come out in polite society. If she had, then none of this might have happened. She might be married off and living an altogether different kind of life.

There had been talk of it, of course. Theresa Darton had made a case for Anna to go to London, but Clement had poured such scorn on the idea that it was never even broached with her father, and her mother had said no more about it.

'It sounds very glamorous.'

'I nearly *died* of boredom.'

'But all those parties . . .'

'There weren't parties. Not fun ones, at least. It was awful. Like being paraded, but the air of desperation was so depressing.'

'Desperation?'

'My mother's, mainly. But it was hopeless for all the girls. There were so few good men. And I absolutely refuse to hitch my wagon to the wrong horse.'

Vita laughed, admiring Nancy's rebellious spirit. After all, she felt exactly the same way about Malcolm Arkwright.

'That's when Edith and I got bored and rebelled. We snuck out of a ball one night and I took her dancing. Let me try this on. I'll show you what a perfect idiot I looked.'

Vita could already imagine the scene – how Nancy might have corrupted Edith, just as she was being corrupted herself. But she didn't care, she realized. Not one bit.

Nancy undid the small pearl button on her dress, undid the hooks at the side and wriggled out of it, so that the silk dress fell in a puddle around her ankles. She hooked a foot into the dress and tossed it away.

As she leant forward to pick up the white dress, Vita saw the full outline of her small breasts beneath her silk camisole. She felt something rush through her. Shock? Excitement? She'd always wondered what it must feel like to fall in love, but maybe it must be a little bit like this. This tummy-tingling feeling of admiration. Because Nancy was simply gorgeous. And so daring and confident. Everything she herself longed to be.

'Look! Horrible.'

'I think you look lovely,' Vita said, meaning it.

'Well, perhaps. Three poor chaps fell hopelessly in love with me when I wore this dress,' Nancy said, swinging her hips and admiring her reflection in the mirror. She sounded wistful and, for a moment, Vita wondered if there was more to Nancy being an outcast from her family than she was letting on.

'I'm not surprised. If I were going to choose a dress, it would be exactly the same as that one,' Vita said, getting up and examining the fine lacework on the hem. 'It's so well made.'

'Mother sent for it from Paris. Much to Mrs Clifford-Meade's upset.'

'Mrs Clifford-Meade?'

'My dressmaker. Well, mother's actually. Lulu – everyone calls her Lulu – set up when she split up with the Major and she had to earn a living. She's frightfully good. I shall introduce you. She has this quaint little shop with a few pieces, but the real magic happens out the back, with her bespoke designs.'

'I'd love that,' Vita said, entranced by this gossipy world

that Nancy was so involved in, but also distracted by the way the designer had tapered the skirt into the waist so elegantly. 'Look at those darts.'

'You're quite the little seamstress, aren't you?' Nancy said.

'Hardly. But clothes – fine clothes like these – are so fascinating. They are like works of art. One day I'll make them myself. That's what I'd like to do anyway.'

Nancy looked down, her face a mixture of curiosity and admiration, as if she were seeing Vita in a new light.

'And in the meantime, I'm serious about that lingerie,' she added. 'Something to tame these,' she said, putting her hands over her breasts and laughing shyly.

'Oh, don't hide them away, darling. They're one of your best assets. Why do you think Connelly hired you?'

Vita looked up at her, startled.

'What? Don't look so shocked. The men come to our club to see beautiful women. It's as simple as that. And you have a quite magnificent décolletage.'

Vita wasn't sure what a décolletage was. She backed away, feeling suddenly self-conscious. Nancy laughed and hopped off the bed, then gave Vita's left breast a squeeze.

'Don't be so coy. I'd be proud of them, if they were mine,' she said. 'But even so, if you want to make some lingerie, you should. Just do it. I can't stand people who talk about such things and never get on with it.'

'Well, I will,' she stammered. 'Can I see what else you have in your wardrobe?'

'Help yourself. But if we're going to do this, I think we need a real drink, don't you? What'll it be?'

'A Gin and It?' Vita said, confidently naming the only drink she knew.

'Yes, good idea,' Nancy said. 'I like your style, Verity Casey.'

37

The Conservatory

Clement sat with the tartan rug over his knees in the cold conservatory, as his mother stood by the birdcage and posted morsels of food through the bars. The birds chirruped noisily inside, and in response she made cooing sounds, as if she were communicating with them. He loathed her for her infantile ways and for her refusal to take part in the real world.

He wasn't sure how much more of this he could tolerate. He tapped his fingers on the arm of his wheelchair, feeling a sense of righteous rage building up. In the distance, he could see the large brick chimney of the biggest of the Darton cotton mills, belching smoke into the grey sky. The sight only made him feel more trapped. He should be there at the mill. Not here.

Martha came in, her head bowed.

'The gentleman is here,' she said.

'Well, send him in. Don't keep him waiting,' Clement snapped.

Mr Rawlings had come from Manchester and was dressed like a man of his class. He had swarthy dark skin, a bushy moustache and a bowler hat and looked reassuringly forgettable – a bonus, for his profession. Clement wondered if he really was as good as his contact at the police force had said. He should be, for the wage Clement had agreed to pay him.

Keen to get his next injection, Clement wasted no time with pleasantries, cutting off his mother when she offered Rawlings tea. They sat awkwardly around the card table, as Clement instructed him on exactly what was required. Rawlings nodded, reassuring him that he would be discreet in his enquiries. His mother twisted a handkerchief in her fingers.

'And may I ask, Mrs Darton, what the incident was that prompted your daughter's departure?' Mr Rawlings asked, making notes in his book.

Theresa Darton, afraid of eye-contact as ever, looked down at the knotted handkerchief in her lap. She had been against the whole idea of a private detective, but Clement had insisted that – as his father had suggested – they take matters into their own hands. Rawlings had agreed to put the notice in the paper, but also to follow up with enquiries.

'There was an incident with Dante, her horse,' she whispered.

'What was that?' Rawlings asked.

Clement silenced his mother with a look and took over. There was no point in Mr Rawlings conversing with her. His mother was deranged, at the best of times, and Anna's recent behaviour had only made it worse. There was no point in dragging out the details of his fury over Dante. He'd been perfectly justified in thrashing the beast. He rolled the wheel-chair away towards the window and gestured for Mr Rawlings to follow.

154

'The point is, my sister is not a terribly responsible person. Not to mention the fact that she's incredibly naive,' Clement said, before adding quietly to Mr Rawlings, as his mother stood and turned away to the birds, 'and there may be some inherited . . . well, problems.' He tapped the side of his temple. 'So you understand it's imperative that we find her and bring her home?'

Rawlings glanced at Theresa Darton and back at Clement and nodded. Clement was relieved, knowing, as always, that such matters were best dealt with man-to-man. He pictured his sister in his mind's eye the last time he'd seen her, and clenched his fist with fury when he thought of how she'd got away. But she wouldn't have gone far. She couldn't have.

'There are no friends she could have gone to?' Rawlings asked. 'Family?'

Clement exchanged a look with his mother. There were no friends to speak of. And certainly no family. Not people who would give Anna shelter. His mother was an only child and her parents were long dead. His father had left his own parents and sisters in Liverpool long ago, keeping the Darton wealth solely for himself.

'No. No. We can't think of anyone,' Theresa said, her voice catching. 'Please, Mr Rawlings. Do see if you can find her.'

'I'll try, ma'am. Perhaps you could give me a description of what she was wearing when she left. And also any distinguishing features she may have.'

38

An Idea Takes Shape

Vita couldn't wait to show Percy the dress that Nancy had given her, but he and Mrs Bell were more impressed with her hair, cooing over her and making her feel more flattered than she'd ever felt before.

After breakfast on Wednesday, Vita went with Percy to the studio in Edward's car.

'He totally forgot he left it at the weekend,' Percy said with an indulgent laugh, as they drove through the streets. Vita looked out at the buds on the trees. It wouldn't be long until spring. She stared out at the shops and buildings, the buses and bicycles, realizing just how much she'd fallen in love with London.

She told him all about Nancy's flat, and about Annabelle's party and Edith's threat, and how he and Edward would have to come to the party with her.

'I intend to make an impression,' she said, pulling the dress out of the bag.

'Where on earth did you find that?' Percy asked, glancing down at the material.

'I found it at the back of Nancy's wardrobe. She said

she'd worn it to a fancy-dress party. She was a mermaid,' Vita explained, stroking the silvery material.

'What's your plan?'

'If you'll help me, I was thinking we'd take off the sleeves and cut it short.'

'Goodness!'

'I know it's drastic, but it's like I can *see* another dress inside this one.'

'Well, anything I can do to assist, let me know,' Percy said, clearly amused by her. 'But first you have to help *me*. The landlord visited unexpectedly and declared my studio to be a fire hazard and has demanded that I get rid of some of my treasures.'

'Oh dear,' Vita said. 'That is a problem.'

They parked the car in the Haymarket, where Edward had asked Percy to leave it, and then walked up to the studio together. Inside the cavernous room, Vita stood by the wall of costumes while Percy made tea.

'How on earth are we going to sort these out?' she asked.

'An impossible task. Agreed?' Percy said, as he lit the stove.

'Don't the theatres want them back?'

'Probably, but I made most of them, so they're sort of my babies. And I'm a magpie – drawn to anything glittery or shiny,' Percy said. 'I have no idea what to do with them.'

'Well, you can't throw them out.'

'Maybe some artful rearranging,' Percy suggested.

Vita started rummaging through the bottom rail, suddenly seeing the landlord's point. There were actually two rails of clothing, not one.

'Oh, look at this one.' she exclaimed, pulling a costume free from the back rail. Percy laughed, seeing what had piqued her interest.

'Ah yes. Boudicca.'

'Actually, that's rather interesting,' Vita said, running her fingers over the conically-shaped bust part. 'This round stitching is very clever. And the ribbon wound like that – to get the shape. What if we copied that idea . . .'

'We?' Percy asked with an amused glance. 'Darling, we're supposed to be sorting out the costumes. Not making more mess.'

But Vita wasn't listening. Instead she was delving under the hanging rail. 'You've got bags of calico here. Oh, and ribbon – just what we need.'

She set to, chopping up the dress and trying to create a replica of the bust section out of calico. Percy, annoyed that she was not helping, watched as he piled up costumes on the bench. But as Vita started to cut, he helped her and soon she was jumping between the mirror and the sewing machine, until she had a garment with dainty curved cups made from the ribbon.

'The edge of the ribbon is scratchy,' Vita said, already trying to improve the design.

'You can use this, if you like,' Percy said, kneeling down to look under the bench. He pulled out a bolt of tangerine-coloured silk fabric and then produced some hooks and eyes on a cardboard sheet.

'Oh, Percy. You're a genius. I really think it might work,' Vita said.

39

Paddy Potts

With the party to look forward to and with her new creation taking shape with Percy, Vita was starting to feel as if her prayers had been answered and there was a God after all. She had to pinch herself that she was actually employed, and when Mrs Winters gave her an envelope with money in it on Thursday night, Vita kissed her.

Thursday's show was the best yet and the audience whooped and cheered, and they had to repeat the whole routine for a second time.

She could understand, now, why the actresses who came into Percy's studio were so clearly in love with the theatre. Even just as a dancer in a show, she was hooked. She loved the adrenaline in her veins, the smell of the thick make-up, the slick of sweat across her body, the applause lingering in her ears as she came offstage with the girls.

As soon as they were behind the wall, however, out of the glare of the lights, the magic was suddenly broken and the girls' postures slumped. But Vita loved these moments of camaraderie too. Tonight, Jane stamped ahead, kicking off one of her shoes.

'The bloody clasp broke again,' she said, doing a funny

lopsided walk down the corridor, making Vita laugh. 'Where's Wisey?'

Mr Connelly was backstage tonight and this was the first time he'd seen Vita's hair. He stopped her as she bustled past with the others to the dressing room.

'Hmm. An improvement, I'd say.'

She wasn't sure if this was a compliment or not, or whether it implied that her hair had been dreadful before. 'Thank you,' she said, patting it. She'd only had the haircut since Monday, but already it felt like she'd had it forever.

Edith, who was just in front of her, stopped, looking between Mr Connelly and Vita, her face thunderous, as if Vita had made some kind of pass at him.

His eyes narrowed behind the cloud of cigar smoke. 'Will you be coming out front?' he asked. 'There's some guests who I'm sure would like to meet you.'

'Yes, give us a moment,' Nancy said, scooping her arm into Vita's and taking her to the dressing room. 'Honestly, that man gives me the creeps,' she said in a confidential whisper. 'I don't know what Edith sees in him.'

'Neither do I. Surely she could do better.'

Because it wasn't as if the girls were short of admirers, Vita thought, as she and Nancy went with Jane, Emma, Jemima and Betsy through the small stage door into the club. Having never received any attention in her life, it was weird to see how they were perceived in the club after the show, and several people applauded them. She could get used to this feeling, she decided.

Nancy smiled at Jerome, who was leading the band, and

he smiled back. Now that the show had finished, the floor was filled with couples dancing in the smoky atmosphere.

Nancy pushed her way to the front of the crowded bar area and winked dramatically at Matteo, the barman. Vita had met him a couple of times and liked the way he spun the glasses dramatically in the air, and how debonair he looked in his shirt and waistcoat. Nancy had told her that Matteo's mother was from Malta, which probably accounted for his swarthy good looks. He was definitely very attractive, and Vita wondered exactly what was going on between Nancy and Jack Connelly's young bartender. They certainly had some sort of arrangement, because Connelly wasn't one to endorse free drinks for the staff, but soon there was a row of glasses in front of Nancy, for her and the girls. Vita offered to pay, keen to repay all the favours she owed, but Matteo winked at her and told her to put her money away.

Jemima left to go and meet her boyfriend, but even just with the five of them, as they toasted one another, Vita felt as if she were part of something glamorous and sinfully good.

Jane leant in close. 'Watch your backs, girls,' she whispered. 'Lolly and Ra are in.'

Vita looked over her shoulder to where two manly-looking women in riding outfits were chatting at the other end of the bar. One of them waved to Nancy, who raised her glass back.

'Ra is a snowbird,' Emma confided.

'A what?'

'You know,' she said, putting one finger over her nostril and sniffing. 'That's why Nancy is friends with her.'

'But who are they?'

'Quite the couple around town,' Betsy said.

'They're together?' Vita asked.

'Oh yes. Famously so.'

'Sapphic love. It's everywhere,' Nancy said, turning back from the bar and joining in the conversation. 'Anyone who is anyone is a lesbian these days.'

She looked over at the pair, and Vita thought about the explosion of sheer moral outrage her father would have if he could see these women flaunting their relationship. 'Well, good for them,' she said.

Nancy gave her a look that made Vita feel as if she'd passed some kind of test. 'Good news, ladies,' she said. 'Paddy Potts is in. Over there. Table at the back.' She pointed over to a man in a smart black suit, a dashing red-and-white polka-dot scarf around his neck. 'He's rich. A banker. And he likes buying us champagne. Come on.'

She grabbed hold of Vita's hand and pulled her through the crowd to the booth.

'Paddy, darling!' she gasped, reaching him and leaning in to deposit a red lipstick mark on his cheek. He was very tall. 'Meet Vita. She's our new girl,' Nancy said, and Vita shook his hand, thinking how sweet it was that he was blushing. 'Didn't you love the show?'

'Of course,' he said. 'I always do. Nice to meet you, Vita.'

But Nancy was already pulling him away, dragging him by both ends of his scarf. 'Come and dance!' she called, wriggling in front of him. 'I won't have you being a shrinking violet at the back.'

Vita laughed, seeing how helpless Paddy was, and how

funny it was seeing Nancy pulling such a large man behind her.

She wondered, for a fleeting moment, what life might be like if she were still at Darton Hall. If she hadn't done anything to Clement and this was just a normal night. She looked out at the jammed dance floor filled with women in colourful dresses, the air thick with perspiration and jazz, and contrasted it with the dry, dull, grey monotony of Darton. Would her father and Clement be forcing an introduction to that horrible man, Malcolm Arkwright? *Probably.* She shuddered, truly grateful for the chance she'd been given, even if it had come at such a terrible price.

Don't think about it. Don't let the guilt in. Not when this is so much fun.

Vita joined in the dancing for a while and then, as Nancy had predicted, Paddy offered to buy them a bottle of champagne, and Nancy, Jane, Vita, Betsy and Emma went to his table.

'You're a shocking flirt,' Vita teased her friend as they waited for Paddy and he waved from the bar.

'So? He doesn't mind. It's all a game,' Nancy said. 'He's very happily married.'

'She's right. You mustn't take everything so seriously, Vita,' Jane added.

Vita decided that she should follow Nancy's lead. After all, Nancy seemed to be very skilled at getting exactly what she wanted. She wouldn't want any husband of hers ever to come dancing alone at the Zip Club, with the likes of Nancy on the loose.

But it seemed that the crowd in the Zip didn't live by the

moral code she'd always known. Here, people came to dance and enjoy life, and the sense of freedom was palpable.

Jane, Emma, Betsy, Vita and Nancy all huddled together at the table, and Jane pointed out the two couples on the other side of the room who had just come in. One of the girls looked decidedly tipsy, and they all talked about how they admired the large bow in her hair. Then Paddy came back with the champagne and put it on the table with their glasses. As he leant over, Nancy whipped the polka-dot scarf from around his neck. She turned to Vita and tied it around her head in a big bow.

'You should have one, too,' Nancy said. 'Doesn't it look lovely on her?' Paddy nodded and, once again, Vita felt sorry for him. She could tell he would be perfectly prepared to lose his scarf, if it meant Nancy being happy. 'Mind you, everything looks lovely on Vita. She has that . . . *je ne sais quoi*.'

She touched Vita's face tenderly, and Vita caught Paddy's eye. He looked a little crestfallen that he wasn't the object of Nancy's affection, but she felt something bloom inside her, as she stood and admired her reflection in the mirror behind the bar. *Oh, it felt so good to belong.*

The music changed to the unmistakable introduction to 'Baby Face' and Nancy jumped up. 'Oh,' she exclaimed, 'come on, girls – it's our song.' She downed a whole glass of champagne and then, grabbing Vita's hand, headed for the dance floor.

40

Motherly Advice

Vita was excited about Annabelle's party on Saturday night and got changed quickly after the show.

'So you remember the plan? I'll meet you at Annabelle's,' Nancy said, hurriedly looking at herself in the mirror. She was wearing her stage make-up and a sky-blue lace dress that Vita had admired before. 'I'll fix my face on the way,' she said, squirting herself with a hefty mist of perfume. 'Toodle-oo, little one. Now chip-chop and don't be late. Tonight is going to be *fun*.'

And with that, she was gone, off in a whirlwind to one of her mysterious pre-party arrangements. Vita waved, trying not to show that she suddenly felt nervous about being alone, not least because she had to make her own way across town to the party from the club. Edith, who was also going, had made it perfectly clear that Vita couldn't come with her, as there wouldn't be room in the car.

When the others had disappeared out to the front of the club, Vita changed into the dress that she and Percy had altered during the week, but she could really have done with some much needed reassurance about her daring fashion choice. It was left to Wisey to deliver the verdict.

'It's unusual . . .' she said, admiring the sparkling fringing. 'I'll give you that. And you'll catch your death,' she said, looking down at Vita's legs, before rearranging Nancy's fur stole. Vita hoped that she meant 'unusual' in a good way. Wisey's hands stayed on the fur, like a hug.

Vita leant forward and gave her a quick kiss on the cheek. The simple gesture surprised them both. 'You sound like my mother,' she said, although that wasn't true. Her mother would never have let her out of the house.

For a fleeting moment she wished her mother *could* see her now. Or was she so beholden to her own husband and son that she would begrudge her daughter her freedom? Vita stamped out the faint flicker of hope. She knew the answer only too well.

'I wouldn't let any daughter of mine out, looking like that,' Wisey said, but her smile was gentle. There was a beat as her warm brown eyes stared into Vita's. 'Should you not at least write to the poor woman, Vita? Your mother, I mean?'

Vita swallowed hard, wondering what the others had told Wisey. She'd provoked a sad response from Jane and Betsy when she'd told them that she didn't speak to her mother and was estranged from her family. She was shocked that Wisey had asked such a direct question. She knew that the girls must have been gossiping about her and saw that Wisey, like them, must be full of unanswered questions.

She shook her head. Contacting her mother – ever again – was totally unthinkable. Wisey hesitated for a moment longer, as if wanting to ask her something, but Vita turned away to the stage door.

On the omnibus to Berkeley Square, however, as Vita pulled Nancy's fur stole tight around her, she felt unsettled. And now, alone for the first time in days, familiar guilty thoughts gnawed at her mind and she pictured her mother looking pale and drawn, her hair turning grey with worry. It must be hard for her to lose Clement, but even worse, perhaps, to have to live with the shame that Anna had brought on their family.

Would the police still be looking for her? Because surely they would have been called. And why had there still been nothing in any of the many papers that she'd scoured? Why would they be hushing up their son's death and their daughter's disappearance?

And what about Clement? They must have had his funeral by now. Had they buried him in the churchyard alongside their grandmother? She imagined his headstone, slick and grey as an eel, standing tall amongst the crumbling graves and tangled weeds.

She pictured her mother, right now, in the conservatory, staring off into space. She wondered what would happen if, just for a moment, she could pull her out of that chair and shake her awake. Tell her that there was a magnificent, wonderful life that she was missing.

Perhaps it was the way Wisey had entreated her to reach out, but now she put her hand on her chest, feeling an unfamiliar pain. Was it guilt or sorrow? She couldn't tell. Somehow Wisey's concern seemed to stretch across the gap between her two lives, and it terrified her.

But she'd had to leave. There'd been no choice.

And now the events that had led up to her departure

167

played out in her mind. She recalled every detail of how she'd marched into her father's study, her righteous fury making her unusually brave. How she'd demanded that he punish Clement for whipping poor Dante so brutally. But her father had said it was Clement's business, and not hers. That she shouldn't interfere with things that didn't concern her, and that she'd never understand. Hunting was for men – not for women to stick their noses in.

She'd pursued the matter and had accused him of turning a blind eye to Clement's cruelty. Not just concerning the horse – but to everyone and everything. And in particular to her. She'd almost told him that she'd found out about the plan for her to marry Malcolm Arkwright, but before she could, Darius Darton had told her not to dare to be so insolent.

'All you care about is Clement,' she'd shouted. 'That's all you've ever cared about . . .'

But then he'd lost his temper – angry that she'd defied him. He'd lashed out at her, striking her across the face.

She held her cheek now, looking at her reflection in the glass window of the bus. For a moment she felt an out-of-body experience, as if she were halfway between Anna Darton and Verity Casey.

No. She'd done the right thing. It was best for everyone that Anna Darton had vanished into thin air.

41

Annabelle's Party

Vita was greatly relieved to arrive at the party finally and find it in full swing. She laughed as she allowed Edward to help her with her fur stole in the brightly lit entrance hall of the house in Berkeley Square.

'So *this* is the creation?' Edward said, admiring her dress. She twirled the string of pearls she was wearing, before settling them into place over her cleavage.

'Oh, and I love your hair. Isn't it magnificent,' Edward said, touching her bob.

'Feel it. Go on,' Vita said, taking his hand and running it over the back of her hair, where it was shaved short like a man's.

'Stop it. You'll turn me,' Edward whispered in her ear, making her laugh at his outrageous comment. She liked being 'in' on his secret. And it was even more fun being at a party with such a handsome man. She felt a big shiver of excitement dance up her spine, as she looked at the crowd of people and heard the band over the burble of conversation.

'Where's Percy?' she asked.

'He said he'd meet us in the orangery. I suggest we fill up

on cocktails on the way. Here we are,' he said, expertly swooping two glasses from the silver tray of a passing waiter.

Vita clinked glasses with him. 'Chin-chin,' she smiled, before taking a sip, then she caught sight of Edith arriving. 'Oh, look. Wait. There's Edith. Don't look, don't look,' she added, making wide eyes at Edward, who was fully aware of the gauntlet Edith had laid down and thought it was a perfect hoot. She'd also told Edward and Percy quite how superior Edith thought she was and how much she delighted in picking on Vita at the Zip Club – constantly undermining her in front of the others. But now, with Edward by her side, Vita felt equal for the first time.

She turned very briefly and saw a look flash across Edith's face. She'd clearly wanted to arrive first, but Vita had been quicker, coming on the bus.

'Where?' Edward whispered.

'Six o'clock. I said, don't look!' Vita whispered excitedly, spying Edith coming towards them. Nancy was still just inside the door, talking to someone she knew.

As Edith came closer now, Edward let out a peal of laughter, as if Vita had said something amusing, then he leant in and kissed her tenderly on the cheek, as if they were lovers. She felt herself blushing, just as Edith arrived. He was such a good actor.

'Oh, Edith, there you are. You remember Edward Sopel,' Vita said, pointedly.

Edward turned to her in surprise. 'No. Have we met?'

He was so charming and so honest that Vita had to suppress a smile, seeing the fury cross Edith's face as he kissed her hand. Vita saw a flush creep up Edith's neck. She was obviously mortified that she'd been caught out. Her eyes darted towards Vita, daring her to say something, but Vita simply smiled back, feeling the moment of triumph.

'Really, Edward?' Edith said, as if he were lying.

Edward looked expectantly at Edith and then at Vita for an explanation.

'We dance together,' Vita explained.

'Oh! You're in Vita's troupe?' Edward said innocently, and Edith bristled even more.

'Edward, don't be silly,' Vita chided. 'It's not *mine*.'

The moment was interrupted by a woman who sashayed into their group, her cigarette smoking in a long ivory holder. 'This looks like an interesting gathering,' she said. She was tall and elegant, like a racehorse, and was wearing a long black evening dress that was covered in sparkling jewels, and long black silk gloves.

'Annabelle, darling,' Edward gushed, kissing their hostess's hand. 'You know Edith, of course, but this is Vita. She's at the Zip too.'

'Oh. I've heard that's *quite* the place,' Annabelle said, looking Vita and Edith up and down. 'So that's where you've been hiding out, Woody?'

She didn't sound like she altogether approved, as she appraised Vita and Edith.

Vita had been caught up in the glamour and excitement of the dance troupe, but she hadn't realized that the social hierarchy she perceived within it counted for nothing, out here in the real world. Here, they were dancing girls – Edith included. Which meant that whatever Edith thought she had over Vita, it wasn't real. They had the same rank.

Perhaps Annabelle sensed that she'd been rather rude, as she smiled quickly. 'It always helps to have some pretty faces around. Oh, and I do like this . . .' she added to Vita, taking her hand and holding it out so that she could admire her dress. 'Where did you get it from?'

'I made it. With a little help from a friend.'

'*So* clever to be so chic,' Annabelle said, squeezing her hand in a friendly way. 'I do admire anyone with a knack for fashion. Some of the people around here have turned up looking ghastly.'

Vita noticed Edith's look of unbridled jealousy.

'Oh, look, there he is,' Annabelle said, a smile breaking out on her face as she flitted off to greet some new guests.

'Stephen Tennant,' Edward explained, nodding over at a man in a cream suit with long, flowing hair. 'If he's here, then it must be a good party.' He seized the moment expertly and guided Vita away, his hand in the small of her back.

She didn't turn back to look at Edith.

'I can feel her eyes,' she whispered to Edward.

'Like daggers,' he agreed. 'Don't look round.'

'Oh, I won't,' she said confidently.

'Always so satisfying to stick it to a bully,' Edward confided. 'Don't you think?'

She smiled and squeezed his arm. Because, with his help, she'd felt a satisfying flush of something very close to victory. Whatever social one-upmanship Edith had tried to pull had failed. And even better, she'd been exposed as a liar.

42

That Man Again

As they arrived in the main hall where the jazz band was already in full swing, Vita sipped her cocktail, trying to identify the unusual taste of the oily orange liquid while doing her best not to spill it, but it wasn't easy. Nancy made moving and holding a cocktail glass look easy, but Vita was pleased when she found a space by the dance floor to rest, and she could stop concentrating on the glass so much. Edward and Nancy were over by the bar and she was alone for a moment.

Trying to strike a nonchalantly sophisticated pose, she looked around the room, allowing herself to wallow in the satisfied glow she felt. Apart from her triumph over Edith, what was far more thrilling was that someone as important as Annabelle Morton had noticed her.

Her father had always said that contacts in business were the most important thing, and Vita had a feeling that this new world she was seeing might one day be to her advantage. Because, standing here, looking around the room, she felt more at home in this world than she had ever done at Darton Hall.

She shifted her position and angled her shoulders, posing

like Nancy so often did. It was true, she thought, what Percy had told her: if you pretended enough, then it became real. Just like she was pretending to be confident now.

And then she saw him, on the other side of the dance floor.

It was the reporter from that night at Blanchard's: Marcus Fox. And now that he'd spotted her, it was too late to run away. She turned, sipping her drink, her bravado slipping away. She glanced back and saw him shouldering his way through the dancers towards her.

'Ah. The dashing Miss Casey. You are looking more ravishing than ever, if you don't mind me saying,' he said, shocking her that he remembered her name. 'I do like your hair.'

Did he mean it? It was difficult to tell whether he was mocking her.

'So am I to take it that you and the very elusive Edward Sopel are an item?' he asked, one eyebrow arched upwards.

She thought of Percy and how she had to be careful, concerning Edward. The last thing she needed was this reporter digging for details. Perhaps she should try and be enigmatic in her answer.

'I don't believe that's any of your business, Mr Fox.'

'You don't have to be so curt, Miss Casey,' he said, mocking her. 'I won't bite. Although I would heartily devour any information that you have about Sopel. He's been giving me the runaround for months, and my readers would dearly like to know what Lord Sopel's son gets up to. With the King in such a flap, there's quite a market for gossip about errant sons. But Sopel's quite the mystery man, wouldn't you say?'

Vita turned away, feeling annoyed. 'I don't want to talk to you. These are people. With lives. It's not a game.'

'That's where you're quite wrong.'

'So you're happy to print gossip? Like you did the last time we spoke?'

He seemed amused. 'I'm simply here to catalogue the comings and goings of the Bright Young Things.' He threw his arm out towards the crowd. 'And you seem to me very much to have arrived on the scene. Annabelle told me you were one to watch.'

Vita took a sip of her drink as he continued. She didn't look at him. She was flattered that Annabelle had made Mr Fox seek her out, but something about this man put her on edge. As if he were waiting for her to trip up.

'I thought you'd be flattered. Most young women in your position would be thrilled with the publicity.'

'Perhaps I'm not like other young women.'

'Clearly.'

What did he mean? She turned to look at him properly now for the first time. And in that instant she had the feeling that he saw right through all her lies.

'I'm curious to know where you are from. You see, I can't place your accent, because it slips sometimes. Like just now. Which, my dear, makes you all the more beguiling. I would hazard a guess that you're from the North of England?'

He smiled slyly at her and Vita felt a warm flush starting in her cheeks. He couldn't possibly know who she really was, could he?

'Bertie, over here,' Marcus Fox said, beckoning over a

photographer. 'Miss Casey, would you mind having your picture taken?'

'Yes, I would. I'd mind very much,' she said, seeing the man in the grey jacket lifting his camera and feeling a rising sense of panic. The last thing she wanted was to be in the paper again – and certainly not with a photograph.

'Good heavens,' Mr Fox laughed. 'A shy one. A rarity indeed. Well, I shall get you one of these days.'

'I doubt it.'

'Oh, I will,' he called after her as she turned and walked as fast as she could across the corner of the dance floor to the French windows, desperate to get away. 'You're a silly girl to set someone like me such a challenge.'

43

Nancy's Plan

Vita was determined to enjoy the party, despite Mr Fox unsettling her. It wasn't hard. There were so many fabulous people to watch everywhere, and Edward and Percy instigated a funny drinking game in the gazebo outside. Then, when the band started playing the Charleston, they all went inside to dance. It was so much fun, crowded in with the other party folk, as the music soared.

When Vita realized that Nancy had been gone for a while, she left the dancing to go and find her. Nancy was sitting halfway up the staircase in the hallway, smoking a cigarette and looking distinctly the worse for wear. Vita sat down next to her, glad to be off her feet for a moment.

'Oh, I'm exhausted!' she exclaimed. 'I don't know how many of those cocktails I've had. They're so strong, but so delicious. I feel quite dizzy.'

She slipped off her silver shoe and massaged the ball of her foot. Nancy raised her eyebrows in tacit acknowledgement, but still didn't speak. Vita sensed that twittering on about her sore feet wouldn't be the right thing to do, so they sat together in silence for a moment, watching the party and all the glamorous people milling around beneath the twinkling chandelier in the drawing room, the occasional flurry of laughter rising above the hubbub of conversation. It really was the most intoxicating atmosphere, Vita thought.

They caught sight of Edith slipping through the doors onto the terrace with Stephen Tennant and his friends.

'Edith hates you,' Nancy said, inhaling the smoke from the cigarette and closing one eye.

'Well, I'd gathered that,' she said, matter-of-factly.

'You know she did date Edward once,' Nancy said.

This was certainly news. 'Honestly? But Edward pretended he'd never met her. He was being—'

'Mischievous,' Nancy said bluntly. 'That's what people like him do.'

'Oh.' Vita thought about this, and how naughty Edward had been to show Edith up like that. She hadn't expected adults to play such complicated games.

'And Edith's jealous,' Nancy continued.

'Jealous? Of what?'

'Of you. That you've come along and taken over. That you had the nerve to muscle into the dance troupe, just like that. When she had to sleep her way in.'

Vita took the cigarette out of Nancy's hand.

'I don't care,' she said, glad to hear that she'd riled Edith. She'd been so horrible to Vita ever since she'd arrived, and she finally felt things were even between them.

She took a drag on the cigarette, feeling the unfamiliar sensation of the acrid smoke in her throat. She'd been practising smoking whenever she could and she was getting the hang of it now. Of course she didn't look as sophisticated as she wanted to – yet – but it was only a matter of time. She risked a glance at Nancy, who finally met her eye now with a wry smile. Vita liked the feeling that she was amusing her friend.

'Imagine . . . Connelly,' Nancy said, and Vita pulled a face. The thought of Edith and Jack Connelly in any sort of romantic clinch was just too grim.

Nancy held out her fingers for the cigarette to be returned, as Vita blew out what she hoped was an elegant plume of smoke. She was glad that her presence had cheered Nancy up.

'You think they actually – you know – do the deed?' Vita asked.

'Do the deed!' Nancy said, rolling her eyes. 'Nobody says "do the deed"!'

Vita had only said it to try and shock Nancy. She was doing her best to be bold, but now she felt a fool for pretending to be worldly. She'd never discussed 'the deed' with anyone.

'You do amuse me sometimes, Vita. Honestly, it's like you were beamed down from another planet.'

If only Nancy knew how right she was. Darton was a different world from this. She shuffled in closer to Nancy and held on to her arm.

'Well, I *am* innocent. That's why I've got you. To show me the ropes. And, Nancy, I want to know,' she implored her friend. 'I really do. I want to know everything.'

Nancy smoked for a minute, then leant in close to Vita. 'D'you know what Annabelle's brother gave me?' she said. She had that cheeky upturn at the corner of her mouth, which Vita knew meant mischief.

'No. What?'

'These,' Nancy said, delving into her velvet pouch, pulling out two pills and showing them to Vita in her palm.

'What are they?'

'What are they?' she repeated in a mock-innocent voice. 'Hmm. Well . . . I would say they're a sort of magic.'

Nancy was teasing her, but Vita still didn't have a clue what she meant.

'Seriously. What are they?' she asked again.

'Well, why don't we go and find out?' Nancy said archly. 'If you're up for a bit of adventure, that is?'

It was another challenge, and Verity Casey would never turn down one of those, would she?

'Always,' she said, letting Nancy pull her to her feet. 'Lead on.'

44

The Bath

Nancy procured a whole bottle of champagne for their secret mission and two crystal glasses, which she gave to Vita to hold. Vita had assumed they were going outside to join the others on the terrace, where she could still hear dancing and raucous laughter, but to her surprise Nancy led her upstairs and along a narrow corridor, then up and up another set of stairs. The further away from the party they got, however, the more drunk Vita realized she was. Nancy was, too, and they staggered up the last few stairs, tripping over each other.

'Sh . . . sh-shh,' Nancy whispered, giggling and then opening a door along the corridor.

'What are we doing?'

'This is Annabelle's mother's bathroom,' Nancy told her. 'I happen to know the man who designed it,' she said, walking across the sumptuous cream carpet and turning on the fancy brass light switch. 'Annabelle's mother is as rich as Croesus. So she had this done.'

The lamps on the walls flickered into life and Vita whistled, awestruck. The bathroom had been redecorated like a sort of temple, complete with pillars and a raised area that housed a sunken marble bath.

'What are you doing?' Vita asked, confused, as Nancy kicked off her shoes and trotted on tiptoe to the bath, leaning over and inserting the plug.

'The first time I took one of these, it was in the bath. I want you to have the same experience,' she said, holding up the velvet pouch.

Vita wasn't sure what 'these' were – only that Nancy must be referring to the pills she had been given. Was that what all this was about? Why she was being so secretive and funny? And what were they doing in a bathroom? She felt drunk and too fuzzy to argue. So far, this had been the best night of her life. She couldn't think of anything she'd rather be doing than having an adventure with Nancy.

'Now, I bet Mrs M has some rather wonderfully scented oil around here somewhere,' Nancy declared, starting to pick up each bottle from the assortment of tasteful containers on the mirrored shelf. She was being so confident and bold, thought Vita. 'Oh yes – this. Smell that. Simply divine,' she said, wafting a bottle of gorgeous-smelling bath oil beneath Vita's nose. She turned on the large silver taps and poured the bottle with a lavish flourish into the running water. 'And, good – hot water.'

She was being serious! Vita looked back at the door. She couldn't have a bath. Not in front of Nancy. And not at a party. What was she thinking?

'Nancy, we can't,' she began, but then was suddenly overcome as she saw the cloud of steam rising from the bath. There really was hot water running out of a tap. She walked over and put her hand under it. It was coming out all by itself. Like a miracle.

'Don't you love it,' Nancy said. 'I often bathe at a party. No one minds.'

She was unwrapping the foil from the bottle of champagne and Vita watched in admiration. All her life she'd been led to believe that only men could do things like open champagne bottles, but Nancy did all those things quite naturally by herself.

'Glasses, quick-quick,' Nancy instructed, and Vita held up the glasses as Nancy popped the cork, which hit the ceiling and then landed in the sink. She caught the froth in the glasses, slurping at the excess bubbles.

'Now, are you ready?' Nancy asked, putting down her glass on the edge of the bath and taking out the pills. 'Let me introduce you to the wild side.'

Vita looked at the small pill in Nancy's hand.

'Be bold, Vita,' Nancy said. 'I'm here, and I promise I won't leave you. You said yourself that life is for living. And if you really want to be wild and daring, then you've got to learn to party properly. So go on.'

Vita pulled a face, tempted to back away, but Nancy's eyes were too challenging. She couldn't refuse. Not now. And if Nancy was promising not to leave her, then what harm could it do? She crossed herself, before putting the pill in her mouth and swallowing it down with a gulp of champagne.

'Now, seriously, get in the bath. It's the best place,' Nancy instructed.

'I can't.'

'Just strip off and get in. It's only me,' Nancy said, as if Vita was being ridiculous.

Vita giggled, tingling all over with nervous excitement, and a few moments later she had discarded her dress, cami-knickers and stockings. In the warm cocoon of the bathroom, she didn't mind being naked, and Nancy made it all feel very normal. She put her feet in and, with a groan of bliss, sat down in the bubbly water.

'I can't believe I'm really doing this.'

Nancy smiled, humming softly as she lit some candles, and then turned off the lights. Shadows danced up the wall. 'Anything yet?'

Vita wondered what she meant.

'No, but this is glorious,' she sighed, letting the feeling of the water seep over her as she closed her eyes. She had no idea how much time passed, or even if she might have nodded off, but the next thing she knew, she felt as if she were melting into the bath and that she had become as fluid as the water itself.

Nancy sat on the side of the bath, watching her closely through narrowed eyes, trailing her hand in the water. 'It feels weird. But good?'

Vita nodded, but she wasn't sure she could speak. She could see whirls of colours everywhere, bright flashes of green and orange. She closed her eyes, but that only made it worse. What on earth was happening to her?

'Wait,' Nancy said. 'I'm coming in, too.'

Vita watched through a fuzzy, euphoric haze as Nancy undressed, flinging aside her clothes, and climbed in the oppos-ite end of the bath. She'd never seen anyone fully naked before, and it struck her how like the statue in her flat Nancy was. How elegant the curve of her back was and the tilt of her pert breasts. No wonder her brother had wanted to sculpt her.

Vita shuffled up, giggling. She was in a bath. Naked at a party. With another woman, but the rest of the world – the party – seemed to have receded and there was only this moment.

'What if someone catches us?' Vita managed to say. Her mouth felt strange, the words difficult to form. She reached for her champagne glass, sloshing the contents in the water as she aimed for her mouth. She giggled.

'I locked the door, but you'd be surprised how many men would love to discover us right now,' Nancy said, easing herself down into the water. 'We'd be their wildest fantasy.'

'Really?' Vita asked. 'Why?'

Nancy laughed her chandelier-tinkle. 'You really are so green, my darling. You don't know the first thing about men, do you?'

She knew quite a lot about men. About men like her father and Clement, but she didn't want them in her head. Not now.

'I suppose not.'

'I bet you've never even kissed one, have you?'

Vita laughed. 'No.'

Nancy sat up. 'I want your first kiss,' she declared, making Vita giggle even more, as she shifted her position in the bath and slid next to her so that their bodies were touching. It felt deliciously slippery, as if their skin was fusing together.

But it wasn't strange. Even so, Vita felt heat rising in her as Nancy moved, the water running around them. She felt a bolt of electricity as their breasts touched beneath the water. She put her arm around Nancy, pressing herself against her.

Then Nancy's face was above hers and she leant down and kissed her fully on the lips.

45

On the Sabbath

Clement liked the way the crowd parted when he limped heavily on his crutches towards them along the church path, a deferential hush falling on the workers who were gathered for the service. Even the birds seemed to stop chirruping in the tall cedar trees.

He ignored the pain as he leant heavily on his crutches, knowing that his limp gave him more power. It gave the message that nothing could defeat him. Not even a prize stallion. He saw the men quickly grab their caps from their heads and the women look down. Not one of them dared meet his eye.

Did any of them know? he wondered. *Did any of them know where Anna was?*

In the silence he heard one of the workers mutter something under his breath. Was that for his benefit? To drive home this nonsense about the charter they'd put together, demanding better conditions? They were lucky to have work, as far as he was concerned. There were plenty more willing to take their places, if they didn't like it.

Inside, as the congregation sang the first pitiful hymn, Clement kept his mouth firmly shut, glaring hard at Father

McDougal, who looked as if he were hurriedly rewriting the sermon he had planned, now that Clement had joined the congregation. Clement knew all too well how the priest might well incite insubordination amongst the workers. After all, he was from working stock himself. His mother had worked in the very first Darton Mill, until the new spinning mule had chopped off her arm. Stupid woman.

Clement afforded himself a sideways and backward glance, seeing a row of the younger mill women in their Sunday best. He caught the eye of one of them and she looked away hurriedly from his gaze. He smiled inwardly, knowing already that he'd seek her out at the end and find out her name and which mill she worked in. He wasn't sure he would be able to go as far as he'd like, with his back in so much pain, but some fresh meat was what he needed to make himself feel human again. As long as she didn't do anything stupid and get herself pregnant. Like that blonde a few years ago. He didn't want any more children turning up at the Hall, like that brat.

'We welcome Master Darton this morning. We're so pleased to see you walking, sir,' Father McDougal said.

Hobbling, Clement thought, as he bowed his head in recognition.

'I shall be leading prayers for both you and your sister.'

Clement heard a shuffle and a murmur behind him. It seemed everyone knew that Anna had run away in the night, having stolen money, and he baulked at the thought that her disappearance made the Darton family seem weak.

He spent the rest of the service imagining what he'd do to Anna as a punishment when she was finally found. He visualized taking an iron bar to her knees and making her feel the pain of never being able to run, cycle, play tennis or ride again, like he never would. He'd make her pay, too, for every moment she had been away.

As the service ended, he limped very slowly down the aisle, giving everyone the chance to see how injured he was . . . and how brave, for enduring the pain his sister had inflicted.

'Sir, if I might have a word?'

It was Harrison, the foreman. He clutched his hat nervously in his hands in front of him.

'What is it?'

'It's about your sister. Miss Darton.'

'What about her?'

'There's talk of getting together a collection. Some money to help with finding her.'

Clement was astounded. He hadn't for one second thought the workers would even consider such a thing. He almost told Harrison to keep his money, but actually why shouldn't the workers pay for Rawlings's hefty fee?

'That's . . . well, very generous of you, Harrison.'

'It wasn't my idea. The girls on the cutting-room floor – Meg and Ruth – and John, too. They're the ones who are worried. Miss Darton is very good to them. They are worried about where she might have gone. Or if she's got lost . . .'

Clement bristled, annoyed at the man's sentimental tone. Annoyed that there had obviously been talk in *his* mills about his sister, when it was none of their business. Anna only flitted in occasionally, and now they were presuming to actually care about her.

Harrison nodded and went to turn away, then thought better of it. He clutched his cap.

'She's a sweet lass. I'm with the girls at the mill. I hope nothing hard has befallen her.'

'Oh, I'm sure she'll have managed, somehow,' Clement said, with a tight smile. 'She can be beguiling when she wants to be. And quite manipulative. I'm sure someone, somewhere, is looking after her. Rest assured that as soon as we've found her, she will come back and apologize for causing such a fuss.'

Harrison frowned at Clement's cold tone. Then he nodded and turned away.

'But thank you, for your idea of the collection,' Clement called after him. 'That will be most useful.'

46

Hungover

Vita woke up feeling wretched. The other beds in the attic at Mrs Bell's were empty and rain pattered on the skylight. She groaned and rolled over onto her back, but her head was so painful, it felt like she'd been hit with a club. And then, slowly, images started to come back . . .

The party. The cocktails. The drugs . . . because, oh yes, there'd been drugs with Nancy . . . *Nancy!*

'Oh!' Vita sat bolt-upright. She clung onto the iron bed-stead, steadying herself for a moment as the room lurched. 'Oh God, oh God,' she whispered, throwing back the cover. She was going to be sick.

In the bathroom downstairs she held her stomach as she retched, and then washed her face and stared at her reflection in the mirror. A whole world of emotions seemed to be tumbling inside her.

What she had done had been *so wrong*. And yet it had felt right at the time. But now the horrifying thought that someone might find out made her feel even sicker.

She checked round the door. *Had anyone heard her?* The house was oddly quiet. It was Sunday, she remembered, thinking of the cold church near Darton Hall and Father

McDougal's obsequious way with her parents. How she'd struggled all her life with her father's pious hypocrisy. But not today. She splashed her face with cold water, washing the memory away.

'Aha! It's alive!'

It was Percy. She turned to him, shocked.

'Come in here,' he said, beckoning her into his room. 'I have tea. And salts.' He looked at her over his glasses. 'You definitely need salts.'

He left the door open and Vita went in, aware that she was in her nightdress and only now noticing that it was on backwards.

'I can't let anyone see me like this,' she groaned.

'We have a bit of time before they're all back from church,' Percy said, putting a record on the gramophone and turning down the volume. 'Mrs Bell has to do all that atoning, for giving a bunch of debauched dancing girls a home.'

Vita smiled weakly, realizing now that she'd promised she'd go with Emma and Jane, who had told her that the curate was incredibly sweet and that together they enjoyed making him blush.

'Oh. I'm going to hell,' she muttered. 'Or maybe I am already *in* hell.'

Percy laughed. 'I don't know what got into you last night, but you were all over the place when you demanded we come home. Edward dropped us both back.'

'Did I?' Vita scratched her head. She couldn't remember getting home. She could only remember . . .

Nancy. Oh God. *Nancy and the bath.*

'It was a good party,' Percy said, eyeing her over the top of his cup.

Vita nodded. 'I suppose.'

'You made quite an impression with that dress.'

She nodded again, shame pulsing around her veins.

'Oh, come on,' Percy snapped, laughing. 'Spill the beans! Who were you with? Because *something* happened.'

Vita covered her face. 'I can't tell you.'

'You can tell me anything.'

Vita felt her heart hammering. Could she tell him? 'If I told you, would you promise not to tell anyone. Ever?'

'Cross my heart and hope to die.'

'Nancy gave me something – a pill – and we . . . I . . . we . . . had a bath.'

Percy spluttered his tea. 'A bath? At the party?'

'Yes!'

'Well, that accounts for the flood then,' he said.

'There was a flood?'

'Yes, quite a kerfuffle. Annabelle didn't have a clue how it happened, but water started coming through the chandelier in the dining room. And then the electrics went and the party was plunged into darkness.'

'Oh, goodness.'

Percy shrugged. 'I wouldn't worry about it. You got away with it.'

How could he be so matter-of-fact? 'But don't you think it's . . . well, strange?' Vita uttered, shocked that her revelation hadn't caused a bigger reaction from Percy.

'What, the flood?'

'No!' Vita said, exasperated. 'The fact that . . . well, I was in the bath. With . . . with Nancy?'

Where was his moral outrage? she wondered. *Why was he being so calm?*

Percy looked at her, his face softening. 'Darling, what are you expecting? Some kind of telling-off? From *me*? I'm the last person on earth to judge you for anything you do. As far as I'm concerned, you can do what you want. As long as you were having fun, then what's the problem?'

'I think I was.'

'Well then, no harm done. Apart from to Annabelle's priceless inlaid oak table. A family heirloom, I'm told—'

'Oh, stop it,' Vita said.

Percy smiled and stood up. 'That's better. Now drink some tea and stop feeling hungover.'

He made her drink two cups of tea and some salts, before fetching her some large slabs of buttery toast and home-made marmalade from the kitchen; and after that, she felt immeasurably better. The music, the rain on the window, the tea in her belly, the soft glow of Percy's desk lamp, but most of all being with Percy, made her feel safe.

She'd spent all of her life looking over her shoulder, expecting to be scolded for every tiny thing she'd ever done. But Percy was right, wasn't he? Last night had just been a bit of fun. Outrageous fun, but there was no harm done, surely? She was in one piece. And why should she beat herself up? Why should she feel guilty? The thought that she didn't have to feel bad about it made Vita feel heady. It had never occurred to her that she could behave so outrageously and actually get away with it.

'Oh, I forgot. I brought you this from the workshop,' Percy said, opening the leather satchel on the bed and pulling out her brassiere. 'I made it up again with the changes we discussed.'

'Oh, Percy. You are so marvellous.'

'I'm very glad nobody stopped me and searched my bag,' he said, laughing. 'Can you imagine how I'd explain that away?'

Vita laughed and then held it up. 'Perfect!' she exclaimed. 'That's exactly how I wanted it to be. Pop outside for a minute and I'll get changed.'

She stripped off to her camiknickers and was pulling on the bra, when the door opened and Percy rushed back in.

Vita yelped, grabbing a scarf from the bed to protect her modesty. Percy blushed deeply as they looked at each other, and then she realized one of her breasts was completely exposed.

'Sorry. It's just that Edward is here. The front door is open and he's over the road, waiting in the car. He doesn't look like he's been to bed.'

'Do you think she saw?'

'Saw who? Edward?'

'No, Percy! Mrs Bell,' Vita said, 'she was just in the hall and I'm sure she saw me. Half-naked in your room?'

'Oh God! No. I don't think so. I hope not.'

Vita rolled her eyes. 'You're hopeless.' She let out a half-amused growl of frustration and flung the scarf away. 'You've seen one, you might as well see them both,' she said, standing in the camiknickers and throwing her arms out to show him. She'd never felt so brazen. Certainly not in front of a man, but this felt like owning her body for the first time.

'Oh!' he said, looking, then looking away, then looking again.

'You see. This is what we're dealing with. This is what we have to subdue.'

Percy shrugged, still pressed against the door. 'It seems a shame. They are quite marvellous,' he said, his cheeks pulsing red.

She'd never felt connected to her body like this before and she wondered if she was still high on Nancy's drugs, but somehow last night had changed her. It had made her feel more feminine than she'd ever felt. 'Now stop gawping and get over here and help me pin this thing,' she said, pulling the straps of the bra over her arms.

Percy pinned it at the back, fumbling with the pins.

'It's still a bit loose. Look,' she said. She turned round, then jokingly bunched her breasts together in an impressive cleavage. 'We could do that with it.' Percy's eyebrows shot up. 'Although I doubt it will catch on.'

'Never say "never",' Percy said. 'As I told you. Fashions change.'

Vita rearranged herself in the bra until it was right, and Percy marked up the material with the special crayon he used. Then he unpinned it again.

'So what are you going to do about Edward?'

'Go and see what he wants. He'll be bored, no doubt, and will want to go somewhere. Do you want to come out with us?'

'No. I'm nowhere near ready. And if you don't mind, I'll stay and copy this one in the other fabrics.' Now that Percy had made the bra, just as she wanted it, she wanted to have a go at making more herself. In fact, she couldn't wait to get started.

47

Mr Connelly's Mood

Vita spent much of the time before she was next due at the club on Wednesday perfecting her brassiere in the tangerine silk. She'd been concentrating so hard that she barely had time to think about what had happened with Nancy. She'd been tempted, late on Sunday night, to go round to Nancy's apartment, but Percy had told her it was best to leave Nancy alone and to get an early night.

On Monday she'd fulfilled her promise and had spent the day helping Percy sort out the costumes in his workshop. Her head was so full of excitement at all the clothes Percy had bestowed upon her that she was rather taken aback when Nancy didn't return her smile, as Jerome thumped out the newest show tune on the piano at Wednesday's rehearsal.

She'd hoped Nancy would be impressed with the outfit she was wearing today: the jaunty mint-green trousers that she'd cropped beneath the knee and a red tunic, along with a pink headband with a large, floppy flower. Teamed with the red lipstick that Nancy had given her, it was quite a striking look.

Mr Connelly had a general aura of grumpiness and dis-approval this morning and it set the girls on edge, as if he were waiting for them to trip up. He'd already given them a lecture about commitment and how they were all to mingle with the guests. Or if they did insist on going out after the show, then they should be checking on the competition. With so many other clubs around, it was clear that he was worried about their future.

'You – who are you, again?' he growled, putting his hand up for Jerome to stop and pointing at Vita.

'Vita . . . Verity,' she said, feeling the attention of all the girls.

'Well, pay attention. And this goes for all of you,' he added, pointing his cigar along the line of girls. 'I want the customers in here to be entertained – in the right way.'

'Yes, Vita. You should practise more,' Edith chipped in. She was wearing a navy leotard today, her blonde hair scraped back. She looked like a proper dancer. 'We can't have you being perpetually one beat behind.'

That was unfair, Vita thought, blushing. She'd been in time, *hadn't she?*

'Sorry,' she mumbled, glancing back at Jane and Betsy, who gave her the briefest of sympathetic looks, but they were trying to concentrate, too, and not get in Connelly's firing line.

'Exactly,' Connelly agreed.

'A little more sleep at the weekends probably wouldn't go amiss,' Edith continued in a low mutter.

Vita caught the snide tone in her comment and bristled. Could it be possible that Nancy had told Edith what happened between them on Saturday night?

'And, good God, what are you wearing?' Connelly asked. He hadn't heard Edith's snippy comment.

Vita looked down at the outfit she was dancing in, then back up at Mr Connelly.

'It's just for rehearsals.'

'Hmm.' Mr Connelly didn't commit himself to an opinion.

Vita glanced now at Edith, whose steely gaze betrayed a knowing look of triumph.

Blushing deeply, Vita began the routine again, her arms linked around Betsy's waist on one side and Jane's on the other. She couldn't bring herself to look at Nancy.

At the time, sharing a bath together had seemed like the most natural thing in the world, when of course it was anything but. And then there'd been the kiss. More than once. And the touching. The intimacy of it had felt so scary and yet so thrilling, as if her body had been waking up for the first time. But now it felt like something she couldn't bring herself to admit. Like another awful secret that she couldn't bear for anyone else to know.

She didn't have a chance to speak to Nancy until right at the end of the rehearsal in the dressing room, after the others had gone.

'How have you been?' Vita ventured.

'Fine.'

There was a small silence. Something about their physical contact had changed everything between them. And not in the right way.

'You seem . . .' Vita persisted.

'What?'

'A bit off.'

'I told you, I'm fine.' Nancy said. 'If you want to come to

199

a party with me and then disappear, and not speak to me for *days on end*, then fine.'

Vita felt relief then, recognizing Nancy's put-out tone. She was cross with her for not getting in touch. That was all. There was nothing more to it. She should have ignored Percy and gone round to see Nancy on Sunday.

'I'm sorry. I did think about coming to see you, but it's just . . . I've been busy. I've been working on something,' Vita said. 'You know – the lingerie. I told you about it.'

'Oh,' Nancy said, unenthusiastically, after she'd told her about working with Percy all day Sunday and then helping out at the studio yesterday. Vita didn't admit how dreadfully hungover she'd been on Sunday.

'But about Saturday,' Vita began, steeling herself.

'What about it?' Nancy said, looking at her directly. 'Is there anything you want to tell me?'

Vita pressed her lips together. She took a deep breath and tried again. 'Only that it shouldn't change things. I mean, I've been thinking about it and it doesn't mean . . .'

'That you're a lesbian?'

Vita blushed deeply, looking down at her hands. This wasn't going well.

'So what if it does? I told you, it's very fashionable to be one nowadays. Anyone who is anyone is a lesbian,' Nancy said matter-of-factly. Vita bit her lip and suddenly Nancy gave a shrill, fake laugh. 'Look at your face! Forget about it,' she shrugged. 'What goes on at parties stays at parties. It's the rule.'

'So you won't . . . I mean, you won't tell anyone? About what we did?'

She wanted to tell Nancy that, at the time, it had been wonderful – not that she could really remember the finer details. Only that they'd been intimate in a way she'd never imagined possible. But now she felt embarrassed. Embarrassed and slightly ashamed.

'You don't want me to tell anyone?' Nancy said, cocking out her hip and staring at Vita. She felt wrong-footed. *Was* Nancy going to tell everyone? It felt dangerous trusting her with such a big secret, when she was such a gossip. 'Then, no, precious one. I won't. Your secret is safe with me.'

Vita nodded and opened the door to find Percy standing right by it, two bales of material piled up in his arms.

'Ah, there's Wisey,' Nancy said and brushed past Percy into the corridor.

'What *is* up with her?' Percy asked, looking after Nancy, but Vita turned away, so he couldn't see her face. She felt close to tears. She felt as if she'd done something terrible, but she couldn't work out what it was.

Because, despite all Nancy's protests, it occurred to Vita now that Nancy might very well be a lesbian herself. That's why she hadn't married. That's why she was outcast from her family. And that's why she'd taken Vita under her wing. Had she been waiting for more from Vita? Some sort of verbal commitment to their shared secret, after Saturday? Because if she had, Vita now felt as if she'd said all the wrong things.

'Can we take Nancy out with us?' she asked Percy, having an idea about how to fix things. 'With you and Edward, I mean? When we next go out. I won't say anything about . . . well, you know. I won't say anything about the two of you.'

'Nancy is a big girl. She can work things out for herself.'

'And it wouldn't be a problem?'

'I don't see why it would. But listen, I have exciting news. Connelly wants you to help with the costumes.'

'What?' Vita asked, momentarily forgetting Nancy.

'Yes, I was chatting to him. Just now. He was saying that he thinks you have natural style.'

48

The Sign in the Fire

Relieved that the air seemed to be clearer with Nancy, Vita threw herself into learning the routine, enlisting Jane and Betsy's help. And, back at home, she worked non-stop on the sewing machine in Percy's room. She was so busy that she didn't have the faintest idea what was going on when Mrs Bell called her and Percy for 'a little meeting' in her front parlour on Friday afternoon.

'There's no easy way to broach this, so I'm just going to say it,' said Mrs Bell, wringing her hands.

Vita glanced at Percy, who was in the armchair, petting Casper on his knee. For once Mrs Bell wasn't wearing either an apron or a headscarf and, dressed in a tweed skirt and matching jacket, looked rather smart.

'What is it?' Vita asked, wondering if she'd done something wrong.

'Yes, whatever is it, Mrs Bell?' Percy asked.

The landlady took a deep breath. 'I don't know what is going on between you two and it's none of my business, I know,' she put up her hand, not looking at either of them, 'but I don't think I can endorse your . . . well, you know . . . without saying something. Not that I don't think you'd make a marvellous couple, don't get me wrong, but I have the other girls to consider – and my reputation. This is not,' she lowered her voice, 'that sort of house.'

There was a moment of silence, then Vita looked at Percy and they both burst out laughing.

'Oh, Mrs B. Honestly, it's not what you think at all,' Vita said, jumping to her feet and squeezing her landlady's arm. 'There's nothing going on between me and Percy.'

'There isn't?' she asked, looking slightly perplexed. 'But I saw . . . well, I'm not exactly sure *what* I saw, and I certainly don't want even to think about it, but on Sunday—'

'We were working,' Percy said.

'Working?' Mrs Bell was clearly confused.

'It's impossible to explain. Wait there. I'll show you,' Vita said.

She ran upstairs to Percy's room and collected the pile of silk-satin brassieres she'd been making. The latest one was the best.

Back downstairs, she showed it proudly to Mrs Bell, who ran the silk through her fingers and held up the bra by its pretty ribbon straps. 'Well, I never,' she said. 'And you, Percy. You know about all this?'

'It's no different to designing for the theatre,' he said. 'And I really think Vita is on to something here. I think she could make a business out of it.'

Vita explained how Percy had been helping her design something for dancing. 'I'm just trying to fathom out how to make them for the other girls. They are fiendishly fiddly.'

'They look it.'

'You see, there are so many variables. Not only in the

cups, but in the central part here.' She showed Mrs Bell. 'You see, this has to work with the straps, and each bit has to be stitched together. This is just a simple pattern, but with time, I'm going to perfect it. Percy's been helping me, and you wouldn't believe how much I've picked up already.'

'She's a fast learner and there's no doubt she has a flair for it,' Percy said, and Vita wanted to hug him.

'You won't catch me throwing out my girdle anytime soon. But if I were a younger woman, I'd certainly want one. I'd say they were top-drawer.'

Percy laughed. 'Top-drawer. You sound like Vita here. Are you *sure* you're not related?'

Mrs Bell smiled. 'I'd be only too proud to have a daughter like you,' she said, and Vita put her hand to her chest. 'Now then, I'm going to light a fire and make us some more tea.'

'Don't on our account, please,' Percy said.

'Goodness only knows when we're going to get more coal, if the papers are to be believed and all this business with the miners gets worse.'

Vita and Percy exchanged a look as she started plucking some paper out of the wooden box in the alcove and scrunching it into balls. She picked up the scuttle and threw in some coal on top of the papers.

'Do me favour, Vita dear, and pass the matches. 'They're on the sideboard.' She lit the fire. 'I'm going to put the kettle on,' she continued, going out into the kitchen. 'Then I want to hear more about this brassiere of yours. I feel like a fool now. Imagine me thinking . . .' She trailed off, putting her hand to her head and making for the kitchen.

'I honestly adore her,' Vita told Percy, watching Mrs Bell go, then walking over to the fire.

'You know, I like that,' Percy said thoughtfully.

'What?'

'Top-drawer.'

'How do you mean?' asked Vita.

'As a name,' Percy replied. 'For your firm.'

'Firm? Gosh, I hadn't considered that it might go that far.'

'Why not?'

Vita thought of her father's firm now, and of the business back home. It had always been a male domain – something that concerned only him and Clement. She'd lost count of the number of times she'd asked questions and had been told to mind her own business. It had never occurred to her that she might run her own enterprise one day.

But with Percy's faith in her, she felt something spark inside her. All those suffragettes in the paper – all those women fighting for their right to be heard – she could be one of them, couldn't she? She could be a woman doing something all for herself, couldn't she? Wasn't it just a case of daring to dream?

'Well, you should think about it, if you want to take all this seriously. I think Mrs Bell's right. Young women will want these,' Percy said.

Vita took a deep breath, letting it sink in. She'd always been told that she wasn't allowed to have ambition; that it was wrong for a girl to feel anything but dutiful. But maybe such ambition had been inside her all along, waiting for this moment.

'Well, maybe down the line – yes, it could be a business.

We could start off small. Build it up. See what happens. And you're right, Percy. And about the name. Top Drawer lingerie.' She put her hand up, miming seeing the words. 'I can see it on the advertising posters.'

'Are you not getting a bit ahead of yourself there, lassie?' Percy said, impersonating Mrs Bell.

'Not at all. Paris. Milan. Rome. We could go big. Huge,' she laughed. She was joking, of course, but Percy gave her a wry smile.

'Why not? Every woman needs underwear.'

Vita bit her lip. 'And you'd do it with me, right? Be partners. Split it all fifty–fifty?'

'Well, it's more your baby than mine. But I'll help you, of course. I suppose we'd better warn Mrs Bell that she's nurturing an international businesswoman.'

Vita laughed. 'Poor Mrs B. You know, I think she was a bit disappointed that our rendezvous was so innocent. She doesn't suspect a thing? About Edward, I mean?'

'Good heavens, no. And you're not to tell her,' Percy said, blushing as he put Casper down on the floor.

'She would probably be much more understanding than you think.'

Percy shook his head. 'She wouldn't be. Believe me. Other people aren't like you, Vita. They don't understand. You're rare. And you're also the only one who knows my secrets, and you must keep it that way.'

'Of course. I promise.'

She turned round to face the fire, putting out her hands to warm them on the flame. And that's when she saw the scrunched-up piece of newspaper burning in the grate and a word jumped out at her.

Darton.

She gasped as she pulled out the sheet of paper, stamping on it to put out the flames on the green tiles in front of the hearth.

'What on earth are you doing?' Percy was on his feet.

Vita knelt down, her heart pounding as she picked up the singed paper.

A tiny part of the picture she instantly recognized as the family portrait that stood on the mantelpiece in the drawing room at Darton Hall. The only family photograph there had been of her, Clement and their parents. She felt sick as she held the charred edge.

'What is it?' Percy asked. 'Vita? What's wrong?'

49

Remembering That Night

Later, as she lay on her bed at Mrs Bell's, Vita felt her guilty conscience like lead in her belly. She hadn't given Mrs Bell or Percy an explanation for her behaviour, telling them that she'd seen someone she recognized in the paper. It must have been the Obituaries page, she reasoned now, still trying to calm down after the shock of it.

It had been like an omen. A rebuke. Just when she'd been feeling so excited about the future, there had been a horrible reminder of her past.

Listening to Betsy and Jane as they breathed in their sleep, she envied them their clean consciences, as fat teardrops plopped over the bridge of her nose and dripped onto the pillow.

Because now everything she'd fought so hard to forget flooded her brain. All the terrible details of that night. The night of the hunt. The irrefutable and awful truth. She gave in and let herself remember it, seeing it all in her mind's eye, as if it were still that night.

She remembered how she'd packed a simple carpet bag, piling in the clothes she owned, trembling and unsure, expecting to be found out at any second, her face still stinging from where her father had hit her. But when she'd managed to leave the house unseen, a new kind of shock at her own daring started to rise within her. She really was leaving. She had no idea where she was heading, only that she needed to get away. Away from this terrible prison.

As she'd tiptoed across the gravel to the back lawn, the moon had cast a silvery light on the stables and she'd decided to go and see Dante to say goodbye. She wanted the poor creature to know that someone in the world cared, even if she was leaving.

The stables comprised a workshop where Mark kept the saddles and tack, and there was a narrow corridor with four stalls off it. In the workshop Anna lit a lantern, her footsteps soft on the cobbles as she crept along to the last stall where Dante was.

As she opened the heavy wooden stall door, he made a snuffling noise and she smiled, knowing it was his way of saying that he was pleased to see her, but even so, he was in a bad way. He'd always been such a placid, beautiful horse, but now he had the metallic smell of blood about him, and his breath was laboured.

'Here, boy,' she said, walking into the stable and hanging the lantern on the hook on the wall, but not before she noticed the shredded skin on his flank. Dark welts of blood glistened in the light from the lamp. She touched his flank tentatively and blood stained her fingers.

She'd wanted to come earlier, but Martha had stopped her, telling her that Mark wouldn't let anyone into the stables. But now she wished she'd defied them. It pained her that her beloved horse had been all alone in the dark and in so much pain.

She moved round to stroke his nose, putting her forehead against it, fighting down the tears. Dante made a whimpering sound.

'I'm sorry. I'm so sorry, boy,' she said, delving into her pocket to retrieve a peppermint. How could Clement have done such a terrible thing? 'He's so cruel. So cruel,' she whispered. 'I wish I could have stopped him. I tried.'

She didn't hear anyone coming, until she saw a shadow looming along the stone wall, and by that time it was too late to run. Clement stood in the doorway, watching her with a sneer on his face. He'd been drinking, and she backed away from him.

'What's this?' he said, picking up her carpet bag and throwing it out of the stall. It landed with a thud on the cobbles in the corridor.

'I'm leaving,' Anna said, too furious with him to back down.

'Leaving? Is that your grand plan?' He sounded so condescending – so scornful – that she felt hot indignation sweep over her.

'I just came to check on Dante—'

'After what he did today! I'm sending him to the knacker's yard tomorrow.'

He didn't look at Dante, only at her, and Anna felt tears stinging her eyes, but she was determined not to let Clement see them. She bit her lips together.

'Oh?' he sneered, his face now leering terrifyingly close to hers. 'You don't approve? What's the matter? You're perfectly happy to sneak around and tell Father your opinions.'

He knew what she'd said to their father? About how he always took Clement's side? About how Clement should be punished for what he'd done to Dante? Had he been spying, or had Papa told Clement all about it? Either way, she felt the force of the pair of them ganging up on her. Nothing in this household could ever be private or sacred.

Anna summoned all her courage to hold her ground. Clement had to be stopped, and if her parents weren't going to, she was going to damned well try. 'You shouldn't have whipped him. Look what you've done.'

Clement took two long steps into the stall and grabbed her by the collar of her coat, yanking her almost off her feet. Her breath constricted as his fist pressed against her windpipe. Dante stamped and snorted next to them.

'I'll whip you for your insolence, you little bitch. As God is my witness, it's what you need, to knock a bit of damned obedience into you.'

He threw her away and she hit her head on the wooden struts of the stable wall. She covered her face, but through her fingers she saw Clement now rolling up his sleeves.

'I'm going to have to teach you a lesson.'

He was going to beat her. That's what he meant. She watched him grab a whip from the rack. He thwacked it into his hand, enjoying the sting of it.

'Please don't, Clement,' she said. 'No . . . no . . . don't.'

'You think you can run away from here?' he said, his voice rising and laden with scorn. 'You think you can defy Father and me and leave? And go where?' His eyes bored into hers, as she backed along the wooden slats to the far wall. Dante's nostrils flared. She caught sight of her terrified face reflected in the black of his eyeball. 'You think you can go running off, telling tales? Is that it? You'd smear our good family name?'

'No, Clement, no.'

'No, Clement, no,' he impersonated her nastily. 'Listen to you. You're pathetic. Father's right. You've always been a disappointment. Well, let me tell you – you're not going anywhere. Come here!'

He raised the whip and took aim, bringing it down hard, but she ducked out of the way, jumping in the hay and tripping, edging further away around Dante.

Her eyes darted towards the door. She had to make a run for it. Before it was too late. She knew there would be no stopping Clement. Not when he was like this.

'I said: come here!' Clement growled, lunging for her.

Dante reared between them and made a terrified whinnying sound.

Anna rushed for the stall door. She got through it, then pushed it shut, sliding the heavy bolt across as Clement yelled her name. Safe now for a second, she pressed her eye up against an empty wood-knot.

She watched as Clement charged at the door, his face a mask of fury. 'Come back here!' he screamed, dropping the whip and yanking at the door.

Dante reared up on his front legs and kicked Clement hard in the back of the head. And then her brother was down, sprawled on the hay, his head at an angle so that Anna couldn't see his face.

She stayed by the door as Dante thrashed; her heart was in her mouth as he kicked Clement hard once more, but her brother's body was limp and turned over in the hay. A trickle of blood came out of his nose. And she knew, in that instant, that he was dead.

She squeezed her eyes shut, shaking all over. What should she do? Go in? Try and save him? No . . . no – it was too late.

Instead, she grabbed her carpet bag and ran.

It was only as she was leaving the stables that she nearly bumped straight into Mark, the stablehand, who had no doubt been woken by Dante's terrible screams. She yelped, hastily backing away from him. Then she was off. She didn't stop. She didn't turn back. She ran for her life.

50

The Grand National

Clement leant heavily on his stick as he watched the horses being paraded around the paddock at Aintree. This was his first trip away from the mill since the accident, but he'd never missed a Grand National and he didn't intend to miss one on account of his sister. When a note had come a few days ago from Malcolm Arkwright, inviting Clement to join him at the race, he didn't hesitate. A day out at the races was exactly what he needed, although his legs were still causing him excruciating pain. He adjusted his position and cursed as his stick sank into the soft turf.

He scanned the faces in the crowd, looking for Arkwright, but all he could see was a sea of hats and overcoats. It was a misty, grey day and there was a chill in the air, but it was perfect running weather and there was an air of anticipation around the paddock. Each horse was being led on a rope, and most of them had blankets strapped over them and headgear, but they were all fine beasts. He could hear the chatter in the dense crowd behind him about who might win. But with thirty obstacles over four miles, it was anyone's guess who might pick up the £500 prize money for the winning jockey.

'I heard you ordered that horse of yours to be sent to the

yard,' a familiar voice said, and Clement turned to see Malcolm Arkwright. He was wearing a top hat, his long wool coat open to reveal a jewel-coloured waistcoat stretched across his belly. He put his thumb into the pocket of it and pulled out a thick gold pocket watch.

'It was lame. I had to,' Clement said, although this wasn't true.

Arkwright didn't look convinced. 'That's not the story I heard.'

How had Arkwright even heard about Dante? Clement wondered. He felt a moment of shame. Maybe the horse hadn't deserved its fate. But no, there was no point in being sentimental. It was just a horse. A horse that had all but paralysed him.

They watched the parade for a while, until the horses were led away to be saddled up.

'So . . . are you a betting man, Mr Darton?' Arkwright asked.

'I'm here, aren't I?' Clement said, looking up at the stands of the racecourse, which were filling up.

'Then I wouldn't mind betting that you have mislaid your sister.'

'Mislaid?'

'I saw the notice in the paper,' Arkwright said, his bushy eyebrows rising. 'But I take it she hasn't come home. She's a spirited girl,' he went on, breathing in, as if Anna was a horse and he was relishing the prospect of riding her. 'Got the better of you, I see.'

'She'll be back,' Clement said, with a dismissive wave as

if he were just humouring Anna and would find her at a time of his choosing.

Arkwright made a satisfied grunt. 'Good. I'm fed up with these young women thinking they can do what they want.'

'I quite agree,' Clement said.

'Votes, indeed,' Arkwright said, laughing and clasping Clement on the shoulder. 'What is the world coming to? String the bitches up, I say.'

Despite Clement's hatred for his sister, after what she'd done, he still felt a sliver of guilt. He knew what a man like Arkwright might do in order to tame her. But she deserved what was coming to her, now that she'd put them all through so much. No, his sister would come back and pay for what she'd done.

'If you are a betting man, then I'd put your money on Jack Horner. Number twenty-one,' he said, leaning in close, as if divulging secret information.

'But that's not your horse,' Clement said, confused.

'Well, I happen to know things. Come this way, Mr Darton. I have a good view from our stand.'

Clement followed Arkwright to the front of the stands where there was a spectacular view of the course, and took a nip of whisky from Arkwright's hip-flask when it was offered. He looked through his binoculars to the starting line, surprised to see a perfect start for once. And then the horses were off.

The crowd gasped as Grecian Wave and Silvo, both favourites, fell at the first fence. Clement watched a man throw down his form card and stamp on it, and a woman in a fur stole laugh at his childishness.

Knight of the Wilderness fell at the third. Clement caught that through his binoculars, too. He rather enjoyed the way the horses' legs buckled, the jockeys tumbling into the throng of hooves. It was thrilling.

'We've still got Becher's Brook to go,' Arkwright said. 'Someone will fall there. They always do.'

Clement watched some young boys chasing behind the crowd, jumping up to get a better look.

He shared the binoculars with Arkwright as the horses continued, and then Bright's Boy was leading Old Tay Bridge and Jack Horner at the last jump. Clement pressed forward to the front of the stand as they roared down the flat towards where they were standing. Old Tay Bridge was leading, but then Jack Horner edged in front.

Clement and Arkwright roared at their success and turned to each other and, for one second, Clement thought they might embrace.

'It's a good omen,' Arkwright said. 'Stick with me, my boy, and you'll go far. You'll see.'

Clement smiled, pleased that Arkwright thought he had the upper hand – for now. Arkwright didn't realize it yet, but Clement's part of the bargain – swapping Anna's hand in marriage for a stake in Arkwright's mills – would give Clement and his father an overall monopoly. And, with it, they would not only be able to pay back the debts they owed, but would secure plenty of contracts in the future. Yes, very soon the Darton name would be the only one that mattered.

51

Nancy's Endorsement

Nancy wasn't miffed with Vita for long, especially as they both had invitations from Edward to join him and Percy for lunch, and then for drinks at The Kit Cat Club after the show. Then, the following Monday, Nancy suggested a shopping trip, followed by an appointment with Mystic Alice.

Nancy had said that her clairvoyant had agreed to see Vita, who had to pretend to be excited about it, when in truth she would rather be working with Percy. Besides, she found the whole thing a little terrifying. Mystic Alice had somehow managed to convince Nancy that she really did have mystical powers. And what if she did? What if she could see into Vita's past?

Seeing Clement's image in the paper had been a terrible shock and a reminder that her family might still be looking for her. But Clement was gone for good, she reminded herself. London was the last place they would think to look, she was sure of it. She was safe. *Wasn't she?* She'd got away with it. She'd rid herself of Clement and her family ties and had started a completely new and wonderful life. Nothing could derail her now, could it?

She decided to try her best to stop worrying about the

future and to concentrate on the present. And it wasn't hard. It was fun walking around the streets and soaking up all the sights of the city and, even though she couldn't afford to buy anything herself, Vita loved window-shopping. Nancy had no qualms about trying on the most expensive fashions she could find; and in a new boutique on Regent Street, she made Vita try on a very smart pinstripe suit.

'Won't I look a bit like Lolly and Ra?' Vita asked, remembering how the infamous female companions at the club dressed.

'It's fun. I want to see what you look like. I'm coming in, too,' Nancy said, sweeping aside the pink satin curtain.

In the changing room, Vita took off her jacket and then plucked up the courage to show Nancy her new brassiere. This was the seventh one she'd made, but she and Percy were convinced they'd worked out the best pattern, and Vita was pleased with the result. This was the one, she was sure of it. She adjusted it, looking down at her cleavage.

'I know it's a bit unusual – the colour, I mean.'

'The colour is the best bit,' Nancy declared. 'I love it. Can you make me one?' she asked, her fingers on the thin straps. She moved her hand down towards Vita's breast, and Vita ducked away, embarrassed by the intimacy of her touch. There was something proprietorial about the way Nancy was looking at her.

'Well, I can now,' she said, slipping on the pinstripe jacket and doing it up. 'It's been so difficult to get it right, but I think I'm there. I should be able to make them in other sizes. Do you really think it looks professional?'

'Absolutely! And you know who would love it, too?'

'No?'

'Lulu,' Nancy said, as if hatching a plan. 'You know, Mrs Clifford-Meade.'

'Your dressmaker?' Vita checked, flattered that Nancy saw such potential in her creation.

'Yes, I'm sure she would. And if she did, she could sell them in her shop.' Nancy's eyes were shining.

'You think she would? Just like that?'

'People need to be told what they want. And you British are so timid,' Nancy quipped. 'So the way I see it: you've had a good idea, so *carpe diem*. Seize the day. That's all it takes.'

'Surely not all?'

'Granted, you need a little chutzpah. But you, little one' – Nancy pressed Vita's nose – 'I've seen you. You have a gift. A natural flair,' she continued, warming to her theme.

'You think so?'

'I *know* so.'

Vita felt herself glowing with Nancy's compliment as they walked out of the store, empty-handed. As predicted, the pinstripe suit had made Vita look exactly like Lolly. Outside, as they dodged a tram to cross the road, Vita discussed the idea further with Nancy.

'Percy and Mrs Bell think I should go into business.'

'There you are then,' Nancy said, as if they'd both proved her point.

'But how?' Vita asked, indulging in the fantasy for a moment. 'Wouldn't I need – I don't know – backing, a bank account . . .'

'A bank account is easy. There's that chap . . . Oh, you know, the banker.'

'Paddy Potts?' Vita said, remembering the man with the polka-dot scarf in the club.

'He's something big at Coutts and Company. He could get you a bank account. Leave it with me. I'll ask him.'

As always, Vita was both amazed and slightly in awe of Nancy's belief that anything was possible.

'And as for selling, you find someone to stock them. Like Mrs Clifford-Meade at first. And then you work your way up. To somewhere' – Nancy stopped and stared up at the famous mint-green facade of the W&T Department Store – 'like here.'

'Nancy, don't be ridiculous.'

'Why not?'

'It's Withshaw and Taylor,' Vita pointed out. 'It's a department store.'

'Exactly. Just where your future customers will shop.'

They stopped to watch the window-dresser who was putting together a display in the window, dressing the mannequin in a slimming cotton brassiere – the advert below claiming it would give the perfect silhouette. 'Yours is much better,' Nancy said. 'It's much more fun.'

'But I wouldn't know the first thing . . .'

But Nancy didn't hear her. She was already on her way through the heavy wooden doors, beaming her flirty smile at the door attendant.

'Nancy, what are you doing?' Vita asked, hurrying to keep up.

Nancy walked confidently up to where they'd seen the woman dressing the mannequin. The window area was blocked off, but Nancy pushed past the screen.

'Excuse me?' Nancy said, drawing the dresser's attention from the window.

The woman, who was wearing some rather fetching linen dungarees, stepped down with difficulty, as Vita admired the rack of clothes.

'We have a meeting, with that chap,' Nancy said, as if they knew one another. 'You know – the buyer. For the female lingerie. What's he called again?'

'You mean Mr Kenton? Lance Kenton?' the woman said, looking confused.

'That's him,' Nancy said, clicking her fingers. 'How could I forget? You've saved the day. Wonderful window-dressing,' she added, before stepping back out to where Vita was standing. 'There we are. Lance Kenton. He's your man.'

'Well, maybe, when I've made *more* than one brassiere.'

'That's the spirit,' Nancy said. 'Oh, is that the time?' She looked up at the clock. 'Come on. We don't want to be late for Mystic Alice.'

52

Mystic Alice

Nancy's clairvoyant operated from a block of flats next to a wine merchant's in St James's, and Nancy leant on the bell for ages, shielding her eyes and looking up towards the very top floor.

'What's she like?' Vita asked.

'You'll see.' Nancy grinned, then pushed against the door as the mechanism opened and they entered the gloomy stairwell with its cast-iron bannister looping up and up.

'She's at the top,' Nancy said, pulling off her hat before taking the stairs two at a time. 'I'll race you.'

They reached the top landing and Vita held on to Nancy's shoulder, laughing as she caught her breath.

A plain brown door was slightly ajar and calypso music was playing softly on a crackly gramophone. Nancy pushed open the door to Mystic Alice's flat and Vita followed her inside, her heart thumping with exertion and curiosity.

The flat was filled with large furniture – an overstuffed sofa and chairs, covered in green and yellow cushions, a bulky sideboard and several fringed lamps were crammed into the tiny space, so that they had to go on tiptoe to squeeze around the sofa. A parrot flapped in a long cage next to the table by the window, which was draped in a knitted shawl.

'Make yourself comfortable. I won't be a moment.' The voice came from behind a bead curtain to another room.

The parrot squawked and flapped its wings.

'Oh, psss-psss-psss,' said a large woman, bustling into the room through the curtain, carrying a jug of orange juice. She was tall, her body clothed entirely in a long purple-and-pink robe. A gold pendant bearing a moon-and-sun emblem hung heavily around her neck. She wore an orange turban fastened with a bright jewel in the front, and looked as if she might be of Caribbean descent, but Vita couldn't be sure. She'd certainly never imagined being in the home of someone so exotic.

Mystic Alice placed the jug carefully on the table, then greeted Nancy warmly.

'This is Vita,' Nancy said. 'You said it was dandy to bring her?'

Mystic Alice's eyes were alarmingly intense as she looked Vita up and down now. She smelt overpoweringly of some kind of musky perfume.

'You will be very successful,' she said, her low voice serious. It wasn't a question. 'I see great things in your future.'

Nancy pulled an impressed face at Vita. 'You see. Told you!'

Mystic Alice's voice lowered. 'But you are a troubled child.'

'Vita here? Troubled?' Nancy asked, clearly not believing it. 'It's just as well I brought her then,' she added, making light of it.

Vita felt herself being sucked into Mystic Alice's mesmeric gaze, as she reached out her large hand and grabbed Vita's, turning it over. She had nails that were so long they were like talons, and they were painted a bright orangey-red. Mystic Alice closed her eyes and breathed in deeply.

Vita pulled her hand away and laughed nervously. This woman – clairvoyant, whoever she was – had already unsettled her.

'Come, come,' Mystic Alice said, ushering them both to the table.

'Don't worry,' Nancy assured Vita in a whisper. 'She's always like this.'

Nancy sat down first and took out her purse, sliding two notes across the red brocade cloth. Mystic Alice made no comment as she picked up the money and folded it, placing it down the front of the V in her tunic.

'What you said came true,' Nancy said enthusiastically. 'After last time. I did find a new friend.' She smiled across at Vita, as Mystic Alice slid a dark cloth from some object on the table, to reveal a large crystal ball. It was exactly like Nancy's, although much bigger. Her eyelids fluttered for a moment and Vita had to press her nails into her palms to stop herself laughing. Surely this was all just an act? She glanced at Nancy, but her face was intense with concentration.

Nancy put her hand on Vita's wrist to tell her to be quiet. Then, when the silence was becoming unbearable, Mystic Alice uttered a low hum that seemed to vibrate out of her chest.

'I see a train,' she murmured.

226

'To where?' Nancy asked, shuffling in her chair. 'I told you I was going to travel,' she whispered in an aside to Vita. 'Paris. I bet it's Paris.'

Mystic Alice's eyes were closed, her fingers with their long nails trembling slightly as they lightly cupped the glass. She drew in a sharp breath and shook her head. 'I see a man. A moustache. And smoke – smoke from chimneys . . .'

Something about the way in which Mystic Alice was speaking was making Vita feel frightened.

'He is powerful. So powerful.' Her eyebrows pinched together dramatically. 'What you said to him – you never, never . . .' She took another sharp intake of breath and made a whimpering sound. 'No . . . no, no, Papa.'

Vita felt her heart pounding. Could it be possible that Mystic Alice was 'seeing' Vita's father and the scene in his study?

'Papa? Whose father do you see?' Nancy asked.

Mystic Alice's eyes snapped open. 'Enough,' she said, deliberately not meeting Vita's eye. She whipped the black cloth back over the crystal ball. Her voice had changed completely now. 'The spirits are troubled today.'

Vita felt a tight lump in her throat. The mere thought that Mystic Alice might have been able to 'see' the argument with her father had been like going back to Darton Hall. And actually being there all over again – even if only in her memory – felt too close for comfort.

Vita could see that Nancy was curious, but she was desperate to know about Paris. 'Do you think it's time I moved on?' Nancy asked, her voice serious for once. 'I was thinking of Paris?'

'Certainly,' Mystic Alice replied, her vivid green gaze not leaving Vita.

'Soon?'

'As soon as possible.'

Vita looked at Nancy in alarm. 'I knew it,' Nancy said. 'I'd better get packing.'

'You can't *leave*,' Vita said, seeing that Nancy had whole-heartedly taken Mystic Alice's comment to heart.

'But I have to, if it's my destiny,' Nancy said.

'And you will go with her,' Mystic Alice said to Vita, at which Nancy reached out and squeezed Vita's hand.

'Oh, goodie,' she trilled with a laugh. 'What fun.'

Vita frowned, annoyed that Nancy had fallen for this woman's hokum – hook, line and sinker. She couldn't have Nancy thinking they were both going to Paris. Because as much as she'd like to go on an adventure, there was no way she could. Not without a passport or papers. Not without revealing that she was already on the run. For all she knew, there might be police at the border looking out for her.

Mystic Alice nodded, as if understanding her inner turmoil. It really was quite unsettling. Nancy put her hands in a prayer position and bowed to Mystic Alice, and Vita held on to her bag, too embarrassed to do any more.

As they were going through the door, Mystic Alice grabbed the top of Vita's arm. Her fingers pinched through the cloth of her coat.

'Watch out for the dark stranger,' she said in an urgent whisper. 'He's coming.'

53

Shaken

Outside on the street, Vita breathed out heavily, but it didn't stop the feeling of panic inside her. She realized that her hands were shaking.

'Well, that was . . .' Nancy put her hand on her chest, letting out a shocked laugh. 'Well! I don't know how to describe it. I've never seen her like that before. I thought she was going to have quite a funny turn at one point. Whose father was she talking about? Wait! Yours? Was it yours?'

Should she tell Nancy? Because this was her moment, Vita realized. The right time to tell Nancy the truth about who she was and where she came from. Surely, after all the intimacy they'd shared, Nancy would understand?

Or would she? If Vita were to open the floodgates – tell her about Clement and what she'd done – then Nancy might tell the others. If she knew one thing about Nancy, it was that she thrived on gossip. She wouldn't be able to keep such shocking information to herself. And one of the others – most likely Edith – would almost certainly be compelled to tell the police.

She felt panicked about all the lies she'd told. One after another, until she'd woven a whole fabric of deceit. Nancy would never be able to forgive her.

'No,' Vita shook her head, feeling more unsettled than she could cope with. 'Not mine. He's dead. Long gone,' she lied, not meeting Nancy's eye. 'I'm afraid I have no idea what any of that was about.'

'Oh,' Nancy said, disappointed. 'You never said. Sorry, old girl. You don't seem to have had much luck with family. Do you?'

'It doesn't matter. I've got friends now,' Vita replied, forcing a cheerful tone into her voice. She grabbed Nancy's arm as they started up the street, her voice catching. 'Let's forget all about it and get a drink.'

'But we're off to Paris, darling,' Nancy said. 'Isn't that exciting?'

'You can't honestly believe that?' Vita said, stopping to stare at her.

'Why ever not? Everything Mystic Alice says comes true.'

Vita was unconvinced.

'Watch out for zee dark stranger,' Nancy continued, imitating Mystic Alice, not letting the subject drop.

'Oh, stop it. Anyway, what would I do with a dark stranger?'

'I can think of plenty of things,' Nancy said, her voice laden with insinuation. 'I think it sounds exciting. What if there *is* someone, Vita? A dark stranger, waiting out there for you?'

Vita thought of Clement. He had dark hair. Was *he* coming for her? From the Other Side?

'I don't want a dark stranger,' she said, too loudly.

Nancy laughed at her reaction, running to avoid the tram that was rattling towards them.

230

'Whatever has got into you?'

'I'm serious, Nancy. I don't need a man bossing me around. Telling me what to do. I'm perfectly happy as I am.' Vita could hear the rising hysteria in her voice.

Mystic Alice had shaken her to her core and reminded her of everything she'd run away from. With all her hard work over the past weeks, she had almost managed to forget that she was Anna Darton. Because Verity Casey was so real. And she wanted Verity Casey's future so very badly.

'Noted. No dark strangers,' Nancy said.

54

A Lead at Last

Having been at home for over a month, it felt good to be back at work. Clement leant on his stick as he entered the mill, putting a handkerchief over his nose to protect himself from the air, which was thick with cotton dust. The mill floor had to stay heated to stop the cotton from breaking, and he felt the familiar wall of humid heat making his skin prickle as his ears were assaulted by the deafening noise of the machines.

He looked across at the giant looms, the spinneys clacking, the huge bales of fabric being made one line at a time, the workers in their overalls and boots manning the machines. It was magical, he thought, the way the strings of cotton were coloured in, until the fabric was created.

He made his way over the concrete floor to the cast-iron staircase and, grabbing onto the rail and wincing with pain, hobbled up to the office.

His father sat behind the large leather-topped desk and hardly looked up. 'You're sure you're fit enough for work?' was his greeting.

'Of course I am.'

'I don't need you here.'

Clement resented his father's words, but tried not to let them smart as he busied himself checking the figures for the latest shipment of cotton from America. Then he signed off on the designs from Barrington and his team.

His father stood looking down through the glass windows at the giant spinneys below, his hands behind his back, his fingers twitching.

'She can't have found out. About Arkwright. Can she?' he said.

He was obsessed, Clement thought. All he could think about was Anna.

'No. There's no way. She certainly must have run out of the money that she stole,' Clement said.

'The money isn't important,' his father said. It almost sounded as if Darius Darton actually cared.

The office door opened and Darius spun round as one of the junior clerks appeared.

'What do you want?' he snapped.

'There's a Mr Rawlings, sir.'

Darius and Clement exchanged a look. A moment later Rawlings appeared at the top of the stairs. He stood while both the Dartons sat and then, after some pleasantries, retrieved his notebook.

'I interviewed the stablehand, a Mark . . . Thwaites,' he said, consulting a page.

Clement's jaw clenched. What had Mark told Rawlings?

'It took me a while to get the information out of him, but it seems he saw Miss Darton on the night she disappeared.'

'He did?' Darius said in surprise.

'She was heading across the fields to the railway tracks.'

Why hadn't that occurred to Clement before? Not only that Mark might have seen her, but also that Anna might have gone over the fields and not along the road. They'd all assumed she must have left Darton by road, maybe picking up a lift from a wagon, which is why they'd only really searched locally. When they'd put the notice in the paper, Clement had assumed that his sister might – at a stretch – have made it as far as Manchester.

'She could have boarded a train?' Darius said, in alarm.

'It's a distinct possibility.'

'Then she could be anywhere.'

'It's a question of making a methodical search. To find out the trains that passed through that night. I happen to have discovered that there was one to London, which was delayed because of a fault. It didn't leave until after midnight.' He looked at Clement and then at Darius Darton. 'I'll find her, sir,' Rawlings said calmly. 'I just need more time and resources.'

'That's no problem,' Clement said, thinking of the workers' collection for his sister. 'Whatever you need. I'll come with you, if necessary.'

'Don't be ridiculous, Clement,' his father said.

'As you wish,' Clement said, bowing his head.

'Leave it with me,' Rawlings said tactfully. 'I have a one-hundred-per-cent success rate. I'll find her.'

55

The Bee's Knees

The brassiere that Vita had made for Nancy was in vermilion red, to go under her favourite blouse, and Vita crossed her fingers at Jane, as Nancy tried it on behind the screen in their dressing room after the show on Thursday.

'Oh! It's simply the bee's knees,' Nancy declared, coming out with her arms wide and admiring herself in the mirror. 'The way the shirt hangs now. Don't you think? And look!' She did a pirouette and some funny jazz-hands. 'I can move. Oh, I just can't wait to show Lulu.'

Vita was delighted that Nancy was so pleased, and even more delighted that she was going to show her dress-maker.

'What's the bee's knees?' Betsy asked, coming through the door and flinging her bag on the chair.

'This,' Nancy said. 'This shirt has never sat right, but now I have a secret weapon.'

'Secret weapon?' Betsy asked, intrigued.

'Vita's Top Drawer underwear,' Nancy said. 'Ta-da.' She lifted her shirt with a flourish.

Jane, Betsy, Emma and Jemima – and even Wisey – were

all suddenly clamouring to take a look. And the more they fussed over Vita's creation, the more confident she felt. And Nancy, of course, was in her element, showing off.

'Can I have one in blue, to go under my silk blouse?' Jemima asked.

'Yes,' Vita laughed, 'but you'll have to wait your turn.'

'And she'll charge,' Nancy said, decisively.

'Well, I wouldn't—' Vita began, but Nancy cut her off.

'You *absolutely* will charge,' she said sternly. 'Come on, let's get out front. This calls for a drink.'

They were all chatting about Vita's potential business out in the bar, when Percy joined them. Matteo opened another bottle of champagne.

'What am I missing?' Percy asked.

'We're toasting her fabulous creation,' Nancy said. 'See – doesn't this look so much better?' She stuck out her chest at Percy, and Vita smiled as she sipped her drink.

'I told Vita that she's on to something,' Percy agreed.

'I know. Mystic Alice says she's going to be wildly successful.'

Vita looked at Percy over the top of her glass. 'Don't ask,' she said.

'Well then, yes – I guess – a business has been born,' Percy said, clearly amused. 'Although can I just point out that there is a world of difference between making one brassiere and selling lots.'

'Only a bit of hard work,' Nancy said, perfectly seriously. 'To Top Drawer!' she proposed, raising her glass to the others. Vita clinked glasses with her, laughing. 'And don't you dare forget who put you up to this,' Nancy told her.

'Oh, believe me, I won't.'

56

The Café de Paris

Nancy had taken Mr Connelly's advice to heart and had decreed they should hit the town to check out the competition, and said she'd heard there was a new cabaret on at the Café de Paris. Vita persuaded Percy and Edward to chaperone them on Saturday night after the show.

Percy had lent Vita one of his leading-lady dresses from the rail – a slinky champagne-coloured dress that made her feel every inch a starlet. Nancy was also dressed up in a sparkling gold dress made entirely of fringing, causing Edward to joke that if the two of them lay over each other, they'd look like rather a fetching settee.

'Go on,' Nancy urged Vita, as they sat in the back of Edward's car. She rolled her eyes and took a deep breath. 'Say it again, say it again.'

''Ey up, our Percy. You'd better hurry up and get down t'pit,' Vita said, in her deep, gruff voice, putting on her best over-puffed Yorkshire accent. 'I'll pay yer half yer wages, and double yer hours.'

'That is too funny,' Nancy laughed.

'Oh . . . oh, do Scottish again,' Percy urged. 'You've got Mrs B spot-on.'

'Hang on, we're here.' Edward pulled over and parked by the kerb. As they got out of the car, Vita reached her arm out for Percy.

Edward had assured them that he knew a chap called Poulsen, who used to be head waiter at the Embassy Club and would be able to get them in on the guest list. But seeing the crowd outside the Café de Paris now, Vita wasn't so sure.

She looked up at the front of the club, with its distinctive signage and ornate revolving door, and raised crossed fingers to Edward as he squeezed his way to the front of the queue, tipping his black top hat to some people he recognized.

A line of well-dressed men and women waited patiently outside, their perfume catching on the breeze, along with the beat of the music coming from inside. Vita counted up the fur stoles and sparkling dresses, and the tailored suits of the handsome young men. It was a rather more salubrious crowd than the one that graced the Zip.

Vita took Nancy's hand as Edward reappeared on the other side of the revolving doors and waved for them to go inside.

'Isn't he a wizard?' Nancy trilled happily, as they shouldered their way through to the front of the crowd. She clearly enjoyed the fact that they were turning heads – that the people waiting thought they were important somehow – but Vita pulled a face at Percy, who found it just as laughable as she did.

'Please, enjoy yourselves,' the host urged them, mistaking them, as everyone did, for two couples. Nancy threw an amused glance at Vita, reaching up to kiss Percy's cheek ostentatiously. 'See you at the bar. Be a darling and get us some fizz.'

In the cloakrooms, Vita and Nancy powdered their noses in the fancy gilt mirrors that reflected the marble washbasins and gold taps. Then Nancy winked at Vita in the mirror. The attendant had left for a moment and she reached into her velvet clutch-bag.

'Look what I've got. Fancy a dab of snow?'

Vita watched as she tipped out some white powder onto the dip at the base of her thumb, or her 'snuff pouch' as she liked to call it. She felt torn: half of her, the good half, wanted to get out of taking any more drugs with Nancy, as they inevitably led to trouble, but the other half – the one so desperate to be daring and outrageous – won. She didn't want to let Nancy down, or for her to think Vita was prudish.

'That's it. Straight up,' Nancy encouraged, holding her hand out to Vita. 'Toot-toot.'

Vita checked once more that they weren't being watched and then dipped her head forward and sniffed up the powder, before rubbing her nostril as the acrid snow stung.

She looked at herself in the mirror. Her pupils were wide from all the champagne she'd had so far tonight, but this felt so good. Then immediately she felt guilty. Because surely it was sinful to have *this* much fun? What if it all ended? What then?

'Look at you,' Nancy said, standing behind her. She ran her hands down Vita's sides and over her hips, in the slinky satin dress she was wearing. 'Did I tell you yet? I do so love this.'

Vita felt herself shudder at Nancy's touch, but as soon as

the moment came, it passed, and Nancy's eyes flashed with mischief in the mirror. Then she grabbed Vita's hand and squeezed it.

'Come on. Let's go and have fun.'

It could have been Nancy's potent white powder, but Vita felt a heady, other-worldly feeling and a definite tingling up her spine as she leant on the balcony. Above them, a grand chandelier hung from the ceiling, which was ruched with silk. Opposite them, a double staircase curved down on either side of the stage where the band played. Way below on the dance floor, elegant couples were dancing. Further back, the tables were crowded with guests drinking cocktails. Standing here, it felt to Vita as if they were right on the pulse of London.

'They say this place is a copy of the dance room on the *Lusitania*,' Nancy said, leaning on the rail by her side.

'The ship the Germans sank?'

'Yes. Wouldn't you love to go on one of those grand ships?' Nancy said. 'Sail away somewhere? Think of all the parties.'

'Not when they sink,' Vita said and Nancy laughed.

'Oh, look, look! We're just in time for the cabaret.'

The compère was introducing the next act, who called herself Delysia. The lights dimmed, then a spotlight appeared at the top of the staircase and a woman in a sequinned sheath-dress descended the stairs, waving an ostrich-feather fan, and Vita remembered a similar fan in Percy's studio. She wondered if it might be the same one: very probably. She was starting to see how interconnected everything was, amongst the clubs and bars. Even here, where the audience was of a more salubrious nature, it was still the same *type* of person. The type she loved being.

Vita could soon see why Mr Connelly was insecure about the entertainment at the Zip, however. Everyone was staring as Delysia began to move, kicking out her gorgeously long legs as she descended one step at a time, her plumed head-dress fluttering.

Then she started her bawdy song in a deep alto voice. It was called 'Does Your Father Know You're Out?', and Vita heard spontaneous applause and laughter from the crowd below, many of whom were now facing the opposite side of the balcony.

'Look – it's him!' Nancy gasped, nudging her in the ribs.

'Who?'

'The Prince of Wales,' Nancy whispered, her face lit up with excitement. 'Over there. Look!'

Vita followed her gaze across the balcony to where a handsome man in a grey suit with a silk cravat was laughing with other people, as he listened to the cabaret.

'Oh, my goodness,' Vita exclaimed, feeling herself blushing with the thrill of witnessing such a moment. Mrs Bell would die, when she heard about this! And how gloriously cheeky of Delysia to sing such provocative lyrics. It was no secret that the King disapproved of his son's prodigious social life.

'Isn't he quite the cat's pyjamas,' Nancy said, grabbing Vita's wrist and making off around the balcony. 'Come on. Let's go and meet him.'

'We can't. I mean, we can't just go up to him. Can we?' Vita said.

'Yes, we can. We can do anything.'

Vita relented, delighted as ever to go along with her friend.

'I dare you,' Nancy said as they got nearer. 'I dare you to talk to him.'

Maybe Nancy was right. Maybe they could do anything. After all, they were here, weren't they? With all the Bright Young Things. With the future King of England. And what did she have to lose? Especially if it meant impressing Nancy.

57

Saying Hello

Egged on by Nancy, and not wanting to back out of the dare, and also because she was now feeling completely high, Vita made her way around the balcony with Nancy to where the Prince of Wales and his entourage were standing.

Delysia was still singing and had the attention of the whole room, so it was easy to move amongst the crowd. Soon they were only a few people away from the Prince.

'Go on,' Nancy urged, pushing Vita forward.

A young man standing next to her noticed Vita and she saw him looking her up and down appraisingly, before smiling and standing aside to let her get through to the Prince. She was glad she was wearing Percy's starlet dress, but even so, she tugged at the neckline, worrying that she was revealing far too much cleavage.

'Excuse me,' she said, shouldering her way through. She could see Nancy in the crowd, holding her hands up in applause.

And then quite suddenly there she was, standing right next to the Prince of Wales. He glanced at her and looked away. Then he glanced back.

For a split second she felt absolutely ridiculous, colour

creeping up her cheeks as she realized that she not only had the Prince's attention, but that of others around him, too.

'Sir . . . I'm so sorry to interrupt,' she said, wondering if she should curtsey. She couldn't believe she was doing this. The man talking to the Prince nudged him and smiled over in Vita's direction. The Prince looked both amused and confused.

'Have we met?' he asked Vita.

'Oh no . . . sir . . . Your Highness,' Vita stuttered. 'It's just I wanted to say . . .'

What did she want to say? What did one say to the Prince of Wales? There was a pregnant pause as the Prince and his friend stared at her.

'It's really very rude of me,' she said, deciding that the truth was the only option, 'but you see, I've rather got myself caught in – well . . . a dare.' She pulled an embarrassed smile and the Prince chuckled.

'A dare?'

'Yes, sir. To . . . to greet you. To say hello.'

The Prince laughed again, amused at her discomfort. 'Well, hello,' he said and Vita extended her hand. He took her hand and kissed it, his blue eyes staring into hers.

'It's an honour,' she said.

'The pleasure is all mine. What is your name?' he asked, one eye now on the crowd, then back to her. He had to raise his voice.

'Verity. Verity Casey. My friends call me Vita.'

'And what do you do, Vita?'

'I'm a designer,' she said confidently. 'Of women's underwear,' she added.

'Oh!' he said, sounding both shocked and amused.

He gave her a smile, and then Delysia had finished her song and the crowd erupted into whoops and cheers and the Prince turned his attention away from her.

But at that moment a man stepped forward with a camera and there was a bright flash as he caught the Prince, who didn't flinch. *He must be used to it*, Vita thought, the bright light making dots appear in her vision.

She ducked down and scuttled back through the crowd to Nancy, who stared at her, her mouth open wide.

'Well? What did he say?' she gushed, clinging onto Vita's arm.

Vita laughed, looking back up at the crowd to check that the Prince wasn't watching. 'Nothing much. He just . . . well. Oh, Nancy!'

She couldn't quite believe what had happened.

'This calls for champagne,' Nancy said, steering her towards the stairs. 'Wait until the boys find out.'

Clutching onto each other, giddy with what had just occurred, they made for the staircase, following in Delysia's footsteps.

'Wasn't she marvellous? Delysia, I mean?' Vita said, seeing the cabaret star drift between the tables to receive compliments.

'We could do that at the Zip. I mean, we're good, but we need to up our game. We could definitely suggest to Mr Connelly having a cabaret act.'

Vita moved out of the way as a very stylish couple passed them. He was wearing tails, a white silk scarf draped around his neck, and was carrying a silver-topped cane. He paused, tipping his hat to them both. He had the most extraordinary hazel-green eyes, she noticed, as she tried to rip her gaze away.

'Good evening, ladies,' he said, but while he was addressing them, his gaze stayed locked on Vita's and she felt a rush in her stomach, unlike anything she'd ever felt before.

She watched him pass by, smelling the woman's perfume. She felt a pang of longing. How wonderful it would be to *be* her. To be with that handsome man with the amazing eyes.

Then, at the top of the stairs, the man turned and looked back at her, seemingly as surprised as she was that they were both looking for each other. Vita bit her lip, her smile seeming to burst out of her. It felt as if they had shared a secret. Although she wasn't sure yet what the secret was.

'Oh, look out! Could he be the dark stranger?' Nancy teased.

58

Mrs Clifford-Meade

Mrs Clifford-Meade, known to her friends as Lulu, was a no-nonsense kind of person. She was in her forties, Vita reckoned, but she looked modern in flared trousers, a waistcoat and a frilly blouse as she met them at the door of her shop in Chelsea. She closed the door and the small bell chimed above their heads. Then she turned the sign round to read 'Closed' and ushered them inside.

'Your mother would kill me if she knew you were here,' Lulu said, kissing Nancy on the cheek. 'And don't for one minute think I'm going to make you anything, young lady, when you know full well that your mother won't pay.'

Vita was amused by the affection in Lulu's voice. She clearly found Nancy a force to be reckoned with, too.

'Then don't tell her.'

'And I told you not to bring that devilish dog.'

'Oh, Lulu, don't be mean to Mr Wild,' Nancy said, kissing the dog, which was in her arms. 'He'll behave this time, I promise. Anyway, this visit is about Vita – my best friend, who I was telling you about.'

Vita smiled, thrilled to be described by Nancy as her best friend.

'You're the one who spoke to the Prince of Wales,' Lulu said, shaking Vita's hand. There was an amused respect in her eyes, and Vita was glad that her daring moment reflected so well on her now. There had been nothing but talk about the Prince of Wales at the Café de Paris amongst the girls.

She stared at the mannequins dotted around the small room wearing an array of beautiful gowns, particularly a pink dress with appliqué flowers. Nancy had explained that Lulu's main work was the bespoke couture that she designed for her 'ladies' in the back of the shop, and now they followed Lulu through a curtain into the large room beyond. Vita watched the dressmakers at their desks, confidently cutting patterns. One of them was pinning the most exquisite long evening gown on a mannequin, appraising the shimmering fabric in the light coming from the large windows.

Vita, mesmerized, longed to stay and watch her, but Lulu led them through another door into a lounge. There was a raised carpeted area, where Vita suspected the models paraded to show off Lulu's clothes, and below it were some comfortable couches and chairs. Lulu sat with them around a low table and poured tea from a metal teapot. Nancy tried to make Mr Wild sit still.

'I don't have much time,' Lulu said. 'So you'd better tell me what this is all about, Nancy. But if either of you is after a job, let me start by saying that I'm afraid I have no vacancies.'

'Oh no, it's not that at all,' Nancy said, then got straight to the point. She described how Vita had made a brassiere – first one for herself and then one for Nancy – and how she had said straight away that Lulu must see them. Vita felt herself blushing as Nancy talked of her 'great talent'. She really was a first-class saleswoman.

'I could have my girls make these,' Lulu pointed out, picking up the pince-nez that hung around her neck on a chain and examining the bra that Vita now presented to her from her bag. Seeing it in Lulu's hand, she realized how amateurish her enterprise must seem.

'But Vita here has the pattern,' Nancy responded, nodding at Vita to elaborate. 'And they've been tried and tested.'

'Each one is quite fiddly,' Vita said. 'But I'm doing my best to make sure each one fits the wearer well.'

'I absolutely love mine,' Nancy went on. 'You can't get a bigger endorsement than that. You know how fussy I am. This is the modern way.'

Lulu gave her a wry smile. 'As you well know, I cut my jackets and dresses to minimize too large a movement.'

'But we want to move,' Vita said. 'That's what us girls at the Zip Club *do* all day. And we want to feel free – and yet safe while we do it.'

Nancy pulled Vita up from where she was sitting. 'Let's show her.'

Lulu laughed and rubbed the side of her face, as Nancy and Vita began a small part of their routine. Mr Wild yapped approvingly. Nancy picked him up and sat back down.

'Poor Vita was either strapped in tight or jiggling all over the place, before she made her secret brassiere,' Nancy said. 'Now look at her.'

'I see your point, Nancy,' Lulu laughed. 'But my ladies are not dancing every night in a club.'

'But they might do. If they had the right support. And

don't you think they'll want a little of the freedom of the Zip Club girls?'

Lulu put her hands up in defence. She sighed heavily. 'I surrender! I'll give you a trial. Genevieve, my assistant, will give you the measurements of five of the ladies that I'm seeing next week. Bring me five brassieres. If any of my customers like them, then I shall commission you properly to make more and I'll sell them in the shop. And pay you, of course.'

Nancy stuck out her bottom lip. 'You're expecting poor Vita to work on spec?'

'I absolutely am. Yes, Nancy. You Americans!'

'I'm so very grateful,' Vita said. 'Honestly.'

'Let's hope Lance Kenton isn't such a meanie,' Nancy said to Mr Wild.

Lulu turned her head. 'Lance Kenton? You mean from W&T?'

'Oh, didn't I tell you?' Nancy said. 'W&T are simply all over Vita's bras.'

Vita was about to contradict her, but Nancy's look told her to be quiet, as they got up to leave. And, as Lulu shook her hand, Vita knew that Nancy's tactic had worked.

'You are the best saleswoman,' Vita whispered to her.

'I know. Aren't we just the dream-team?'

And once again Vita felt a sickening pang of sadness when she thought about Nancy leaving for Paris.

59

The Telephone Call

Clement leant on his stick in the dark hallway and pressed the cold black Bakelite of the telephone receiver against his ear. The call from Rawlings had interrupted their breakfast.

'You think it could be her?' he asked again. The line crackled disconcertingly. He knew that Martha was probably listening in.

'She fits the description perfectly. I have the address here. I've seen her entering the building. Shall I call the police? Ask them to escort her home?' Rawlings asked.

Clement felt hope bursting in his chest at the prospect of trapping his sister. 'No. No, that won't be necessary. Stay there and keep an eye on her. Follow her and find out where she goes. I'll come myself to collect her.'

The door to the drawing room opened as he put down the receiver, and Clement knew straight away that his mother had heard his conversation.

'Is it good news, dear?' she asked tentatively. She had a canary in her hand and was petting its yellow feathers. It chirruped loudly, as if it were about to fly away, but his mother grabbed it and held it tight.

'She's been found,' Clement said, stumping down the hallway towards the stairs. 'I'm going to get her.'

'Where is she?'

'London.'

'London?' Theresa Darton sounded almost excited. 'All that way?'

Clement turned on his mother, seeing something odd in her expression. It was almost as if she were proud, rather than surprised, that Anna had made it so far.

'Yes, but I'm bringing her home. And then she'll be sorry for making us all worry so.'

60

A Summons From Mr Connelly

'There,' Vita said, poking her tongue out and twisting the last bit of wire into the feather spray that she'd created for tonight's costumes for the show. She held it out to Percy, who took it from her and pinned it onto the back of Edith's bodice.

'What are they supposed to be?' Edith asked, suspiciously.

Vita didn't tell her the design for the new routine had been inspired by Mystic Alice's parrot. Since Jerome had played them the jazzy Latin American number to which they were to choreograph their performance, the theme had taken on a life of its own.

'Latin American.'

'I look like a bird,' Edith said disparagingly.

'That's the point. Higher,' Vita said, 'so that it plumes out behind, here.' She gestured to Edith's head.

'I think it looks smashing,' Percy said, positioning it correctly. 'Oh, Vita, you are so clever. They look so flamboyant. If I'm not careful, you'll have my job.'

'Who's getting whose job?' Nancy asked, walking in and grabbing her dancing shoes. 'Oh . . . are these for tonight?' she said, distracted by Edith, who was looking cautiously at

254

herself in the mirror. 'They're quite something. Do we all get one?' Edith gave her a look that implied that she thought Nancy was being sarcastic. Nancy eyeballed her in the mirror. 'I mean it. You could say something nice, for once.'

'Thank you, Percy,' Edith said in a conciliatory tone.

'All Vita's idea,' Percy said, putting his hands up. 'I didn't think she'd pull it off in time. This girl sure can work miracles.'

'Well, I nearly didn't,' Vita laughed. 'I've only had two hours' sleep. After the show I'm going straight back to Mrs Bell's. It's hard enough doing the costumes, but with the brassieres for Lulu, too, I'm done in.'

She noticed Edith stiffen. She'd made no secret of the fact that she didn't approve of Vita's 'little cottage industry', as she called it. She was annoyed that the girls were so excited about it.

'I don't know why you're wasting your time, Vita,' she said, leaning forward to check her lipstick in the mirror. 'Nobody is ever going to take you, or your so-called "business", seriously.' She gave a derisory snort and then left the room, her tail-feathers quivering.

'She's just jealous,' Percy said, but Vita felt Edith's words pinch. Edith was right. Who *was* ever going to take her seriously? It was all very well for Nancy to flounce around, expecting everyone to do her favours, but in the real world business didn't work like that.

In the wings, Edith became even more riled when Jack Connelly appraised the dancing girls.

'Wonderful,' he said, looking genuinely impressed. 'Well done, Vita. Very imaginative.'

Edith scowled, but Vita smiled back at her. It was annoying that she was always so superior. She had nothing to be so snarky about, Vita thought. Things were clearly going well between Edith and Mr Connelly, and she had been promoted to head up the new cabaret they were rehearsing.

'I want you all out front afterwards. No excuses,' he added, pointing his cigar at them. 'There's some admirers of yours, who have specifically asked for you, Vita.'

'Oh?' she said, pulling a face at Jane, but there was no time to ask anything more, as they received their cue to get onstage.

Mr Connelly slapped Edith's bottom as they danced past.

'I'd never let a man play my emotions like that,' Jane whispered.

'Me neither,' Vita agreed. 'Who needs *men*?'

61

Some New Admirers

The routine was a hit, judging by the applause in the club, but it took the last vestiges of Vita's energy. After the show she could hardly be bothered to take off her stage make-up, flinging on her oldest dress in the dressing room. She dragged her feet as she followed Nancy back into the club.

'I'm so tired,' she moaned. 'I don't want to meet anyone.'

'Oh, buck up,' Nancy said with a grin. 'You can sleep when you're dead. Let's see what old Connelly wants, and then we'll hop in a cab to "Les A".'

Out in the club, Jack Connelly was installed in a red leather booth at the back, an ice-bucket housing two bottles of champagne on the table in front of him. Edith, who had glammed up into a white dress after tonight's show, sat demurely beside him, like the cat who'd got the cream. Vita wished now that she'd made more of an effort with her appearance.

The other guests had their backs to her, but they took their cue from Jack Connelly, who stood up, all false bon-homie, as he beckoned them forward.

'There you are. Girls, I'd like you to meet some of your new admirers. This is Mr Archie Fenwick and—'

But Vita didn't hear the rest. Because as soon as he turned round, she knew it was him. The man from the Café de Paris.

She stared, tongue-tied for a moment, feeling the weirdest sensation in her stomach, and a tugging inside her that she hadn't felt since she'd been in the bath with Nancy. She felt herself blushing.

'Hello,' he said, and for a second it was as if the rest of the club faded and there was only his face, his voice . . . his smile. He had those amazing eyes that she'd been so drawn to the first time she'd seen him, and high cheekbones, with a mole halfway up the left side. But it was his mouth that most intrigued her. She had to deliberately stop staring at his lips.

'Well, introduce yourself,' Mr Connelly said with a laugh.

'I'm Verity. Verity Casey,' she said, but her voice sounded strange as he took her hand and shook it.

'Would you care to dance, Miss Casey?' Mr Fenwick said, not letting go of her hand. She hadn't even been aware of the music, but now he led her away from the others towards the dance floor and pulled her effortlessly into his arms to join the crowd dancing the slow foxtrot.

He was a confident dancer, but then someone like him must have had lots of practice, Vita reasoned, as he guided her round the dance floor. She thought briefly of Annabelle Morton's party and of the countless men she'd met there, but none of them had been anywhere near as dashing as Archie Fenwick. She thought, too, of the woman he'd seen her with at the Café de Paris. Surely he must be engaged? How could such a catch be single?

She felt furious with herself that she hadn't worn her

green dress, instead of this awful dowdy grey one. And fixed her make-up.

'I've seen you before,' he said.

'I know. But we've never met.'

'It feels like we have. But then I've been to see you three times in the past week.'

He said it so matter-of-factly that Vita laughed. She pulled back to look up fully into his face. 'Three times?'

'Of course. When I realized it was you. I haven't been able to stop myself.'

Was he teasing her? Surely he was. But then he smiled shyly down at her and she could see that he meant it.

'I would hazard that I could give your routine a go myself.'

'I'm flattered,' she frowned. 'I think . . .'

He smiled and turned her round in his arms.

'You've really been looking for me?' she checked.

'Ever since I saw you on that staircase I've been trying to find you amongst all the dancing girls in London. I overheard you talking to your friend, you see.'

He looked at his hand around hers, as if he were holding the most precious thing.

'I'm sure there are better shows in town,' she said.

'That may well be, but they don't have you in them.'

She bit her lip, amazed at his easy compliment. *He actually meant it*.

'Well, you've found me now.'

'Yes, I have,' he said, and when he smiled, she saw what he must have looked like as a boy.

And still the fluttering inside her continued – and seemed

to increase with each moment that she was in his arms. Nobody had ever cared enough about her to track her down. Or to come and see her. She let this new, unsettling sensation seep into her. If Archie Fenwick had been able to find her so easily, then what would happen if her parents started looking? She'd been convinced that she'd been hiding cleverly, but what if she hadn't?

They danced further around the dance floor, but the song was coming to an end.

'Would it be terrible if I told you a secret?' he said.

'You can tell me anything you want,' she said lightly, but her heart sang at the thought that he'd want to share anything at all with her.

The music stopped briefly, as the band prepared for the next number. She stayed in his arms, his hand around hers. Everyone was moving around them, but they remained quite still.

'Well, the thing is—'

'Oh, Vita, it's our favourite!' Nancy interrupted them as the band struck up with 'Baby Face'. She tugged at Vita's arm, pulling her away from Archie before shouting at him, 'It's our song.'

Vita was jolted away, feeling horribly torn. She couldn't blame Nancy – after all, this was one of their dances – but as Nancy lifted up her leg now in a high kick and then turned to bump her hips provocatively with Vita, she felt embarrassed.

'"You got the cutest little baby face",' Nancy sang, but instead of joining in, Vita watched as Archie took a step back away from the dance floor.

She wondered if he was already regretting how much he'd

told her. She could see him thinking that the person he'd thought she was didn't match up to the brazen dancing girl before him. She smiled her best showgirl smile at him, but he didn't smile back; instead he looked down at his shoes.

Nancy looked confused, too. Her eyebrows knitted together as Vita turned to her. 'Come on, kiddo.' She gave Vita a quizzical look, putting extra fervour into her steps.

She had no choice, Vita realized, smiling at Nancy and putting some effort into the dance, but her heart wasn't in it. She could see Archie turn his back and walk away from the dance floor.

What was his secret? What had he been about to say? Something about them? Something about his feelings towards her? She was sure of it, but the moment was gone and it was as if a barrier had gone up between them.

She tried to look for him, but then she saw his head near the back of the crowd. Was he heading towards the door? Was he *leaving*?

'Oh, I do love this one,' Nancy said. She blew a kiss to Jerome, who was conducting the band, and Vita wondered meanly if Nancy had told him to play their song, just to get her away from Archie.

'I've got to go,' Vita told Nancy.

'Go where? Come on, stay.'

'Just a minute,' Vita said, rushing through the dancers and the crush of bodies. She saw the back of a man's head – it must be Archie – as he made his way up the steps towards the doorway.

'Mr Fenwick,' she called. 'Wait . . .'

She caught up with him, and he leant in towards her. 'I'm

so sorry, Miss Casey,' he yelled over the music. 'I have just seen the time. I have to go.'

'You have to go?' she asked. 'But—'

'It was so nice seeing you again.'

He squeezed the top of her arm, hardly meeting her eye, and then ran two at a time up the steps to the door, and Vita was left looking at the space where he'd been. She thought of following him, but then he hadn't been able to get away fast enough. Away from her.

Deflated, she tried to smile as Nancy caught her eye and beckoned her back to the dance floor, but instead she went back to the table where Mr Connelly and Edith were.

'Who on earth was that man you were dancing with?' Nancy asked, catching up with her at the back booth, out of breath and brushing down the ruffled sequins on the front of her dress. 'He looked frightfully serious.'

'Archie Fenwick,' Edith said, smugly. 'His family used to own half of Gloucestershire, apparently. He's one of those Eton types. Part of that set.'

Her tone and the sideways look she now threw at Vita made it clear that she thought being an Eton type made Archie way out of Vita's league.

'What set?'

'You know the type. They always use people.'

Vita immediately felt riled. She was annoyed at Edith's assumption that Archie was using her in some way. Just because he was wealthy. He certainly hadn't seemed like any sort of 'type' at all.

'He seemed to have the hots for you,' Nancy said, nudging her in the ribs.

And you ruined it, Vita wanted to snap.

'Anyway, if he's here, then you know he's probably after one thing,' Edith said.

That was rich, coming from her! She had no problem flaunting her relationship with Mr Connelly. She had no right to imply that Vita or any of the other girls were loose.

Vita excused herself and nodded at Nancy to join her at the bar. She didn't want to listen to Edith's opinions about Archie Fenwick. She wanted to hold on to everything he'd said and the feeling she'd had when she was in his arms. But why had he left her?

62

Perfect Seams

In Percy's bedroom, Vita examined in the mirror the bags under her eyes and smudged away last night's make-up from below them. They had stayed late at the club – Vita hoping all the time that Archie would come back. But he hadn't and she'd drunk far too much, succumbing to a few dabs of Nancy's 'marching powder' in order to stay awake.

She felt soiled now, her flagrant partying ways at odds with the kind of nice girl she wanted to be for Archie, but Nancy had been very persuasive.

Vita folded her arms and looked out of the window at the white sky. She wondered what Archie was doing right now. Whether he was even in London. Whether he was looking out at the same clouds. Had he thought of her at all since he'd walked out of the Zip?

She couldn't stop herself picking over their meeting again and again. If he'd gone to all that trouble to find her, why had he left so soon? He'd obviously been annoyed that Nancy had interrupted them, but it was most odd. They'd only been dancing. Everyone else seemed to love the exhibition they made of themselves. So why had Archie been so unimpressed?

Perhaps he had disapproved of her closeness to Nancy. Or perhaps he was the kind of person who wouldn't allow her to have friends and would want to guard her jealously? In which case he most definitely wasn't for her.

As if it were a choice. She caught herself slipping into fantasy land again.

Edith was right. Archie Fenwick was way out of her league. And, as she'd said, probably after one thing. But Archie wasn't like that. Was he?

She knew she was indulging the old, romantic part of herself, but she couldn't help it. Why had he become so scared? Why had he left her?

'Stop it,' Percy said, looking at Vita over the top his glasses.

'What?'

'That man you danced with. I can tell you're still thinking about him.'

She turned away from the window to face him. He was sitting at the small table, his legs tucked under the sewing machine. Percy looked at her, then put a pin in his mouth, before squinting down at the treadle. It was a relief to be able to talk to Percy about Archie. She could never tell Nancy how she'd been feeling, but Percy seemed to understand.

'It's just . . . he *can't* have been looking for me amongst all the dancing girls in London. He was only saying that to flatter me. Like he probably flatters dozens of women.'

Percy grunted in agreement, before the hum of the sewing machine started up for a minute and then stopped.

'So I should forget him. I know. I know you're right. But, Percy, he was *so* handsome.'

'Looks aren't everything,' he said, with a wry smile.

'I know, but . . . I've never felt like that. Like I felt when we danced together.'

'If it's meant to be, then it's meant to be,' Percy said.

'You really think so?'

'Of course I do. I'm a firm believer in fate.'

Vita sighed. 'I want to believe in fate. I really do. But the fact is – he left.'

'He'll be back.'

'You think?'

'Why wouldn't he be? You're gorgeous.'

Vita was immeasurably cheered by how sure he sounded. 'I think Nancy put him off.'

'Nancy would put any man off. She's terrifying. And she guards you like a fierce terrier.'

It was odd hearing Percy talking about Nancy like this. Like he disapproved of her. Vita almost confessed how, sometimes, she felt that Nancy wanted more of her than she was prepared to give.

'She wants me to go to Paris with her.'

'Oh?' Percy didn't sound convinced by the idea.

'Well, obviously I'm not going,' she said, putting him straight. 'I'm not leaving here. Not now. Not ever.'

'Good,' Percy said. He concentrated on the sewing for a moment. 'The Folies Bergère had better watch out, if Nancy is on the loose.' Even Vita had heard of the famous club in Paris. 'You mark my words, she'll head straight for trouble.'

'You don't sound like you really approve?'

Percy sighed. 'Nancy is one of those people who likes to detonate things and then leave a mess.' He made a gesture like a bomb going off. 'Like this, for example. She bamboozled us into making brassieres for her dressmaker and, even if we pull it off and get another order, it'll still mean that everything will change.'

'Change how?'

'I'm not sure, but that's what I'm worried about. I find it stressful enough doing my job, as it is,' he admitted.

'Don't you want to be part of Top Drawer?' Vita couldn't keep the panic from her voice. She'd thought they were partners. Equals. She'd forgotten how busy Percy was already.

'Vita, I will do whatever it takes to help you, but really, this is your baby, not mine. Is it what you want?'

'Yes, Percy. Yes, it is. I need this.'

'Well then, we'd better get to work.'

Vita went over and examined the stitching on the camiknickers he was sewing. She had insisted that the new brassieres were better off being shown as a set, and was determined to go the extra mile to impress Lulu, even if it meant more work.

He flicked up the lever at the back of the sewing machine and held up the camiknickers.

'Oh, Percy. You are so clever. Look at those perfect seams.'

'Making nurses' uniforms in the war had its advantages after all.'

She grinned at him and held her hands out. 'Pass them over. I can't wait any longer. I'm going to try them on with the brassiere.'

Vita felt a new-found confidence come over her – a strength in her unity with Percy. Because she was talented, wasn't she? Albeit with Percy's help.

If Mrs Clifford-Meade was impressed with this batch of brassieres, as Vita was pretty confident she would be, looking at Percy's workmanship now, then she might order some more. And, more importantly, pay her. And then she would truly be on her way. To where, she wasn't sure. But it suddenly felt as if Nancy might be right and she had a future laden with possibility.

63

The Girl

Clement hated the capital city. Well, he hated parts of it – like this busy street, with the cabs and cars and noise. A light drizzle was falling and the street lamps were flickering.

How had his sister survived here for this long?

She must have found a job, he supposed. But as far as he was aware, Anna had no skills to speak of. Or maybe she'd already learnt the hard way: that the only way to make money was to sell herself.

Still, no matter if she'd garnered a little experience. Arkwright wasn't to know. He just wanted young flesh. And young flesh with a little life in it was always the best kind.

Clement took the notebook out of his pocket and looked up the address again, scanning the row of tall buildings. Rawlings had met him at the station and had assured him that he'd seen Anna here, only an hour ago, and that she hadn't left the building. He'd even told Clement that her room was right at the top.

He knocked on the door, but just as it opened two young women were leaving.

'Can I help you?' one of them asked. She had blonde hair and a pretty face.

'I'm looking for Anna,' he said, as charmingly as he could.

'Anna?'

'She's my sister.'

'Oh, well, in that case, go on up. The top landing. But if you see the landlady, don't say we let you in.'

'I won't. Good day,' Clement said, smiling. He watched the two women trot down the front steps. The one with the curly hair looked back in his direction and he tipped his hat.

And then he was inside. Somewhere in the house, judging by the smell, someone was cooking suet and he could hear music through the walls. He walked forward, leaning heavily on his cane, hope blooming in his chest when he saw his mother's coat hanging on the peg in the hallway. He touched it, seeing Anna's red beret in the pocket. He took it out and sniffed it, noticing one long, dark hair tangled in the brooch. Then he looked up at the steep stairs.

'I've got you,' he whispered, fingering the small iron bar in his coat pocket.

64

Delivering the Goods

As it turned out, Mrs Clifford-Meade was with a customer when Vita arrived to deliver the brassieres and camiknickers, and she had to wait for a while in the shop. Nancy was walking Mr Wild around the block.

Vita didn't mind the wait and she was glad that she was on her own and not with Nancy. She felt a mixture of pride and nerves as she sat with her carpet bag on her knee. Would Lulu be as impressed as she hoped she would be?

In the back room, Vita laid out the brassieres one by one and Lulu checked each one over, peering at them intently through her pince-nez. 'You've done a very good job, I must say.'

Vita knew the praise really belonged to Percy. 'I'm glad you think so. I took the liberty of making matching camiknickers.'

'Matching?' Lulu sounded surprised, as Vita pulled them from the bag.

'Why not? I think they're pretty, don't you? I think there's something nice about having a set. If it was me, I'd want matching knickers.'

Lulu nodded, impressed. 'I will see what my customers

271

think, but you know, I have a feeling there will be great demand for these.'

'I can make you some more. Any time.'

'You are quite an ambitious young woman, aren't you?'

'I don't always intend to be a dancing girl,' Vita said. 'I want to make something of this. Something of myself. Designing these . . . well, I think I've found a passion. I know that sounds silly.'

'It doesn't at all. Passion and hard work – that's what it takes. And to be bold. You know, one of your sets is going to Amelia Grey. Do you know who she is?'

Vita shook her head.

'She's a suffragette. And a bold one. She always says that one has to kick down the doors to get what one wants.'

Vita took in this information. It felt wonderful to know that something she'd invented was going to someone like Miss Grey.

'Now then, let me pay you. Have you decided on a price?'

'Well, I know you could make them yourself,' Vita began nervously. 'And I know other people are already stocking brassieres—'

'The price, Verity,' Lulu said. 'You don't have to justify yourself to me. I'm sold. If you're going to be a business-woman, then be one.'

Vita laughed, embarrassed. 'Well, in that case . . .'

She named the price she and Nancy had discussed, cross-ing her fingers, and Lulu nodded. 'It's good doing business with you,' she said, as she handed over the bank notes from the small metal box she kept in her desk. 'And here's an advance,' she said, adding more to the pile of notes. 'I want more. As many as you can make.'

As she left Mrs Clifford-Meade's to go and meet Nancy near W&T, Vita felt the same as she had that first morning she'd woken up on the train: as if life was there for the taking. She just had to hold on and keep holding on. For as long as she could. For as long as she had.

And what if she had more time? What if her reinvention had worked? And was real? Couldn't Verity Casey be not simply a dancing girl, but much, much more?

She'd been so hung up on thinking about Anna Darton and the status that she'd thrown away – how it meant she could never be with someone like Archie Fenwick.

But this, she thought, looking at her reflection in a shop window as she waited for Nancy, and feeling the bulge in her purse, *well, it changed everything*. Because she could be successful in her own right. As a businesswoman. And yes, it would be hard, but that didn't matter. She would make it successful. And then she'd be able to travel. To Paris . . . New York. Those dreams – they could be real. Couldn't they?

She saw Nancy rounding the corner, pulling Mr Wild by his lead. 'Well?' she called, and Vita grinned.

65

Miss Proust

'Miss, I'm afraid we don't allow dogs,' the door attendant said as Nancy and Vita pushed through the revolving door into W&T.

'We have an appointment with Lance Kenton,' Nancy said, as if the man were insane. 'We shan't be long.' She paused and looked back again. 'What's his secretary called again. Miss . . . ? Oh, Vita, what is her name? She's on the fifth floor, isn't she?' she said to the doorman.

'You mean Miss Proust?' he replied. 'Room six. On the seventh.'

'Thank you, my good man,' Nancy said, exaggerating her American accent, putting her hand on his lapel and pushing a note into his top pocket. He blushed.

'Are you sure about this?' Vita asked, as Nancy strode confidently towards the lift, past the shoppers. A smart-looking sales assistant was selling a felt hat to a gentleman, and he tipped it to her and Nancy as they went past.

'Suits you,' Nancy called out brazenly. She was doing her usual trick, Vita thought – of pretending that she owned the place. She knew she ought to be embarrassed, or at the very

274

least tell her to stop, but Nancy's confidence was rather magnificent.

Even so, she wished she hadn't told her what Mrs Clifford-Meade had said about Miss Grey and kicking down doors. Nancy seemed to be taking it literally. But she'd insisted on striking while the momentum was with them.

Inside W&T, Vita was distracted by the wooden counters displaying some gorgeous china brooches, and by a whole section with an array of wonderful hats. On the counter was a jar of coloured feathers. Percy would love it here.

'Come on, follow me,' Nancy instructed, heading towards the lift, past some stylish women who were trying on hats.

'But we can't just go in there and demand a meeting,' Vita whispered.

'Why not? Are you, or are you not, the girl who spoke to the Prince of Wales,' Nancy asked, clearly enjoying herself, 'and told him that you design underwear?'

'Yes, but—'

'And the girl who has just had a repeat order from one of the most discerning dressmakers in town?'

'Yes.'

'Well then,' Nancy said, as she strode out of the lift, looked at the board and scanned down it for the number of Mr Kenton's office, before hurrying along the corridor, checking out the numbered offices. When she reached number six, she didn't knock, but flung open the glass door.

The secretary sat behind a large wooden desk. 'Can I help you?' she asked, her fingers hovering over the keyboard of her shiny black Remington.

If Nancy was nervous, she didn't show it one bit. Instead she puffed up her chest and shifted Mr Wild under her arm.

'Ah, Miss Proust, I was just passing here with my latest protégée,' she said haughtily. 'I'm not sure if you've heard yet of the Top Drawer range, but, knowing Lance, it's entirely the kind of thing he'd want to know about first.'

The secretary looked wrong-footed, and Vita could tell she was scrabbling around in her memory to place Nancy.

'Is he here? Lance?' Nancy demanded, craning her neck to look through the frosted glass of the office behind her.

'Is he expecting you?' Miss Proust asked, clearly intimidated.

'No. It's an impromptu call.'

'I'm very sorry, but I'm not sure Mr Kenton has any appointments available.'

'Oh, that's a shame,' Nancy said, breathing out, as if thoroughly disappointed. 'Now that we're here. We will be back again, though. Um, Verity darling, what day is it that we're seeing Selfridges?'

Her eyes bored into Vita's, forcing her to roll with the deception that Nancy was creating. 'Wasn't it on . . . Wednesday?' she ventured.

'Oh yes! Wednesday week. That's right,' Nancy bluffed.

Miss Proust sized them up and then flipped through the pages of a large diary.

'Why don't you and your . . . associate—'

'Verity. Verity Casey,' Vita said, offering her hand. The secretary shook it limply.

'Yes . . . well, why don't you come back after that. Let's see . . .' She turned the diary around slightly so that Vita could see the pages. They were filled with appointments and she flipped over several pages. 'We're into May before there's anything. How about then? On Thursday the thirteenth, at twelve? Would that suit?'

'The thirteenth. Isn't that unlucky?' Nancy asked.

'Only for some,' Vita said, before smiling at Miss Proust. That gave her a month. It wasn't long, but it was doable. 'Book us in,' she said.

66

Roses

Having agreed to the meeting, Vita spent the next few days in a whirlwind, veering between panic and excitement. Percy was delighted that Mrs Clifford-Meade had been so pleased with her consignment, but rather alarmed that Vita had secured a meeting with W&T to present Top Drawer.

'But we'll have to look like a proper business,' he protested.

'I know. But we can do it.'

'Can we?'

'If we don't sleep. Oh, goodness, look at the time. If I don't leave now, I'll be late for the show.'

Vita hurried to the Zip Club, her mind whirring with plans. She almost bumped straight into Nancy, who was getting out of a taxi. As they reached the stage door, Jane, Betsy and Jemima were waiting for Vita. Betsy clapped her hands excitedly.

'Oh, she's here,' Jane said, shushing the others and pushing the girls aside, so that Vita could pass.

'What's going on?' Nancy asked.

'Just wait and see!' Jane grabbed Vita's arm and pushed her through into the dressing room.

Three colossal bunches of fragrant pink and white roses filled all the space on the dressing table. They were so overwhelming, it was as if the small room had been transformed into a garden, and they filled the stuffy air with scent.

'Who on earth are they from?' Jane asked.

Vita fingered the impossibly beautiful, downy petals.

'There's no name,' Nancy said, examining the blank cream envelope as she waggled it provocatively in front of the girls.

'Well, open it, for goodness' sake,' Betsy said.

Vita felt something tingling in her stomach. Could they possibly be for her? Might they be from Mrs Clifford-Meade?

Wisey bustled into the room. 'Haven't seen flowers like those since the opening night of *Tosca* at Drury Lane,' she said, approvingly.

Nancy shrugged and peeled back the flap, then took out the card inside. A large cat-like grin spread across her face.

'Dearest Verity,' she read out and Jane and Betsy gasped, Jane reaching for Vita's arm and squeezing it tightly. 'Tonight, eleven p.m. I'll tell you the secret.' She looked up, her eyes wide. 'Vita. They're for you!' she said, a tease in her voice. 'From the dark stranger!'

'You watch yourself, my girl. The flashy ones are always hiding something,' Wisey said.

'Don't listen to her,' Jane admonished. 'He must be serious, if he's had these delivered.'

'I can't meet him,' Vita said, panicking.

'Why not? It's just a man asking to see you. It's not a big deal,' Nancy reassured her. 'Go and have fun.' But Vita sensed a hint of forced bravery in her encouragement.

'I haven't got anything to wear.'

'The red,' Nancy said, nodding over to the rail.

'But that's your favourite.'

'You can borrow it,' Nancy replied, with a shrug.

She really was too lucky to have a friend like Nancy.

'But don't overdo it, kiddo. After today, let's face it, you really don't have any time for a boyfriend.'

67

Champagne and Oysters

The band, Kettner's Five, was playing 'The Girl Friend', the hit from the Broadway musical, as Archie and Vita were seated at their table by a smart and very subservient waiter. She glanced around the oak-panelled dining room, spotting the other waiters flitting between the tables, holding silver trays aloft between the well-dressed diners, the air filled with the sound of conversation, the clank of silver cutlery on bone china and the chime of cut-glass crystal.

'Doesn't it make you want to dance,' she told Archie, jangling her shoulders in time to the music. She felt quite giddy after the large glass of champagne she'd just drunk, way too fast, at the bar, and her body fizzed with nervous energy. 'Isn't she cute, isn't she sweet,' she sang along to the melody, but suddenly she felt embarrassed. Might Archie think she was singing the song about herself? *As if she might ever be his girlfriend.*

Maybe she should stop trying to behave as if she were Nancy and be more demure, but she really was *so* nervous.

'Whenever we go out dancing, we always dance to this one.'

'We?' Archie enquired.

'Nancy. And my friends Percy and Edward.'

He looked taken aback. 'That sounds like quite a cosy foursome.'

Vita laughed. 'Oh, it's really not like that at all. Percy works with us on the costumes. And Edward – he just helps us get into places.'

She bit her lip, seeing Archie's reaction. Admitting that they all used Edward for his money and status now seemed crass. She tried to make amends. 'That sounds wrong. He really is quite a hoot. In fact, you might know him. Edward Sopel?'

Archie's thin smile faded altogether now. He put his napkin down on his lap and didn't say anything. The waiter presented the menus, and the champagne bucket was brought to their table and their glasses filled. Archie ordered oysters, but his tone was overly formal as he asked her for her preference. She told him she'd take his advice, but he didn't meet her eye. What had she said? Why was he suddenly so frosty?

'Well? Do you know Edward?' Vita pressed, when they were left alone. He nodded briefly. '*And?*' Why was Archie being so guarded?

'I don't . . .' He paused. 'I don't approve of his . . . well, sort.'

'His sort?'

'He's a homosexual,' Archie whispered, his eyebrows drawn together.

Vita leant forward. 'Don't say it like that.'

'You mean, you *know*?' Archie suddenly stared up at her as if seeing Vita in a new light and she blushed.

'He's a friend,' she said indignantly. 'What he does in his

own time is nothing to do with me. But as far as I'm concerned, he's nothing but a gentleman.'

She didn't meet his eye, but fiddled with her cutlery. If Archie knew about Edward, then maybe he knew about Percy, too. What if her bragging about their friendship got Percy into trouble?

'I'm sorry,' Archie said with a sigh. 'Let's not start on the wrong foot, dear Vita. It's just . . .'

'Just what?' She felt close to tears.

'I remember Sopel from school, that's all. He got one of my friends expelled. And, before that, into the most frightful trouble. He's all smiles and charm, but in my opinion he isn't a good man. I don't like him thinking that he's a friend of yours. If I'm honest, I really don't approve of homosexuality of any kind.'

'What about women?' Vita asked.

'Women and women?' Archie exclaimed. 'Goodness me, Vita. That's even *worse*.'

She was shocked by how clear-cut his opinions were. She thought of Lolly and Ra at the club, and then of her own shameful secret with Nancy – and how horrified Archie would be, if he were ever to find out. But then her defensiveness kicked in. How could he make such sweeping generalizations, when each situation was different? Besides, she knew far more about Edward than she did about Archie himself. If he was going to judge her friends like this, then perhaps she should leave.

'People have made mistakes in their past,' she said, her voice shaking. 'And—'

'Yes, they have,' Archie interrupted hastily, putting his

warm hand over hers in a sort of absolution. 'It sounds to me as if you have so much more fun with your friends than I ever have. I'm jealous, if you must know.'

She looked up into his eyes.

'Your life is . . . different from mine. That's all. I'm not judging anyone. Least of all you. You're . . . well, you're wonderful.'

She smiled tentatively at him, touched by his compliment. Archie smiled back and then the waiter came and poured more champagne.

After that, the conversation flowed easily, and soon a whole platter of oysters arrived and was placed on a silver stand. Vita giggled, peering round it at Archie. She'd never eaten oysters before and asked him to instruct her.

She forced the first oyster down, chewing it briefly, feeling the saltiness flood her mouth and trying not to gag, reminding herself that this was the height of sophistication.

'What do you think?' he asked, watching her intently for a reaction.

'They're . . . interesting.'

'Try these ones. These are different,' he said, pointing to the oyster shell in front of her. She ate another one, enjoying it more this time. 'More creamy, don't you think? We always have them as a special treat at Hartwell. Jeffers, our butler, has a man who brings them from the coast.'

'Hartwell?'

'Our estate,' he said.

His *estate*? He said it so casually, as one might say 'our motorcar', and Vita remembered Edith's declaration that his family was loaded.

'We used to have competitions to see how many oysters we could eat in one go.'

'We?' she asked, cheekily echoing their earlier conversation, just to make sure the air was clear between them.

'Horace and me.'

'Who's Horace?' she asked, dabbing her mouth with her napkin and taking another slug of champagne. She was drinking too much, but she couldn't help it.

'He was my brother,' Archie said, before suddenly taking a sharp breath. 'The war, you know. Terrible thing . . .'

'I'm so sorry.'

She looked at him as she slowly put down her champagne glass. It was on the tip of her tongue to tell him about Clement. That she was missing a brother, too. But she couldn't. As much as she longed to share this common bond, she knew she didn't have the right to mourn with people like Archie, who lived with the hole where their brave brother should be.

Because she was glad that her brother was dead. It was a sinful, terrible thing to think, but now Vita held her breath and allowed herself to say his name in her head, testing how painful it was, like tentatively touching a scar. *Clement*. If only he could see her now. Eating oysters in a London restaurant. With someone as sophisticated as Archie. He'd go that strange puce colour he went when he flew into one of his rages. Then he'd ruin it for her.

He'd been like that over everything she'd ever possessed, every person she'd liked. Most days now she shuddered inwardly at the thought of Clement and put him resolutely out of her mind, but this was the first moment she felt triumph as well as the sickening guilt that sometimes stopped her in her tracks. Because Clement couldn't get her now, she reminded herself. Sitting opposite Archie Fenwick, she felt safe. Whatever happened in the future, it would be of her own making and not Clement's.

'Let's not be glum, my dear,' Archie said, suddenly composing himself and smiling. 'What's done is done. And, as they say, you can't change the past. So let's drink to the future.'

He raised his glass and Vita smiled, clinking her glass against his. 'To the future,' she said, smiling back at him. *Please, God, let it involve you*, she thought.

68

Georgie

Archie was a good talker. He warmed to his theme over dinner, describing the river and lake where he and his brother had fished as boys, and the tall trees they'd climbed at Hartwell. It sounded like a charmed childhood – especially the way he depicted it – as if those days had a kind of golden glow. He was so good at description that Vita couldn't help picturing it all, is if it were a movie.

'Did you ever travel somewhere special as a child?' he asked, eventually.

She shook her head, wishing he'd continue and not ask her about herself. She didn't have the courage to tell him that the wider world away from Lancashire was a mystery that she'd only read and heard about from her parents. Parents who had taught her that the world was a dangerous and unsuitable place – particularly for her. That her place was at home. Doing what she was told.

'No. My parents had a . . . business,' she said, suddenly trying to invent a suitable lie on the spot. 'We had to stay nearby. But I long to travel,' she hurried on, keen to change the subject. 'Paris, New York, Rome – I want to go every-where. Paris, mainly. My friend Nancy is going there. So she says.' She sighed for a moment, feeling upset once again at the thought. 'I wish she wasn't.'

Archie smiled at her. 'Paris isn't so far. You can visit.'

Looking across at him, she felt herself expanding – blossoming like one of those glorious blooms that had filled her dressing room. He seemed to take it for granted that dancing was something she was only doing for now, and that her horizons were much grander, as if she were on some sort of predestined life journey – the same kind as people like him did, in which foreign travel and new adventures were the order of the day. And for one dizzying moment she started to believe that she might be.

'Tell me about where you grew up,' he said.

'There's not much to tell,' she lied, as the facade of Darton Hall rose in her mind like the smoke from the chimney stacks at the nearby mills. 'My parents were ordinary folk . . .'

She pictured her mother and father, and how irritated her father would feel to be described as ordinary. But it was true. She could see that, now that she'd seen life in London. Her parents were hard-faced and stern, stuck firmly in a bygone era. She thought of the staff who cowered under her father's steely command, and the grudging respect of the workers.

'My father was never the same after the war,' she said, with a shrug. *He was richer, harder, meaner*, she wanted to say; one of the few industrialists who had capitalized fully on other people's misery. He'd positively relished the war, cheating the authorities so that Clement had been saved from fighting, on a technicality, and had stayed in the comfort of his own home.

'You said they had a business?'

She thought of the mills – that claustrophobic, horrible heat, the spinning mules eating the cotton as fast as they could. In her mind, it was like an inferno. Like hell.

'Oh . . . yes,' she stalled. 'They sold fires.'

'Fires?' Archie sounded shocked.

'You know, fireplaces for homes,' she stalled, thinking on the spot and feeling her pulse race, trying to conjure up the kind of family that a girl like Verity Casey might plausibly have. Anything that would never give any hint of the truth about Darton. 'That sort of thing. Furnishings,' she elaborated, 'antiques.' She winced inwardly, aware of the thin ice of deception that she was now treading. Fireplaces? It sounded far-fetched, even to her.

'Oh,' Archie said and she looked up. She could tell that she'd disappointed him. She could hear it in his voice, but then she realized a moment later that it was something else bothering him.

'Archie?' A young woman in a heavily jewelled dress and a mink stole was standing by their table, and Vita twisted round to look at her. 'I thought it was you!'

Vita's knife clanked against her plate and she picked up her napkin, as Archie stood to greet the young woman.

'We were expecting you earlier,' she said, sticking out her lip.

Her heavily made-up eyes danced with mischief as she looked at Archie and down at Vita, making it clear that she assumed Vita was the reason he hadn't fulfilled his social obligation. This wasn't the same woman she had seen with Archie at the Café de Paris, Vita realized. She was another one of Archie's set . . . an even prettier one.

'Do meet Miss Casey, Georgie,' Archie said. 'She's from the Zip.'

'Oh, really? Well, how do you do,' the woman said, extending her hand to Vita, who noticed her perfectly manicured nails and diamond bracelet. A sinking feeling settled in the pit of her stomach as she smiled weakly. Having just spoken of her working-class parents – albeit having invented them – the contrast between the two women couldn't be more marked.

Everything about Georgie was so groomed, and now Vita felt how tatty and home-made her red dress really was. She thought of Nancy and wondered what she would do in this situation, but inside she felt herself shrivelling.

Then Vita remembered Nancy's rule – that paying someone a compliment always bought one time.

'Oh, I do love your stole,' she ventured confidently as soon as she got a moment, deflecting the conversation away from Archie.

'Thank you,' the woman said, pulling the fur up to her chin and stroking her jawline luxuriously with it. Her diamonds sparked. 'Isn't it wonderful? It's not mine,' she added in a confidential whisper. 'It's my sister's. Maud would positively skin me alive if she knew I had it on.'

'She would,' Archie said affectionately.

'So don't you blow my cover, you,' she said, extending a finger and pressing Archie's nose. 'And I won't blow yours.'

Archie looked embarrassed.

'Don't be a stranger, Archie,' she said, giving him a look charged with meaning. 'Toodle-oo.'

Archie sat back down in his seat and didn't meet Vita's

searching gaze. What had all *that* been about? Was she an old flame of his? She certainly acted like there was far more to their relationship than she was letting on.

'Is she . . .' Vita began.

'She's a childhood friend,' he explained quickly. 'My mother is her godmother. Georgie's a little exuberant, but sweet underneath.'

69

Archie's Secret

Vita couldn't stop thinking about 'sweet' Georgie and how much she'd soured the evening, as her crème brûlée arrived. Why did she feel so unsettled? Was it jealousy? Because Georgie was so rich and beautiful? Or was it indignation? Because Georgie had ever so subtly looked down her nose at Vita? Or perhaps it was the nagging feeling – not from anything particular she'd said, but simply from her manner – that she and Archie were sharing some kind of 'in' joke.

But, as Vita kept having to remind herself, she wasn't Anna Darton. She was Verity Casey. A dancing girl who didn't have anything at all in common with Archie's friends. The kind of girl who had no right to Archie Fenwick.

She thought about telling Archie about Top Drawer, but she had the feeling it would only make things worse. Georgie most probably had her clothes made by the likes of Mrs Clifford-Meade. Telling Archie about her connection might lower her even further in his estimation. She didn't want to tell him about getting the meeting with Lance Kenton, either. Or the dubious way in which Nancy had secured the appointment. It was all too new and too fragile to stand up to Archie's scrutiny.

'Do you want to know the secret?' he asked in a soft voice, and she looked up into his earnest gaze. And she saw then that he knew exactly how she felt.

'All right then.'

She wondered if Georgie was looking back at them. And if she might be seeing this. She admired Archie for not caring, as he took her hand over the table.

And she knew that he was about to be honest. And that he deserved her honesty, too. That if she were ever to fall in love with him – which, looking into his eyes now, might be a distinct possibility – then she had to come clean herself. And tell him her secret. He deserved it. The truth.

He was silent for a moment, as if steeling his nerve, and then he spoke.

'Well, it's the damnedest thing, but you see, ever since I saw you that night at the Café de Paris and our eyes met, I haven't been able to get you out of my mind. Not for a second. It was like a thunderbolt. Like I realized: *well, there she is, old chap.*'

How could he make it sound so simple? How could he be so brave? State the truth so unashamedly and openly? She couldn't believe he'd admitted it. That he'd felt it, too. It hadn't just been her. There really had been a spark.

And now he was presenting that truth like a gift. He'd made it real. Real *and* true – and it terrified her.

'And I was going to tell you that night. When I came to see you. But then you were dancing with your friend, and I lost my nerve. And I acted . . . well, I acted like a bashful idiot.'

A round, fat silence seemed to suspend itself over them, as Archie's words, which had been so softly spoken, seemed to get louder and become a declaration. A declaration that changed everything.

But then the waiter came to pour more drinks and the moment was broken, the silence punctured, leaving only a tense husk. Archie pulled his hands away from hers and gave her an anguished grimace. The waiter fussed, wiping away crumbs on the pristine white tablecloth, and Vita watched, reeling from what Archie had said.

It had been on the tip of her tongue to grab his hand back, to say, *Me, too. I felt it. I know what you mean. This . . . thing. This thing between us is real.*

And to say those words would have been to hold his hand and jump over the precipice into the unknown.

But the crucial few seconds in which to think made her head override her heart. And now she couldn't bring herself to look across at Archie. She couldn't bear the honesty of his gaze. She was sitting right opposite him, but she felt as if she were being pulled away . . . far away – back and back . . .

Back to the past. Back to who she really was. And what she'd done.

She didn't deserve him. He was too good for her. What was she even thinking: being here . . . encouraging him? When he was wonderful and she was a criminal, someone who would never be worthy of him.

'Would you excuse me?'

Vita walked in Nancy's heels, as sedately as she could, to the cloakrooms. Inside the cubicle, she leant against the door and let out an anguished moan. Because she knew what she had to do.

70

Who Would Win?

He didn't like to think about London. It had been a relief to come home and put the whole thing behind him. And he was glad to see there was still no mention in the news of the girl in London. He wondered if she'd even reported his visit.

As the car crept along the road, he noticed that the sudden April shower had given rise to some sun. Clement stared out at the distant green hills and remembered what he'd done with a calm detachment, marvelling at how easy it had been to enter the girl's room and violate her. He doubted the girl – Suzanna, she was called – would be walking straight for a week, but it had felt good to let off some steam. And she had looked so very much like Anna. The surprise on her face, when he'd struck her, turned in his memory now. It only made him relish even more the prospect of the same look from his sister.

The low sun was shining through the windows of the pub in dusty orange shafts as Clement limped in. Rawlings was at a table in the far corner, nursing a bottle of stout. The delivery of the landlord's beer had been held up, he explained, ordering a bottle for Clement, too.

Clement was glad of the respite from the headache of the

mills and to have some time away from the sombre presence of his father, who was annoyed that Clement had employed Rawlings and yet Anna still hadn't been found. Clement, however, had defended his decision. Nobody wanted his sister brought home to heel more than he did.

'So. As you know, she was the wrong girl,' Clement said, as they drank.

'I'm sorry, Mr Darton. Truly I am. I was convinced it was her. She had your sister's coat and hat. Anyone would have assumed—'

'I know. But that doesn't change the fact that Anna has disappeared into thin air.'

Clement looked at Rawlings's inscrutable face. He owed the detective money for his work so far and it was only fair to pay him, but he baulked at this, when the result he wanted was so far out of his grasp.

'I can keep looking,' Rawlings said. 'In London, I mean. I've arranged a lift down as far as the Midlands tonight, if you want me to carry on?'

'But where will you start? Anna left that boarding house and vanished. She could be anywhere,' Clement said, repeating verbatim what his father had said.

'There will be a breakthrough,' Rawlings assured him, as Clement handed over the money he owed in a brown envelope. Rawlings looked inside at the pile of notes. Clement was glad now of the collection from the workers. He felt a perverse kind of pleasure in giving it to Rawlings, when he knew how much those families needed it. If only his sister realized how many people she was letting down.

'But what if there isn't?' Clement said.

'Well, that will depend,' Rawlings said.

'On what?'

'On whether your need to find her is stronger than her need to hide.'

Clement clinked bottles with Rawlings. He didn't need to answer that. Because if this was a contest, he would win. Of that he was sure.

71

Is He Stalking You?

Hard though Vita concentrated on banishing Archie Fenwick from her thoughts, it wasn't easy. For every time she told herself she'd done the right thing in leaving Archie in the restaurant, another voice in her head told her that she'd been a fool. There had never been anyone like Archie before.

If only she hadn't been so fixated on coming clean and airing her troubled conscience. After all, she'd been happy to lie to Percy, Nancy and the girls about who she was. They had no idea that she was really Anna Darton. So why had the compulsion to tell Archie been so strong?

Perhaps it was because she wanted to be honest with the man she fell in love with. And although it had been far too soon to tell if Archie was 'the one', he was by far and away the closest she'd ever come.

Or maybe the urge to tell the truth had simply been because Archie might have fallen in love with Anna Darton. And they might have had a real chance of happiness together. But as Verity Casey, a dancing girl at the Zip, what hope did she really have? Was Archie, as Edith had suggested, just after a fling? But he hadn't seemed the type. He'd been serious . . .

respectful. As if he genuinely cared about her. *Well, there she is, old chap*. His voice echoed in her mind.

Vita tried to play down the date with the girls, who all wanted to know if Archie was really as dreamy as he seemed to be. Vita had said that he wasn't for her, but Wisey had raised her eyebrows and made faces at the other girls, and Vita suspected they all knew that she was lying.

The only thing that was saving her from her constant tortured thoughts of Archie was making up the orders for Mrs Clifford-Meade, which took up every spare moment. Mrs Bell, impressed by Vita's appointment with W&T, sent up sandwiches and tea to Percy's room whenever Vita was working up there, and bragged to everyone she could about the new business.

Nancy, however, was quickly annoyed that Vita was so busy. On Thursday she'd announced that Percy and Vita were working far too hard. She'd insisted on taking them for tea at her favourite French café in the Haymarket, where the *millefeuille* was 'to die for'.

'Carter's – Friday night,' she'd then declared, as she'd poured a large china pot of Darjeeling tea. 'The theme is Roman. I was thinking that you could run us up a toga each, Vita,' she'd demanded. 'And I'm not taking any excuses – from either of you,' she said in such a bossy way that she'd made Percy and Vita laugh.

Vita had to admit that the tea and the delicious cream cakes did cheer her up and, after that, she'd thrown herself into the new challenge, making them costumes. She'd almost convinced herself that things were back to normal and that the whole idea of Archie Fenwick was nonsense, when Nancy nudged during her first dance of the night on Friday.

'It's him. Your fancy man – Archie,' she whispered, as they waited, counting in their cue.

'What? Where?'

'I saw him. At the back. I'm sure it's him. Do you think he's stalking you?'

Vita tried desperately to see past the lights into the smoky club as she wiggled her hips to the raucous trombone. There was a part in the dance where the girls had to whoop and cover their mouths. This week, when they'd all put the routine together, it had been fun to be provocative. They had fallen about laughing in rehearsals – joking about what a bawdy lark they were having – but now she felt self-conscious as she bent over and looked over her shoulder, aware that the dance was designed to show off the contours of her buttocks. She was aware, too, of the strings of pearls that barely covered the space left by her daringly low-cut silver top. The thick make-up on her face, her black eyeshadow and glossy red lips felt sticky and false.

What must Archie think of her provocative dance, if he really was here? And why *was* he here? To remind himself that she was only a dancing girl? Had he come here to mock her, to disapprove? To pay her back for walking out on him, the way she had?

She couldn't help feeling that the answer to these questions was an overwhelming 'yes', and it took all her strength to get through the routines with a big false smile.

She'd felt so strong when she'd left Kettner's. So resolute that she was doing the right thing – the noble thing. But now she couldn't seem to find the same resolve. Instead, she felt weak with a mixture of longing and fear. Longing to see Archie's face again, and fear that he might be horrible to her.

As Vita hurried backstage to the dressing room with the girls, Nancy was prattling away about the arrangements for the party, and it took every ounce of Vita's acting ability not to break down. Nancy – completely oblivious to the torrent of emotions that she was going through – looked surprised when Vita jumped at the knock on the door.

'Goodness, Vita. Whatever is the matter?' Jane asked.

'What if it's him?' she hissed.

'Who?' Betsy asked.

'Archie, of course.'

She remembered now how she'd played down the date with the girls – telling them all that Archie hadn't been her type.

'Oh. Well, shall I get rid of him?' It was Jemima who turned to the others as she headed for the door.

Vita shook her head, and something in her look spurred Nancy into action. She jumped ahead of Jemima and opened the door. Vita glanced in the mirror and saw that it was Archie and took a sharp intake of breath.

'Come on, girls, let's leave her to it,' Nancy said, deliberately adding lots of drama to her voice. Jane, Jemima, Betsy and Emma all left with Nancy, who tiptoed past Archie in an exaggerated way. 'I'll be out front with the others, if you need me,' she said in a loud stage-whisper. 'But don't be long. We're going to Carter's, remember.'

72

Take It From the Top

Now that the door was closed, the music from the club was suddenly muted. For a moment Archie stared at his hand on the door handle, as if he still might leave. Vita turned round so that she wasn't looking at him in the mirror, but at his back, but even the sight of that made her tremble all over. Archie Fenwick was here. Alone with her in the dressing room.

She wished it wasn't such a mess. The vases were still filled with the remnants of his flowers, but they were way past their best and petals littered the countertops.

'I'll go, if you want me to,' he said.

She felt breathless, hearing his voice. Of course she didn't want him to go.

They both started talking at the same time.

'Verity—'

'I'm so sorry—'

He turned round now and his eyes met hers.

'I mean – about . . . the other night,' she said. 'You . . . you wouldn't understand.'

'I could try.'

She owed him an explanation. And not just about why

she'd run out of the restaurant. She owed him an explanation about everything. About who she was. About her family. About Clement.

'The thing is . . . I can't possibly be the girl you want me to be,' she said. Tears crowded her, threatening to over-whelm her.

Why did doing the right thing have to be this hard?

He reached her now. 'And what do *I* want *you* to be?'

He sounded offended at the assumptions she'd made.

'I don't know. Someone who could . . .' she began, but she couldn't continue. She'd been so sure of all the arguments she'd had for not getting involved with Archie. It had seemed so logical in her mind. So impossible. And yet . . . and yet here he was. Right in front of her. 'I'm not like her.'

'Like who?' He looked confused.

'Like Georgie . . . that girl. At Kettner's.'

He let out an astonished laugh, as if everything made sense. 'It was Georgie. It was *Georgie* who put you off?'

Now he'd said it, she could see how petty she must seem to him. How vain and insecure.

'It's not just that,' she persisted. 'I'm not someone who – someone who . . .'

Tell him. Just tell him, a voice inside her screamed. *Come clean. Make him see why you could never be with him. Tell him that you're on the run. That you did something unfor-givable in your past. Something that could ruin both of your lives, if anyone were ever to find out . . .*

But the words seemed to desert her.

'Someone who could have feelings for me, too? Is that what you're trying to tell me? That this is all one-sided?'

Archie said. He sounded sad. He lifted her chin so that her gaze met his. 'Look me in the eye, Verity Casey, and tell me honestly that you didn't feel that spark, too. I've thought about you every minute of every day since I first met you, but if you really felt nothing, well, I'll go.'

She didn't say anything.

'See, you can't, can you?' he said, his face softening now. 'That's what I'd hoped. Because you've been driving me crazy. I've sat out there, trying to pluck up the courage to see you. Terrified that you'd reject me again. But you can't. Because this is real. I know how it feels, to be scared of it. Because nothing like this has ever happened to me before, either.'

Her eyes stayed locked with his as she took in the enormity of his confession.

'And I know we're different,' he continued. 'Both of us are from different worlds. And that's why we've run away from each other. Me first, and now you.' He made it sound like they were equals, when they were anything but. 'Don't you think I'm just as confused as you are? I didn't expect this to happen, but it has. And I don't know what the future may bring. But I can't live my life being afraid of what might be.'

She felt her puffed-up resolve pop. It was hopeless. Hopeless to do anything but listen to him. Because Archie was so brave and fearless and strong and, in that moment, she'd never admired anyone more.

'I don't want you to be afraid, either. You see? Because I don't want anything from you. Anything at all. Only that it fills me up with this feeling – this feeling I can't describe – when I'm near you.'

'Oh,' she said, her tears spilling over, even though she was smiling. 'Come here,' she went on, throwing her arms around him, holding him close.

'Shall we try again?' Archie said, pulling back and putting his knuckles on her cheek. 'Take it from the top, as you dancers say.'

'Yes,' she said, laughing. 'Let's take it from the top.'

It was Wisey who interrupted, bustling into the changing room. And, as the door opened, Vita knew that Nancy must have said something.

'You know I don't approve of closed doors,' she said to Vita.

'We were just . . .' Vita began, pulling an embarrassed face at Archie and hurriedly wiping her eyes.

'Leaving. We're leaving,' he said decisively. His eyes glittered at her.

Vita could feel Wisey's gaze on Archie.

'Can we go somewhere? Just to talk?' Archie whispered, as Wisey approached, clearly intent on shooing him outside.

She thought about suggesting going out front to join Nancy and the others, but she didn't want him to be scared off by Nancy again, or to encounter Edith and Mr Connelly. And even if Nancy didn't scare him off, she'd certainly insist on dragging Archie along to the toga party.

'Two minutes. I'll see you out there by the stage door.'

Archie left, and Wisey dumped all the costumes over the back of the chair.

'He's the one, is he?' she said, meeting Vita's eye in the mirror. 'The one you've been mooning over.'

'Yes.'

'Hmm, well he's easy on the eye, I'll give you that,' she

said. 'You be careful, though, Missy. He looks like a heart-breaker to me. And I've seen a few in my time.'

'Can you tell Nancy that I'm sorry, and I'll see her at Carter's later? Tell her I'll get there as soon as I can.'

'She won't be happy.'

'She'll understand,' Vita said, but even as she said it, she knew Nancy would be cross.

73

Gordon's Wine Bar

Outside, it was raining heavily and Archie put his coat over their heads. 'I don't have the car tonight,' he said and she laughed at his apologetic tone, delighted to be sheltering with him like this.

'It doesn't matter. Let's go to Gordon's. It's just down the road. Villiers Street.' She'd been there with Percy and Jane and she liked the cosy ambience of the tables down in the vaults under the stone arches. She desperately wanted to be somewhere alone with Archie, where no one would be watching or trying to eavesdrop. She wanted to savour him all to herself.

In the candlelit corner right at the back, Vita shook out her wet paisley scarf and put it over the spare chair beside her. She wondered what kind of places Archie went to with friends like Georgie.

'It's perfect,' he said, as if reading her mind, and then ordering them a carafe of red wine from the waiter. A woman in the far corner started playing an accordion softly.

'I expect you're used to smarter places,' she said.

'I have a club, if that's what you mean. The Athenaeum. You've probably heard of it?'

She shook her head. 'It's one of those gentleman-only places, I take it?'

'You don't approve? Don't tell me you're a suffragette,' he teased. She hadn't meant it to sound the way it had, but now that she had the opportunity, she felt herself being bold.

'I wouldn't mind being one. If it meant men and women became more equal.'

Archie looked surprised. 'Well, I agree actually. If you must know, I much prefer places like this, where people can just be – people . . . like themselves,' he admitted. She smiled. Archie really couldn't be further from the likes of Clement and her father if he tried.

He reached his hands across the scuffed wood and held hers for a moment. His touch was warm and reassuring.

'So here we are,' she said, grinning.

'You know it's my fault,' Archie said.

'What is?'

'All of this . . . between us. I was like a bull in a china shop. That first time we met and we danced at your club. And then I bamboozled you at the restaurant. I'm not very good at keeping my feelings to myself. Mother tells me I always wear my heart on my sleeve.'

The way he'd said 'Mother' so formally brought to mind someone strict and imposing.

'It doesn't matter,' she said. And it didn't. What he'd said about not knowing the future – that was all that mattered. 'Oh, Archie, I've felt wretched about what I did.'

The waiter placed their wine down on the table and Archie poured her a glass. They clinked the rims of their glasses together, their eyes locked.

'To us,' she said.

'To us,' he replied, before hurrying on, 'But this "us" business. I want to do things, you know, properly,' he said, and Vita laughed.

'Things?'

'You know. Taking you out. That sort of thing. Courting . . .'

Vita bit her lips together, touched by how earnest he seemed. 'And exactly how many women have you been courting?' she asked teasingly, before realizing how rude it sounded.

'Oh. Well . . .' he was blushing. 'Not many.'

'I see. What about her?'

'Who?' Archie looked confused.

'Georgie.'

'Good gracious, no! Georgie? No, she's far too much of a handful for me. And you?' he asked. 'Any dark skeletons in the cupboard that I should know about?'

She should tell him now, she realized. Now the opportunity was here, but as she looked at his face in the candlelight, she knew she couldn't. Not now. Not ever. She shook her head.

'No other admirers?' he probed. 'I bet there are. I bet the club is packed full of them.'

'No! No one. Seriously.'

He sighed and gazed at her. 'Well, now that's out of the way, I want to know everything else about you,' he said.

'Everything?'

'Every tiny thing,' he said.

'Like what?'

'Like – I don't know . . .' He smiled, his eyes shining, trying to think of something off the top of his head. 'What are your favourite flowers?'

'Daffodils, definitely,' she said, before realizing her mistake. 'Oh, and roses. Your roses were spectacular.'

'But you prefer daffodils? I shall make a note next time I'm in Harrods.'

He'd got those flowers from Harrods? They must have cost him a fortune.

'It's just, they remind me of being a child . . .' She thought of the moor behind the Hall and how much she liked riding Dante to where the field gate between the hedgerows afforded a view over the countryside: the valleys dotted with cows, the dark woods and the misty hills beyond. She pictured herself and Dante trotting along the lane, the daffodils crowding each bank.

'Was the shop near the countryside?' he guessed and she nodded, but she couldn't look at him.

Tell him, that voice told her, but she stamped it down. *Tell him about Darton.*

'No, but Archie, now we're talking about it, I do have a secret I should tell you about. You see, I'm not just a dancing girl.'

She took a sip of wine and, buoyed up with courage, told him about Top Drawer. How she'd had a genuine need for some proper underwear, because of the dancing, and how Nancy loved it and now Mrs Clifford-Meade was interested.

'Underwear?' he asked, with a surprised laugh. 'Is that what you call it?'

'Isn't that what it is?'

'Well, I suppose so, yes, but—'

'It's no laughing matter. Let me tell you, for most women it's dreadful. All wrong. It's uncomfortable and doesn't do the job properly.'

'The job?'

'Yes, of holding us in, or up, or giving us the right shape or support.'

'You've really thought about this.'

'Of course. It's something that applies to every woman. Every single woman you know.'

'I don't like to think about the women I know and their "underwear".'

'Well, you should.'

Archie laughed, but she furrowed her brow.

'Mrs Clifford-Meade says they've been wildly popular and has placed another order. And I have an appointment to present them at W&T. You know, the department store?'

And as she said it, she realized how proud she was of this business that she was starting and how much she wanted Archie to believe in her. She could see, from his expression, that she'd already gone up in his estimation.

'Vita, that's wonderful,' he said.

'I think it could be a real business,' she said. 'I mean, one day. If it were to take off. I feel foolish for dreaming about it, but the potential is enormous. My head is crowded all the time with how I could improve the design.'

Archie nodded, taking it all in. 'Why do I have the feeling that you will make it happen?'

'You think I could?'

'I have a feeling, dear Vita, that you could do anything you want,' he said.

And she realized that all she wanted right at this moment was what she had. To be sitting holding hands with Archie Fenwick in the candlelight.

74

Betsy Confides

Much later that night, when she finally got back to Mrs Bell's, Vita's head was filled with every detail of her date with Archie.

'He sounds divine,' Betsy said. 'And he's so handsome.'

'Did he kiss you?' Jane asked.

'No, but oh, I *wanted* him to.' She smiled dreamily, remembering how they'd talked and talked, and how Archie had called her a cab on the Strand and they'd stood staring at each other in the rain, the future kiss between them so tangible that they'd both laughed.

'What's he waiting for?' Betsy asked.

'He's being a gentleman,' Jane answered. 'It was only the first date. Well, second, but the first one doesn't really count.'

Vita fell back on the bed, hugging the pillow. The springs creaked. She rolled over onto her side and looked at Jane's and Betsy's eager faces. She should really have gone to Carter's to join Nancy, but after Gordon's had closed, Archie had got the cab to bring her home, and now she was glad she was in her bedroom and not at a raucous party with Nancy.

'So if he kissed you, you'd kiss him back, wouldn't you?' Betsy said.

'Yes. Yes, I would,' she replied, her voice betraying the longing she felt.

'With tongues?' Betsy clarified, and Jane bashed her back with the cushion.

'I'm only saying, because as soon as tongues are involved, he won't be able to help himself, and you don't want to get knocked up, Vita.'

In her typically dramatic way, Betsy had gone from her current state of never having been kissed by a man to being knocked up by one – which Vita was pretty sure meant getting pregnant.

'Don't scare her,' Jane said, before adding, 'You do know about the birds and the bees?'

Vita sat up and hugged the pillow to her chest, feeling a deep blush starting within her – a kind of wash of shame, when she thought about Nancy in the bath and how they'd kissed. What would the girls think, if they knew? Would they be horrified?

But that night with Nancy didn't really count, did it? It wasn't the same as how she felt about Archie. Back then she'd been naive, and high on Nancy's crazy pills. But Archie? Well, Archie was real.

'Have you seen – you know, a man's parts?' Betsy whispered. 'You know it gets big and hard? And it has to go all the way inside you?'

Jane hit Betsy again with the cushion and they all laughed.

'What she means to say,' Jane clarified more gently, 'is that sex can be wonderful. That it's not all about the man's feelings – physically, I mean. Women should feel just as much pleasure.'

314

'Really?' Vita asked.

'I don't think there's any shame in giving yourself to the man you love,' Jane said.

'Even if it doesn't work out,' Betsy said, with a sad sigh.

'You've done it?' Vita asked.

Betsy nodded.

'What was it like?'

'Oh, Vita,' Betsy said. 'It was the best thing ever.'

Vita listened wide-eyed as Betsy described her lost love, Alasdair, and how they'd first made love in his parents' bedroom.

'Weren't you scared?' Vita asked.

'No. Not at all. I wanted him. It seemed the most natural thing in the world to give myself to him.'

'What happened?'

'Alasdair would have married me. He said he was going to, but then he had an accident at the docks and he was never the same.' She tapped her forehead. 'It was awful. A real bump to the head that left him simple, and he had to live with his grandparents. I got the chance to come to London and I left, but I always wonder what might have been.'

All of her life Vita had been taught that women had to succumb to a man's will. That she should marry and be dutiful. She'd always looked at her mother and found it impossible that she'd ever conceived children. She'd seen the anatomical pictures in her father's science books in the library at home, but she'd never understood that a man and a woman's intimacy might be something pleasant.

But Betsy's experiences opened up another possibility. And with it came the realization that she wasn't wrong for feeling desire. Desire was normal. *Wonderful*, according to Betsy, who had described how natural and easy it had been. And Vita allowed a new and thrilling question to blossom in her mind until she could think of nothing else: would she and Archie ever be lovers?

'Why don't you show her?' Jane whispered to Betsy.

'Show me what?' Vita asked.

'We've got some magazines. I'll lend them to you, but you mustn't let Mrs Bell see them.'

'I won't. I promise.'

Betsy's eyes flashed at Jane, and then she climbed off the bed and lifted up the mattress and pulled out a brown paper bag.

'They're from France,' she said, so you won't be able to read them, but you can look at the pictures.

'Thank you,' Vita said, taking the mysterious package and opening it up, before gasping at the image on the front of a naked woman. 'Goodness.'

She felt herself flushing all over as she flicked through the pages and saw the images of men and women together. The others were looking at her closely.

She could feel a dull ache between her legs and her throat went dry.

'It'll give you the general idea,' Jane said.

She nodded and laughed over a couple of the pictures with the girls, but the ache was still there when they all turned off the lights. She lay wide awake in the dark, thinking of Archie and how much she wanted him. And when she dreamt, she dreamt of being naked in Archie's arms.

75

At the Flicks

The girls had agreed to meet for the newsreel the following day. Vita had been to the cinema once or twice, but the Plaza off Leicester Square was by far the most opulent place, with a thick red carpet in the foyer and gold cornicing on the ceiling. Vita noticed the ushers eyeing up the girls as they waited by the giant film poster.

When Nancy and Edith arrived to meet them, Vita went to give Nancy a big hug, but she shrugged her away. Vita wondered whether Nancy was cross that she hadn't made it to Carter's, until she realized that Nancy was swaying slightly and smelling strongly of alcohol. She grabbed hold of the rope bannister as they made their way up the shallow red steps.

'Good party?' Vita ventured as they took their seats, choosing a row near the front.

'Actually it was the best party ever,' Nancy replied, stubbing out her cigarette in the ashtray. She was cross then, Vita surmised from her tone, and from the cold look she gave Vita now. Even though Nancy always said that every party was the 'best party ever'.

'I'm sorry I didn't make it,' Vita said, wondering whether

Nancy had even been to bed. 'It just got so late – I mean, by the time we'd finished talking at Gordon's.'

'Chitter-chatter,' Nancy said meanly, making puppet-mouths of her hands. Vita felt her disapproval keenly. She hadn't intended to upset Nancy so much, but clearly she had. 'He's worth it? This lover-boy of yours?'

'Oh, Nancy,' Vita gushed, almost bursting to tell her friend how she felt, and hoping that all the emotion she was feeling would soften Nancy's mood. 'He's wonderful.'

Nancy's eyebrows knitted together. 'I thought you said he wasn't your type.'

'Oh, but he is.'

'He'd better be, if you're going to miss out on the best nights in town.'

'I won't do that again. I promise,' Vita said, but even as she said it, she knew she didn't mean it. 'It probably won't amount to anything,' she went on, feeling now as if she should play down the whole thing. But even saying those words made her feel disloyal.

'So, has he got any eligible friends?' Jemima asked, as they settled into the row of deep-red velvet seats.

'I'll ask him. He's taking me out for lunch at the Serpentine tomorrow,' Vita said.

'Another date,' Jemima commented, impressed. 'He must be keen.'

'I wouldn't be under any illusions,' Edith said. 'Because I told you before. He's just after one thing.'

'You don't know anything about him.'

'Oh, grow up, Vita. Men like *him* think girls like *us* are easy.'

'Archie doesn't think that.'

Edith tapped her forehead as if Vita was being an idiot. 'Why did he come to the Zip then? To find a wife?'

Vita was still fuming at how mean Edith had been as the Pathé newsreel started, but she was soon distracted from Edith's nasty comment by the black-and-white footage of the miners who stared back into the camera. There was talk of a strike. Vita looked at the miners' grubby faces, dismayed that their world seemed so far away. She wondered, fleetingly, how things were in the mills back home. Would her father's workers start protesting about their working conditions, too?

Then the newsreel had moved on to the latest update on the Prince of Wales and his fast friends. A montage of snapshots from recent publications filled the screen. And there, on a society page inside what looked like *Vanity Fair*, was the Prince laughing and applauding Delysia at the Café de Paris and, next to him, the unmistakable profile of a girl turning away.

Nancy let out a loud gasp. 'Oh, goodness, Vita. Look! That's you. It's *you!*'

She nudged Vita so forcefully that Vita spilt the box of chocolates Jane had passed along to her.

She blushed furiously. 'Oh my,' she said.

'Vita, you're famous,' Jane said, clapping her hands. 'Quick, let's go and buy *Vanity Fair* right now.'

'We can get it afterwards,' Vita said, feeling flushed and unsettled, glad that the newsreel had moved on.

'What's the matter?' Nancy asked. 'You don't look very excited. Aren't you pleased?'

'I don't like being in the press,' she said.

'Well, you'll have to get used to it. You can't be a shrinking violet, if you want your business to take off.'

319

76

The Serpentine

The next morning, Vita was surprised to see a protest in favour of the miners as she parked Jane's bicycle near Speakers' Corner and made her way into Hyde Park, where a man on a soap box was addressing the large crowd.

'Keep the red flags flying high,' he shouted, eliciting a cheer. Vita hurried on, but the path was blocked by a group of miners with sunken cheeks and fiery eyes. Their dark suits and grubby collars were so familiar that she felt as if they'd marched here straight here out of the newsreel pictures. They passed her and she felt unsettled by their scrutiny. She wondered what they'd do to her, if they really knew whose daughter she was.

At the tea rooms by the lake she took a table, looking out at the shadows of the clouds on the water. The miners had reminded her so much of home and now, as she thought of Clement's face – the blood trickling from his mouth, his leg bent at an odd angle – bile rose in her throat.

What had happened to Dante? she wondered. Clement would have taken him to the knacker's yard. He'd told her that's what he was going to do. And her father would have insisted upon it, when they'd found Clement's body. In her mind's eye, she saw Dante's black eyes beseeching her – a bullet hole between them. A bottomless hole, which was all her fault.

The presence of the workers she'd had to pass to get here seemed like a personal rebuke now. As if her past was crowding in on her. A reminder of all the lies she'd told Archie. What would happen to him and to his reputation, she wondered, if she was caught and brought to justice?

And then there was the small matter of her picture in *Vanity Fair*. She'd gone way up in Nancy's estimation – the picture being quite a coup with Wisey and the girls – but the whole thing had made Vita terribly nervous. She'd bought a copy straight after leaving the cinema and had studied the photograph for ages. It had been obvious to Nancy that it was Vita, but nobody else would be able to tell it was her, would they? No, of course not, she assured herself. It would be impossible to identify her. She'd changed completely: her hair, her clothes . . . everything was different.

'You look very serious.'

It was Archie. He looked extremely dapper in his light trousers and he was carrying a straw boater.

'Didn't you think I'd come?'

'No . . . yes, I mean, of course I did.'

'I'm a few minutes late because I have a present for you,' he said, lifting a small package wrapped in brown paper from his inside pocket. It was tied with string, and under the string lay two fresh daffodils.

She opened the package. Inside was a leather-bound book of poetry. He'd written on the first page. 'For dearest Vita, from Archie Fenwick,' she read out. She rubbed her finger over the black ink, thinking this was the first time she'd seen his writing. 'Thank you,' she said.

'I've marked the page with the poem. You know, the one about the daffodils,' he said. '"Beside the lake, beneath the trees . . ."'

'"Fluttering and dancing in the breeze",' she said, joining in. She put the poetry book against her chest and hugged it. 'I shall treasure it.'

Over tea and egg sandwiches, they chatted easily – about the possibility of a strike at first, and about all the miners she'd seen.

'Mother says it's a disgrace,' Archie said. 'Unlawful. She's scared of Bolsheviks, of course.'

'I think the miners should stand up for what they believe,' Vita said. 'Everyone should.'

Archie smiled kindly at her, his eyes staying locked with hers, and then the waitress came over.

'Was Nancy cross you didn't make it to the party the other night?'

'She said it was the best party ever. It must have been, as she stayed out all night.' Archie looked shocked. 'She doesn't do that all the time,' Vita added.

She felt disloyal to Nancy. Why was she trying to make herself out as more straight-edged, and distancing herself from Nancy, when she'd been more than eager to go to any party that Nancy would take her to? She felt guilty for painting Nancy as the wild one. She sensed that Archie disapproved of the time she and Nancy spent together, so she didn't tell him about the picture in *Vanity Fair*.

'My life seems very dull in comparison,' Archie said.

'You're lucky to have those girls at the club. Perhaps you'll permit me to take you all out after the show one night? Possibly to the American Bar? That's nearby. I want to meet them all.'

'And they certainly want to meet you,' she said. She restrained herself from telling him that Archie was the biggest gossip they'd had for a while. Apart from how she'd said hello to the Prince of Wales.

'That's settled then. Gather the troops and I'll do my best to keep up with you all.'

Vita felt herself glowing at the thought of another date already.

'And before then, I've booked tickets for the opera.'

Vita laughed at how keen he was.

'You do like opera?' he checked.

'Who knows? I've never been.'

After they'd finished their tea, Archie suggested that they go boating on the lake. Vita gathered up the daffodils and put one in Archie's buttonhole and the other in her hat, before pinching a few of the sugar lumps from the bowl for Mr Wild.

'I'm a good rower,' he assured her. 'We have a lake where I fish at Hartwell.'

'Hartwell. You mentioned that before.'

'I think it's the most beautiful place on earth,' he said. 'You have to see it. The woods, the skylarks – it's breathtaking really. Especially at this time of year. I'll take you there.'

She was touched that he wanted to share it with her, but even if he was serious, how would it ever be possible for her to go away with him? It was only now that it occurred to her how hectic her schedule at the Zip Club was. And with the lingerie business taking off, she hardly had any free time at all.

But the thought of being in the countryside with Archie caught her imagination and for a heady moment, as they rowed out into the middle of the lake, she pictured herself alone with him at Hartwell. And as soon as she thought that, she remembered the images in the magazine that Jane had given her. She tried to push the thought away, but pictured Archie now without his shirt.

'What would you do, if you could do anything at all?' she asked him, admiring his strong arms, now that he'd rolled up his sleeves. She ripped her eyes away, feeling the hot sensation between her legs.

'Mother wants me to go into business.'

'That's not what I asked.'

He smiled. 'What would *I* like, you mean? You know, not many people have ever asked me that.'

'So? I'm asking you now.'

He looked bashful and let go of the oar for a moment. He rubbed his cheek and looked at the water as they drifted. 'Well, if you must know, I'd like to finish my novel.'

'You write?' She was surprised, but then, no, she could imagine him typing, with that terribly serious look that he sometimes got on his face.

'You're the first person I've told about it.'

She smiled, flattered that he trusted her so much. 'What's it about?'

He described the plot to her, about a young soldier taken prisoner in the war, and she listened dreamily as he told her how he wanted to rent a villa in Italy and write in the early mornings and walk in the hills. How he felt passionately that he must say something about his generation. She pictured herself living with him, working on her designs while his typewriter clattered in another room. How they might eat their own home-grown tomatoes for lunch and she'd help him with his plot.

They talked, too, about her order for Mrs Clifford-Meade.

'I do so admire your entrepreneurial spirit,' he said. 'It's most unusual.'

'For a girl?' she asked.

'That's not quite what I meant,' he said bashfully. 'For anyone, but yes, if you must know, for a girl. Certainly none of the girls I've met have your talent or vision.'

'I guess I have nothing to lose,' she said honestly.

'You're very special,' he said, the sunlight reflecting on his face, and he sounded so sincere that she felt a strange emotion, making it impossible to breathe.

Archie sat forward and stroked a strand of her hair out of her face and stared into her eyes. Her heart hammered as her lips moved towards his.

But then they were jolted apart. A boat had crashed into theirs and a man in the other boat waved effusively, as Archie held on to the side of the boat.

'What-ho, old chap,' the man called. 'We thought it was you. Heading straight for the weeds.'

Archie looked furious. 'Oh no,' he said. 'It's Diggers, from Oxford.'

'He never could command a punt – and no better in a boat,' the man called teasingly to Vita. He was wearing a pink jacket and a boater and had red cheeks. His friend in the boat looked positively sozzled, and Vita saw that he was clutching a beer bottle, which he raised in salute. They both looked like pompous prigs, and she could tell that Archie was embarrassed.

They talked for a minute, exchanging pleasantries, but Archie didn't introduce Vita, despite Diggers clearly being curious. Then Archie made an excuse and turned the boat round and rowed back fast to the dock.

Vita asked about Diggers, and Archie looked annoyed. He told her that they were part of a set that he had tried desperately to move on from.

'Sometimes I long to reinvent myself,' he said. 'Just go away and become someone entirely different.'

'I don't want you to be different,' Vita said, but her heart was in her mouth. What would Archie say if he knew that she'd done exactly that? And, more importantly, what would have happened if they'd actually kissed?

77

A Spark of Hope

Now that he was in London again, Clement seemed to see his sister everywhere. There was a girl cycling near Hyde Park yesterday and he could have sworn it was Anna. It must be the medication Doctor Whatley had given him, he thought, or the intriguing message from Rawlings that he'd got a lead and that Clement was to meet him to discuss it.

He was meeting Rawlings at the Lyons Corner House on Coventry Street, but he hadn't expected the place to be so cavernous, or so crowded. Every table was filled with chatty young women, and Clement couldn't help scouring each face for Anna. Where had she gone, after leaving the boarding house in Bloomsbury? Could she possibly be here?

He couldn't shake the feeling that she was close.

He sat and observed the scene while he waited for Rawlings. It was a cheerful, noisy place, the high-corniced ceiling lit with bright chandeliers, the walls decorated with fancy wooden Doric columns. Behind the counter, which ran the length of the room, there were giant silver urns of tea and coffee, and the counter itself was filled with a display of cakes and all sorts of food.

'She's another fine Nippy,' he heard the man at the table

behind him say, admiring the waitress who sped past with a tray, her narrow hips swerving to avoid his groping hand. She stopped at Clement's table and put down his pot of coffee and milk and positioned herself away from the man, although she looked over her shoulder and smiled at him. She obviously hadn't minded the attention.

Clement was astounded by her self-confidence. Is that what women were like in London? He appraised her now, seeing how her smart black uniform, with the starched white linen apron and the buttons sewn on with red thread, made her look appealing. She had a nice smile beneath her monogrammed white cap.

'Tell me, is it always this busy?' he asked.

'Oh yes, sir. Never stops. We're open all through the night, you see. We serve up to five thousand people a day,' she said proudly.

And this was just one coffee shop, Clement thought. How on earth was Rawlings going to find Anna, when there were so many people?

She looked down at the newspaper he'd been reading, at the picture of the new Princess.

'Elizabeth. Such a pretty name, don't you think,' the waitress said, and Clement had to force himself not to roll his eyes. He'd never understand the sentimentality that women felt over such things. What was the point in celebrating a royal baby, if it wasn't going to be a monarch, which the new Princess most certainly never would be.

The waitress smiled, but Clement ignored her. He wasn't going to leave her a good tip, so there was no point in her trying on her friendly chat with him. He turned over the paper and then saw Rawlings come through the door and waved to him, feeling his leg ache as he stood on his stick. When Rawlings was settled at the table, Clement got straight to business.

'So? Do you have anything? Why couldn't you tell me what it was on the telephone?' he asked, knowing already what the answer would be. In a metropolis this size, finding his sister was surely an impossible task. He wondered how long it was practical to keep paying Rawlings.

'I don't know . . . maybe.'

'Maybe?' Clement was annoyed. He wasn't here on a maybe. It was a whole month since the Grand National and he had to deliver Anna to Arkwright soon, if he stood any chance of his plan going ahead.

'I'm not sure if this is anything?' Rawlings said, delving inside his jacket for a rolled-up magazine. 'I was in the tea room at the National Gallery and I happened to see a woman reading this. I bought a copy.'

Clement was confused as he handed over an issue of *Vanity Fair*. He opened the magazine to the folded-over page.

'Do you think it could be her?' Rawlings asked.

Clement stared at the long legs of the woman turning away in the picture, wearing a backless evening gown. It couldn't be Anna, could it? Dressed like that? And with . . . *with the Prince of Wales?* He brought the magazine closer to his face. 'It can't be.'

'It certainly looks like her, though, doesn't it? Although her hair is different, of course.'

Clement thought back to the stylish young woman he'd seen riding the bicycle. He was imagining things, surely. And

Rawlings was, too, if he thought this could possibly be his sister. It was absurd . . . unthinkable that she'd got so close to the future King of England. He shook his head and was about to hand the magazine back when Rawlings said, 'Only I remember that, when I asked you if your sister had any distinguishing features, you mentioned a mole on her shoulder. And it was only when I looked afterwards that I saw this.'

Rawlings now produced a magnifying glass from the inside pocket of his jacket and handed it to Clement. He pointed at the picture, and Clement leant forward to inspect it more closely. Sure enough, there was a mole on the girl's shoulder . . . and it was exactly the same as Anna's.

God damn it. The man was right.

'It can't be,' Clement whispered, feeling his pulse race.

'I'm going to make some enquiries at the Café de Paris, if you would like to come with me?' Rawlings continued. 'However tenuous, a lead is a lead.'

However, when they got there, Poulsen, the man on the door, was useless.

'I couldn't really say,' he said, scratching his moustache as he looked at the picture.

Clement nodded to Rawlings, who licked his finger and added another note to the one he had in his hand. Poulsen eyed the notes greedily.

'But she *was* here. It says here: "The Prince of Wales listening to Delysia." It was only a few weeks ago. You must remember?'

'We have all sorts in here. Mostly society types. She looks like any number of the young ladies. Could be a Tiller Girl, if you ask me, with that figure.'

'Tiller Girl?'

'You must have heard of them? The dancing troupe.'

Clement and Rawlings looked at each other.

'Only, if it was me looking for someone like that, I'd start with the theatres and clubs. Or, if she's a society sort, try the opera maybe?'

78

Opera Glasses

Vita and Archie's seats were in the royal circle of the Royal Opera House, but were no more comfortable for it, and by the end of the first half Vita was struggling to sit still. She had to admit that Lotte Lehmann made a good Countess, and Elisabeth Schumann as Susanna was a skilled actress, but the heat in the auditorium, along with the dilapidated coat with the ostrich-feather trim that Percy had found to go over her dress, didn't help. Too embarrassed to hand it into the cloakroom, she'd folded it over the back of her seat, but feathers kept sticking into her and migrating upwards and tickling her nose.

She knew she ought to be impressed by high art, but she'd never understood people's fascination with opera. It was difficult to follow the plot, despite Archie's occasional translation of the Italian libretto.

'Shall we leave?' Archie's voice was close to her ear. Vita turned to face him, nearly knocking him in the face with her opera glasses, and they both burst out giggling. 'I thought this would be a good idea, but . . .'

They escaped the opera, annoying the other audience members as they shuffled past, before running hand-in-hand down the staircase and through the grand foyer of the opera house.

Outside on the pavement, Vita laughed, breathing in the balmy air.

'Oh no!' she said, realizing she still had the opera glasses in her hand.

'Keep them,' Archie said. 'I won't tell, if you don't.'

She grinned at him and put them in her coat pocket.

'Where shall we go?' he asked.

'I don't know. It's nice to be outside. Let's go for a walk,' she suggested.

'Here, let me carry that thing,' Archie offered, holding out his arm to take her coat. 'Wherever did you get it?'

'Don't you like it? It's one of Percy's theatre creations.'

Archie raised his eyebrows. 'I can tell. You and your feathers!'

She remembered her hat at the Serpentine and how he'd laughed at her when the feather annoyed her.

'You, my dear Vita, are in need of a proper coat,' he said decisively.

She thought for a second of her mother's coat. The one she'd sold to Suzanna. It had been a very good coat, and she hoped Suzanna had made good use of it. She shuddered now to think what might have happened to her, if she'd had to stay in that boarding house. She wouldn't be here now, if it hadn't been for Nancy rescuing her – and then dear Percy.

'I'm holding out for a fur coat,' she laughed, pretending to wear one, 'something gorgeous.'

'I see,' Archie said. 'And in the meantime you're content to make everyone sneeze.'

She tucked her arm through his as they strolled through Covent Garden.

'So I take it you won't be hurrying back to the opera?' he said.

'Maybe one day. Although I'm not sure I understand the appeal. Besides, I have my fill of being in theatres. Even one as grand as that.'

'Oh, you're right. I didn't think. Sorry,' he said, stopping suddenly.

'Don't be sorry, Archie,' she laughed. 'One can't really compare the Zip Club with the Royal Opera House. They are at rather different ends of the spectrum, wouldn't you say?'

'I wanted to impress you.'

'You did,' she smiled. 'I'm sorry if I ruined it for you. I couldn't concentrate. Life is too exciting at the moment.'

'I agree. Opera is perhaps one of those things we're told we're supposed to enjoy,' he said wistfully. 'Perhaps I'll force myself to develop a taste for it, one day. Just like I might force myself to eat mushrooms.'

'You don't like mushrooms?'

He pulled a face and stuck out his tongue. She thought of Cook suddenly, back at the Hall, and of how, when Anna had been little, Cook would let her go and pick mushrooms out in the woods. That was until Clement had found out and had stopped it, claiming that Anna could well poison the whole family. How wonderful to be free of him criticizing her and stopping her every move.

'Look, we're nearly at Percy's studio,' she said, spotting the entrance to the cobbled road. She could see the lights of the tavern opposite and a glow in Percy's studio window.

'You know. I told you about him. He helps me with the brassieres. He really is my dearest friend. I'd love to introduce you, if he's still in. You have to see his studio. It's simply my favourite place.'

Archie nodded and, as they walked, Vita caught sight of them in the glass window of the Italian café. What would Giovanni, who always gave her a discount on her pastries, say if he could see her now? She felt so proud to be on Archie's arm.

'You know, I told you a lie the other day,' he said.

'Oh?'

'I do think about one person and their underwear. Almost all of the time.'

'You do?' She stopped and stared into his eyes. He nodded and looked at her lips. And then his face was moving towards hers and he kissed her.

79

Top Drawer

Vita still felt as if she were walking on a cloud – even the following day, when they all gathered at Percy's studio for the girls' fittings.

'It sounds pretty much like the perfect first kiss,' Jane said, munching on one of Percy's biscuits. He slapped her hand.

'We've got a presentation in a few weeks. You're to look your best,' he warned.

'You liked Archie, didn't you, Percy?'

'He's quite wonderful,' Percy agreed. 'You look good together.'

Vita smiled, delighted with how well their impromptu call had turned out last night. They hadn't stayed for long, but she'd taken Archie out into the secret back alley to cut through to the Strand and he'd kissed her again.

Jane jumped off the bench as Vita called her over to the dressing curtain. Betsy admired her brassiere in Percy's long mirror, turning one way and then the other.

'Once you all have your brassieres, and hopefully they fit, I want your comments, so that Percy and I can make a proto-type of the one that could potentially be manufactured.'

'So what's the plan exactly?' Jane asked. 'When we go to W&T?'

Vita looked at Nancy. 'Ask her. It was her idea,' Vita said.

'I was thinking that we could do part of our routine, maybe?' Nancy said.

'What routine?'

'What if we sang "Top Drawer" to the tune of that number we did the other day? You know the one, da da da daah.'

'And maybe that dance to go with it?' Jane added. 'Or something more ballet-like?'

She mimed a few ballet moves and poses, making the others laugh.

Jane jumped up on Percy's worktop and pulled Betsy up after her. Vita grabbed the brassiere off it as she did a shuffle ball change, as if in front of an audience. 'Top Drawer, Top Drawer, you need look no further for . . .' she sang.

Suddenly Jemima burst into harmony and Vita laughed as she climbed up next to Betsy and made up the song. Percy chucked Betsy his ivory-topped cane and she gestured for a top hat and then, with the cane and hat, she did the dance in her brassiere, standing in a row with Jane and Jemima, pointing their feet in unison.

Vita laughed, but with the made-up lyrics, they were certainly getting across the selling point of her bras.

'That's exactly what I had in mind,' Nancy said, clapping.

'But I have no idea how this man, Mr Kenton, does his orders,' Vita said.

'So what? It's a start, isn't it?' Nancy said. 'What's the worst that can happen?'

'Yes, come on, Vita, be brave,' Jemima chipped in. 'It'll be fun.'

There was a knock at the door and everyone froze. 'Oh, goodness, who could that be,' Betsy said, 'catching us all out in our smalls?'

Percy went to the door to see who it was.

'It's Ida,' he said, 'from the Adelphi.'

The young woman had a curious look on her face as she saw all the girls from the Zip Club in various states of undress, up on Percy's workbench, until Vita explained what they were doing.

'You wait till the Adelphi girls hear about this,' Ida said, admiring Nancy and Betsy in their brassieres. 'Can I tell them?'

'Sure,' Nancy said. 'But you'd better be quick. They're going to sell like hot cakes.'

80

The Mysterious Studio

Clement looked across the street through the steamed-up window, as Rawlings finished his plate of liver and onions in the small café near Earls Court Tube station. For the last five minutes he had been describing how he'd followed a young woman that he was convinced was Anna, but Clement wasn't so sure. He'd got the wrong girl once before, and with this girl he'd clearly been following a hunch.

'She was with a man? What kind of man?'

'A gentleman. Although they did kiss in the street, so maybe he has other intentions.'

Clement clenched his fist. The thought that Anna might have been cavorting around Covent Garden at the opera with some suitor made his blood boil. What kind of life was she living? Being photographed with the Prince of Wales and then being taken to the opera. Whoever she was with almost certainly didn't know who his sister really was – or what she was capable of.

'I followed her then, to a studio,' Rawlings said.

'A studio?'

Rawlings looked down at his notepad. 'It belongs to a

Percival Blake. He's something to do with the theatre. A cos-tumier, I believe.'

'And you think it was her?' Clement leant back in the chair and made a spire out of his fingers. It didn't sound like his sister, but then again, she had always had her own fashion sense. He could imagine how Anna would be drawn to such a person.

'I can't be certain, but it certainly resembled her. As I said, I was only in the area by happenchance. I went because the opera was on that evening. I thought it was as good a place as any to start.'

Clement nodded at the man's diligence. It seemed to have become a point of personal pride for Rawlings to find Anna.

'And where did she go, after she'd visited this Percival Blake?'

'Well, that was the strange thing, sir. I waited across the road in the public house . . .'

Clement noticed his cheeks flushing.

'You didn't see her leave the workshop?'

'No, sir. And I stayed until closing time.'

'So you must have missed her?'

Rawlings looked bashful. It was on the tip of Clement's tongue to remind him that he'd boasted about being one hundred per cent successful.

Clement nodded. 'Very well,' he said. 'Let's start with this Percival Blake.'

81

The American Bar

Vita knew the miners' strike was really happening when she saw a scuffle on the street outside the Zip Club on Saturday night. A couple of men – miners, by the looks of them – were shouting, and two burly policemen were trying to move them on.

'What on earth is that all about?' Jane asked, as they made their way up the street towards the Savoy Hotel, where they were meeting Archie at the American Bar.

'Haven't you been reading the papers?' Emma said. 'They've been locked out of their mines, apparently. They've been told to work longer hours for less pay.'

'That's not fair,' Jane said with a frown.

'They say everyone will come out in solidarity, but we'll see,' Betsy added. 'What will we do if everyone goes on strike?'

'Oh, do your miner's accent,' Nancy said to Vita, and then added to the others, 'It's so funny. Did you know she can do a brilliant Yorkshire accent? She's such a good mimic.'

Vita frowned. It didn't seem appropriate to do her impression now. She'd been so happily living in her bubble of the theatre and Percy's studio that she had hardly thought about the miners since she'd seen the protest in Hyde Park. But now that she glanced behind her at the desperate-looking men, she sympathized with them.

She knew their conditions were worse than those at the mill – and *they* were pretty appalling. She knew how dangerous and unhealthy the mills were, and how her father demanded long hours for the pitiful pay he gave his workers. But Darius Darton had always ignored anyone who spoke out, and few of them dared. He made no secret of the fact that he thought the strikers were nothing but communist agitators. He called them 'traitorous scum' who should be imprisoned and shot.

She thought now of the rows of workers' cottages that raked across the hillside, and remembered her mother's disdain as they drove along those streets on Boxing Day, handing out parcels of food. How Theresa Darton had always considered the workers to be so far beneath her. How she'd never thought them grateful enough.

She remembered a child – one of the mill workers' children – turning up at the back door of the Hall in December. She'd held out her hand for food, barely able to talk, and when Martha had asked what she should do, Vita's father had been outraged, setting the dogs on the little girl. Vita had run out of the back door of the kitchen to look for her, hiding a hot loaf of bread in her coat, but she hadn't been able to find her.

How far away her family's nasty, selfish, enclosed world had felt until now, but seeing the miners reminded her of home.

She remembered Harrison now, the kind foreman, and

Meg and Ruth, the ladies on the cutting-room floor. She wondered what her parents had told them about her disappearance. It pained her to think they must feel so disappointed in her.

She told herself not to be sentimental. That was her old life, and here was her new life – with a handsome man waiting to buy her cocktails. But still her conscience niggled.

'No, come on. I don't want to be late for Archie,' she said.

The girls often talked about the American Bar at the Savoy Hotel, but this was the first time Vita had been there. The bar was crowded, noisy with the chime of cocktail glasses and the tinkle of conversation. The flamboyant pianist, resplendent in tails and with a carnation in his lapel, sat at a large, shiny grand piano, singing over all the noise. Vita heard a flurry of laughter from the bar as they walked down the stairs.

She could see the girls scanning the assembled guests in the bar, waiting for them to be noticed, and Vita felt as if all eyes were on them, especially now, as the music suddenly changed and the pianist broke into the tune of the last number they'd all danced to in the club. She could tell, however, from the smiles of the well-dressed women, that the Zip Club girls were something of a novelty. Vita couldn't blame them. Their club was so much more seedy than this bar.

Archie applauded and beckoned them over to the booth he'd reserved. Vita grinned, accepting his kiss on the cheek, then tucking her arm into his as she introduced the girls. But when she caught Nancy's eye, Nancy looked unimpressed and bored.

After Archie had ordered champagne, they all settled

down in the booth and Jane started talking about how they'd started planning for the presentation, and what they were going to do, and how word had already spread to the girls at the Adelphi about Vita's clever design. They all talked excitedly until the band started playing the Al Jolson song they loved, and then they started singing in unison, 'When the red, red robin comes bob, bob, bobbin' along'. Vita could tell that Archie was embarrassed by them singing, but she didn't mind. This was how she was in their group, but even so she stayed with him in the booth when the others got up to dance.

She watched them as she snuggled closer to him, but then became aware of someone leaning over the top of their booth.

'Oh, hello, Vita,' she heard someone say. It was Annabelle Morton, the hostess from the birthday party. Vita felt herself blushing as she leant in to kiss her. Annabelle smelt of exotic perfume and was wearing a very chic black silk dress. 'I thought it was you.'

Vita smiled, flattered that Annabelle had recognized her, but her stomach clenched in sudden anxiety. Nancy had absolutely promised not to say anything, but what if Annabelle knew that it had been Vita and Nancy who had caused the flood? And – God forbid – if she did know, she wasn't going to mention it, was she?

Vita introduced Archie, aware that her cheeks were throbbing.

'Well, aren't you quite love's young dream,' Annabelle said, an amused look in her eye. 'She's quite the talk of the town, you know, Mr Fenwick.'

Vita frowned slightly, her heart beating frantically. *Oh no, oh no . . .*

'Lulu Clifford-Meade was telling me all about a fantastic young woman from the Zip Club, and I knew she must mean you,' Annabelle continued.

Archie looked surprised, but in a good way, and Vita felt relief flood through her. Annabelle didn't suspect a thing about the bath, after all. And now, as she carried on, she wanted to kiss Annabelle, each word of praise making her feel more and more puffed up and proud. Then when the music slowed and Annabelle flitted away to someone else she recognized, she waved her hand at Archie and Vita. 'You must come for dinner,' she called over.

Vita snuck a look at Archie. Would he ever consider going to dinner with her at Annabelle's? Somehow she felt as if, with such an invitation, her status had changed entirely. But Archie didn't comment. Instead he pulled her to her feet and they took to the floor for a slow dance.

'Oh, Archie, this is so much fun,' she said. 'Being out like this.'

'I like your friends.'

'And they think you're the cat's pyjamas,' she said.

'Is that so?'

She grinned at him.

'Darling Vita. Would you consider . . . ?'

'What?'

'We can only see each other for such a short amount of time. I have to drive out to Hartwell next weekend. It's the annual cricket match, and it would be marvellous if you'd come. What do you say?'

She'd love nothing more than to see Hartwell, too, but with the schedule of the shows at the club, it was impossible.

'I can't.'

'You can't or you won't?'

'I would ... maybe ... but there's no way Connelly would let any of us have a weekend off. I'm afraid it's quite out of the question. Anyway, I need to prepare now for the presentation.'

'But if you could, you would?' Archie clarified.

'Yes,' she laughed.

'Oh, Vita. Darling, darling Vita, I want to be with you so much.'

'And I do, too.'

'We'll find a way. After all, a lot can happen in a week.'

82

The Lipstick Mark

Clement had spent an enlightening few hours in the small public house opposite the studio that he was watching. He observed the locals, amazed at the different nationalities in the pub – the Irish, and the Italians in particular.

He had been planning on going back to Darton and leaving Rawlings in charge, but the railway workers had come out in support of the miners and in the past couple of days the whole country had come to a grinding halt. He'd had a cable from his father saying that the Darton workers were out, too. He knew how furious his father was, but what could Clement do when he was stuck at the other end of the country? And it was all his sister's fault that he was here.

There was much talk of the strike in the pub, and there had already been a fight between two workers, one of whom the landlord had dragged out onto the street. Clement, head down in the corner, was keeping his opinions to himself.

As the evening wore on, the workers left and the theatre folk came in and now there was music – a man with a flat cap playing popular tunes on the piano. Two bawdy girls joined him by the piano, while the barman polished a silver tankard, a wry smile on his face.

Was this the kind of crowd that his sister had been mixing with? Clement flinched as one of the girls stepped her foot up onto the velvet stool next to him. He could see the dimpled pink flesh at the top of her stocking and felt something stirring within him. Then – still singing – she parked her bottom on his knee. The other men in the bar laughed and clapped, but Clement was not amused. Her eyes, heavily made-up with kohl, flashed at him and she kissed his cheek.

He stood up and the crowd jeered, as he took out his handkerchief and wiped the lipstick mark away. He made for the door on his cane, just in time to see the man – the one that Rawlings had mentioned, Percival Blake – approach his studio door opposite.

Clement hurried as fast as his limp would carry him across the cobbles. He almost didn't make it, but just as Blake was unlocking the small wooden doorway, Clement grabbed him from behind, pressing the blade from his pocket-knife to his kidneys.

'Where's Anna? Where is she?'

'Don't hurt me.' The man's voice was high, his eyes bulging behind his tortoiseshell glasses. He dropped his keys on the cobbled road.

Clement twisted Blake's collar from behind, causing him to choke.

'I said, where is she?'

'Who?'

'Anna. Anna Darton.'

'I don't know anyone by . . . that name – I swear it,' he choked.

'She comes in here. A girl. You know her.'

348

'There are lots of girls: actresses ... dancers. I don't know. I don't.'

'Oi!'

Clement heard a shout and looked round. The girl from the tavern had come outside. 'Don't leave me, handsome,' she called.

He growled in frustration. Could Rawlings have got this wrong? He'd been most insistent that Anna had been in and out of the workshop.

Clement held Blake by the scruff of the neck for a second more, wondering what to do. Then his instinct kicked in and he pushed the man hard, so that his face hit the doorframe. It felt good to hear his skull connect with the wood. To hear his glasses smash.

Blake cried out, and Clement kicked him as he went down. Then he bent and picked up the cane that had clattered to the pavement. Yes, this would do. He liked the ivory top. It would look just the part at the gentlemen's club tonight.

83

The Coat

Vita, Jane and Emma crowded around Mrs Bell's wireless in the front room, listening to Stanley Baldwin appealing for calm. As of this morning, more than one million workers had come out on strike, and traffic was at a standstill.

Mrs Bell was full of doom and gloom about how she wouldn't be able to get milk, but Vita was happy to carry on with her sewing. It was annoying that she couldn't get to Percy's studio, but she managed to get Jane, Betsy and Emma's brassieres finished for the presentation, and a few more ready for the consignment for Mrs Clifford-Meade.

On Wednesday she walked with the girls to the Zip, her head full of how much she still had to do.

She was discussing it all with Nancy, and how and when she was next going to get the brassieres to Lulu, when Jerome came to their dressing room carrying a mysterious cardboard package with a decadent white silk bow.

'What's this, then?' Nancy asked as he set it down on the leather chair.

It was a gift, clearly, and they both knew it might be from Archie. 'It came earlier. I saw the delivery boy. Said it was for you, Vita,' Jerome said.

'Oh, so I see the strike doesn't apply to some people,' Nancy commented.

Vita unwrapped the bow, wishing she wasn't being scrutinized by Jerome and Nancy. And now Wisey stopped in the doorway to see what was going on.

Inside the box was some crisp tissue paper and, below that, something soft. Vita lifted the mink coat out of the box and held it up, as Nancy let out a slow, impressed whistle. She held it up, pressing the impossible softness to her cheek. This must be because of what she'd told Archie. About wanting to own a fur coat.

'Blimey, that's something,' Wisey said, leaning back on the doorframe.

'I can't accept it,' Vita said, suddenly putting the coat down.

'I'll take it,' Jerome said. 'I could sell it for a month's wages.'

Seeing Vita's desperate stare, he turned and left with Wisey, who laughed as she went out.

'People will think . . .' Vita began, hoping Nancy would understand.

'People will think *what*? Everyone knows you and Archie are together. They assume you're lovers. The least he can do is buy you a fur coat, for ruining your reputation.'

'We're not lovers,' Vita said, suddenly indignant. But then she remembered Annabelle at the American Bar. Nancy was right. Annabelle had assumed they were lovers.

'You're not? You mean you haven't done it?'

'Of course not. If I had, I'd have told you.'

Vita felt wrong-footed. Had going out with Archie

351

changed things so much between her and her friend? Had Nancy really thought Vita would keep something that big from her?

'Why ever not? What are you waiting for? A *proposal*?'

And now Vita understood what a fool she was being. Everything between her and Archie felt so wonderfully noble. But from everyone else's point of view . . . well, she was just a dancing girl being courted by a handsome, rich man for his own amusement.

'You wouldn't understand,' Vita said.

'Wouldn't I? Aren't you forgetting that I *know* all about you?' Nancy said. Her eyes narrowed and Vita realized she was referring to the bath. 'I know you in ways he never will.'

'Stop it,' Vita said in a panic. 'You said you'd – I mean, you wouldn't . . . ?'

'Calm down. I'm not going to break up your little romance,' she said. 'But I don't see what the hold-up is. If you want him, why haven't you taken him?'

Vita stared at her, amazed that Nancy could think that way. That people could simply be 'taken'. But then, she supposed, why wouldn't she think like that? Nancy got whatever she wanted. She prided herself upon it.

'Perhaps you haven't given him the right signals?' Nancy suggested.

'What kind of signals?'

'I don't know, but this is a pretty big signal that *he*'s serious,' she said, stroking the coat. Vita saw a look of envy cross her face. 'He wouldn't buy you a fur coat if he didn't want you, would he?'

'I guess not,' Vita said.

'So go get your man.'

Vita laughed. 'Just like that?'

'Yes, oh, but wait. You'd better take this,' she said, delving in her handbag. She pulled out a small paper bag.

'What is it?' Vita asked, looking inside.

'Birth control.'

'Birth what?'

'Just be practical. Get him to wear it. It'll stop you getting pregnant.'

Vita felt herself blushing furiously. How could Nancy be so matter-of-fact? So brazen about something so shocking?

'What?' Nancy said. 'It's the modern way. Always stay in control, kiddo,' she said, tapping Vita on the nose. 'Remember that.'

'I can't. I mean, I wouldn't know how to even begin to ask . . .'

'Stop being so English,' Nancy said. 'You don't have to apologize to anyone. Be bold. You can do it.'

Could she? Vita felt herself quaking now. Much as she wanted Archie, this seemed far too real. What would it be like, if things went further than a kiss? But Nancy gave her that look – the look that forced her into being Verity Casey, the girl who had come from nowhere and was living a dream life. The look that told her she had to grab hold of life and live it to the full. She took the bag now, with a nod. 'I can do it. You're right,' she said, trying to believe it.

84

The Prototype

Vita made her way from the theatre up the alley to Percy's studio with difficulty, as she was carrying the coat in the box. She stopped, remembering kissing Archie in this very place, and looked up at the thin sliver of blue sky way above, feeling her tummy tingling. 'Oh, Archie, what have you done to me?' she said out loud.

She was still suppressing a smile as she pushed through the door into the studio.

'Ah, there you are. Just in time for tea, as usual. So what do you think?' Percy said, as she manhandled the box onto the workbench. He was standing by the kettle, his back turned to her, and she saw him put out his arm towards the mannequin. 'For the presentation.'

There, in its full finished glory, was the latest brassiere. Only Percy had embellished it according to the girls' suggestions and had made the ribbons pink. It was wonderful. Stylish, practical and yet feminine, too.

Vita rushed over, all thoughts of Archie and the coat forgotten.

'That's it. That's absolutely *it*, although I'd go slimmer

354

still on the straps,' she said, fingering the silk and pinching it in. 'Maybe. But it looks wonderful.'

'I'm glad you like it.'

It was only now, as Percy turned round with two cups, that she saw he had a black eye, and that one of the lenses of his glasses was missing. She gasped and covered her mouth, rushing over to him.

'Percy! What on earth happened?'

'Oh, that,' he said, putting the tea down and gingerly touching his cheekbone.

She put her hand over his. 'Percy?'

'I walked into the door. Stupid, really—'

'Was it Edward?'

'No! Of course not. Some stranger attacked me. I can't really remember much about it. Only that he took my cane.'

'The one with the ivory top?'

Percy nodded sadly. She knew it had been a gift from Edward. 'Did you call the police?'

He gave her a look. 'Me? No! Besides, I didn't see the man. There were a lot of drunks about. The strike has made everyone go crazy. But I'm perfectly all right,' he said, putting both his hands on her shoulders.

'Promise?' she asked, feeling worried.

'Promise. Now you have work to do. Try it on.'

Vita frowned, but realized Percy really did want to let the matter drop. She slipped behind the curtain that Percy had rigged up in the corner of the studio and tried on the brassiere, enjoying the way it felt on her body.

'Do you want to see?' she called to Percy.

'Of course.'

She smiled, pulling back the curtain.

He stood back. 'Oh, Vita,' he said, clapping his hands together with a satisfied grin.

'Do you think people will like it?'

'They'll love it.'

'I love it, too,' Vita said, admiring herself in the mirror, placing her hands on her slim waist. 'If we get the order from W&T, then we could make some and start selling them straight away.'

Percy let out a short frustrated laugh. 'Yes, but how? That took hours. You and I are at breaking point, as it is.'

'So we need to find an investor. So that we can afford to pay someone to sew them.'

'But that would involve people – other than me – seeing how good it looks. And that might be difficult.'

She pressed her lips together, an idea forming.

'Archie,' she said.

'What about him?'

She tapped her forefinger on her lips, spying her own silken curves through narrowed eyes. 'His mother wants him to go into business.'

'So?'

'So what better business than this?'

'Well, I hardly think . . . I guess you know him better than me,' Percy said, rubbing the remaining lens of his glasses on his jumper.

'He's our best shot. So I'm going to show him,' she announced, Nancy's dare suddenly making perfect sense.

'What? Now?'

She went over to the box and pulled out the fur coat, and Percy whistled, impressed.

'Why not? Seeing is believing. We want him to invest. I'm going to show him what he should invest in.' She took hold of Percy's wrist and looked at his watch. 'I've just about got time before I have to be back for the show, but it'll be tight.'

'I'll drive you,' Percy said. 'I don't know what you're planning, but I have my suspicions. And they're not good. Come on. I still have Edward's car.'

85

Surprising Archie

Archie's house was a white stucco affair in a smart crescent overlooking Regent's Park. Vita stood on the steps, watching Percy drive away, pulling the collar of her fur coat tightly around her neck and wondering if anyone had heard the bell-pull. This had seemed such a good idea back in Percy's studio, but now that she was here – wearing only her new underwear, heels and the fur coat – Vita felt her nerve deserting her. It had been such a daring idea. Something she couldn't wait to tell Nancy about, but now she felt ridiculous. She ran her tongue over her teeth, hoping the bright-red lipstick she was wearing hadn't left any kind of mark.

What if Archie wasn't home? Or, worse, what if Archie was the kind of man who didn't take too kindly to surprises? Maybe she should go and find Percy, who had said he was going to take a much-needed evening stroll in the park for quarter of an hour. She was about to turn away when she heard footsteps and the door opened.

A butler stood in the light, on a polished chequered marble floor. His grey hair was oiled back from his wrinkled forehead.

'Good evening. May I help you?' he asked.

'I wondered . . . I mean, is Mr Fenwick in?' Vita said, determined to front this out. She flashed her most friendly smile.

The butler remained unresponsive. 'He's expecting you?'

'No. This is an impromptu call.'

'I'm afraid Mr Fenwick is occupied at the moment.'

'May I wait to see him?' she asked, jogging her knee beneath the coat, the chill of the night air reaching the top of her stockings. She almost turned on her heel and ran, but then she thought: *what would Nancy do?*

Vita seized her moment. She was damned if she was going to come this far to be stopped now. She took two steps up towards the butler, who drew back, alarmed.

'He will thank you, I promise. My name is Miss Casey. Perhaps you'd be good enough to tell him I'm here.'

The butler relented, opening the door.

The hallway was dominated by a large staircase that wound down towards the marble floor, but there was so much space, it would make the most fabulous venue for a party.

The butler reluctantly showed her through an ornate door on the right into a library. A large fireplace dominated the far wall. The mantelpiece was filled with pictures, and Vita went over to examine them, once the butler had left her alone. There were pictures of Archie and his mother, and a large black-and-white photograph of a stern-looking man in military uniform.

She turned round, surveying the rest of the room. There were two floor-to-ceiling bookcases crammed with books, both modern and old. She thought of her father's study, and of the last time she'd been in it and had stolen his money. She walked over to the desk and sat in the swivel chair, running her hand over the green leather top of the desk. It felt thrilling to be in Archie's private space. *Was this where he wrote his novel?* she wondered.

Suddenly the door opened and she jumped up.

Archie was formally dressed, the bow tie at his neck looking as if it might choke him.

'Vita! What are you doing here?'

'Surprising you,' she said, holding on to the front of the coat. She glanced over his shoulder at the library door. 'Is your butler still there?'

'No.'

'We're alone?'

He looked flustered. 'Well, yes. For a minute, but, you see, I'm right in the middle of—'

She ran across the room and kissed him hard on the lips.

'Thank you,' she said, pulling back. 'For my coat.'

He grinned bashfully. She loved catching him off-guard like this.

'It looks good on you.'

'But better off,' she said, opening her coat to reveal her underwear.

'Oh . . .' he said. 'Oh, my goodness.'

'You like it?' Vita asked, walking towards him. His eyes were wide, glued to her body. 'You said you wanted to see me in my underwear,' she teased.

He reached out for her then, pulling her towards him. She felt his hand around her breast and a deep moan escaped his lips. She felt herself responding as he kissed her hard and deep. Then, after a long moment, he gasped, pushing her away. He wiped the back of his hand across his lips, to smear away her lipstick. 'We can't.'

His cheeks were pink as he plunged his hands into his pockets.

'It's not that I want you to go. Not when you look . . . well, when you look like that. You look incredible.' He puffed out his cheeks. 'Jeepers!'

Vita looked down. 'I'm glad you like it.'

'I do.'

'That's why I'm here. Because, you see, I made it.'

'What?'

'I made it. Well, Percy helped me – but this is it. The brassiere I designed by myself. The one I'm presenting to W&T.'

'Seriously?' Archie looked genuinely shocked. 'I thought you'd been to a fancy boutique.'

'I told you: I want to be a designer. I'm setting up a proper business. Selling these.'

'Goodness.'

'And that's where you come in.'

'Me?'

'Yes. You could help me, couldn't you?'

He looked as if he'd been put on the spot. 'Well, I don't know . . .'

'But you said yourself you were looking for business opportunities.'

'Yes, but—'

'If I had a proper plan,' she clarified, 'of how I saw the business growing, would you consider it?'

But Archie was prevented from answering, because at that moment the door swung open.

A tall woman in an old-fashioned black dress with a high lace collar stood in the doorway. She looked at Archie and then her stern gaze fixed on Vita, who hastily drew her coat shut, but not before the woman had seen how little she was wearing underneath it.

'I didn't realize you had a guest,' she said to Archie, her look conveying the level of disapproval that she clearly felt.

Vita felt sick.

'Mother,' Archie said, bowing his head. Vita could see his cheeks pulsing. So *this* was Mrs Fenwick? 'This is . . .'

'I'm Verity. Verity Casey,' Vita said, proffering her free hand, while the other one kept a grip on the coat. Mrs Fenwick stayed rooted in the doorway and Vita let her hand drop. Her gaze was still on Archie. 'My friends call me Vita.'

'Oh? Would your . . . *friend* . . . like to join us,' his mother asked, 'rather than hiding away in here?' Her words were friendly enough, but there was a steely edge to her voice that made their meaning perfectly clear.

'I'm just leaving,' Vita said, looking at Archie and then back at his mother. The skin around his eyes was drawn tight. Even if his mother intended to honour her invitation, there was no way Vita could possibly stay, when she didn't have anything on underneath her coat.

'We were discussing a business matter, Mother,' he said as an explanation.

Archie's mother drew herself up, her lips a thin line, and Archie blushed even more deeply. For a second Vita was

362

confused, then she blushed too, astounded by what Mrs Fenwick had obviously inferred from his comment.

'An investment,' Vita explained, widening her eyes at Archie and trying to salvage some dignity. 'In a business. High-end. You could say . . . the future. For women,' she spelled out. 'Your son has been offered the business opportunity first, but if he doesn't grab it, there'll be other investors soon.'

'I'm sure,' Mrs Fenwick said, finally looking at Vita. 'But, you see, Archie is in the middle of entertaining, so such opportunities will have to wait until *business* hours. Archie? The others are waiting.'

Vita didn't look at him, quickly following Mrs Fenwick instead, as she left the room.

'Vita?' Archie whispered, catching her arm.

'I'm sorry. I don't know what I was thinking, coming here,' she said. She'd been so caught up in getting Archie to see her in her underwear that she hadn't considered he might be busy. Or that she might have had to meet his formidable mother.

'Can I see you? Tomorrow?' he said.

'The girls and I are going to join the protest in Trafalgar Square.'

'Then I'll meet you on the steps of the National Gallery.'

She nodded, but now the door opposite was open and Vita saw beyond it to the dining room, laid up with a full dinner service. A silver platter with a large joint of pork steamed in the middle, and the waft of delicious food reached her.

Two women rose to their feet, one older, the other younger, but dowdy-looking, her dark hair piled into an elaborate bun. They looked at Vita curiously, and then at Archie behind her.

'Goodbye, Miss Casey,' Mrs Fenwick said, holding open the front door.

86

At the Club

His father came to London so rarely, it hadn't occurred to Clement that he might still keep up his club membership, but it had only taken a couple of calls and Clement had been welcomed into the gentlemen's club and given a tiny single room in the attic for the duration of his stay in the capital.

He leant back on the green wing-backed chair in the club's breakfast room, going over what Rawlings had told him, eating the remains of his marmalade on toast. He liked the ambience of the bright room, and the men who gathered here. Over the past few days he had enjoyed some rather stimulating conversations regarding the strike, and the suffragettes. It comforted him that he'd found a place where he was amongst like-minded fellows.

He'd also become aware of a feeling of freedom. London felt like such a different world from Lancashire, and he was beginning to understand how Anna had found it so easy to cut off her old life. It felt good to take a break from all his responsibilities and the austerity of the mill, and to enjoy some fine food and wine. But he was aware now of how out of place Rawlings looked, as the detective sipped his tea from the bone-china cup, before scratching his moustache.

Clement hadn't admitted that he'd attempted to extract information from the Blake fellow. He'd been too embarrassed that he'd botched his attempt. Anyway, after the ordeal of having had to deal with that whore who'd spotted him, he'd been keen that Rawlings take over the surveillance of Blake's workshop.

'So you saw him with a girl? Was it Anna?' Clement leant in closer. Were they any nearer to tracking Anna down?

'I couldn't tell.'

'What did she look like?'

Rawlings referred to his notebook. 'She was wearing a fur coat.'

'And where did they go?'

'I'm not sure. I didn't have time to follow them. But I took the number plate of the car.' He licked his finger and flipped over the page. 'I have a friend at Paddington Green who will be able to trace it.'

Clement nodded, satisfied, and sat back in the chair. He thought briefly again of the woman in the tavern. How it had been so easy to lure her to the darkened alley. How she'd been so eager at first . . . and then *not* so. Oh yes, this was turning out to be a very enjoyable adventure.

'He says he can tell me the information by the morning. Although it's tough, with the strike. All his constables are gathering in Trafalgar Square, so I hear. There's a protest.'

'Is that so?' Clement said, his lip curling. He'd had another telegram from his father this morning, to say that Darton Mills, the press – everything was at a standstill. 'Well, I hope your friends in the police will quash any rebellion. This strike really is quite outrageous.'

87

Trafalgar Square

Vita hadn't expected Trafalgar Square to be so full. There seemed to be people protesting everywhere. She shielded her eyes, scanning the swarming crowd. Betsy and Jane were in there amid the fray with a placard.

It was a ridiculously hot day for early May, the sun scorching down, and Vita was rather enjoying flaunting her pink hat, which she'd teamed up with a pale-green sleeveless dress to which she'd added a lace sailor-collar. She was wearing her favourite coral-red sandals and had made a matching silk rose for the dropped waist of her dress. She'd hoped her demure appearance, in contrast to her fur coat last night, would put Archie at ease.

She stood nervously holding two melting ice-creams, searching every face for Archie's. And then suddenly she saw him, and her jealousy over the young woman she'd seen at his house vanished, as his face lit up in a smile.

He laughed, taking the ice-cream from her, and they sat on the steps, watching the crowd.

His eyes locked with hers, and the memory of the kiss they'd shared suddenly seemed so powerful. She looked at his lips, feeling desire rising in her.

'So, about last night,' Vita said eventually, plucking up the nerve to broach the subject of her visit. 'Your house is very nice.'

'Oh, it's not ours,' Archie said.

'Oh?'

'*Our* house has been turned into some ghastly modern flats. "Bachelor flats" they call them. Mother can't bear to have it mentioned. She carries on, pretending she owns the whole of Regent's Park.'

He gave her a look, and Vita sensed a whole world of stress behind his flippant remark.

'Was she very angry that I'd visited?'

He didn't answer for a moment, watching her lick her ice-cream. He trailed his finger up her arm. 'It doesn't matter what she thinks. What I think is that you're the smartest woman I've ever met,' he said. 'Who looks a knockout in her "underwear", by the way. I have not been able to get that image out of my head ever since.'

She wanted to ask Archie if he thought she was smarter and more talented than the girl he'd been dining with, but stopped herself. His compliment was satisfying enough and she didn't want to appear petty or jealous. She had to be assertive.

'Does that mean you'll invest?'

'Yes. Well, perhaps – yes, it does,' he said. 'How can I not, when it's the most interesting proposition I've had to date?'

'You really would? You would back Top Drawer?'

He nodded.

'Oh, Archie. Thank you. You won't regret it. I'll make you double the money. Triple. I promise.'

'But . . .' He paused.

'There's a but?' she asked.

'Yes, I mean . . . no. It's just – I'd rather any investment stayed private.'

She pulled a face and let him off the hook. 'I understand. You can be a silent partner. How is that?'

'I didn't expect to get a word in anyway,' he joked.

They chatted about her plans for the business, and she told him more about the presentation at W&T and how the girls were going to help her.

Archie listened, his eyebrows furrowed. 'But if you get a big order, it'll be expensive making them by hand.'

'I know. And demand will grow quickly, so we'll be looking into manufacturing capability down the line. I know of some textile factories in Leeds. We'll be talking to them.'

Archie looked genuinely astounded. 'How does a girl from a small village know about all this?'

Vita didn't tell him that she'd been watching her father all her life. That thinking big was in her blood.

'It can't be that difficult,' she shrugged. 'I can do it.'

'And the dancing?'

'Well, I can't do that forever,' she said. 'Besides, I want to make my own money, doing something I'm passionate about.'

Archie looked thoughtfully at her. 'That's very modern of you.'

'I am modern. Hadn't you noticed?' she said, squeezing his arm. She watched him finish the rest of his cone, and then he wiped his mouth with his handkerchief. 'I don't want to be one of those women who sits around waiting for a man to marry her.'

It had popped out, but now that it had, she realized what a daring thing it had been to say. She risked a sidelong look at Archie. They'd never come close to discussing marriage before.

'Don't you want to get married?' he asked, putting his handkerchief back in his pocket, then he hurried quickly on. 'You know . . . eventually.'

She laughed. Was that a proposal? She could see Archie thinking the same thing. He looked terrified.

'Of course. But nobody should marry anyone unless they're completely and totally in love, don't you think?'

Archie didn't say anything. 'Quite,' he replied, but he avoided her eyes. Was there something he was hiding? He wouldn't consider marrying for any other reason than love. Would he?

There was a small silence and then Vita changed the subject. 'I should join Betsy and Jane in the fray. Old Connelly is going to have a fit when they don't turn up tonight.'

Archie stopped. 'Oh? Are the girls not at the Zip tonight?'

'No, we're joining the workers. Nancy thinks it's a hoot. She's having a strike-party at her apartment.'

'And are you going?'

'Well, if they strike, I will too, obviously. But I don't think I'll go to Nancy's for very long. To be honest, I'd rather be working on Top Drawer.'

'I have a better idea,' Archie said.

'What's that?'

'Come with me to Hartwell.'

'Today?'

'Yes. Right now, in fact. If the girls are boycotting the club, then what have you got to lose?'

'But I haven't got any clothes. Things for overnight?'

'It doesn't matter. We can sort all of that out. Come on, Vita. Say yes. *Please?*'

88

A Dubious Hotel

Clement was not in a good mood as he was jostled by the crowd in Trafalgar Square. It seemed as if the whole world had descended on London, the sheer volume of bodies making it impossible to think straight.

He felt sweat dampening his armpits beneath his jacket and cursed his sister once again. The strike reminded him every moment of home and of the money the mills were losing. They had to get back into production soon or they would miss the deadline for the ships to America.

But the workers seemed only to get more fervent in their support of the miners, despite the Prime Minister appealing yet again for calm. It was outrageous that the whole country was being held to ransom like this. How dare all these workers defy their employers. Didn't they know their place?

He'd come to Trafalgar Square, knowing that Harrison and some of the other men were here from the mills. He hoped his presence would dampen their fervour, but he'd been caught in the crush and taken for one of the protesters. Someone handed him a red flag on a stick and he dropped it, grinding it under his foot.

He was relieved when he spotted Rawlings shouldering his

way through the crush towards him. Rawlings helped Clement out of the crowd and, although Clement could hardly hear him, he could tell that Rawlings was pleased with himself.

'We've got him, sir.'

'Who?'

'Blake. Percival Blake. He's one of *them*, sir.' He raised his eyebrows.

'One of who?'

'A queer,' he said in Clement's ear. 'And that's not all.'

'What do you mean?'

'The car that Blake was driving. Guess who it is registered to?' he shouted. He'd just come from a meeting with his contact at the police station.

Clement watched the men climbing up on the giant statues of the lions, like ants.

'Who?'

'None other than Edward Sopel.'

'Sopel? Should I know him?'

'Lord Sopel's son.'

Clement nodded slowly, letting this information sink in. He'd read about Sopel in the papers. He was sure of it.

They were walking down Whitehall now, and Rawlings nodded to a public house and they ducked in, away from the crowds. At the bar, Clement ordered two tankards of ale.

'I followed Blake in the car just this morning. He went to Clifford Court,' Rawlings said, once they were left alone at the end of the bar.

'What's that?'

'A hotel. The kind of hotel where people rarely stay the night.'

'I see.'

'I did some asking around. It seems that Sopel pays for a room there quite regularly.'

'Goodness.' Clement was impressed. Rawlings had certainly scored, linking this Blake character with Lord Sopel's son.

'In my experience, sir, it takes only a very small amount of pressure in this situation for the right information to come to light.'

Clement nodded and then clinked tankards with Rawlings. He'd done a good morning's work. It felt as if he were aiming a rifle and Anna was finally coming into focus on his scope. He couldn't wait to pull the trigger.

89

In the Country

As Archie's motorcar slowed along the country lanes, Vita breathed in the air, holding up her hand as blossom drifted towards her from the trees above.

'To be out of the city,' she sighed, realizing how much she'd missed the fresh air. For weeks she'd been in a bubble in London, her life revolving around the club, Mrs Bell's and Nancy's social life, but this felt like popping free.

'We're here,' Archie said, pulling the car over. He got out and reached under a stone to find a key and then unlocked some large iron gates. They squeaked loudly as he pushed them against the gravel. 'This isn't the usual entrance, but it gives the best view of the house,' he said, getting back into the car.

A long avenue of horse-chestnut trees, resplendent with their candle-like white blooms, stretched ahead and Vita couldn't help feeling nervous about what to expect. Hartwell was so dear to Archie's heart and he'd mentioned it so many times, she could see how much he wanted her to love it, too. But when the house came into view, she didn't have to pretend.

'Oh, Archie, it's glorious,' she told him and he grinned.

On one level, it reminded her of Darton Hall – inasmuch as

there was a drive up to the house and a very large porch – but whereas Darton was cold and dark, with sharp edges and mean-spirited black windows, Hartwell was altogether softer, with curved ashlar-stone bay windows on the ground and upper floors. Pink roses blossomed in urns at the front and, as they approached, a Labrador dog limped out of the doorway.

'There's Benson,' Archie laughed affectionately.

Archie came to a halt outside the front of the house and a very old manservant appeared. Vita, who had hurriedly collected some essentials from Wisey at the Zip Club, unknotted her scarf and took off her sunglasses, feeling her cheeks smarting from the wind and sunshine. A flurry of blossom whipped into a mini-tornado as she stepped out of the car.

'Hello, Jeffers, old chap,' Archie said jovially, slapping the servant on his shoulder, before crouching down to pet Benson, the aged dog. 'I've brought Miss Casey to meet you. Is Bobby here?' he asked innocently.

Archie had explained that the servants would almost certainly gossip if they thought Archie was alone with Vita, so he'd come up with a ruse. His friend, Bobby Chartwell, was coming for the cricket, but Archie had it all planned so that he and Vita could be alone tonight.

Jeffers, who seemed to be an even older version of Jenkins, the butler in London, nodded his head gravely towards Vita. 'Mrs Hopson got a wire. Mr Chartwell has been delayed. With the strike, you know. Terrible business. He's hoping to be here in the morning before the cricket.'

'Oh, bother. Looks like it's just us, Vita dear. Do you mind dreadfully?'

'Not at all.'

'Will you be wanting lunch, sir?' Jeffers asked.

'A picnic, I think. What do you say, Vita?'

'Sounds tickety-boo,' she said, remembering Nancy's favourite phrase. The servant's face remained impassive.

'Very good, sir . . . Miss,' he said, nodding his head deferentially, before shuffling back inside as Archie grabbed their suitcases from the car.

'Looks like his hips are playing up again,' he whispered to Vita.

But Vita was still on a high from being treated as Archie's equal and she smiled. She wouldn't mind betting that she was shortly to be a very hot topic of gossip amongst the household staff.

Inside, Hartwell was as lovely as it was outside. A round mahogany table housed a vase bursting with Sweet Williams. There was a large window seat halfway up the stairs. Vita knelt on it to look at the back of the house.

'Aren't the gardens lovely?'

'They were laid out by Capability Brown,' Archie informed her. 'I can't wait to show you around.'

They went along the first-floor corridor and then Archie opened a door.

'This is you,' he said.

She smiled at the small four-poster bed with the pretty coverlet of needlepoint roses. He went over and pulled back the shutters, and daylight flooded the small room with its pretty lace-covered furniture. She thought of the cold guest room in Darton and the black floorboards, and how very few guests had ever been to stay.

As Archie smiled at her, she knew there was no way she'd ever be able to sleep in such a lovely room, knowing he was in the same house. Being here with him – all alone – did that mean he expected . . . what, exactly? She didn't know, but whatever it was made her feel breathless with excitement.

'Come on, let's go and explore,' Archie said, grinning at her.

She followed him out into the corridor and he ran down the stairs two at time, before rummaging in a deep cupboard.

She could hear him saying something, but his voice was too muffled, but then he came back out. 'Roller skates,' he declared, holding up two sets of adjustable wheels. 'It's the only way to get around.'

'You're serious?'

'Quite. Mother desperately disapproves, but Horace saw them in New York and brought them home. We had great fun,' Archie said, sitting down beside her on the stairs. 'He used them on the crossing, too. Said it was the only way to get around the cruise ship.'

She smiled at him, watching his fringe fall into his eyes.

She laced the skates onto her shoes. They were too big, but they held, and shakily, with the help of the newel post, she got to her feet. She was used to skating on the pond at Darton when it got cold enough, but this was an altogether new sensation. She concentrated hard as she felt the skates on the hard tiles beneath her. She slipped a few times, Archie having to catch her elbow, before she got the hang of it.

'That's it. Come,' said Archie. 'This way.'

He set off down the corridor at speed and she had to hurry to catch up with him, holding on to the walls occasionally and trying not to upset any of the vases on the occasional tables they passed.

At the end of one corridor Archie turned suddenly, like an expert, and stopped by a grand double door. He caught her as she fell into his arms.

'I knew you'd be a natural,' he said.

He opened the door and she followed him inside, gasping at the splendour of the chandelier. He padded over the carpet to the floor to ceiling shutters and opened the brass catch. Dusty sunlight illuminated the vast room.

'Don't do that,' he said.

'Do what?'

'Look so cute that I just have to kiss you.'

He came over to her and grabbed her playfully, and Vita lost her footing and, as the wheels whipped from under her and she fell backwards onto the sofa, Archie crashed on top of her, but neither of them was hurt. She felt the weight of him pressing down on her as they both laughed. Then he tenderly stroked the hair out of her face and kissed her.

'We'll get caught,' she whispered, smiling up at him, even though she didn't want the kissing to end.

'That's the beauty of roller skates. It'll take old Jeffers an age to get down the corridor. He could never catch us.'

There was a moment when they both realized what he'd meant by 'us' – as in himself and Horace.

'Do you miss him dreadfully?' she asked, putting her hand on Archie's cheek and staring into his eyes. 'Horace, I mean?'

'Yes. Especially when I'm here. The whole place is haunted with memories.'

He stretched out his arm and lifted a silver-framed photograph from the small table next to the sofa.

'There. That's him.'

Vita wriggled from beneath him so that she could hold the photograph. The similarity between Horace and Archie was quite striking. In the picture, Archie was staring up adoringly at his brother.

'You're better-looking,' she said.

'Don't say that,' he said. 'Horace was better-looking . . . better at everything.' She could hear the sadness in his voice. 'He was so bright and clever. Really the apple of my mother's eye. And for all this time I've just kept thinking that it should have been me. Me that went to war. But I was too young to go. I guess I'll always have to live with that.'

She wished she could comfort him. Her heart ached that he had shared something so personal with her. She wished she could come clean and tell him about her own family. How she knew what it felt like to be an underling to a superior sibling. That she, too, knew the pain of never feeling good enough. The feeling of knowing that your parents love your brother more, and always will.

For one heady moment she thought about what it might be like to say the words. Let them fly out of her up to the ceiling-rose above. Let Archie be a witness as she unburdened her guilt.

But would he understand? How could she explain the daily torment Clement had put her through, without making herself seem weak? How could she explain how feeble and pathetic her father had always made her feel? How hard it had been to stand up to him? How she'd longed, all her life, to be free? That she'd always known that Anna Darton's wasn't the life she was destined to live, but that she'd found out that Verity Casey's was.

Archie was such a decent man. He'd never deliberately lock someone in a stable with an angry horse, however much they deserved it. And, worse, when Archie still mourned his own brother so desperately, hearing what she'd done quite deliberately to her own brother would be unforgivable. There was no way around it.

But how she ached to tell him who she really was. That his family and hers, under any other circumstances, might have approved of their courtship . . . encouraged it, even. She thought of her father, smoking a cigar in this very room, mixing with Archie's set. She could almost picture it.

But that would never happen. She could never risk telling Archie anything about the Dartons. As painful as it was, her secret had to stay just that.

90

The Perfect Picnic

Archie procured a picnic lunch from Mrs Hopson and, as soon as they were out of sight of the kitchen window, they held hands as they strolled down the garden and through a gate into a wood. Sunlight came in diagonal shafts through the trees, lighting up the carpet of vivid green grass and wild flowers. Butterflies danced in their path and birds chirruped high in the branches above. Vita sighed and smiled. To be alone like this with Archie, somewhere this beautiful, filled her with a happiness she'd never known. And more than that – a sense of anticipation that made her tremble inside.

'I want to show you my favourite view in the whole world,' Archie said as he led her through a tunnel cut into a giant rhododendron bush. He ducked and held her hand until they came through to the other side. Vita gasped as she took in the astounding view. Flawless English countryside swept away from them down into a valley. In the distance a river twinkled in the sunshine. Cows grazed in the field beyond.

Archie walked a little way further, then spread out the blanket from the basket in the dappled shade of the huge hornbeam.

'When I was little we used to own everything as far as the eye can see, but now it's only up to that river,' he said.

'It's beautiful,' she replied, flopping down on the rug and kicking her shoes off.

He opened the wicker hamper he'd been carrying and lifted out a flask. 'It's Mrs Hopson's elderflower, I bet,' he said, pouring some liquid into a silver cup. 'Oh, look. Jeffers put in strawberries. He grows them in the vegetable garden. They're heavenly. Here,' he said, dangling the strawberry over her mouth so that she had to lean up to reach it.

'Oh, my goodness,' Vita said. It was delicious. Archie leant over and kissed her luxuriously. She longed to tell him that each kiss felt like a door closing on her past. Like he was layer upon layer of goodness, burying everything bad that had ever happened. Each kiss was a salvation that she grabbed onto.

'How long has your family had this place?' she said eventually, breaking away. She leant back and stared dreamily at Archie, as he told her about his great-great-grandfather making a fortune abroad and how he'd commissioned Hartwell from a famous architect of the day.

'You're so lucky to have it still. So many beautiful homes have been demolished lately,' she said, thinking of two stately homes that she knew of personally in Lancashire that had been flattened in the last two years. It was even worse in Derbyshire and Yorkshire. 'I mean, I can understand why the houses go, but it seems such a shame when such a grand vision is lost.'

He smiled at her. 'You know, I can't put my finger on it, but there's something about you that doesn't add up.'

'Add up? Whatever can you mean?' she said. She looked down, feeling her heart fluttering.

'You're too bright.'

'You mean for a dancing girl?'

'That's not what I mean. You just seem a bit of a mystery to me. That's all. I mean, why don't you talk about it, Vita?'

'What?'

'Your childhood? Your family? Where you come from?'

'Because there's nothing much to tell,' she lied.

'Nothing? You're not nothing. You're everything.'

'It's boring,' she said. 'This is what matters now. Us.'

'But I want to know—'

She silenced him by putting her finger on his lips. 'Don't,' she told him. 'I don't want to talk about it because I don't want to be that person. This life – that I've made for myself – is the one I want. I'm not like you, with your traditions and family ties. It's not the same.'

The afternoon grew hotter. When the shade went, they left the picnic spot and Archie led her down to where the river opened out into a lake. She hadn't seen it from the top of the hill, but the secluded spot, surrounded by trees, was a perfect sun-trap. There was a summer house on the far side of the lake and, below them, a wooden jetty stretching out into the still water. Insects buzzed and the mirrored surface broke occasionally with rippling circles.

'Come on,' said Archie. 'Let's have a swim.'

'We haven't got any swimming costumes,' she said.

Archie laughed. 'Well, there's no one around. Horace and I always used to go skinny-dipping.'

Vita blushed.

384

'What?' Archie laughed. 'There's no point in being coy now! I've already seen you in your underwear.'

He pulled off his clothes quickly, leaving his underpants on. She watched him run along the jetty, before jumping at the end and diving in boyishly. He surfaced and flicked his hair, his face lit up in a grin. 'Come on,' he called. 'It's easy.'

'Don't look,' she said, unbuttoning her dress before pulling it over her head. She could feel herself shaking. Was she really going to do this? And if she did, didn't that mean she was giving herself to Archie?

Yes, was the answer, screaming in her head, but as much as that scared her, she didn't care. Right now all she wanted was to be with him in the water.

She stripped off down to her slip and tiptoed lightly down the jetty.

'The best way in is to run and jump,' he said, treading water, still facing away from her.

She took a dive in and the cool water was instantly delicious on her skin. She surfaced, gasping and laughing.

'The bottom,' she said. 'I can touch it. But it's muddy. Oh, and slimy!'

Archie filled up his mouth with water and squirted it in an arc. 'It's perfectly safe,' he said. 'The last of the eels went ages ago.'

Vita did a little wriggle in the water. 'Don't!'

Archie swam up to her and pinched her waist, then caught her in his arms.

She felt the cool water and his hot skin, and she moaned as he kissed her. The water sparkled all around them.

'Oh, Vita,' he breathed. 'I want you. I want you so much.'

And she wanted him, too. She thought of Betsy in their bedroom. How she'd described this feeling. How natural it felt to give yourself to someone when they were the right one.

'I want you too, but . . .'

'But what?'

'Won't you think . . . I mean, won't you think of me differently?'

'How could it change anything about the way I feel about you? Apart from to love you more.'

She stopped breathing for a moment, watching the sunlight on the drops on his eyelashes, feeling the enormity of what he'd just said. She stared into his eyes, seeing so clearly that he meant it.

'I mean it, Vita. I love you. I've wanted to tell you since I first met you. Is that crazy?'

She kissed him again. 'No, but . . .'

'We don't have to,' he said, kissing her again, more passionately this time. 'We don't have to do anything at all.'

'We do. I mean, I want to. So much.'

'Here,' he whispered, taking her hand and putting it around him, underneath the water. She felt her breath, hot and shallow, as he moved his hand with hers so that she squeezed and massaged him.

'Come with me to the boathouse,' he whispered.

91

The Boathouse

Vita was shivering uncontrollably as they entered the boat-house, but not with cold. She was aware that her thin slip was see-through and clinging to her, as Archie moved some wooden chairs out of the way and made a pile of cushions on the floor. She'd picked up their clothes from the jetty and she dropped the pile of them in the corner.

'Here,' he said. 'It's safe, I promise. No one will find us here.'

He lay down on his side and reached his arm up to her and she knelt down beside him. She could see his hardness, erect against the hairs of his flat stomach, waiting for her. She thought how strange it was that although this was the first time she'd seen a man in the flesh like this, it seemed natural. As if she'd always known his body.

'I've never done this before,' she said, her voice timid as she lay against him and she stared into his eyes.

'Oh? I thought you might have – I mean . . .'

She shook her head. Had he really thought that? Is that what Edith meant when she said everyone who came to the club thought the dancers were *those sorts of girls*.

'That sounds so rude,' Archie said, clearly ashamed. 'I didn't meant that at all. Maybe we should wait.'

'No!' she cried, kissing him. 'I want you. I want it to be you. Now.'

She looked into his eyes, a drip of water hanging from his fringe.

'Are you sure?' he asked her and she nodded, and he pressed himself against her and kissed her deeply.

'But . . . that doesn't mean – you see, I'm not that sort of girl,' she breathed as he kissed her neck.

'I know. You're mine. That's the only sort of girl you need to be.'

And then he was removing her slip and it was as if they had both crawled across a desert to get to one another; the relief felt so intense as their limbs twisted around each other and their naked torsos pressed together.

'What about . . . I mean, Nancy gave me something, but it's back at the house,' she admitted.

'Oh yes, yes,' Archie said, as if remembering. 'I have something. Wait.'

She watched as he knelt up and grabbed his trousers, rummaging through the pockets. He undid a small package, with his back turned to her.

And then he was above her, staring right at her. They kissed for ages and then he pushed into her. She gasped at the sharp pain and then she felt an untightening, a delicious yielding, as if she were a flower opening up for the first time. And then she was lost.

Afterwards they lay together, her head on his chest. She ran her fingers over the springy hairs, delighting in knowing his body. She had wondered what it might feel like, to have given herself to a man, and she felt a grin spread over her face.

Archie leant down and looked at her. 'That's a big smile,' he said. 'You look like the cat that got the cream.'

'I feel like the cat that got the cream,' she said, leaning up and putting her chin on her hands. 'I feel . . . undone.'

'Undone?' Archie questioned, a tease in his voice. 'And it's a feeling you like?'

'It's a feeling I like very much,' she said, her laugh dissolving into kisses.

They made love again then, more slowly and with more talking and laughing, discovering each other's bodies as they connected together. Both of them agreed that they seemed to fit each other perfectly.

Vita could have stayed there forever with Archie, but when the light started to fade, it was time to go back to the house. Before they did, Archie took out a pocket-knife from his trousers and carved their initials in a heart on the floor.

'There,' he said and she laughed. They kept stopping to kiss and then giggling, exploring this new knowledge that they were lovers. But then, as the house came into view, Archie stopped holding her hand.

'It's like you're my knight putting your armour back on,' she told him.

'I have to,' he said sadly. 'I know only too well that everything I do here gets watched. I bet Mrs Hopson and Sally are looking at us right now from the first-floor window.'

Vita shielded her eyes and looked at the house, wondering what they saw. Wondering if the staff could possibly know what had just happened and that everything was different. Everything. She and Archie were in love and she'd given herself to him completely. She had no idea what would happen next, but life would be altogether different.

'I shall try and look normal then,' she said, 'but I don't really feel it.'

92

Starlit Sky

Back at the house, Vita changed for dinner in her room, but when she looked at her reflection in the mahogany mirror, she blushed, then laughed. She wondered what Nancy would say. Whether she'd approve. Because this certainly felt like the most courageous, daring thing she'd *ever* done.

But the big question was: what did it mean, now that Archie had told her that he loved her? Surely that changed everything? Anna Darton was dead and gone for good. She was Archie's Vita now. Nothing else mattered.

They ate dinner together in the dining room, Jeffers serving them formally from silver platters. Vita was impressed that such formality was being observed. Clarissa Fenwick obviously had very high standards. But she'd be able to match them, wouldn't she? She could convey class and breeding just as well as anyone in Archie's set, she was sure of it.

Archie made small talk about estate affairs and the village cricket match, but she wasn't listening. She knew that, with every word, he doing his best not to catch her eye.

After supper he declared that he was off for an early night, pressing a note into her hand:

Don't for one minute think that you're sleeping alone.
Or sleeping at all. When the clock strikes eleven, meet
me in the corridor. Bring the robe from the back of
your door and the quilt from the bed. We're going to
the roof.

Vita lay in a state of nervous agitation, reliving every
moment of the boathouse, her ears straining to hear the clock
strike.

After an eternity, when the old grandfather clock started
to chime, she crept out of the bed and opened the door and
looked along the corridor. Sure enough, she saw Archie's
head poke out from the stairwell and he beckoned her to
follow him. He put his fingers to his lips.

She gathered the quilt from the bed and followed him
along the upper corridor and then to an attic room, where a
shaky electric light illuminated the shadowy eaves. At the far
end was a hatch and Archie pushed it open; they climbed out
onto the flat roof, and he pulled the quilt from her.

It was a perfect night, the sky clear with stars starting to
come out. To her surprise, Archie had already prepared for
their visit and there was a candelabrum full of flickering
candles, along with a bottle of champagne and two glasses.

'We can talk up here,' he said, twisting the wire on the
champagne cork, which flew out and the champagne gushed.
There was a distant plop as the cork landed in the fountain
in the driveway. 'You could stay in my room, but Jeffers has
the hearing of a bat. He'd be on to us in seconds.'

She snuggled into him, and Archie wrapped the dressing
gown around her. She stroked the hair on his chest.

'It's wonderful,' she said, holding out the glass.

'You're wonderful,' he said.

They drank champagne and then they kissed for ages.

'I just can't stop,' he laughed. 'You're too kissable. Is it crazy that I love you this madly?'

'Not when I love you, too.'

He stroked the hair out of her face. 'In fact I think I can safely say that I will always love you,' he said. 'No matter what.'

'You don't mean that. You can't say you'll love a person no matter what.'

He pulled back and looked at her. 'Yes, you can. You *know* when your heart is captured.'

'But you hardly know me. I mean, not really.'

'I know enough to know that you have a good soul.'

Vita felt a knot form in her throat as she thought of Clement's immobile body in the barn and the trickle of blood from his mouth. 'But what if I'm not?' she managed.

He took her palm and kissed it. 'I don't know what silly ideas you have, but I *see* you. I know that you are a decent, kind, loyal, sweet, intelligent, amazing person.' He emphasized each word with a kiss.

She felt her tears falling then.

'Why are you crying?' he asked.

'Just because . . .' she said, taking a deep, shuddering breath. She should tell him. She absolutely should tell him. That she hadn't been honest. That she'd led a whole life he knew nothing about.

'Shhh, my love,' he soothed. Come here,' and he pulled her into his arms and then pointed at the sky. 'Now look.'

She nestled into his arms, feeling hopelessly torn as she gazed at the canopy of stars. She *must* tell him, she resolved. Now that she'd given herself to him, she'd come clean. Give herself entirely.

And that was when she saw a bright light dash across the sky.

'Archie. Look! Did you see that?'

'Yes. Yes,' he said. 'A shooting star. Make a wish.'

Vita closed her eyes and wished with all her heart that she would one day be free of her guilt over Clement, and that she and Archie would be together.

'What did you wish for?' he asked.

'I can't tell you. Otherwise it might not come true.'

93

Edward Is Cornered

It wasn't difficult to locate Sopel. After a few easy enquiries, it turned out that he was a member of the club next door to Clement's own on Pall Mall. Clement and Rawlings had no problem getting past the doorman at the grand marble pillars.

The club was opulent, with a lavish marble staircase and large oil paintings of bygone military heroes on the walls. After some discreet questions to one of the liveried butlers, Clement was told that he could find Sopel at the bar on the first floor and they headed up there, following the sound of raucous laughter. Clement felt his back twinge painfully as he stumped up the steps and he was glad of Rawlings's support – his arm gently cupping Clement's elbow. He would have to make this short and sweet and then retire for his injection.

The bar was crowded with groups of loud men and was thick with smoke. A large wooden bar dominated one side, the mirrored wall behind it covered in exotic-looking bottles of gin and whisky.

'That's him,' Rawlings whispered, and Clement looked over to the young man in evening dress at the bar. He was handsome, and Clement could immediately sense the entitled air that he had about him, as he held court with a group of men. As they started to drift towards a table, he waited until Sopel was alone for a moment at the bar and then nodded to Rawlings. They walked directly towards him, standing on either side of him.

'I say, fellas, what do you think you're doing?' Sopel began, but then he saw the cane Clement was holding. He stopped and Clement felt a frisson of satisfaction to see this confident young man looking so rattled.

'Recognize it?' Clement said.

'Who the devil are you? What's the meaning of this? I am entertaining company this evening, so if you'll excuse me.'

'Percival Blake.' Clement said softly, leaning in close. The barman was pouring drinks, his back turned to them.

Edward scrabbled for words to deny it. 'I have no idea . . . no idea what you're talking about or who you mean.'

'We have pictures of you two together,' Rawlings lied. 'Meeting at your hotel. Clifford Court.'

'So there's really no point denying it,' Clement said. He gave Sopel one of his hard stares. 'And my colleague and I were thinking how unfortunate it would be if the pictures were to get into the hands of the press. Or . . . your father.'

Sopel mouthed something wordlessly for a moment. 'What is it that you want? Money?' he whispered, his gaze flitting across the room to where his friends were waiting for him.

'We just want some information from Mr Blake. That's all,' Rawlings said. Clement admired his deadpan tone.

'What information? What's he done?'

'Get him to meet you at that hotel room,' Clement said.

'There's no need for you to be present. We can do the rest. Make the call. And when he's there, call this number.'

Rawlings handed over a card with the number of Clement's club on it. 'Ask for Mr Darton.'

94

The Cricket Match

Vita finally crept back to her room at dawn, after having made love with Archie under the stars all night, whereupon she fell into the deepest sleep of her life. When Mrs Hopson woke her, it took her a moment to remember where she was. If the old housekeeper knew what Vita had been up to in the night, she didn't let on.

Embarrassed that she'd overslept, Vita hastily washed her face, got dressed and hurried downstairs. She found Archie in the breakfast room in cricket whites. Bobby Chartwell, his friend from London, had arrived earlier in the pony and trap, Archie explained, and the two men were full of bonhomie. She knew straight away that Archie had told him what had happened between them. Bobby's eyes glinted with the knowledge, and she felt herself blushing under his gaze.

Archie had told Vita that she'd 'simply adore' Bobby, but Vita didn't like him on sight. He was the kind of priggish bore, with a red face and a honking laugh, that Nancy would roundly mock, if she'd been here.

They had clearly been talking about the plans for later that evening and Vita felt a dart of apprehension. She'd been anticipating another night alone with Archie, but now that

Bobby was here, that wasn't going to happen. The grandfather clock in the hallway chimed. Was it only twelve hours since she'd left her room to join Archie on the roof?

'So, we'd better get a move on,' Archie said, clapping his hands together. She could see a flush in his cheeks. 'Can't let the side down. Can you bear to watch?' he asked her, as if she were just a friend – one who might want to spend some time alone at the house.

'I'm looking forward to it,' she lied, staring at him hard as she picked a grape from the fruit bowl and put it in her mouth. She waited for a special sign from him – a touch, a look – but Archie and Bobby were clearly excited about the match.

As they sped down the drive in the car and along the lane beside the impressive drystone wall of the Hartwell estate to the village green, Vita shivered, looking up at the grey clouds mounting. She couldn't help thinking about the last time she'd been in the car, only yesterday, and how different she felt now.

'Hopefully we'll get the match in before the rain,' Archie said over his shoulder to her. 'You can watch from the pavilion, Vita, just to be on the safe side.'

When they parked by the village green and Bobby vaulted over the low door of Archie's sports car, she still she didn't get a second alone with Archie. They were the last men to the pitch, and as Archie and Bobby hurried onto the green, she saw several men greet Archie fondly. He waved his bat over at her. 'Don't worry. They're all very friendly,' he called to her.

She blew him a discreet kiss and then made her way into the wooden pavilion and queued up for a cup of tea, looking round at the mixture of women, who were all chatting animatedly by the urn. She felt their stares as she got herself some tea, and went to the front porch with her bone-china cup and saucer to watch the game start.

'Veronica,' the woman ahead of her said, turning to Vita and shaking her hand roughly. She was tall, with a cricket jumper over her summer dress and a large floral scarf tied round her head. 'We're next-door neighbours of the Fenwicks. I've known Archie since we were this high.' Suddenly she put her teacup down on the wooden balustrade and shouted loudly, deafening Vita, 'Go on, darling. Run for your life.'

Vita followed her gaze out to the cricket green, where a young boy in a white cap was running.

'My eldest,' she explained. 'He's under strict instructions to beat his father.'

Vita smiled and nodded. 'He's here?'

'The husband? Yes . . . ghastly man,' Veronica added, but Vita couldn't tell whether or not she was joking. 'He's the bowler next to Archie.'

Vita followed her gaze to where Archie stood, surrounded now by a group of men discussing tactics.

'We're friends from London,' Vita said, wondering if Veronica was trying to guess their relationship.

'Only friends? Shame. It'd be lovely to have London people here. It's so boring. And now all the traditions are going. It's devastating that this is the last Hartwell match.'

'The last one?'

'Didn't Archie tell you? But that's why he's here.'

'Why the last . . . ?'

Veronica put a large piece of cream cake into her mouth and licked her fingers. 'Because they have to sell up. Clarissa is completely broke. The cricket green is part of the house sale.'

'Sale? But I thought . . .'

'Alas, the only way the Fenwick family can survive is if dear Archie were to find himself in changed circumstances.'

'Changed circumstances?' Vita asked.

But Veronica didn't answer, because now the spectating became rather animated. Vita joined in, shouting for Archie, and it felt good to be included with the wives, but still her mind churned with this new information. Why hadn't Archie mentioned that Hartwell was for sale, when they'd had a whole conversation about country houses? Veronica must be wrong.

The match 'tea' was actually a lunch and Archie, who had scraped to victory with his boys, was in a jubilant mood. She watched him as he socialized, longing for his eyes to search her out.

'You're looking at him as if you could eat him whole,' a woman – a friend of Veronica's – said to Vita.

'Oh,' Vita said, laughing. 'Really? I was just daydreaming.' She was making it sound even worse.

'Who can blame you? You'll have to join the queue. Everyone around here has been in love with Archie Fenwick forever. But it looks like it's too late.'

Vita wondered exactly what the woman meant. That she had been in love with Archie, but now saw that Vita had claimed him?

Veronica joined them as Archie came over, and Vita

wondered if he knew that they'd all been talking about him. She was gratified when he smiled at her, and Vita felt the woman beside her stiffen as she saw the look between them.

'Why don't you come over to ours. What do you say, Arch? Bring Vita, here.'

'Oh, no. Ron, that's so sweet, but we can't,' Archie said.

'He's got to go back to London,' Bobby said, slapping Archie on the shoulder. Archie turned, his eyes flashing at Bobby. 'Well, he's taking me,' Bobby clarified. 'Bloody strike means there are no trains, and I absolutely promised we'd be there tonight.'

'Be where tonight?' Vita's voice sounded shrill, even to herself.

'Didn't he tell you?' Bobby said and she saw Archie's cheeks go pink. 'Three-line whip at the club, I'm afraid. Pals' thing, you know. When one of us old buggers gets married, we have to give the fella a good send-off. The lads sent me down to make sure Archie puts in a show.'

'Oh? Who's getting married?' Vita asked, but at that moment there was a loud clap of thunder and everyone jumped, and all the remaining players ran for cover in the pavilion.

'I said I'd drive Bobby,' Archie said, his tone placatory. 'I'm sorry we can't stay longer. You'll come with us, won't you, Vita?'

'It'll mean being squashed in the back, old girl,' Bobby said, as if trying to put her off.

'I don't mind,' Vita replied, but she did. And she minded even more when Archie didn't meet her enquiring gaze. She'd missed Nancy's party for him – no doubt incurring Nancy's wrath – and yet he wouldn't miss a party for her? Why was he doing what this awful man said? Why was Archie going back to London, when she was quite happy to stay here with him for another night? And why hadn't he told her about needing to sell the house? Most importantly, where was the Archie of last night, who'd told her he'd love her forever?

95

Squashed in the Back

The heavens had opened by the time they got back to Hartwell and rain hammered down on the canvas roof of the car. Vita had hoped Archie might try and wriggle out of the arrangement that Bobby had insisted upon, especially over tea, when both Jeffers and Mrs Hopson expressed their concerns about it being too wet to drive. But Bobby was having none of it and, all too soon, Vita was squashed in the back, just as he'd predicted.

She sat, glowering, finding it hard to breathe as Bobby smoked in the front. It was difficult to follow the conversation, because the engine was so loud and the windscreen wipers struggled to cope with the rain. Vita shivered as a leak in the side-window blew cold spray into her face. Archie lost his grip of the tyres several times and, as the journey continued, Vita's worries turned to fear that they'd ever make it in one piece. She was relieved to see the river and the skyline of London through the gloom.

'You don't mind, do you?' Archie asked her, as he parked by the kerb on Pall Mall, next to the white stucco building round the corner from the Haymarket. With the honking motorcars and all the people on the street, it felt as if they'd been swallowed by the city, and yesterday's tranquil picnic seemed like a year ago, but Vita was delighted to be able to stretch her legs as she stepped out of the back of the car. 'I'd take you home, but we're late as it is.'

'You go, then,' she said, feeling the imposing building looming over them. 'I'll be fine. I can walk from here.' She shivered, her clothes wet from where she'd been sprayed in the car. Archie opened the boot and produced an umbrella.

'Here, take this,' he said, putting it up for her and handing it over.

She tried not to let her pent-up tears fall, as she huddled from the rain under the umbrella. She felt bereft. Archie was really leaving her. The magic of last night – of everything they'd shared – had gone.

Archie watched Bobby disappear inside the building and then he pulled her into an embrace. 'I'm sorry,' he whispered. 'Bobby is quite the world's worst gossip. I didn't want to give him any more ammunition than he already thinks he has.'

Why did it matter so much to him that she remained a secret? So what if Bobby knew? She didn't care if the whole world knew they were in love.

As if reading her thoughts, he held her face and kissed her with infinite tenderness on the lips. 'Oh, my darling,' he said. 'Today has been torture.'

She felt relief bleed through her. 'I know.' She kissed him back then, until she was pressed right against him and, embarrassed at the spectacle they were making, he moved back from her.

'Will I see you?' she managed.

'See me?' he asked, shocked. He held her shoulders and

looked into her face. 'Of *course*. Remember everything I said last night?'

How could she ever forget? She nodded, drowning in his gaze, longing for him to repeat it all.

'Well then,' he said.

'Come on, old chap,' Bobby called, coming back around the porch. 'Everyone is waiting.'

'You'd better go,' Vita said, nodding, clear at the understanding between them, although she longed to throw herself into his arms – to make him promise they'd never be apart.

96

The Cheque Book

Mrs Bell was serving supper as Vita came in. As she entered the parlour, she felt the weight of what had just happened hit her. The wireless crackled with a familiar dance tune, but suddenly Archie and his club and his friends seemed a million miles away. It was as if he'd been consumed by his world and she'd been cast back to hers, and *their* space – that magical place where the two of them could just be together – seemed to have vanished.

'Where on earth have you been? The girls said you went away?' Mrs Bell said, looking at her with knitted eyebrows. 'Casper, shoo,' she said, nudging the cat off Vita's chair.

Vita nodded, sitting down heavily in the chair, feeling too exhausted to make an excuse. She suspected that the gossip had been rife here in the house, from the way Mrs Bell looked at her now. Casper jumped back up on her lap and Vita petted him, burying her face in his fur, suddenly wanting to cry.

'Well, did you?'

'I went to see a friend,' she said, looking at the plate of ham and boiled potatoes, wondering how she was ever going to eat. She thought of Archie dining in his smart gentlemen's club, and the contrast with her boarding house couldn't be more marked.

There was the noise of footsteps on the creaky stair and Percy came in and grinned, sitting down opposite her.

'There you are,' he said, not noticing her glum expression. 'Look what came to the studio.' He handed her a thick white envelope.

Vita put Casper down and looked inside, before pulling out a cheque book. She turned it over in her hand and opened the page. 'Coutts and Co.,' she read, running her fingers over the loopy writing of the private bank's insignia. 'Proper cheques,' she said, her mind suddenly flooding with the enormity of their forthcoming presentation and what it might mean. 'Paddy Potts came through after all, thanks to Nancy.'

'Look at those,' Mrs Bell said, admiring them. 'Aren't they beautiful? Such a lovely design.' She nodded. 'This business of yours is on its way now.'

Percy leant in closer. 'It's all very well having a bank account, but it's empty,' he reminded her. 'Did you ask Archie for his investment money? We need contracts, and a lawyer, too.'

'I know, but . . . I couldn't exactly ask him. It would have seemed—'

'Inappropriate?' Percy whispered, putting it bluntly, and she winced.

'It wasn't like that,' she whispered back. 'He'll be good for the money. He promised.'

He would be good for the money, wouldn't he? Vita worried now that she'd forced Archie to make a commitment, when he might not have as much money as she'd thought, if his mother was having to sell Hartwell.

But they still had the house in London – albeit rented. Anyway, she shouldn't listen to other people's gossip. Who knew what Archie's finances were really like?

'Well, eat up. It's just as well you're back. We have work to do, if you want this presentation to be any good. It's only five days away.'

After dinner she helped Percy in his room, making up the bras on the sewing machine for Mrs Clifford-Meade. At least she was getting better and faster all the time.

They listened to the comedy show on the wireless, but Vita was in no mood to laugh. She knew she wasn't being logical. She knew that Archie was – right at this minute – at a party, but she longed for one tiny word of reassurance.

'So I take it things went well,' Percy said, as the news came on and he turned down the wireless. They were both bored of the strike.

'They went very well, until his friend turned up and ruined it.'

'And this Archie fellow – he's the one, is he?'

'Oh, Percy,' Vita cried, putting down her sewing. 'If being in love is like this, I can't bear it.'

'Welcome to the world, kiddo,' he chuckled in an American accent.

They worked on in silence. Vita longed to tell him everything – how magical it had been at Hartwell – but she worried now that if she admitted what she'd done, Percy would think less of her. She hadn't made a mistake, had she?

She pinned the fabric, pressing the seam beneath the foot of the sewing machine, but she was hardly concentrating, her mind filled with thoughts of Archie on the roof. He'd meant what he'd said, she knew it. Under those stars, there really had been true love. Of that she was sure. She had to hold on to that.

'Are you going out with Edward tonight?' she asked Percy eventually, once she'd finished the seam.

'He wanted to meet, but I won't see him until we're all sorted for the presentation. I told him I had other priorities. I think it's good to say no to him once in a while. It must have worked, because he's invited me to the hotel, but I said I wouldn't be available until Thursday.'

'Goodness. Thursday,' she said, thinking about the presentation and wishing that she could be like Percy and focus.

'It's going to be great,' he said, grinning. 'I think Top Drawer is going to be a big hit.'

'You think so?'

Percy gave her a quizzical look. 'Come on! Where's my Vita gone? You're so quiet. Where is my ray of sunshine?'

'I'm here,' she said, with a sad smile. 'I'm just tired, that's all.'

Later, in her room, she undressed slowly, remembering how it had felt to be naked in Archie's arms. Had it only been last night?

She tried to remember everything he'd said – how he'd declared that he loved her, and would love her forever. It should be enough, but somehow it wasn't.

But Archie loved her, she reminded herself. He'd told her over and over again. She wasn't sure exactly how, but they would find a way to be together. She had to have faith. She *must* have faith, she told herself.

97

Tickets to Paris

Vita woke to the sound of the wood pigeons on the chimney and lay in bed fretting, as relentless questions pecked at her mind. Where was Archie now? What was he doing? Who was he with? What had the party at the club been like? Which one of his friends was getting married? Would he invite her to go with him to the wedding? And if he did, what would she wear?

She kept reminding herself of what he'd said on the roof-top – that he loved her and always would – but being apart so suddenly like this was torture. Unable to bear being in the house any longer, she got up and got dressed. She had a couple of hours to spare before she had to meet Percy in the workshop.

She was out of breath from the bicycle ride across town when she got to Nancy's apartment. Nancy was wearing a camisole and a long, billowing silk dressing gown and sun-glasses – even though she was indoors. Her toenails were freshly painted bright red and she held her hands up, as her fingernails were drying. 'Paris red,' she explained.

'Oh,' Vita said, remembering with a jolt that Nancy was still planning on leaving, to go to Paris.

'So,' Nancy said, cupping her hand and blowing on her fingernails as she surveyed Vita, sliding her glasses down her nose. 'You finally did the deed, then?'

Was it that obvious? Vita bit her lip, concerned now that there was something in Nancy's tone she hadn't heard before. Something cruel. She'd thought Nancy would be proud of her for being so daring. 'Don't say it like that.'

'Like what?'

'Like I've done something wrong. I thought you'd be pleased. For me.'

But as soon as she said it, Vita knew it wasn't the truth. A part of her had known all along that Nancy would be jealous. Maybe she'd somehow hoped that losing her virginity to Archie might give her some kind of status, but now she wished she'd gone straight to Percy's studio.

Nancy relented, pulling her into an embrace. 'I am, I am. Just annoyed that you missed my party. So come on in and tell me all about it. Excuse the mess,' she said, gesturing to the stacks of glasses teetering on the tables. Records were scattered all over the carpet. A breeze blew in through the open balcony door, but the air was still thick with smoke. Through the open door to Nancy's bedroom, she saw two people sprawled asleep under the black cover.

'Come in the kitchen,' Nancy said, lighting up a cigarette.

Vita sat on Nancy's chair and cuddled Mr Wild as she relived every moment of her night away with Archie.

'But now I feel . . . I don't know. Like he's keeping things from me,' she said, immeasurably cheered to get all this off her chest. 'Like I'm not seeing the whole picture.'

Nancy sighed and took off her sunglasses. She pinched

the bridge of her nose. 'Oh, for goodness' sake, Vita, I won't have you losing your head over a silly man.'

'He's not a silly man.'

'Of course he is. To have treated you like that. He doesn't deserve you.'

Vita hadn't expected Nancy to react like this, and much as she wanted to defend Archie, he had been a bit mean – *hadn't he?* It had never occurred to her that Archie might not be good enough for her. Only the other way round.

'Anyway I have exciting news, too,' Nancy said. 'I've bought a ticket to Paris. Well, two. One for me and one for you.'

She went over to the sideboard and took out two paper tickets for Le Train Bleu from the drawer. She put them down on the table and Vita picked up one of them. She stared at Nancy, then back at the ticket. It was leaving next weekend. How could Nancy be so sure that the strike would be over by then and that travel to France would be possible? But then she remembered that events inevitably conspired for Nancy to get her own way.

'But the presentation? It's on Thursday.'

'Oh,' Nancy said, and Vita saw that she'd entirely forgotten.

'So there'll be orders, won't there?' Vita said. 'Well, hopefully there will be.'

'And?'

'And so . . . I can't possibly come with you. I thought you wanted me to do Top Drawer. It was *your idea*,' Vita said.

'You could run it from Paris,' Nancy said, with a shrug. 'Why not?'

414

'Because . . . because everything is here. And Percy. I can't do it without Percy.'

'You mean *Archie* is here,' Nancy said, looking put out.

Vita resented the way Nancy was making her feel as if she had to choose between Nancy and Archie.

'Yes. Archie is here. My whole life is here.'

'But I've booked the tickets now. All this strike business is so dreary. Come on, Vita. Don't you want to get out of here? Have another adventure?'

'No,' Vita said, aghast that Nancy was behaving like this. How could she describe the strike as dreary? Didn't she have any real idea what it was like, for real people out in the real world?

As for having an adventure? Well, hers had only just started. And she'd thought Nancy would be sharing it with her. For a moment Vita considered begging her to stay, and articulating how much she wanted her help with Top Drawer, but she could tell from Nancy's haughty look that it would be pointless. She had made up her mind.

'Well, you'll be missing out,' Nancy said.

98

The Presentation

Mrs Bell paced in front of the wireless.

'Can you believe this? They derailed the Flying Scotsman,' she said, turning off the news, which had been on constantly since the weekend. She'd been following every detail of the strike, and Vita had been getting regular updates.

'It can't last forever,' she said.

'Everything feels so odd, doesn't it?' Mrs Bell went on. 'I don't like seeing the army trucks. And goodness only knows when we'll get more milk.'

Vita picked up an apple from the fruit bowl on the sideboard and bit it. She squeezed Mrs Bell's arm.

'Are you sure your presentation will go ahead?'

'There's no reason why it won't,' Vita said, wistfully, thinking of how enthusiastic she'd felt at the American Bar with Archie.

Oh, Archie. She longed for some contact with him and toyed endlessly with the idea of going to his house, but having encountered his mother once before, she knew she had to wait for Archie to come to her.

When the strike broke on Wednesday and the girls all gathered at the club, Vita looked out into the darkness, willing Archie to be in the audience, but he wasn't. By Thursday, the day of the presentation to W&T, her nerves were shredded. Percy must be sick of her, she thought, as she packed up all the underwear sets they'd made for the girls.

'Don't worry about Archie,' he told her. 'If it's meant to be, it's meant to be.'

'He could have found a way to wish me luck,' she said, realizing that her fear was turning into anger.

'Put him out of your head and concentrate on the presentation,' Percy said, kissing her.

'I wish you were coming.'

'You don't need me,' he told her.

She knew that Percy was way behind on the costumes for the chorus girls at the Apollo, so he was staying behind to get them finished, before meeting Edward. Vita made him promise to meet her at the Zip Club later.

'Knock 'em dead,' he said, as she left.

Nancy, Edith, Jemima, Jane, Betsy and Emma were all waiting for her outside the department store.

'Thank you all,' Vita said, relieved to see they were all here. Even Edith had come. 'Edith,' she nodded.

'I thought I might as well see what all the fuss is about,' she explained.

'Let's go and change,' Vita said. 'We don't want to be late.'

She handed the brassiere sets out to each of the girls from her carpet bag, and they headed for the changing rooms on the first floor.

Upstairs, Miss Proust seemed annoyed that so many girls had turned up for the meeting, but Nancy, behaving as if they owned the place and this had been prearranged, bustled them through to Mr Kenton's office. Vita was amazed at how easy Nancy found it to bamboozle people.

Mr Kenton stood up at the intrusion. Vita hadn't known what to expect, but she was surprised to see that he was young and dapper-looking, with fair hair and a tanned face. Nancy helped herself to one of his cards from his desk, after he'd shaken her hand and she'd introduced Vita as if she were some kind of thrilling act.

'Miss Casey?' he said, shaking her hand. 'I wasn't expecting so many of you.'

'I hope you don't mind, but I brought the girls from the Zip,' she said.

'I thought this was about your brassieres?' he said, looking confused as the girls started to take off their coats.

'Oh, it is,' Vita said, 'but, you see, it's much better to show you how they really look when they're worn.'

Lance Kenton's eyebrows shot up. This was certainly an unconventional approach, but Vita didn't care. She had to make him see in order to understand.

'Oh no, that's not how we do things here—'

'Let's hit it, girls,' Nancy said.

Before Mr Kenton could protest, she and Betsy cleared a space so that they could move, and then Jane produced a tuning fork, which she tapped and held on his wooden desk to get the right note. Then together in close harmony, the girls started to sing: 'Top Drawer, Top Drawer, you need look no further for . . .'

Vita watched Mr Kenton's face as the girls started to strip off. 'Flexible,' Betsy sang, doing a handstand so that Jemima caught her legs. 'And practical, too,' the girls sang. 'Go dancing or running – it'll hold up for you.'

There was a knock on the door and Miss Proust came in, but Lance Kenton held up his hand to stop her interrupting. The girls had all stripped off now and headed into the tap-dancing part of the routine. Vita had to smother a smile when she saw the look on Mr Kenton's face. He was loving this – despite himself. She could see it. His foot was tapping ever so slightly.

She glanced over at Miss Proust, whose hand was over her mouth, her eyes wide, as the girls wriggled their shoulders and sang, 'And perfectly safe for you.' They finished with a final pose, each one with one arm up, one foot forward. Vita clasped her hands together. They all looked magnificent.

She nodded to the girls and clapped her hands and they relaxed from their poses. Mr Kenton looked down at his shoes, as if they might have the answer. Vita felt terrified for a moment. Maybe he thought she was mad. Maybe she *was* mad, thinking this might work. Had she made a fool of herself?

'I'm quite bowled over, Miss Casey,' he said. 'I don't know what to say.'

Edith stepped forward and placed her hand on the desk, leaning towards him. 'It's not just us who are fans of these brassieres. Vita has several other stockists interested,' she declared.

'And we know that, as a store, you pride yourself on stocking only the latest fashions, so we would hate you to miss out,' Vita said, backing Edith up.

Lance Kenton looked cornered.

'Show me that order again, Vita,' Edith said. This was entirely unrehearsed, but Vita got up and showed Edith the blank page in her book. She had no idea what Edith was playing at, but it certainly caused Mr Kenton to pay attention.

'Did they confirm it?' she asked in a stage whisper.

Nancy came forward and peaked over Edith's shoulder at the book. 'Yes. They're starting with fifty,' she said.

Vita stole a glance at Lance Kenton, who was eyeing up Edith. Then Vita turned away and got out her carpet bag and placed it on his desk. She took out the prototype samples and laid them in front of him. 'This is what we're going to manufacture,' she said confidently. 'Because this is what women want.'

Lance Kenton drew in a long breath, his eyes dancing. He exhaled and shook his head, as if he were surprised at himself as well as surprised at the whole situation. 'Well then, young lady. Let's get down to business,' he said.

99

Archie at Last

They all linked arms as they walked jubilantly towards the Zip Club in the sunshine, Vita holding aloft the purchase order that Miss Proust had written out. Nancy had seen someone she knew in the street and was lagging behind, but Vita didn't mind.

She couldn't believe how well the meeting had gone and she chattered animatedly, analysing everything that had happened.

'And, Edith, you were brilliant,' she said, meaning it.

'I should have my own business,' Edith said. 'I've always thought that.'

'I can't wait to tell Percy,' Betsy said. 'One hundred. It really is a proper order!'

'And that's just for starters,' Emma reminded them.

'You'll have your work cut out now,' Jane said, as they all turned down the alleyway to the stage door.

'Don't I know it. Oh, my goodness,' Vita said, her heart soaring as she saw Archie waiting by the stage door. He crushed a cigarette beneath his foot. Vita had never see him smoke before, but it didn't matter; she was too excited to see him. She broke away and rushed ahead of the girls.

'You're here. Oh, Archie, wherever have you been?'

She had so many questions – about the party the other night, about his money worries – but they all faded now, and his eyes met hers.

'I'm sorry. I had things to attend to. Mother—'

She cut him off with a quick kiss and then there was raucous greeting all round. Archie looked bashful. Vita beamed at him, drinking him in. 'You're here now, and you'll never guess what? We did our presentation—'

'She got an order,' Betsy interrupted.

'It was marvellous, Archie,' Jane said. 'We all did our dance.'

And then Jemima and Emma chipped in, too, telling Archie all about their meeting and how impressed Mr Kenton had been.

'Vita was wonderful,' Jemima confirmed. 'You should have seen her in action.'

Vita blushed, soaking up their praise while checking Archie for a reaction. 'So this means,' she said, trying to suppress her grin, 'it's a proper business. Just like I said.'

She wanted him to be happy. Not just for her, but because of what it meant. Because of this afternoon, she was really on her way. To making money. To being so much more than a dancing girl.

'Come on, come on, ladies,' Nancy said, arriving now and flouncing into the dressing room. 'Oh,' she said, seeing Archie, who was looking more and more out of place amongst the girls.

He ran his hand over his hair.

'You remember Nancy,' Vita said, not meeting Nancy's

eye. 'She helped get the order. Oh, Archie, you should have seen their faces.'

'You should have,' Nancy confirmed. 'We're having a celebration later, after the show. You'll stay, won't you?'

'Maybe; it's just that I can't stay for the show. I have some things to do first. That's what I came to say.'

'Surely they can wait. We need to celebrate. Please don't go.'

'Come on – out, out,' Wisey said, bustling into the changing room. 'No gentlemen out the back. You know the rules.'

Archie tipped his hat to the girls, who blew him kisses. At the door he turned round and looked at Vita. For a moment he held her eyes, as if she were the most precious thing in the world.

'I love you, Vita,' he whispered. 'You know that, don't you?'

'Come on, break it up,' Edith called, watching them. 'In case you'd forgotten, we have a show to put on.'

'I'll see you afterwards,' Vita said.

He turned and headed back down the corridor to the stage door.

'Is he always that serious?' Jane asked.

'Come on, stop gossiping and get ready,' Edith said.

'And you'll have to make the most of me, darlings,' Nancy said. 'This will be one of my last.'

100

Clifford Court

In the cramped bathroom of the hotel suite in Clifford Court, Clement pressed himself into the shower stall, his skin crawling with revulsion when he thought of the kind of activities that must go on in this very room.

As it was, he could hardly bear to be in the same space as the chap Rawlings had found. He pressed himself against the wall, trying to distance himself from the young man, who was dressed in a flimsy silk robe, the tattoo on his neck visible above the collar. Rawlings had termed him a rent boy and had picked him up in an insalubrious part of town. *How old was he?* Clement wondered. Probably no more than twenty, but his eyes were old and knowing as he glanced at Clement now.

Rawlings seemed to be handling the situation well, talking calmly to the young man, but now Rawlings held his fingers up to his lips for them all to be quiet.

Clement heard the door to the hotel suite opening.

'Woody? Are you here?'

It was Percival Blake.

Clement listened intently, wondering if Blake was reading

the note on the bed. It was typewritten: *Get in and get comfortable.*

He heard a low chuckle. 'I'm not sure why you're being so mysterious,' Blake called out. 'If you're even in there. But, yes, I've missed you, too.'

Clement cringed, hating the affection in Blake's voice. He gave him a few more minutes.

'All right. You can come out now,' he heard.

Clement nodded to the young man, who opened the bathroom door. Rawlings went next with the camera, catching the moment. Hopefully he got the perfect shot of the naked young man walking towards an equally naked Percival Blake in the bed.

'What are you doing? What is this?' Blake cried. 'Where's Edward?'

Clement came out of the bathroom as Percival Blake clutched the covers to him. Rawlings kept on taking pictures as Blake held out his hand in front of his face.

'Stop it. Stop!' he shouted.

Rawlings nodded to the young man, who went back into the bathroom wordlessly to get dressed.

'We want some information about Anna Darton,' Clement said, approaching Blake in the bed.

'It's you. You . . .' Percy let out a cry, recognizing his voice. He scrambled against the green headboard with the covers clutched to his chest.

Clement leant in and threw the copy of *Vanity Fair* on the bed, with the picture of Anna and the Prince of Wales circled. 'Her – that's Anna. Tell me where she is.'

Blake's eyes widened in recognition. He looked pathetic

now as he shook his head. 'I don't know her. I don't know who you're talking about.'

'God damn it, man. Tell me what you know. I need to find her.' Clement clasped his hand around Blake's throat, but still the man shook his head.

'I don't know anything,' he said.

Rawlings put his arm on Clement's, and Clement let go.

'Mr Blake. Think about this. We have evidence of you meeting a young man to commit a sexual act.'

'I've never seen him before in my life.'

'Do you know what will happen, if we have you arrested?' Rawlings continued. Clement saw Blake's eyes well up with tears. 'And to your friend, Sopel, too.'

'Edward?'

'Yes. He was the one who set this up for us.'

Clement watched the shock register on Blake's face.

'We only want to know where she is.'

'I don't know,' he said in a whisper.

'You do.'

Percival Blake shook his head vehemently. 'You can beat me again, if you have to. But I'm not telling you anything. Do you hear me?'

Clement looked at Rawlings.

'Very well,' Clement said. He nodded to Rawlings, who picked up the telephone next to the bed. 'Operator, can I have Paddington three-o-five?'

Clement raised his eyebrows at Blake. There was still time for him to give up what he knew about Anna, but Clement saw a stubborn defiance in his eyes.

'Inspector. I'm sorry to bother you, but there's an incident at Clifford Court. A gross act of homosexual indecency. I suggest you get one of your officers here to make an arrest. Yes, sir. The man in question is Mr Percival Blake.'

101

Make It Real

After the show Vita felt the exhaustion of the past few days and the excitement of today hit her. It felt overwhelming that she'd made such a big commitment to W&T, and she didn't feel right celebrating without Percy.

As she wiped off her make-up, she had to smother a smile. *They'd really done it. They'd really got an order from a department store.* She wanted to patter her feet in jubilation. And Percy! He was going to be *thrilled*.

And Archie would be, too. She thought of him earlier and how he'd told her he loved her. *Why had she ever been worried?* she wondered. Everything was perfect.

She hurried out to the front of the club to find him.

'He'll turn up soon enough,' Nancy announced as they stood by the bar. Matteo gave them a bottle of champagne, but Nancy insisted on shots, too. She was clearly intent on getting smashed.

'Only two more shows and that's it. I'm off on the train to Paris from Charing Cross right after the show on Saturday,' she told everyone. 'I've still got a spare ticket, if any of you want to come, too?' Nancy pulled a blank face at Vita. She was still annoyed that Vita wasn't going. And now, as

Nancy gushed on about how fabulous Paris was going to be, Vita couldn't help feeling offended. How could Nancy leave, without so much as a backward glance? Wouldn't she miss them all? Miss *her*?

'I've a good mind to go with you,' Edith confided.

'You would?'

'He's never going to commit,' Edith said, flashing her eyes over in the direction of Jack Connelly. 'And who knows what will happen to this place. It's a miracle it's still open.'

Vita remembered now when she'd first come here with Nancy for the audition and there'd been a fracas at the back.

'You think it might close?'

'I know it will. It's only a matter of time. I've seen the books. And I know he's cooked them. It's simply a case of when he's found out. You know, Vita, I wish men weren't so damned dishonest.'

Vita stared at Edith, amazed by this confession.

'Oh, don't look like that. I don't need your pity. Besides, you'll be all right,' Edith said. 'You and Percy have your business. You can do that. I just want . . .' She sighed heavily. 'I want a fresh start, you know?'

As the hour after the show ticked by, a sense of uneasiness crept over Vita. Percy and Archie should be here to celebrate with them, yet there was no sign of either of them. She kept looking around the smoky club, seeing how much it had filled up and willing Archie to walk through the door. She remembered his earlier declaration of love, but now she also remembered how sad he'd seemed.

But as soon as she was dancing in his arms, everything would be perfect, she told herself. In the meantime, she set about dancing with the girls, savouring every moment they still had together, until Nancy grabbed her.

'You remember Marcus, don't you?' Nancy shouted, pulling Vita off the dance floor.

Vita felt her skin bristling as the journalist turned his attention towards her, looking her up and down.

'So you're not just a dancer, I hear,' Fox said.

'I beg your pardon?' Vita asked.

'A new business?'

Vita felt annoyed. She didn't want Marcus Fox to hear about Top Drawer. Not yet. Not until she was ready. But it seemed the cat was already out of the bag. How could Nancy be so indiscreet?

'Please,' he said. 'Allow me to do you a favour. A mention of your new enterprise in my column will boost sales no end.'

There was something about him that made the hairs on the back of Vita's neck stand up, and the way he'd said 'enterprise' was so condescending.

'Here she is,' Nancy said and, to Vita's horror, she saw that Nancy had brought over a photographer to where she was standing.

'Oh, please,' Vita said, holding up her hands. 'Don't. I don't want a picture.'

'Don't be silly, Vita,' Nancy said. 'Marcus can't do his feature without your picture. You have to sell yourself,' she said, giggling as if she'd been very clever. 'Marcus said the newspaper wants more stories about modern young women like you.'

'But I don't want a photograph.'

'Oh, take no notice,' Nancy confided to the photographer. 'She's been photographed with the Prince of Wales.'

Vita winced as the photographer's bulb popped unexpectedly in her face. Nancy frowned, then fussed around, fluffing up Vita's hair.

'Come on, old girl. Don't be a sourpuss. You're going to have to get used to it, if you're going to be successful,' Nancy went, before turning and smiling at the camera like a Hollywood starlet. 'Take another one. Vita, smile this time.'

But as she tried to smile, Vita felt terrified. She knew Nancy was only attempting to help, but she wished she hadn't interfered. Whatever was Marcus Fox going to print in his column now? And with her picture, too?

It was one thing to have been in that picture with the Prince of Wales, where nobody would have been able to recognize her, but this was altogether different. It might not seem so to Nancy, but then Nancy didn't know how much Vita wanted her face to stay out of the press.

Fox looked at his watch. 'Just in the nick of time for tomorrow's edition,' he said, smiling and beckoning the photographer to go with him. 'Goodbye, Miss Casey.'

There was something far too final about the way he said it. Vita scowled as she saw the salacious look on his face, but she was distracted by Nancy, who had seen someone she knew.

'Oh, look, she's here,' Nancy said, holding her hand up to wave.

Vita saw a familiar-looking woman come down the steps from the street entrance into the club, and Nancy darting through the crowd to greet her.

431

'That's Nancy's new friend,' Jane told Vita. 'We met her at Nancy's party. Betsy and I don't like her.'

'It's Georgie,' Vita said, moving towards where Nancy was now embracing Archie's friend. How did Georgie know Nancy?

'Oh, look – it's you,' Georgie said, clapping her hands together when she saw Vita.

Vita accepted her kiss on the cheek. She looked at Nancy for an explanation, but her friend looked away. How were Georgie and Nancy suddenly friends?

'Where's Douglas?' Nancy asked.

'Oh, he'll be along in a while,' Georgie said. 'He had a beastly hangover after going to the club on Saturday night. It was quite a do, I gather. And the poor chap has had to work all week, with everyone on strike. Tough luck, I say. He has to save up for the right ring.'

She jangled her finger in front of Vita's face.

'You're engaged?' Vita asked. Had this Douglas – her fiancé, by the sound of it – been at the same party at the club as Archie on Saturday night? Perhaps it had been Douglas's engagement send-off? Odd that Archie hadn't mentioned it.

'Let's just say it's imminent.' Georgie exchanged a look with Nancy, who raised her eyebrows, her red lips suppressing a smile. Vita knew that look well. They had a secret, she was sure of it.

Georgie discarded her coat and looked around as she made her way to the bar with Vita and Nancy. Her diamond headband looked far too glamorous for the Zip.

'So, little birds have been chattering,' Georgie said excitedly to Vita, linking her arm through hers.

Chattering about what? Vita wanted to know. She looked across at Nancy, who deliberately didn't meet her eye again. Had she told Georgie about Archie? About the fact that they'd spent the night together?

'You know, poor Clarissa is in quite a flap,' Georgie said, leaning her head in towards Vita.

'About what?'

'Why, about Archie taking you to Hartwell of course,' she said.

Her words were gossipy and light, but her eyes were steady and cold as she delivered them.

Vita felt them plummet into the depths of her belly and, with them, a terrible sense of foreboding. Had Clarissa Fenwick already found out? And if she had, what did it mean? She hated that Georgie was delivering this information. She hated that she and Archie had been gossiped about like this. She felt tainted, as if it were written large above her in lit-up letters that she and Archie were lovers, when what they had shared had been so private and magical.

She forced herself to be bold – and not show how she was churning with emotion. 'Oh?' she said as nonchalantly as possible, as they reached the bar and Georgie accepted a glass of champagne from Nancy.

Meanwhile her mind was racing. If Georgie and Mrs Fenwick knew, then did that mean Archie had made his feelings for Vita public? Had he told his mother they were in love? Because if he had, that meant that he'd been true to his word. He did love her. He was going to make it possible for them to be together.

'My dear, it really is quite a scandal,' Georgie continued

cheerfully, almost gleefully, after she'd taken a slug of champagne, as if this had been Vita's intention all along.

She grew more suspicious now of Georgie's tone. What exactly did she mean by a 'scandal'? Was Archie in trouble?

Georgie looked down at Vita. 'So? Tell all?'

Vita was damned if she was going to give her anything. 'There's nothing to tell,' she lied. She didn't look at Nancy, but she felt the hairs on the back of her neck standing up. She knew, without a doubt, that Nancy had told Georgie everything. She'd always been a gossip, but Vita had never guessed she'd betray her like this. 'I hear you went to Nancy's party?' she said, changing the subject.

'Oh, yes. You missed an absolute blinder, Vita.'

'So I heard,' she said coldly.

'And did Nancy tell you?' Georgie continued.

'Tell me what?'

'Mother is redecorating, so we're all moving out for a while. And guess where I'm moving?' Georgie said.

'Into my flat,' Nancy answered. 'Oh, now you're here, come and dance,' she said to Georgie, pulling her away to the dance floor.

'Oh, I wish I'd been to your Zip Club before. Isn't it fun!' Georgie trilled.

Vita shook on the spot where she was, loathing Nancy for being so duplicitous and hating herself for the wave of jealous indignation that she felt. The second she'd turned her back and gone to Hartwell, Nancy had replaced her with Georgie. And now she was making it perfectly clear where her affections lay.

Well, good riddance to her. Vita was glad now that Nancy

434

was going to Paris. Who needed a friend who wilfully shared secrets, as she so obviously had?

She wanted to cry with fury – and with fear, too. What was happening? What exactly was the fallout from the scandal that Georgie was so pleased about? She had to find out. She had to see Archie *right now*. Nothing else mattered.

102

Archie Is Not at Home

Out on the street, Vita wrapped her fur coat around and managed to get one of the few cabs on the Strand. She sat in the back, willing the journey to be faster, as she made her way to Regent's Park. She looked out of the window, thinking about Georgie and Nancy at the Zip Club right now. Would they be gossiping about her? Would they even have noticed that she'd gone?

Her mind was whirring as the cab arrived in Regent's Park and she asked the driver to slow down, peering up at the houses until she found the right one. Telling the driver to wait outside, she ran up the steps to Archie's house. There were only a few lights on as she rang the bell. She'd been so sure Archie would be here, it was only now that the possibility that he might not be actually hit her.

It took an age, but eventually she heard movement on the other side of the door and Jenkins opened it slowly.

'Is Mr Fenwick at home?' she asked hurriedly, annoyed at the slow butler and his disdainful manner.

'I'm afraid not, madam.'

'Who is it, Jenkins?'

It was Mrs Fenwick. She brushed past him and looked

down at Vita. Then she looked up the street and beckoned her inside.

At first Vita thought that she was being graciously accepted into Archie's home. But then, as Clarissa Fenwick closed the door, she realized how mistaken she'd been. There was nothing gracious about the look on Archie's mother's stern face.

The butler shuffled away and then they were left alone in the dimly lit hallway. A clock ticked loudly on the wooden side-table next to them. Vita was not invited into the drawing room or the study.

It was now that she remembered Archie's warning – about how most people were frightened of his mother. She'd laughed it off, but now she felt scared.

'I hope you are not here again about your so-called "business",' Clarissa Fenwick started. 'What was it Archie said?' She put her fingers to her lips, as if trying to recall. 'Oh yes. That's it – underwear.'

She said it as if it were a horrible joke and Vita felt her face flushing.

'It is very much a business,' Vita said. 'We have orders and—'

'I doubt that.'

'It's true. Ask Archie.' She forced herself to try and sound brave. 'He can make his own decisions.'

Clarissa Fenwick's eyebrow rose sardonically.

'That, my dear, is not the case. And if he's told you that, then I'm afraid you have been gravely misled.'

'But—'

'And I sincerely doubt he would . . . invest,' Clarissa

Fenwick said scornfully, 'in the kind of woman who has to bare her body to get money?' She eyed Vita coldly.

Vita blushed, remembering how Mrs Fenwick must have seen her in her underwear in the study.

'Oh, don't think I don't know everything my son does,' she said, and Vita was wrong-footed. She said it with such conviction that she knew in that moment Georgie had been right: Clarissa Fenwick knew all about Hartwell and what had happened there.

'But he's promised to—'

Clarissa Fenwick held up her bony hand. 'He's promised many things to many people, my dear. Not least of all to his fiancée.' She stared at Vita, her eyes boring into her.

Had she heard right? *Fiancée? Did she just say 'fiancée'?*

'Oh? Didn't you know? Archie and Maud are engaged to be married.'

Maud? Georgie's sister? 'Married?' she managed.

'Oh yes. I think you met her – well, almost met her – here, that night you so rudely turned up unannounced and uninvited.'

Unannounced and uninvited. Her insulting words hit hard, as they were intended to. Archie's mother drew herself up, her beady eyes staring down at Vita, a glint of satisfaction in them as she saw her aimed barbs hit home, like a pipette of poison, as her revelation sank in.

It had been Maud dining with Archie that night . . . with the two mothers . . . drinking champagne. They'd all been celebrating Archie's engagement?

Clarissa Fenwick, satisfied now, smiled as Vita put her hand to her chest, as if she couldn't contain the physical pain

438

there. 'So I really must thank you. You've served your purpose very well.'

'My purpose?' Vita's voice was barely more than a whisper.

Mrs Fenwick gave her a blistering look, then leant forward to speak confidentially. 'Why do you think Archie came to see you in that dreadful club of yours? Why do you think he sought out a common dancing girl? Hmm?'

Her eyes twinkled with menace, but Vita couldn't breathe. She couldn't take any more.

'I couldn't accept my son going into his marriage as a virgin. And I wouldn't countenance him going to a prostitute. So I found the next best thing . . . you.'

103

Georgie's Threat

Percy's studio was locked up and, despite Vita's pounding on the door, the inside remained resolutely dark. Vita turned and pressed herself against the wooden door, looking up at the yellow street lamp, her eyes clouding with tears.

She needed Percy. She needed the comfort of his studio, his kindness and his warmth. Only Percy could dispel the poisonous words Clarissa Fenwick had uttered.

She felt a low, dry sob escape her. She kept telling herself over and over again that it couldn't be true. Archie wouldn't do that to her, would he? Not after everything that had happened between them?

He couldn't *possibly* be engaged, could he?

She thought of how tenderly he'd held her in his arms under the stars at Hartwell and had told her that he'd love her forever. He'd meant it. She knew he'd meant it. He couldn't be with someone else, could he?

But the stark facts, illuminated by Clarissa Fenwick's revelation, reared up like boulders in her path. Like the fact that the party at the club had been for Archie – that's why he'd had to go back to London so suddenly. *He'd left her to go to his own engagement party.*

Which meant that he was *already engaged* when he'd taken her to Hartwell. He'd used her – just like his mother had said.

Which is why he'd come the theatre earlier tonight to say goodbye. *Because he knew she'd find out.*

Each fact seemed like a physical blow. She dragged herself back to the club to look for Percy, torturing herself over and over again with the thought of Archie and Maud. Together. Engaged.

She pictured them together, holding hands. Archie touching Maud's face the way he'd touched hers, slipping a ring onto her finger.

And she heard Edith's warning, too, in her mind: *he's probably after one thing.* Could she have been right all along? Because she'd fallen for it, Vita realized. She'd given herself away. Given herself entirely, believing Archie when he'd told her that he loved her. Believing – stupidly, she saw now – that they would somehow find a way to be together.

Back at the club, the crowd was thicker and there was an edge to it. Everyone was drunk, the band loud, the dancing raucous.

'You have to help me,' Vita pleaded with Georgie, steering her off the dance floor through the mass of sweating bodies. Georgie was clearly high – probably with Nancy's snow. 'I must speak to Archie. Do you know where he is?'

'He won't want to speak to you, Vita. He's with my sister right now,' Georgie said, shaking off her grip. '"Otherwise engaged", you could say.'

'But he can't – he can't do this,' Vita said, her voice breaking, tears spilling down her face, her anguish lost in the smoky atmosphere of the club. 'He can't marry her. Not after . . .'

'There's no point crying, Vita. The deed is done. And it'll certainly be common knowledge by tomorrow. Mother has the announcement going in *The Times* in the morning.'

'But Archie doesn't love her. He loves me.'

'Oh, look at you,' Georgie said, pinching Vita's cheek condescendingly. 'You poor thing. Did you really think Archie would be with someone like you?'

'What do you mean?'

'Well, you're a dancing girl, darling. Hardly a match for Archie.'

'You don't know that. You don't know me.'

Georgie put her hand on her hip and looked at Vita through narrowed eyes.

'Yes, I do. I know you're a little tart who flaunts her bosoms around town.'

'Flaunts? It's a business!' Is that really what Georgie thought? Vita felt the blood booming in her ears. How dare she call her 'a little tart'.

'I don't know why you're so offended. You got the best part of the deal.'

'The deal?'

'Clarissa and I agreed that Archie should get some experience before he married. And when Nancy mentioned you, I knew you were just Archie's type. So he got to spend a night with you.'

'Nancy? *Nancy* said that,' Vita gasped. 'Nancy knew . . .'

'Oh yes. It was Nancy who suggested you.'

Vita felt sick. She shook her head, covering her ears. It

wasn't true. Archie loved her; he'd told her earlier. And Nancy was her friend.

'No. I don't believe you. You must have tricked him somehow. I have to stop him. He's making a huge mistake.'

'I wouldn't do that, if I were you,' Georgie said, leaning in close. 'You see, if you do anything to stop his engagement, I'll tell him exactly who you are.'

Vita felt saliva flood her mouth. There was something coldly sober about Georgie suddenly. She couldn't possibly know where Vita was from, could she? She couldn't know that she was really Anna Darton?

'I'll tell Archie everything about your little lesbian relationship with Nancy. And let me tell you, Archie won't be impressed. He really doesn't approve of that sort of thing.'

104

At the Police Station

Vita went back to the dressing room, so furious that she banged the door with her fist.

Jane was with Betsy, neither of whom noticed Vita's mood, as they were lolling over each other.

'Get these two out of here, would you?' Wisey said to Vita. 'I don't know what's wrong with you all tonight. I've never seen everyone so tight.'

She shook her head at Vita, who scooped up Betsy and Jane. She got them into a cab to take them home and then helped them both upstairs before Mrs Bell saw them.

She thought about going downstairs, but she was too tired and heartbroken to see Percy now. He'd been quite wrong about fate making it possible for her and Archie to be together. They weren't ever going to be together. Not now. Not ever. She helped Betsy get Jane into bed, and then Betsy flopped down on her quilt.

'Oh, that was a fun night,' she said, but Vita ignored her, lying instead on her own bed and staring at the ceiling.

In the morning, she dragged her feet downstairs, having hardly slept.

'There you are! I've been dying to hear all about it!' Mrs Bell said excitedly, coming out of the parlour.

'About what?' Vita said.

'About the presentation of course,' she said. 'How did it go?'

'Oh, that.'

So much had happened since then that Vita had almost forgotten. But Mrs Bell was on tenterhooks, and Vita guessed she owed her an explanation. So she told her all about the girls, and about how she'd been given an order.

'You don't seem very happy about it,' Mrs Bell said, her brow furrowed. 'I thought it was what you wanted.'

'There's been a lot going on. At the club and . . .' Vita swallowed hard. 'I'm sorry.'

How could she explain to Mrs Bell the level of betrayal she felt – not just from Archie, but from Nancy, too. She couldn't even begin to explain, without having to admit how foolish she'd been. How stupidly naive. How she'd been thinking like Anna Darton, when all along Archie only ever saw her as Verity Casey: a working girl. Someone he could easily exploit. And Archie had simply indulged her over Top Drawer – no doubt making fun of her behind her back, with Georgie. He'd never had any intention of investing . . .

'Vita?'

'It's nothing.'

But her voice caught and, as the tears came, Mrs Bell pulled her into a hug. 'There, there, lassie,' she soothed. 'Come and sit down and tell me all about it.'

Vita nodded miserably. 'Oh, Mrs Bell, you have no idea.

I've been such a fool. You see, I thought I was in love. I *am* in love,' she said. 'Only . . .'

'Oh dear, oh dear,' Mrs Bell said. 'Let me fetch a cup of tea and you can tell me all about it.'

But while she was in the kitchen, the doorbell rang and Vita heard Mrs Bell going to answer it. Despite everything, Vita longed for it to be Archie. Hoping that he was here to make everything better.

'Vita? It's someone for you,' she heard Mrs Bell say, and Vita rushed through to the hallway.

But it wasn't Archie. Matteo was standing by the door. Vita had never seen the Zip Club's bartender in daylight. He looked younger than he did in the club, his dark fringe flopping in his face.

'Oh, hello, Vita,' he said.

Mrs Bell looked round at Vita, a stern look on her face. Vita knew the old woman didn't approve of gentlemen callers.

'Matteo? What is it?' Vita asked, seeing the sombre look on his face.

'It's about Percy. You see, I've just found out that he's been arrested. I thought you'd want to know.'

'Arrested? But why?'

'I don't know.'

'Where is he?'

'Is everything all right, Vita?' Mrs Bell asked, clearly curious.

'Yes, yes – I just have to go out.'

'But I've made you tea.'

'I'll be as quick as I can.'

She grabbed her coat and walked out with Matteo, who'd come on his bike to deliver the news.

'He'll be at Paddington Police Station, I reckon,' he said.

'Thanks, Matteo,' Vita replied, waving to him as he set off on his bike.

She hurried straight up the road and caught a bus to the Tube, and then headed to Paddington. The police station was housed in a dirty brick building with thickly recessed windows. She watched two grim-faced constables coming out of the large green doors, ejecting a woman in a brown coat.

'You can't keep him in there. He was only striking. He has a right to strike, you know! And it's all over now!' the woman shouted. She brushed herself down, clearly furious. 'You be careful in there, Miss. They're right brutes, they are.'

Vita went through the door and queued at the small glass window, where a harassed-looking officer told her to wait across the hallway in the waiting room.

The minutes ticked slowly by, and Vita watched a fly bash itself against the glass of the high window in the waiting room. At this rate, she was going to miss the show. It hardly mattered now, though, she supposed. If Edith was right and the Zip Club was going to close, what difference did it make?

Besides, she still couldn't face Nancy. Not after Georgie's revelation. About how it had been Nancy who'd set her up with Archie. That Nancy and Georgie had known each other all along. Which meant that Nancy was part of Archie's set. The very set Edith had warned her about. *They always use people.* How indignant Vita had been at the time, but how right Edith had been.

'Please can I speak to someone about Mr Blake?' Vita asked, leaping up as she saw a different policeman pass the doorway. He looked her up and down in a disparaging way as she approached. 'I've been waiting for hours.'

'Who are you?'

'Vita. Verity Casey,' she explained. 'I'm his friend.'

'And what kind of friend is that?'

Vita heard the insinuation in his voice. 'I work with him.'

'And what work do you do, Miss, may I ask?'

She almost told him about Top Drawer, but stopped herself. 'I'm a dancer. At the Zip Club,' she said, knowing that she was only making things worse because, just like Georgie and Archie's mother, he probably thought she was some kind of immoral woman of the night.

'It figures that Blake would consort with your type,' he said with a tut.

'You don't know Percy. He wouldn't harm anyone,' Vita protested. 'If only you'd let me see him.'

'Well, I'm afraid that won't be possible. It seems he had a little accident last night, when we brought him in. Turns out he rubbed his cellmate up the wrong way. Didn't they tell you? He's in the infirmary.'

'The infirmary?'

'He got beaten up,' the policeman spelled it out. 'Happens occasionally. With his sort . . .'

How dare they fail to protect Percy? Whatever he'd done, he didn't deserve to be beaten. She remembered Percy admitting how much he hated violence. And how he lived in terror of the kind of people who might want to punish him for who he was.

'Please let me see him.'

'Look, Miss, I would walk away if I were you. No good will come of this. There is an eyewitness who has more than enough evidence to incriminate your associate, Mr Blake. The magistrate takes a dim view of homosexuals, believe me.'

'But Percy . . . he wouldn't hurt anyone.'

The policeman looked down his nose at her. 'His sort – they hurt society. I'd leave, if I were you. Before you make things even worse than they already are.'

105

Marcus Fox

Clement stood by Marcus Fox's desk in his office, watching Fox smoke, his feet up on the desk, revealing his garish socks. Fox's collar button was undone, the fat knot of his tie loosened. The office was cramped, with piles of papers teetering on the desk, and the air was filled with the sound of clattering typewriters.

With Percival Blake absolutely refusing to talk – even when Rawlings had physically threatened him – they'd had no option but to hand him over to the police. Clement could see the man quaking in his boots, but he'd still refused to say anything at all about Anna. *What on earth did Anna have on him?* Clement wondered. Because surely Blake wouldn't do that out of loyalty? But then he was constantly surprised by how strange folk in London were.

And none more so than this reporter, Fox. After the lengths they'd gone to, Clement had nearly choked on his toast when Rawlings had plonked down today's paper on the table beside him, with the face of his sister and her floozy friend staring up at him.

He'd read the article, wide-eyed with shock, the reporter talking about the Zip Club – a den of iniquity and vice that laundered gang money. And Anna? Anna was a dancer there. A *dancer*.

'Of course I know her. I was there when the picture was taken. If that's the one you're after, then it's the very lovely Verity Casey.'

'Anna Darton.'

'Excuse me?'

'She's Anna Darton. I'm her brother, Clement.'

'Is that so?'

'We own Darton Mills in Lancashire.' Clement drew himself up, annoyed that the journalist wasn't showing him more respect.

Marcus Fox rubbed his hands. 'I knew she was from up north. I wondered what dark secret she might be hiding. She's been quite elusive, that one.'

'You've spoken to her?'

'My dear fellow, I know all about her. About her friends, her business—'

'Business?'

'She's been resourceful, I'll give her that. Got herself a load of orders with a big department store for this underwear of hers.'

Clement shifted on Blake's cane, leaning forward to check he'd heard right. 'Underwear? What do you mean, man?'

Fox gave him a lewd smile. 'Oh yes, it's all legit. I was going to give her a mention, but the story about Jack Connelly was even better. I got a tip-off. Stitched him up royally, we have.'

Clement was flabbergasted. Anna had achieved all this since she'd left home.

'She's no fool, you mark my words,' Fox continued, hauling his legs off the desk. 'I've looked into it. One of my sources says that if she plays it right, she could make a fortune. They seem very excited at W&T about it. They're going to stock her brassieres, you know.'

Clement felt a righteous fury rise up in him. How dare Anna achieve all of this? How dare she carve another route into the future – away from the mills, away from their father – when his own path was so set in stone. And how *dare she do it for herself.*

'I just need to know where she is.'

'Then it'll be my pleasure to introduce you. She'll be dancing tonight at the Zip.'

106

Confronting Edward

Mrs Meyrick had short, wavy brown hair and was wearing a fur-trimmed gold kimono that was far too young a garment for a woman of her age. 'He'll be in there,' she told Vita, waving her hand towards another room.

The '43, her club in Gerrard Street, was busy, even though it was only eight o'clock in the evening. Vita walked across the bare floorboards to where various tables were dotted, around which sat an array of men and women – several already in evening dress. In the corner, a man stood by a wooden upright piano singing Noël Coward songs. In any other circumstances Vita would have wanted to stay and mingle and drink, but now she was on the lookout for Edward.

She saw him then, through another doorway, carrying two large glasses of gin towards a table of people.

'Hello, Vita,' he said when he saw her. 'What are you doing here? Aren't you supposed to be at the Zip?'

She walked over and pulled Edward away from his friends.

'Have you heard about Percy?' she asked in a hurried whisper.

'What about him?'

'He's been arrested?' she said, staring at him for a reaction. She saw his jaw clench and, for a second, his eyes shifted guiltily. 'Did you know? Were you with him?'

'Is that what he said?' Edward hissed and, as his dark gaze met hers, in that moment it suddenly became clear to Vita that he knew much more than he was letting on.

'No. I went to see him, but he's in the infirmary at the police station. He's been beaten, Edward.'

Edward took a breath to steady himself, as if this information pained him. Then he looked across at his friends, holding up his hand to show that he was coming.

'You know something, don't you?' Vita implored. 'Edward, tell me. This is Percy. *Our* Percy. You have to help.'

'I can't.'

'You can. You can vouch for him. Get him out of there. Do you know what they'd do to someone like Percy in jail? He hates violence.'

Edward pressed his lips together and shook his head. 'I'm sorry, Vita. I can't have anything to do with him.' He went to move away, but she put her hand on his arm to stop him. He stared down at it.

'But why?' Her voice was louder than she meant it to be. Edward frowned and pulled her away to the door. He clearly wanted to get rid of her.

'They had information. Information about Percy and me.'

'They? Who is after Percy? What has he done?'

'I have no idea. I don't want anything to do with all of this. I won't speak about it any more.'

'Edward! Please!'

'Didn't you just hear what I said? It's not my problem,' he hissed. 'Now, please, go away.'

He shrugged her off and headed back towards the table. She watched him go, aghast that he could be so callous. For a moment she was tempted to run over – tell the two women and the man that Edward was with exactly what kind of person Edward Sopel was, but then she remembered Archie's warning at Kettner's. Edward was the kind of man who liked to get people into trouble and walk away. She'd just never thought he'd do that to poor Percy.

107

Mrs Bell's Stand

Since the show had already started, Vita decided to miss the rest of it and go back home. She simply felt too wretched to face the girls. By the time she got to Mrs Bell's, however, everything seemed even worse. She ran to the front door as Mrs Bell opened it and flung herself into the old lady's arms.

'Oh, Mrs Bell,' she sobbed, 'it's just too dreadful.'

Mrs Bell took a step backwards, pulling Vita inside and hastily shutting the door. Vita had been dreading telling her the news about why Percy had been arrested, but it seemed to have reached their landlady already.

'It's a terrible business,' she said. 'I'd have never have thought it of Percy . . .' She dabbed at her eyes.

'Someone deliberately set out to trap him.'

Mrs Bell frowned. 'Trap him? As well they might. I can hardly believe it's true. He is a homosexual?' she said in a hoarse whisper.

'I know, but—'

'You knew?'

'Yes, but—'

'All of this right under my nose. In my own house,' Mrs Bell snapped, and now Vita's tears stalled. She remembered what Percy had told her about people not understanding, but she'd never thought Mrs Bell would be like this.

'No, Mrs Bell, it wasn't like that—'

'I can't have you here,' the landlady said, putting the tissue in her apron pocket and drawing in a deep breath. She didn't meet Vita's eye. 'Have you even seen the papers? What they said about your Zip Club? Mrs Bradbury brought it round. "A den of iniquity and vice" indeed. There's even a picture of you and that American girl. You both look drunk.'

Vita looked at the paper now, her heart racing with shock. The photo of herself and Nancy was terrible. There was no mention of Top Drawer, but instead there was what looked like a scathing attack on Jack Connelly.

'That's just a malicious journalist. You can't . . . I mean—'

'I'm afraid you can't stay. My brother-in-law is coming to pack up Percy's room. I can't bring myself to go in there.'

'But he'll be coming home here. It's all a misunderstanding.'

'No, he won't. Not here. And that goes for all of you. I want you to leave, Vita. I'm sorry, but that's how it is.'

'I can't leave. Percy and I have a business. I have orders to fulfil.'

'It's immoral,' said Mrs Bell bluntly. 'All of it. Immoral. I should never have taken any of you in.'

Vita stared, dumbfounded, as Mrs Bell marched away from her down the corridor into the kitchen. 'I want you out by the end of the week,' she called. 'Tell the others.'

Vita was shaking as she went upstairs. How could Mrs Bell be so callous? How could she throw them all out with so little notice? Where would they go? And poor Betsy and Jane. They had done nothing wrong . . .

She pulled out her carpet bag from under the bed and crept down to Percy's room. She switched on the light by the bed and then started packing up all the patterns and bras she'd made with him. She took his notebook, too, knowing how much his ideas book meant to him. As she put it in her bag, a photograph of Edward fell out.

What on earth had Percy done to get arrested? She couldn't begin to imagine. He'd always been so careful and discreet. It was Edward who'd taken the risks.

But now it was Edward who'd clearly got him into trouble. And poor Percy would have taken it, to protect his friend. She thought again of Archie's warning about Edward, and how angry she'd been at his suggestion. But he'd been right.

And thinking about Archie made her think of Maud, and a fresh bout of tears assaulted her.

'Oh, Percy. Oh, what are we going to do?' she whispered, clutching the book to her chest and sobbing.

108

The Last Show

The ripples caused by the article about the Zip Club kept spreading. Jane and Betsy were distraught when they found out that Mrs Bell was intending to throw them out. Jane woke their landlady up on her return from the club to try and reason with her, but that only made things worse.

They spent Saturday clearing out their room and trying to work out where they were going to stay. By the afternoon, after several phone calls, they had found lodgings for the two of them with Betsy's cousin, all the way over in Tottenham, but Vita was still unsure what on earth she was going to do.

Wisey was at the stage door as they all finally made it to the theatre. It had taken all of Jane and Betsy's powers of persuasion to make Vita come with them to the show.

'What time do you call this?' Wisey said, opening the stage door. 'Mr Connelly is tearing his hair out. That article in the paper has put everyone in a terrible mood. He reckons this might be the last show, if the police show up. Here, take this,' she said, pushing a metal clothing rail towards Vita and the girls, 'and shove it out there for a minute. There's no need for it back here, now that Nancy and Edith have packed up. Like rats escaping a sinking ship, they are.'

'Edith has packed up?' Jane asked.

'Didn't you hear? After that newspaper piece, she's going to Paris with Nancy.'

Vita kicked the rail, which was now stubbornly blocking the door, and closed the stage door with a thud.

'Oh, and this came for you,' Wisey said, digging in her overall pocket and handing Vita an envelope. 'It was left out front. No doubt from some poor admirer.'

'Why poor?' she asked, as she shoved it in her coat pocket.

'Well, you're taken, aren't you? Or you were,' Wisey said, and Vita felt the colour rise in her cheeks. Wisey knew about Archie? Which meant all the girls did, and no doubt they'd all been talking about her behind her back. 'I did warn you, didn't I?' Wisey whispered. 'I told you to keep your nose clean and not let anyone take advantage.'

Vita was about to protest that Archie hadn't taken advantage of her, but that's *exactly* what he had done, she realized. She could see how hopelessly naive and stupid Wisey must think she was. Vita pushed past her into the dressing room, trying not to cry.

'Girls, thank God!' she heard Jemima say, as Jane and Betsy put up their hands in greeting. 'We thought we were going to have to do the show alone.'

'Where have you been?' Edith asked.

'I say, are you quite all right, old girl?' Jemima asked, seeing Vita's blotchy face. 'We were worried about you last night when you didn't show.'

Vita shook her head, her eyes full of tears.

'Are you glum about Archie?' Nancy asked. 'Because if you ask me, you're so much better off without him.'

'How could you?' Vita managed, tears threatening to choke her.

'Come on. Don't be like this,' Nancy said. 'You'll spoil the last night.'

Furious, Vita drew herself up, wanting to let rip and tell Nancy exactly how betrayed she felt, but before she could, Edith was in front of her. She slammed her costume against her.

'Save it, Vita. We're on in two minutes.'

Vita turned her face away from Nancy, deciding to pick a better time to fight this particular battle. She changed in a hurry, hardly bothering to finesse her make-up. Who cared what she looked like now?

'Let's go,' Nancy said, hurrying them all out into the corridor. 'This is it, ladies. The last time we'll be together.'

'Don't,' Jane wailed. 'It's too awful.'

'Make it a good one,' Edith said, with a rare smile.

Vita stumbled onto the stage, flinching at the bright lights. She watched the others high-kicking and she joined in, her body moving automatically, but her voice was a hoarse croak. It felt as if she were watching herself from the top corner of the room.

How jubilant she'd felt after the presentation, but now everything had turned to dust. She stared out into the darkness, knowing the audience was out there, but Archie wasn't. And never would be again. She felt tears overwhelming her as they took their final positions.

'I know, it's sad, isn't it?' Betsy said, squeezing her hand, as they took a bow. 'But cheer up, Vita. You don't have to worry about the future – it's such amazing news about the order.'

'Ladies and gentlemen, this is the last show from our current line-up,' Mr Connelly said to the audience, putting his hands out to the girls. 'Come and join us all for a drink,' he said to them. 'You can change later.'

They broke the line and Mr Connelly helped them down off the stage one by one, as if he'd always been the most chivalrous boss on the planet. Vita was behind Edith, who refused his hand.

She saw Jack Connelly lean in. 'Come on, Edie. Don't be like this. Can't we part as friends?' he asked, but she ignored him and he shrugged at Vita. 'I'll never understand you women,' he said, as an aside to her.

Vita caught up with Edith. 'Are you really going with Nancy?'

'It looks like it,' she said.

At the bar, Jack Connelly gave them all champagne and toasted Nancy and Edith on their way. 'Are you all right?' Vita asked, seeing how hard Edith was trying to hold it together.

'Not really. But thanks for asking,' she said. 'I thought he was going to fight for me. For the club – for us all – but he only cares about himself.'

Nancy was holding court, carefully avoiding Vita's eye. They needed to speak and, for a moment, it looked like they would when Nancy pulled a face and walked directly over to her and Edith.

'Oh God, it's that dreadful toady Marcus Fox coming right towards us. Don't turn round. Don't look. Come on, Edith, we have to get a move on,' Nancy said in a hushed whisper, grabbing Edith's arm. 'I have to get Mr Wild, then

I'll see you at the station.' She quickly touched Vita's hand, as if everything was normal between them. 'You'll come and wave us off, won't you, darling?'

How could she be so blasé? Vita wondered. She'd thought they were close. That they were best friends even, but now she saw that Nancy was only interested in herself.

'New horizons for us all. Isn't it exciting?'

Edith and Vita exchanged a glance. Neither of them shared Nancy's enthusiasm. Vita marvelled once more at her thick skin and her ability to move on without a backward glance.

She didn't have time to answer before Marcus Fox arrived.

'So. All change, I hear,' he said, as he stared at Vita.

'Please leave me alone, Mr Fox. You've done quite enough damage with your article. I'm surprised you even got in here. I wouldn't let Mr Connelly see you, if I were you.'

She watched as Nancy linked arms with Edith and went quickly back up onto the stage, the girls crowding around them to say goodbye. A feeling of utter desolation swept over Vita. She'd thought she'd found a sisterhood – friends for life – but now she saw how flimsy and transient it had all been.

'I won't be staying. It's just that we missed you last night. I brought a friend to meet you,' he said. 'Ah, here he is now.'

And that's when Vita turned round and the world seemed to stop. Because the man walking towards them was leaning on an ivory-topped cane. He had a scar on his face, his once-handsome features now disfigured, but it was unmistakably *him*.

'Hello, Anna,' Clement said, his eyes burning into hers.

'You've found each other at last,' Marcus said. 'I should so like to be a fly on the wall for this, but I shall leave you two to get reacquainted.'

109

Walking Ghost

He was alive? All this time she thought she'd killed him, but *Clement was alive.* Vita stumbled away from her brother. She'd believed she was about to be caught for murder. All that subterfuge – the lengths she'd gone to, to hide from Archie who she really was – and Clement was *alive* . . .

'So this is where you've been hiding.' Clement's voice was calm, but laced with the venomous sneer she knew so well. 'Although not very effectively, I might add. I found you, you know, before I saw you flaunting yourself in the paper.'

She stared now at the cane he was carrying. The ivory-topped cane. Percy's cane. Had Clement hurt Percy to get at her? Was it because of Clement that Percy had been arrested?

'Recognize it, do you? Belonged to your little queer friend.'

'Percy,' she whispered. 'What did you do to Percy?'

'Nothing, really,' Clement said, clearly enjoying how shocked and upset she was.

'He was arrested.'

'Oh, that. Yes. We got that awful man, Sopel, to lure him to their love-nest. It was all very easy.'

Still she backed away, but he grabbed her, the familiarity

465

of the pain making it so much worse, as his fingers crushed her upper arms.

'Uh-uh,' he said. 'You're not going anywhere.'

She tried to wriggle free, but his vice-like grip simply got tighter. 'Listen to me very carefully. Don't make a fuss. I'm taking you home,' Clement said.

She heard the word 'home' and an image of Darton, windswept and bleak, rose in her mind.

'I can't. I won't. Let me go.'

He looked startled that she had defied him, and then his eyes flashed with anger.

'Oh no. You see . . . now I've found you, I shall never let you go. Never. Not until you've paid for what you did to me.' He tapped Percy's cane on the side of her knee. 'Your dancing days are over, young lady.'

And there it was. That demonic glint in Clement's eye, and all the terror she'd known as a girl came flooding back. She had to do something. Fast.

'Emma, over here,' Vita called, grabbing her opportunity. 'Betsy. Emma. Come here.'

'What are you doing?' Clement hissed.

Vita waved to the girls, who had said their goodbyes to Nancy and Edith. 'Please let me introduce you to Mr Darton,' she said, trying to stop her voice trembling.

'You look familiar,' Emma said. 'Have we met?'

'Don't let Mr Darton go anywhere,' she instructed, her eyes boring into Betsy's. 'I'll be right back. I'm just going to change,' Vita said, running for the stage.

110

The Getaway

She knew the minutes were precious. Backstage, she ran for the corridor and grabbed Wisey. 'Don't let anyone come back here. Do you hear me?'

'Whatever's wrong, Vita? You look quite crazed.'

'I have to get away. I have to get away.'

She raced through the door of the dressing room. Edith was packing up the last of her make-up from the dressing table.

Vita slammed the dressing-room door and pressed herself against it.

'Fuck,' she said. '*Fuck!*'

'Vita!' Edith exclaimed, watching now as Vita paced towards the dressing table and away, pulling off her feather headband and throwing it to the floor.

'Oh, Edith,' Vita said in a shuddery breath. 'He's alive.' A startled sob escaped her. She put her hands to her head. She had to think. 'Oh God.'

'Who?'

'Clement,' she said in a shuddery breath. 'My brother. I thought he was dead. I thought I'd killed him, but now he's found me . . . You don't understand. I've got to get away,' Vita said, with a sob. 'I've got to run.'

'Vita, calm down.'

'I can't calm down,' she cried. 'You don't understand. You don't understand what he's like. What he's capable of. He's the one – the one who has hurt Percy.'

'I heard Percy got arrested.'

'And it's my brother's fault. He'll do anything to get at me. To destroy me. He threatened me . . . He'll hurt me, and everyone and everything I care about,' she said with another sob. She picked up the carpet bag. 'Poor, sweet Percy. You know, this is all we'll have left. Our patterns and our plans. This is what Percy and I have worked so hard for. And now I've got to get away. Far away,' she said, grabbing her coat. 'So if Clement comes in here, please do one thing for me and stall him.'

'Stall him how?'

'I don't know. Any way you can think of.'

'Where are you going?' she asked as Vita hurriedly put on her coat.

'Anywhere. Just as far as I can get. But, Edith, I want you to know that you were right all along.'

'About what?'

'About everything. About Archie and how he would use me. I was such a fool. Such a naive little girl when I got here, and you let me stay and for that I will always be grateful.'

Edith blinked, looking shocked.

'Good luck in Paris, Edith. Say goodbye to Nancy.'

She made for the door, but Edith sprang across it and blocked her path.

'I don't know what's going on, but I have a feeling you won't get very far. At least not without these.'

Edith held up her ticket and passport.

Vita met Edith's cool gaze, her heart pounding as she thought of the lifeline Edith was offering. And Edith meant it. She could see it in the way her eyes were shining.

Vita looked again at the passport and the ticket. The ticket to Paris – another world away. 'But . . . why? Why would you give me those?' Her eyes met Edith's.

'Because you have something I want in return.'

'What?' Vita asked, truly perplexed.

'That,' Edith said, jutting out her chin at the carpet bag. 'I don't really want to go to Paris. I want a fresh start, that's all. A way to support myself that doesn't involve dealing with the likes of Jack Connelly. I was so envious of you at that presentation.'

'You were?' Vita couldn't believe Edith was saying this.

'Don't you see? I want what you have: the orders and the patterns. Give me Top Drawer, Vita, and you can have these.'

Vita gasped and then took the ticket. 'But Nancy . . .'

'Nancy wanted you to go all along. Not me. She'll be thrilled you've taken my place, believe me.'

Vita wasn't so sure, not after the way Nancy had been behaving, but there was no time to argue. She leant forward and kissed Edith's cheek and then, checking the corridor, headed for the stage door and ran.

111

The Blonde

Clement felt his head throbbing with panic as he pounded on the door of the dressing room with his fist.

'Just a moment.' He heard a girl's voice.

'Sir – please, sir. I don't allow any gentlemen back here,' the older woman said, trying to block his way, tugging at his jacket. He turned and shoved her, startling her, and she staggered backwards against the bar along the wall. 'Well I never,' she said. 'In all my—'

'Where is she?' Clement shouted, before the door opened and a blonde girl leant against the doorframe, as if she had all the time in the world. She was quite striking, Clement noticed. She was wearing a pink silk gown with lace trim, loosely opened. Despite his fury at losing Anna, he felt something stir within him.

'Hello. I don't think we've been introduced,' she said calmly.

'Have you seen Anna? I mean Verity. Vita?'

'Vita? Oh yes, she's around somewhere,' the blonde said. There was something about her. Something about the way she wasn't afraid that he found most distracting. He had to

470

force himself to look away from her eyes. She was quite mesmeric. Like a cat.

Remembering himself, Clement pushed past her through the door, but the blonde girl was alone in the dressing room. 'Where is she?'

'Oh. I thought she was here. She must have left,' the girl said with a casual shrug. 'And you are . . . ?'

'Clement Darton. Her brother.'

'Her brother? How fascinating. She never mentioned you.' She barred the door with her arm, now that he tried to get out. 'She's naughty. Hiding someone so handsome.'

Clement felt himself blushing. Nobody had described him as handsome before. And the way she was staring at him: boldly, brazenly, but powerfully, too. He thought of all the women he'd taken, but none of them had made him feel like this. She was quite unsettling. And now he was stuck. Normally he would have used force – hit her, maybe – but he couldn't bring himself to behave as he normally would.

'You look quite tongue-tied, Mr Darton,' she said teasingly. 'Aren't you going to ask me my name?'

'Yes . . . I mean, Miss, I really have to go.'

'It's Edith. Edith Montgomery,' she said. 'You can find me in the directory.'

Clement blushed furiously at her wanton advance, then he remembered himself and why he was here.

'Excuse me,' he said, pushing past her. He ran out of the door, knocking aside the older woman to get to the stage door, but it had been locked from the outside. He threw himself against it and it gave slightly, but was blocked by some kind of bar.

'Damn it,' he yelled furiously. He should never have let Anna out of his sight.

Back in the club, he stumped across the stage. 'She's gone,' he growled to Rawlings, who was looking around for Anna over by the band.

Rawlings was faster and Clement let him go ahead while he grabbed his coat and, ignoring Mr Connelly who had bought him a cocktail, made it up the stairs and onto the Strand, scanning the pavement left and right.

And then he saw the girl in the fur coat and heels. She was running along the pavement. A man was chasing her. It was Rawlings. He'd almost caught her.

Clement held his breath, watching, but at the last moment Anna jumped off the pavement and ran straight across the road, holding her hand up to a bus. Rawlings barrelled after her.

Clement heard the horn and a loud thud, as the bus made contact with Rawlings. He turned his head away, but not in time to avoid the blood-splatter against the front of the bus, up the windscreen. A woman on the pavement screamed as the bus hit the lamp post.

Clement moved as fast as he could into the road and looked past the bus, to the other side, trying to see his sister.

But she'd gone.

112

Le Train Bleu

Vita walked as calmly as she could down the passageway of the moving train, searching for the carriage number on the ticket that Edith had given her. She caught sight of her reflection in the glass, as the train gathered speed out of Charing Cross.

She couldn't believe how much she'd transformed herself since the last time she'd been on a train. Back then, when she'd been Anna Darton coming to London for the first time, she'd longed for everything about her to be different, but now she felt a pang for that innocent little girl. She'd wanted so much to be flagrantly immoral and now, still in her smudged stage make-up and fur coat, she looked exactly that.

She shuddered at the thought that she'd only just got away. She couldn't stop picturing the man who'd been chasing her. The sound of the impact of the bus hitting him behind her seemed to resonate deep in her bones. She wondered if the man – undoubtedly connected to Clement – had survived the hit. She doubted it.

She'd always expected to be caught out for what had happened on the day of the hunt, but she hadn't expected that it would be Clement himself who would track her down.

She thought now about how he'd hit Percy's cane against her knee. How she'd known, with absolute certainty, that he'd do whatever he could to destroy her and anyone she cared about.

Like Percy. Her poor, sweet Percy. She thought of Percy's black eye. That must have been Clement. Why else would he have Percy's cane? He must have taken it when he attacked Percy.

She let out a sob when she thought of Percy in the police infirmary. Running away like this wouldn't help his cause at all, but her need to get away from Clement had been stronger than her desire to help Percy. She hoped Percy would forgive her one day or that she could somehow find a way to help him. She didn't know *how* yet, but she would.

She put her hand in her pocket to see if there was a hand-kerchief to mop her tears, but instead found the envelope Wisey had given her earlier. She'd forgotten all about it.

Taking a big, shuddering breath, she ripped it open. Inside was a piece of paper folded into three. She opened it, her hands shaking. It was then that she saw the pressed daffodil taped to the paper, and another, smaller piece of paper fell out. It fluttered to the floor and she picked it up, seeing that it was a banker's draft made out to cash. The signature read: 'A. S. Fenwick'.

Archie.

She pictured his face when she'd given the daffodil to him. Did this mean that, after everything, he still believed in her? In her business?

The business that she'd now given to Edith.

Or was it some kind of guilty pay-off? Consolation

474

money, for treating her like a whore? But somehow she couldn't find it in her heart to be angry with him.

I think I can safely say that I will always love you, no matter what. His words echoed in her mind. What if Archie really had meant them? What if he still meant them? He'd been manipulated by his family and forced into agreeing to marry a woman he didn't love, simply because Maud was rich and she could save Hartwell. She resented Archie for being so weak, but she couldn't hate him. She couldn't hate him because she loved him, too. Even though she'd lost him now, for good.

She jolted as the door behind her opened. Nancy was standing in the compartment doorway.

'Oh, my goodness, Vita!'

'Surprise!' Vita said sadly.

'Look at the state of you.'

'Oh, Nancy.'

'What's happened?'

'I had to run.'

'Run? What are you talking about?'

'It's a long story,' Vita said. Mr Wild yapped and jumped up on the seat. Vita stroked him and he licked her hand. Nancy slid the compartment door shut and they were alone.

She let out a sob. 'Oh, Nancy. Everything that could go wrong has . . .'

Nancy put her arms round Vita. 'There, there, kiddo,' she said. 'You cry it out. Everything will be just dandy. You'll see.'

Vita broke then. She cried for Percy, and for herself and for Archie. She cried for the loss of the Zip Club and her friends. And she cried from relief, too, that Clement was alive and that she wasn't a murderess. And relief too that, once again, by the skin of her teeth she'd got away from him. She was still so angry with Nancy for betraying her, but her arms felt like such a comfort and, as Nancy soothed her, she felt herself calming down.

'Have you got anything to drink?' Vita asked eventually, when she'd finally managed to curb her tears. She shook her friend off, annoyed that Nancy had comforted her.

'Of course. Matteo gave me a farewell bottle of champagne.'

'That'll do,' Vita said, wiping her face. She took a deep, long breath. 'Although, to be honest, *you* are really part of the problem. I'm so upset with you.'

'Oh, don't be a sourpuss,' Nancy said, taking the bottle and the champagne glasses out of her bag.

'There's nothing to celebrate.'

'You're quite wrong. You're *here*. That's enough.'

'Well, I might not be for long. I'm not sure I'm going to get away with being Edith Montgomery.' Vita looked at Edith's picture in her passport, thinking of the logistics of lying once again about her identity.

'Oh, I'm sure you can pull it off,' Nancy said. 'After all, you're not even called Verity Casey.'

Vita looked up, her heart thudding.

'What? You knew?'

'Of course. You told me everything that night in the bath.'

'Did I?' She felt her cheeks pulsing as Nancy nodded. She couldn't have, could she? Vita hardly remembered what had happened after their kiss. Only waking up the next day.

'You told me everything about . . . what was it? Locking

your brother in the stable and running away, before they made you marry someone ghastly?'

'I told you that?'

'Oh yes. You were most insistent that you'd killed your brother, but by all accounts, it sounded to me like it was the horse's fault, not yours. Not that I could persuade you of that. And you may think I'm an incorrigible gossip, but I didn't tell a soul. I didn't even let on to *you* that I knew, when I realized you had a memory blank.'

Nancy had known all along who she was? Vita rubbed her forehead, trying to take it all in. But Nancy couldn't now claim some kind of moral high ground, after all the trouble she'd caused. 'But you told Georgie. About us . . . and the bath.'

'Only to prove that you were up for some fun.'

'So that you could set me up with Archie?'

'Oh, Archie, yes. I had to. For my own sanity.'

'*Your* sanity?'

'I had to do something drastic to stop being so in love with you.' Nancy pushed a strand of hair over Vita's ear. 'And don't worry. It worked. I'm over you,' she said, with a sigh.

Vita held her breath, suddenly remembering how jealous Nancy had been of Archie and how it all now made sense.

'Oh, Nancy, I—'

'Don't say any more about it. I'm fine.'

'I didn't know.'

'I know. But I'm still sorry Archie hurt your feelings. That wasn't my intention. It was just supposed to be a bit of fun to get you over being so hopelessly naive, before coming to Paris.'

Vita was reeling. 'Wait! How did you know I would come to Paris with you?'

'Because you had to. Because it was your destiny. *Our* destiny.' She twisted the cork on the champagne bottle.

Vita shook her head. Nancy was crazy. Was this because of her obsession with Mystic Alice?

'Which is why I told Edith to give you her ticket.'

'You did?'

'And for a moment there I didn't think she would, which would have been awful. You know how much I wanted you to come along.'

'What do you mean?'

'Dear Vita,' she said, making Vita hold a cut-glass flute and pouring the fizz into it, 'you are like me. You're an adventurer. Only, *un*like me, you are exceptionally talented.'

'Talented? What are you talking about?'

'Top Drawer, of course. The business. Your talent.'

'But I've given it to Edith.'

'Did you? Damn. That wasn't part of the plan.' Nancy bit her lip. 'You didn't bring the samples?'

'No. I gave them to her.'

'Well, no matter. She won't do anything with them. She'll be embroiled with another unsuitable man before she knows it.'

'Nancy, I don't understand?'

'Don't you see?'

'See what?'

'Think of how much you've achieved with next to nothing. With your vision, you can make a fantastic success of yourself. With my help, of course. That's why we need to go to Paris together. Because that's the home of lingerie. That's where we'll make it big.'

'But I have an order? *Had* an order,' Vita said, struggling to take in everything Nancy was saying.

'A tiny one. Anyway, we can write to Mr Kenton from Paris.'

Despite everything that had happened with Clement and Percy, Vita felt a glimmer of hope. Nancy really meant it. She really believed in her.

'So,' Nancy said, 'what do you say? To us – and to Paris. Let the adventure begin.'

113

Free at Last

Clement walked in through the door to Darton Hall, his stick clicking on the tiles. He hung his hat up on the peg, thinking how exhausted he felt. He'd just come back from the mill, where his father had addressed the workers and laid down the law. There would be no insubordination from now on. It almost felt as if life had got back to normal. Except that, after what had happened in London, it would never be normal again. Not when it all preyed on his mind so much.

Not when his sister had gone. And Rawlings, too. The poor man. Clement had grown fonder of the detective than he liked to admit, but at least his death had meant that he hadn't had to pay him. But he still wondered if Rawlings had any family. They must have been informed by the police by now.

He placed the blame for Rawlings's death firmly at his sister's door and, as the days ticked past after she'd slipped away, Clement's indignation only grew and grew.

After some consideration Clement hadn't given himself up as a witness in the bus accident that had claimed Rawlings's life. His association with the private detective had all been too messy to explain to the police. He'd wanted to keep the focus on Percival Blake, but the damnedest thing had happened. When he'd gone to collect the negatives that Rawlings had given him from the studio in Soho, the wretched man behind the counter had managed to destroy them. Which had meant that Rawlings's evidence incriminating Blake had gone.

Clement had thought about denouncing Blake anyway and telling the police what he'd seen, but he hadn't wanted to have the Darton name dragged through the papers, or for it to be his word against Blake's. Besides, if he and Rawlings had been linked to Anna, there might well have been repercussions concerning the girl in King's Cross.

Which had meant that Percival Blake, that awful little queer who'd protected his sister, had got off scot-free. Clement had been standing across the road and had seen him leaving the police station – that older woman from the Zip Club had been outside and had pulled Blake into a motherly embrace and led him away.

Whatever had been the appeal of that sordid club for his sister, he wondered, when it harboured such lowlifes? But then again, Clement's mind wandered back to that girl – the blonde one, Edith, who'd been in Anna's dressing room. He passed the mirror in the hall and remembered how she'd told him that she thought he was handsome. He pictured her now, standing by the door, that sly smile on her face, and how it had made him feel completely topsy-turvy.

He'd been back to the club to find her, once Anna had given him the slip, but the police had arrived to shut down the Zip Club and he hadn't been able to get inside. But the blonde must know where his sister had gone. Or know someone else who would know. Yes, Edith Montgomery: she was his key. He'd find the first excuse he could and go back to London to look her up and establish what she knew.

He found his mother in the conservatory, standing by the open doors, her face to the sunshine. Clement walked towards her and then noticed that the aviary doors were open and the cage was empty.

'What have you done?' he asked in alarm.

'Don't speak to me,' Theresa Darton said.

'Mother?' Clement felt an unexpected flush rise in him. She'd never used that tone with him before.

'That came,' she said, not turning round, but gesturing to a letter open on the small table.

Clement picked it up:

Dear Mother

I am sorry not to have written before, but I have been making a new life for myself in London. I write this in haste, but I needed to tell you a few things. It was Clement who made me run away. He threatened me, as he has done all my life. Well . . . you know. You know the kind of man he is. I thought Dante had killed him and it was my fault, so I ran. But I was already on my way. Did you know that Clement and Father want me to marry Malcolm Arkwright? Well, I shan't. When I marry, I will marry for love. I will not come home and have Father and Clement bend me to their will. You always told me that my independent spirit would get me into trouble. And it has, Mother. Glorious, wonderful, life-changing trouble. And I wouldn't have missed a second of it.

It may surprise you to learn that I have found a passion. A new business that I intend to make successful. I am going to live abroad, so please do not waste your time trying to find me. I do not need anything from you. I am coping splendidly well by myself.

Clement felt fury pulse through him, making his cheeks burn. How had Anna known about Arkwright? Who had told her of the plan? Not Arkwright, surely? How dare she blame him for running away. How dare she . . . *defy* him, like this. Her tone – the sheer independence of it – drove him to distraction. He thought of Rawlings and how he'd said that finding Anna would depend on whether Clement's need to find her was stronger than her need to hide. Clement had been so sure he would win. And he almost had, but she'd got away and now she was going abroad. Where on earth would he start to look for her now? And how, without Rawlings?

Growling, he crushed the paper in his fist. At the sound, his mother turned and he stared at her, expecting her upset and outrage at Anna's letter to match his own. But instead her eyes were blazing.

'Mother?' he said, aghast at the look on her face.

'One of us is free, Clement,' she said. 'Now let her go.'

Author's Note

I hope I have evoked an era, although it must be said that this is entirely a work of fiction. I've tried to be historically accurate where possible, but have taken a large dollop of artistic licence as well. I have used some lyrics from songs of the era in the text: 'You got the cutest little baby face' (from 'Baby Face') in chapter 61, 'Isn't she cute, isn't she sweet' (from 'The Girlfriend') in chapter 67 and 'When the red, red robin comes bob, bob, bobbin' along' in chapter 81.

I found some books very helpful in my research, in particular Judith Mackrell's brilliant *Flappers*, D. J. Taylor's *Bright Young People*, Stella Margetson's *The Long Party* and Barbara Cartland's memoir, *We Danced All Night*.

Joanna Rees 2019

Acknowledgements

Firstly, for the opportunity to write this book, I'd like to thank my wonderful publisher, Wayne Brookes, who is quite simply the best. Thanks to Jeremy Trevathan, Stuart Dwyer, Alex Saunders, Mel Four and the whole team at Pan Mac – all of you make being one of your authors a true privilege. A very big thanks, too, to Susan Opie who made this book so much better with her insight and encouragement.

Thanks to everyone at Curtis Brown – including Alice Lutyens and my amazing agent, Felicity Blunt, and thanks, as ever, to my publishing fairy godmother, Vivienne Schuster.

There are several people I'd like to thank who have helped me along the way with my research: theatre historian Alan Strachan, dress designer Harriet Gubbins and journalist Shan Lancaster – for both her pearls of wisdom and her moral support.

My guilty pleasure has been West End musicals and seeing so many of them in the name of 'research' with my lovely sister has been brilliant. The glitter of *Dreamgirls*, the tap dancing of *42nd Street* – keep 'em coming, Catherine.

There are many people who have helped me during the process of writing this book: my girlfriends – you know who you are, I love you all; my family – in particular my very own sparkling showgirls, Tallulah, Roxie and Minty. But most of all, my love and thanks to my leading man, Emlyn, the person who keeps the whole show on the road. And lastly, Ziggy, my beautiful boy, who has sat in my study with me, keeping vigil, before demanding I take him out to see the sea. No dog could be a better writer's companion.